UNMITIGATED CHAOS

COLLECTED SHORT STORIES

FROG JONES
ESTHER JONES

Impulsive
Walrus

CONTENTS

INTRODUCTION

So it's the fall of 1999, and I'm living in Streeter Hall—objectively the best dormitory on the EWU campus (fight me). Specifically, I'm living on the Fifth Floor of Streeter, a floor that has been designated as the "liberal arts" floor, but that may as well simply be called the "floor of weirdos."

Life's pretty good.

Not only am I living in a fun place, surrounded by fun people, I'm also dating. I've been seeing this gal named Esther for the last eight months, and it's been going really well. We've been on some dates, we've had some fun. We're young, we're in love, and it's great. She's also a resident of Streeter 5, which is super convenient, and the world is basically our oyster.

Now, she's taking a creative writing course. And I'm an English major myself. So she comes to me with a short story she's working on for class and asks me to revise it.

There are points in any and every relationship that test the strength of the bond between people.

I don't remember anything about that story. But I do remember that the next forty-eight hours of my life were a blur of frustrations, accusations, tears, and recriminations. Asking someone for feedback on a story is laying yourself bare to them, and receiving feedback from a person you love turns out to be too emotionally complex for a pair of nineteen-year-olds. Suffice to say, we did not handle it in a professional manner.

After it was done, and the story handed in, we made a vow. Never again would we read each other's work. The emotional tension of laying oneself bare to someone whose approval you want so much was simply too much for us. Our relationship came very close to ending, and so in order to preserve the relationship we both agreed that we would never, never do that again.

You're holding this book in your hand already, so you can figure out what comes next.

It's now 2011. We've been married for nine years. Our relationship is in a very different place than it was in 1999. To put it bluntly, we are very familiar with the smell of each other's farts. There comes a point when you recognize all the flaws of the other person and decide that you love them anyways. That point is years in the rearview for us now.

We're both working at a small law firm in Colville, Washington—me as an attorney, her as a paralegal. This is a slight problem, as we also live in the Spokane Valley. We're commuting ninety minutes one way every day, and spending three hours in a car together. Conversation topics get stretched pretty thin in these circumstances.

In her off time, Esther is meeting with a friend of ours named Crystal. And the two of them have started doing writing projects together. This is a thing I encourage—but, staying true to our pact, I stay the hell away from it. The two of them have decided that they are going to enter the League of Extraordinary Writers competition at Spocon together, each with a short story.

During one of our commutes, Esther begins talking about the fact that almost all of her feedback from Crystal is positive.

She doesn't feel like she's improving the story much. And then she says some words that send a shiver up my spine and forever changed the trajectory of our lives.

"Will you take a look at it?"

For twelve years—twelve years—we had adhered to our promise. We'd kept this promise longer than we'd had our marriage vows. Not looking at each other's writing was one of the great cornerstones of our relationship, and now my darling wife had proposed taking a sledgehammer to that stone and busting it wide open.

The rest of that commute was filled with a conversation. You have to understand, this was so taboo to our relationship that the conversation about how to keep this safe and acceptable to all people's emotions had to be detailed. Her proposal sat on the emotional level of, say, asking to bring a third party into our marriage bed. It was a big deal.

We got the rules worked out. We agreed ahead of time that I was going to go in full-force and tear the thing apart as I saw fit. We had safety words. Esther was free to put the thing in the shredder if my comments were too much. In short, we approached this venture with all the trepidation of someone about to touch the third rail of the subway line.

And so, with a faint heart, I opened the zero draft of Blood and Spirit, the first piece of Esther's writing I'd looked at in twelve years. Perhaps over those twelve years she had honed her skills to the point where I would simply be blown away by the story. Perhaps Crystal's positive feedback was a sign that Esther had become a flawless wordsmith. Perhaps what I was about to read would change the face of fantasy literature forever.

Guys...it sucked.

I mean, it was bad. Told out of order, weird sentence structures, missing appositives, the whole gamut. I read it through once to come to grips with what I had to do. Then I followed our pre-set safety protocols and went back to speak with my beloved wife.

"Hon," I asked. "I am seeing some problems with this. Are you sure you want me to go the full nine?"

"Yup," she said. "Hit me. I really want to do well in this competition, so give me what you got."

You have to envision me making one of those cartoonish gulps at this moment. I knew—knew—that my comments stood a chance of endangering our marriage. But on the other hand, Esther had asked me to do this. So I picked up my red pen, and I set to commenting.

And then I handed it back to her.

What followed was something of a revelation. You see, a twelve-year-old relationship is in a much different position than an eight-month-old one is. This time, she wasn't using the comments as a potential barometer of how I felt about her—I had already well-established my love for her. This time, it really was about the story.

And so the gateway opened at last for us. We started talking —really talking—about the story. About the worldbuilding behind the story. Suddenly, those ninety-minute car rides involved us building this fabulous world together. A world of summoners and demons, of mafia-like Groves and the cops that hunted them. Those of you who are familiar with the Gift of Grace series will recognize what I'm talking about. This is where that began.

And damned if Esther didn't win that competition. Blood and Spirit triumphed, and suddenly we started to gain attention. Since that time, almost all of our writing has been done in tandem. We've had others warn us that we're endangering our relationship, but now we can laugh that off. We're fully aware of the emotional pitfalls surrounding them, and now we know how to step around.

The result has been amazing. Yes, we've got the critically-acclaimed series of urban fantasy novels, and those are great. But the ride has also included being invited to so many different anthologies. We've become a sort of background singer in the genre fiction world—we've been published alongside Brandon Sanderson, Todd McCaffery, Jody Lynn Nye (twice), David Farland, Charlaine Harris, and Mike Resnick, to name a few. Our short stories span science fiction, fantasy, weird west, cyberpunk, and any number of places that blend them.

In these pages are a collection of eighteen stories. All of them were written at different times, and for different reasons. Each one is accompanied by a bit of behind-the-scenes commentary from yours truly, a sort of commentary-track for the collection. We're the only thing tying them together—they have very little in common with one another. Indeed, when looking at our body of short fiction work as a whole, we could only find one phrase to describe it:

Unmitigated Chaos.

BLOOD & SPIRIT

...What can I say about Blood and Spirit that I didn't already say in the introduction?

This is it. The first thing we wrote as a team. The beginning of the entire Gift of Grace series. The first step to our entire writing career.

Andrea and Cythymau have become a part of our lives in the last decade. They're fully-formed people who walk around in between our heads. Looking back on this story, where they first emerged into the world, is always an extremely nostalgic experience for both of us.

Gift of Grace didn't start with Robert, and it didn't start with Grace. It started here, with Andrea, and I'm glad to finally see it published for distribution to let people start that series at its true starting point.

This story has been heavily revised since its initial publication in the 2011 League of Extraordinary Writers anthology. We were not actually that good, then. But it's kept its core, and it tells the same story—it just does a better job of it.

1
BLOOD & SPIRIT

WITH JUST ME, our cozy farmhouse felt empty, chillingly silent. No warm smell from Gran's baking wafted from the kitchen. No constant motion as Mom worked her next quilt from her well-worn recliner. Just me, Andrea Rothstein, alone, on the couch.

I turned the dial on the rabbit-eared TV in the corner, hoping sound might fill the stillness.

Instead, a local newscaster confronted me, talking about the only thing *worse* than this stifling silence.

"There was a failed attack by summoners at the general hospital today. Witnesses inside the hospital report that two deceased women, now believed to have instigated the attack, lost control of five shadowy, wolf-like demons, which are now believed to be at large," the news anchor said.

And then, on the screen, appeared pictures of the two women who'd passed. The same two women who *should* have been filling this house with the warmth of family.

Those bastards.

Mom and Gran had prevented those demons from attacking the hospital. They hadn't summoned them. They'd died warding the hospital to keep it safe. And apparently everyone they'd died to protect didn't have the wits to tell the difference between sic'ing demons on somewhere or holding them back.

The newscaster continued, "The demons are described as red-eyed, giant wolf-like creatures wrought of smoke and flame. They're also reported to have very deadly claws and teeth. The demons have been sighted in several populated areas, including the memorial park."

I bit my lip, wresting with ugly emotions welling up inside me. I wanted to believe these bastards got *exactly* what they deserved—no more than they deserved—because my family had already sacrificed their lives to save their ungrateful butts.

"The demons are now suspected in many more deaths, and disappearances in the immediate area of the hospital. The public is advised to lock their doors and shelter at home as authorities devise a strategy for dealing with this unprecedented attack in our small community."

Okay. When the newscaster laid out the situation like that, I had to admit maybe Mom and Gran *hadn't* saved very many people with their fight at the hospital. But that would mean they'd died for no reason, and I couldn't stand that.

Then the TV went to commercial and began bragging about how Brim coffee was the official coffee of the Olympic Games or some such.

With an angry twist of the dial, I turned the TV back off. The authorities would be coming for me, too—probably soon. Summoning was hereditary and illegal, and my entire living genealogy (as of yesterday) just made the news for their supposed atrocities.

I wanted *not* to care what happened to this town, these people. I *wanted* to be the kind of person who could consign everyone to their fate and run away. But this was my hometown. I'd grown up watching Mom and my Gran mend the Weave— the fabric of reality— to keep this place as the

4

idealistic, peaceful community all of my school friends believed it to be.

And I desperately *needed* to be the type of person Mom would be proud of, especially if she and Gran were no longer here to cheer me on. They both would've told me to act. To protect my friends and neighbors, even if they never understood what I did, or why. Mundane authorities wouldn't be able to fix this.

These demons would wipe our remote farm community off the map before any outside summoners could reach it.

The checkered kitchen curtains blew cheerfully in the breeze from the open window, blissfully ignoring the agonized decision beginning to form within me.

I walked over to the worn table where Mom and Gran had shared so many meals. Neither of them would ever sit here next to me again. But *I* was here. And I knew what I *had* to do if I wanted to honor everything they'd lived for. If I ignored that, I wouldn't be able to live with myself.

That left me one option. I had to summon otherworldly help.

I found a grease pen at the back of a junk drawer and started drawing futhark-style runes onto the kitchen tabletop's polished surface with a shaky hand.

Altair had been a guardian spirit of my family for generations. I needed his help to banish these demons. But Mom's Grove book, our family's book of summons, had been destroyed in their disastrous fight, so I could only write from memory. Several times I paused, stuck on a particular rune, struggling to remember.

Summoning an otherworldly Visitor is already inherently risky. You're pulling something into our reality that wasn't originally there, and you can create voids in reality, or any number of bad outcomes if the two Weaves don't stay in balance. Not to mention that there are any number of things—

like the current demon pack—that can slip in uninvited. Writing out the final rune, I squinted at the summons.

I closed my eyes, trying to envision the page as I'd last seen it. Had I gotten it completely correct? It felt *about* right—as good as I could hope for. Nervous tension cramped my stomach turning it to acid, but regrets fixed nothing now.

If I did nothing, everyone would die. If I messed this up, most likely nothing would change. That made this my best option to protect everyone and preserve my family's legacy.

Taking a deep breath, I popped the top off a container of cow's blood, then grimaced at it. I lifted the container, tipping it. The blood oozed over the runes, before slopping messily over my hand on the upswing and onto the floor as well.

Piss and shit. Just one more thing I'd have to clean up.

I inhaled slowly. I didn't have time to give in to my emotions now. If I took too long the blood would dry, lose potency. Then I'd have to start over.

Gingerly lowering my hands into the sticky puddle, I spread my fingers over the runes and closed my eyes to concentrate.

I extended my Sense. The room around me became a part of me. I felt every curve in the wooden floorboards under my feet, the veneer of paint and wax on the table in front of me, the electricity creating the lights.

Carefully, I threaded my Sense through the runes, groping to find the guardian spirit I needed on the other end. At the far end of the summons, my Sense felt a target...but met with resistance when I tried to retrieve it.

Odd, I thought. *Well, maybe odd. Not like you've done this before, Andrea.*

Taking a deep breath, I cleared my throat and spread my fingers more firmly over the runes, willing myself to stretch farther, push through this resistance and find the guardian I sought over the vast distance separating him from this Weave.

The specter of failure began coiling tighter and tighter

around my guts. I felt my Sense catch, hook onto something. This must be the spirit, I thought.

I tried to pull my Sense back, bringing whatever I'd found with me. It remained stuck, refusing to obey. Tension filled me from toenails to fingertips, as every inch of me braced for what could be inevitable failure.

Finally, shouting in despair, I slammed my Sense through the runes, trying to jar loose whatever was preventing me from bringing back Altair.

Maybe I was just not strong enough. Talented enough. The awful, terrible reality where I was alone and powerless to change anything gripped me like a vice. I lifted my hands from the summon, then banged my fists down in frustration.

The force of that impact jarred and reverberated up my arms and through me. My Sense recoiled back through the runes, making my eyes sting. The shock and noise from my fists echoed, spreading throughout the empty house. Blood flew up from the table, splattering my cheek, and I flinched away.

Opening my eyes, I gazed hopelessly around the room. No spirit had appeared next to me. What a giant, useless mess I'd made. The shadows had lengthened outside the open window, but I hadn't changed anything. There was nothing more I could do here.

I dropped my head onto my hands, not caring as my cheek hit the sticky mess on the table. Cleaning this all up was going to be pain in the ass, anyway. What was one more spot to wash?

I'd known I couldn't do this. Summoning a guardian spirit was hard enough—it was sheer hubris to think I could do it *without* a Grove Book.

I sighed, then continued, "What am I, crazy?" My voice echoed, too loud in the empty house. I choked, a sob caught in my throat.

"Hmm, mayhap," a quiet voice answered me. "But many are, you see. You would not be alone in that."

My eyes snapped open, and I jerked upright, my hair matted to my cheek.

A tiny man stood on the table in front of me, only about a foot tall in height. He wore archaic-looking polished leather armor, but his feet were bare and taloned like a bird's. Intricate, whirling, blue rune tattoos covered his face and all his visible skin.

"Whuft, child! What a sight you are! It is customary to clean yourself up before inviting guests, hmm?"

I gaped at him.

"I was quite shocked by your summons." His lips crinkled up into a wide grin and his eyes twinkled at me merrily before he continued, "However, today, I am inclined to forgive your abrupt invitation, even if you are next door to bedlam. It has been an age since I've had a good conversation with anyone." He glanced at the runes beneath his feet. Then he turned, pacing slowly across the table, inspecting my writing.

I sat there, stunned, not sure what had just happened. Altair should've appeared as a normal-sized human, not a small, bird-like spirit.

"Whuft, child. I have never seen such dreadful scribbling. Ambitious, but extremely crude, hmm? What was this supposed to be?" the spirit asked, tapping his clawed foot against one of the runes.

"That's dagaz," I said.

"Ah, No. That's opila." he said, glancing up at me. "You do know those runes are two very different things, yes?"

"Oh, yes," I said. "I must've remembered it wrong. But at least it worked. I had try something. I couldn't just leave things the way they are."

"What *things* could not you leave alone?" he asked me, quirking an eyebrow, then glancing back down to the table, "I doubt very much you meant to wrench me out of my cozy little cave so abruptly. To tell truth, I am amazed you managed such a difficult feat with just this crude attempt." He leaned down to inspect one of the runes a little closer, not caring as he left bloody hen tracks all over.

"Uh," I cleared my throat. My mind raced frantically as I remembered everything I'd ever heard about summoning a spirit outside of a Visitant Pact.

It all boiled down to: *Never, ever do it.*

But here he stood. Maybe I could get him to agree to a pact first?

"I-I meant to summon Altair Griffiths, an ancestral spirit that's guarded my family for generations. I wanted to ask him for advice and assistance in banishing demons that have already killed my family and my Grove." I cleared my throat uncertainly. "I sincerely apologize for calling you, who I have no claim to. I invite you to my hospitality and swear I mean you no harm, under the Visitant Pacts of 1615." I finished in a rush, knowing I had messed everything up, but hoping he wouldn't call me on it.

He looked at me considering for moment, an arrested look on his face. The pause stretched just long enough for me to start to feel a tickle of hope.

Then he crushed it.

"Whuft, child! I am not this Altair, and I will be invited properly, or not all, if you please. I know nothing of this 1615, but no pact binds without naming the parties agreeing to be bound. If you invite me nicely, I may be able to help you yet." The spirit tutted his tongue at me and shook his head, but his expression stayed mischievous and amused, his eyes still sparkling joyfully as he added, "For a fair price, of course."

I couldn't see what he found so amusing about my situation. "I-uh, I don't—"

"Go fetch your materials so we may do this properly, yes?" he said, "I am feeling very magnanimous, since your recklessness has opened up a few new possibilities to me. It may be this outrageous attempt will work out to our mutual benefit."

The words caught in my throat but I forced them out anyway. "I don't have my Grove book, or anything else to fetch. I did this from memory, which is probably why it didn't work right."

The spirit stared at me for a minute, his face frozen. Just when the silence had become so unbearable I'd opened my mouth to break it, he spoke first.

"Mayhap you are ignorant and reckless as well as being mad. If you reach blindly into other Weaves you could bring back anything, yes?"

"I thought I knew what I was doing," I said. "I *didn't* reach blindly."

He whistled. "And yet, here you are with me. I do not know whether to be appalled or impressed with you, child. I suppose where knowledge lacks, fortune has filled the void."

"Something killed Mom and Gran. Demons so strong my family already failed against them. So if I summon and fail, or if you refuse to aid me, what do I have to lose? These demons destroyed what I hold most dear. All I can do is stand in Mom's place. Everything is truly lost if I do nothing. What should I fear? What other choice do I have?"

"Ah, so you do know this is a choice—and a foolish one—then?"

"It's only foolish if it doesn't work," I said stubbornly.

"Have it your way. Children can be so contrary," he said. "Has anyone witnessed these demons' form up close? Not you, I think, or you would not be alive to talk to me."

"I haven't seen it in person, but I saw black smoke in some of the news reports. They slink along the ground, and suddenly strike out of shadows and alleys. They're wolf-like, and it sounds like they're bigger and more active at night."

"I do not know this 'news' you speak of," He clucked his

tongue. "But it sounds likely to me your Weave has attracted a pack of Lycaon. Very terrible." The tiny spirit paused for a moment, folding his arms over his chest and appearing lost in thought.

"Please help me, sir. I promise I will make it worth your while. Somehow. My word on that."

"Such grand promises you make to me. Yet you currently have few things of value to offer," the small man said. I held my breath as he continued, "I will allow that does not mean you have nothing. I may be able to help you, but I do not think you would like my price."

"I'll pay any price if you can banish these demons." I said stubbornly.

"And if the price I ask is for your life?" he said, watching my expression intently.

"Even then, I will pay it." I said grimly, ignoring how my stomach knotted with nerves. I looked at the small spirit critically. "But are *you* sure you can banish it? You seem pretty small to stand up against a otherworldly terror that has already taken out two summoners at once." I gestured at his diminutive stature doubtfully.

"Do not doubt my abilities," he answered confidently, "If we enter an agreement, you and I, I will be bound to fulfill it, as will you."

I nodded, considering his words.

"So here is my offer, young daughter of blood. I will aid you. I will give you my power, my abilities, my knowledge. But, so we have a fair trade, in return you must give me your life, even if that means you never again open your eyes on this Weave when this is done."

I bit my lip, tasting blood. My heart hammered in my throat. Would I do it? My mom and gran's death, I had to make it worth something. Even if that meant making a pact with a spirit I didn't know.

"Done." I said, keeping all my terror and sadness in a small, tight ball at the pit of my stomach.

"Whuft! My *plentyn*, as I said, no pacts can be entered without names. If we are to do this, you must give me your full name."

"I am Andrea Iris Rothstein."

"Andrea Iris Rothstein. You have bargained away your life, forsaking this Weave, in order to gain the knowledge, abilities, and aid of Cythymau. I, Cythymau, in return for your life and all the future potential it represents, agree and pledge to uphold the terms of this bargain. What say you?"

I knew enough about otherworldly pacts to make sure I asked for exactly what I wanted in my response back. I didn't want any room for him to say I hadn't asked him to rid this Weave of the demons. "I, Andrea Iris Rothstein, confirm that I will relinquish my life to Cythymau in return for his aid as stated, as long as that aid includes banishing the demons that killed Mom and Gran from this Weave."

"So shall it be." Cythymau said.

"So shall it be." I repeated, for good measure. Not like I had any idea if that was required or not.

He took a small stone dagger out of a holster on his polished armor, and suddenly stabbed downward, pricking the back of my hand. I yelped, but he was already nicking his hand and pressing his wound against mine.

I waited for a thunderclap, or some other world-shattering sign of the universe "witnessing" our agreement.

Instead the small Visitor knelt, drawing out a new set of runes in the blood still on the table, and a portal opened where the checkered kitchen curtains had just been waving. He jumped up, landed on my shoulder, and then the world turned sideways. I felt as if I'd been turned inside out and then jerked back upright.

I found myself in a roomy cavern lit with wall sconces. The

stone floor was even and polished, and shelves lined the walls, no matter where I looked. One wall held floor-to-ceiling scrolls, the small alcoves stuffed to bursting. The rest of the shelves held curious runed objects I had no reference for.

"Welcome to my storeroom," Cythymau said. "It is small but sufficient for our purposes."

"Excuse me?" I said, feeling severely out of my depth.

He began rummaging through the shelves, hopping his small bird-like figure about, shoving this and that under the breastplate of his armor, or putting things in the pouch tied to his hip. I didn't recognize any of it.

Spreading out four pieces of parchment, he picked up a plumed quill and began drawing elegant runes but layering them over each other in a way I'd never seen any summoner do before. Usually, one drew runes out in a long chain, not made into one compound emblem like he seemed to be creating.

"Will those work?" I asked him dubiously.

"Whuft, my *plentyn*. They will work a great deal more effectively than yours, yes?" He sprinkled sand over the parchments to hasten the ink drying.

"You take the stone dagger that is on the stand over there. Put it on your belt. Quickly now, we must make haste." He said pointing.

"Okay," I said, picking up the holstered dagger. It looked like smooth obsidian, its surface covered with the same compounded rune emblems. I unfastened my belt and threaded the holster through it with fingers that felt like ice.

He watched me, his eyes bright. "Now, try taking the dagger out. Hold it like so," he said demonstrating a low stance, the knife held up in front of him in a loose grip.

I fumbled clumsily, cutting my thumb on the blade, but managed to copy his posture.

He tutted. "Whuft, child. I suppose now that you have blooded it, try to channel yourself through it, yes?"

I closed my eyes and threaded myself through the shining runes on the dagger. Lines of energy threaded through Weave, reinforcing the weft and warp, spiraling through this world like a million starburst-shaped spider webs. It wound around Cythymau and everything I could Sense in the small room. And between Cythymau and me stretched a twisted thread, like snarled fishing line, messily connecting the two of us.

"Well, my *plentyn*?" the spirit asked, his voice impatient.

"There's something threaded through the whole Weave here. It looks like poinsettias layered over each other into some kind of tiled pattern or something. And there's something tangled up connecting the two of us."

"Good, very good." Cythymau said. "We can work with this. Well done."

"Really?" I said opening my eyes. "That's good?"

"It is a very promising start, shall we say, hmm?" The small spirit hung a key around my neck and handed me a curious runed box not much bigger than my palm. Both appeared to be crafted of carved bone.

"Once we have trapped the Lycaon, you will use this, yes?"

"What is it?" I squinted at it to see the runes better.

"A seal," he said cheerfully, still sounding amused.

"Uh, care to explain?" I said dubiously.

He quirked an eyebrow at me. "You blood it, you use it, hmm?"

"I didn't bring any blood with me," I pointed out.

"Living beings are little more than blood and spirit. I am sure you will find a way to improvise when the time comes, yes?" He rolled up the parchments he'd written, and stuffed them in a satchel, slinging it over his shoulder and checking the main holsters and straps of his armor. "We must go." He pressed his still-bloody palm to the runes, and the portal sprang back to life.

"Wait! But how will we trap them?" I said, feeling panic crawl up my throat now we were about to do this for real.

"I will create the barrier. Your purpose in this will be distraction, and to trigger the seal when I say. I assume you are a fast runner." I opened my mouth to object, but we were already headed through the portal. The world turned on its head, leaving no time.

We exited the portal in the hospital's vast parking lot. Cythymau hopped out in front of me, his small form bobbing in a half-walk, his arms extended for balance. High up on the light poles, lettered signs divided the lot into quadrants so that stressed family and friends could find their cars after visiting their loved ones.

It was not quite dark yet. The sun lay against the horizon, sending long, dark shadows streaming across the pavement.

Cythymau glanced around. "I targeted the portal's location on the disturbance in your Weave, so what we're looking for should be near," he said.

At the corner of the lot behind a big blue truck, I saw movement.

Something that looked like black smoke roiled along the ground, flowing through the shadows and into the lot toward us. For the first time, I got a good look at what we faced.

And then I wished I hadn't.

What first appeared as smoke became a flickering, loping five-member pack of giant, red-eyed, wolf-like demons, blazing like a hungry, dark, wildfire, as if wolf and flame had melded into one malevolent entity. The leader's scythe-like claws glinted in the waning sun, like flashing sparks through smoke. The whole pack ran so fast I couldn't tell if their paws actually touched the pavement or not.

I was supposed to distract these? My stomach squeezed, and I wondered how I was supposed to stay alive long enough to do that.

Cthythymau gave my ankle a little push that had surprising strength behind it, given his small size. "Whuft! A moving target is much harder to catch than a stationary one, yes? Remember to draw them to the center— under the 1N sign should suffice."

And with that, he started running himself. I didn't have time to watch what he was up to. The Lycaon pack would be on me in seconds if I did nothing and I didn't like my chances if that happened.

I gritted my teeth and started running, dodging between a row of cars, and heading for the island in the middle of the lot.

Raising my Sense, I became hyper-aware of everything within ten feet of me. I could tell exactly how far I had to go, how many steps it would take. When the pack of Lycaon got close enough to cross into its periphery, I'd feel that too.

I grabbed a rock from next to one of the trees in the parking lot, wound the rock back in my best junior-league softball fast pitch and let it fly. The rock arced high, as I'd intended, but landed with a loud *thunk* to the pack's left.

I pulled the dagger out of its sheath with my right hand and gripped the runed box with my left, waiting just a fraction of a second more. Just long enough to make sure the pack had turned, following me and not Cythymau. I dodged full-tilt behind a fifteen-passenger van.

Clearing the van, I glanced back toward where I'd come from. The churning black mass flowed up and over the ambulance bay, rushing effortlessly toward me, as if the vehicles in its path weren't even obstacles.

So much for any kind of hide-and-seek plan. I might as well high-tail it to Cythymau's designated spot, and figure out how to keep from dying afterward.

Three rows left. Two. They were almost on me now. Sensing one lunge at me, I dodged, but felt a tooth nip my ankle. Reflexively, I stabbed out my knife to fend it off. I felt, Sensed the blade slice solidly into the Lycaon behind me. Then the giant wolf crashed into me, sending me careening away. I barely caught myself, reflexively peeling off some of my momentum with my Sense.

The Lycaon chasing me started an enraged unworldly howl that reverberated inside my skull, making my ears ring. I crashed headlong into a large red truck and came to an awkward stop, unable to go any farther.

Apologizing internally to the owner, I Sense-summoned one of the parked cars and placed it on its side in front of me to use as a shield. Wedging myself between that car and the truck, I waited for Cythymau's signal.

The car's frame vibrated suddenly, taking a violent blow from the other side. I saw red eyes and gleaming fangs, as one of the Lycaon peered over the car's hood. The eyes disappeared, and long scythe-like claws came fishing for me from under the truck. I stabbed downward, spearing the paw.

An0ther Lycaon flowed over the top of the truck and snapped at me in my small space. I forced my small dagger in under its jaw, stabbing up into its skull.

It let out a spine-chilling howl as a sheet of burning blood splashed me. Jaws and claws lashed out at me, forcing me to dodge away and clamber up and over the car.

The Lycaon on the other side of the car pounced, his jaws snapping shut just short of my scrabbling legs. I spun on it. Then I lashed out with the dagger, plunging it deep into the Lycaon's chest. Black blood, looking like old engine oil, flowed out, coating me.

Not fast enough. The Lycaon's teeth bit into my shoulder, and I could feel its fangs piercing just over my collarbone. I used its body and the car behind me as shielding, keeping the other four Lycaon at bay.

This wasn't going to last long.

"Are you ready yet?" I yelled to Cythymau.

"A moment more," came his lilting voice.

17

Everywhere the Lycaon's blood touched me, my skin crawled with frissons of unnatural energy.

Cythymau skidded to a stop and placed some kind of parchment tag at the edges of the parking lot where he stood. He slapped his hands down on the parchment. I thought I saw light play over his skin for a moment. But it could've been a trick of the setting sun.

A massive barrier sprang up, enclosing me and the pack of Lycaon at its center. Each corner was anchored by another of Cythymau's parchment tags. I wrestled with the knife, feeling it plunge into the Lycaon's chest. The demon's teeth savaged my shoulder. The air inside the barrier began whipping around in a torrential gale. I felt like some kind of lodestone in the eye of a tornado.

I hadn't expected banishing whatever these things to affect the weather or damage the parking lot. In fact, I'd never seen summoning as flashy or as overt as this. Mom or Gran would never have approved.

The runed box tumbled free of my preoccupied hands, my blood raining across it. The remaining Lycaon snapped at me with their jaws, and I curl into a smaller ball, hiding behind the bulk of the dying one.

Lightning suddenly lanced down from the black clouds, sizzling through me, through the Lycaon around me. I felt the power of the universe, of reality itself scour me.

I let the energy flow through me and into my blood on the runed box. The cube expanded, growing until it was as big as the truck it sat next to, then pushing the vehicles aside.

For a heartbeat or two it pulsed, then began sending out fingers of brilliant electricity, reminding me eerily of the arcs from a tesla coil. Until it found me. I vibrated with the weight of the energy it pumped into me, through me, the key around my neck acting as a lightning conductor.

As the energy sliced through all my nerve endings, seizing all my muscles, I thought, *Ah. This is it. This is how I die.* At least I took these demons with me. I comforted myself with savage satisfaction.

The runes on the box's surface crackled and pulsed with brilliant energy. It suddenly opened, drawing the Lycaon into itself, then just as abruptly folding back shut.

Lightning rained down all around me, striking me and the area inside the barrier again and again in an unabashed fury. The air inside the barrier became so electrified I could not see out.

I had become some kind of tuning fork for the universe.

The barrier suddenly burst, shattering into a million fragments of light and force. It was there one moment and vanished the next, quickly fireworks.

The only evidence of the fight was the giant glowing runed box beside me, the overturned vehicle, my own blood, and the smell of ozone lingering in the air.

My eyelids felt heavy, drugged as if when I shut them, they may not open again in truth.

But to my surprise, I still lived.

Inside the cube, I could see the unwounded Lycaon thrashing.

Cythymau walked over, plucked the key from around my neck and used it to shrink the box back into a size no bigger than an acorn.

He looked to me and pointed, "Smash it," he said. "And we will be done here."

I staggered over, placed my heel on top of the thing and put my whole weight on it. It fractured as easily as blown glass.

A high, hooting laugh filled the night, just as the street lamps blinked on overhead.

Bewildered, I swung my head to look at my new mentor. In that fraction of a second, he'd changed. He was no longer small, or bird-like.

He now stood taller than me, at least six feet, if not more. His polished armor remained, and the tanned crows' feet at the corner of his merry, dark eyes, but his smile was too... too intense. It chilled me to my core. As I watched, his blue tattoos gained brilliance. A cloak of energy began to hum around him as he drew the excess power still throbbing in the evening air into himself.

As I watched, he snapped the key I'd worn in half. I blinked. Thunder clapped overhead, and one last lightning bolt touched down next to him.

"What did you just do?" I asked.

"What did *we* just do, my *plentyn*." He gave another hooting laugh. "It is not every day that I am given the chance to strike such an excellent bargain. Though you are definitely ignorant, I am well-pleased with our pact. But we must go, before the last of my wards fade and the constables of this Weave find us. Since you have gone to these lengths to protect the inhabitants here, I am assuming you would prefer that I am not forced to end any of them."

My head throbbed. I felt like my whole body was weighed down by wet sand. "Uh, that's right." I said. "Okay."

I tried to walk, staggered, and the new, tall Cythymau picked me up. He slung me across one shoulder like a sack.

"Why am I still alive?" I asked him as he strode back toward the open portal. "I thought that was your price. When do I die?"

"Whuft! Your *death* has no worth to me. It was your *life* I bargained for."

END

THE CURSE OF KHENTI-AMENTIU

All right, all right. So, as I said in the introduction—our method of writing short stories is to assign one of us to a sort of point position.

What I didn't say in the introduction is—this may have started with Esther taking point on "Blood and Spirit," but it's this story that cemented it.

Esther came home from the Friday of Spocon 2011 as one of the finalists for the League of Extraordinary Writers competition. "Blood and Spirit" had been well-received, and as a finalist she got all kinds of attention. She ended up hanging out with actual authors at the convention. Behind-the-scenes. She was being lauded for her writing ability.

Now, I will admit this next bit makes me something of a dick, but I got jealous. After all, I knew I was almost as good as her, and I'd had a pretty significant hand in that story, but she got all the attention. Why weren't these people heaping praise on me for something they knew nothing about?

So when she came back and told me that the great Maggie Bonham of Sky Warrior Books was asking for Zombie stories—

and that they were due in two days—I said screw it. While she spent Saturday getting more attention lavished on her for being a great writer, I'd be taking point on a zombie story to get our first publication credit. So there.

Which is what I did. Not one who's a big fan of zombie stories, I put a twist on it to entertain myself as much as the reader. I set a zombie story within ancient Rome, because I wanted to put the premier military of the ancient world up against, well, zombies. By the time I was done, I had a story that I'd fallen really in love with.

And then Esther came back from Spocon, and revised the heck out of the story much as I'd done to "Blood and Spirit." The story that results...the one in the pages to follow...was just as much a collaborative work as "Blood and Spirit" was. We put both our names on it. With one exception, we haven't deviated from that pattern since.

But there's other wonderful memories tied to this story that have nothing to do with petty envy or spite. Because this is the story that got us our first acceptance letter. It's the first thing we had professionally published, the first story for which we were paid (not much) in currency of the realm. "Blood and Spirit" opened the door to being professional authors for us. "The Curse of Khenti-Amentiu" represents us walking through it.

For that, this story will always have a special place in my heart.

2

THE CURSE OF KHENTI-AMENTIU

I ENTERED the world amidst destruction, during the naming celebration of Augustus Caesar, on the fourth day of Februarius. That day, the earth shook beneath us, the buildings crashed to the ground, and the reek of death lay about the city. In the middle of chaos, my mother lay on her back, attended by her slaves. She screamed, then died as she pushed me into the world.

I took the name Fabricianus, the crafter, to commit myself to rebuilding my city. I attended the College of Pontiffs, to study under the *Flamen Vulcanis*. For five years, in Rome itself, the high priest of the god of fire and craftsmanship taught me. I learned the ways of the *lares*, the household spirits, and of the *Flamenis*, our Gods. Most of all, though, I learned how to rebuild. I learned the dispassionate arts of math and science. I learned how my god would aid me to regrow the city I loved.

And grow it did—as did I. I worked at my forge and timbers and my chest became rippled, my arms whipcord strong. From the awkward, bookish youth of my time in Rome, I grew out long, dark brown hair, and my complexion became deeply tanned from hours spent in the sun. Despite being a priest from one of the patrician families, I looked like a plebe.

Now, as a man grown, seventeen years of age, I stood before one of the buildings I had helped rebuild. The scent of perfume wafted out the door. Rebuilding this brothel had been one thing; going inside was another. I knew, of course, what happened inside these places in a general way. Large frescoes on the side of the public baths depicted the acts that men and women engaged in behind closed doors. I felt the appeal, of course, but also a little fear. I took a deep breath and held it for a moment, then released it.

"Nervous?" asked Theodosio, my elder brother. "Your first time in here."

I was. But I also wasn't going to admit it. "Why would I be? I'm just hoping their ladies are pretty enough for me." I flashed Theodosio a grin that helped the lie, and I let my swath of brown hair cover the jitters in my eyes. He slapped me on my back and went before me. I had no choice but to follow.

Inside the brothel was...a large selection. The frescoes on the wall advertised the services available. Theodosio, ever the bold one, spoke to the *materfamilias* of the house. A slight young girl with dark olive skin and black hair came into the *larium* and led me back to her room.

I saw Theodosio following us, and I believed for a moment that he intended to witness every moment of my first time. This horrified me; I did *not* want my elder brother to witness my first, fumbling attempt with a woman. I kept looking over my shoulder at him, and he returned my nervous glance with that charming smile of his, the one that let you know absolutely nothing of what was happening in his mind.

It failed to reassure me.

Fortunately, he turned into the room just before my companion's, and entered it with a smile. Inside, a woman snarled at him in a foreign tongue; some slave from the outlying regions, no doubt. Theodosio had varied tastes.

As to myself, well, it was over quickly, and once done it was hard to see what I had been nervous about. The girl I had lain with gave me a pleasant smile—I'd at least been a *quick* customer, if not a skilled one. I roused myself from the bed, placed a denari on the stand, and headed back towards the larium to await Theodosio, whom I believed would take somewhat longer than I had.

I was wrong.

Mere seconds after I passed Theodosio's door, I heard that snarling voice scream, in Latin this time, "May Khenti-Amentiu see my sacrifice and hear my words for what they are. A curse I bring on this house, this city, this empire, and you. A curse!"

Khenti-Amentiu...I didn't recognize the name from my time at the College of Pontiffs. It must have been some foreigner's powerless God. I thought Theodosio played at some game with his new catch, but suddenly I heard a shout from him, and then he ran out of his room, clutching at a wound on his shoulder.

"That crazy whore just bit me!" Blood began to seep through his toga. I looked behind him, into the room, and saw his naked foreign slave had stab herself between her two lovely, exposed breasts with a curiously snake-shaped dagger.

Probably a good move; she would have been crucified otherwise, and most likely she knew it. She collapsed onto her knees, her head bowed, and no breath in her body. It struck me as a grotesque scene, at once ghastly and erotic.

"*Lares*," I said, trying to keep my voice as even as possible, "she really sacrificed herself just to bite you?"

"I think she was going for my neck."

"It seems she preferred her dagger to yours," I cracked in a half-hearted attempt to lighten the mood. "What have you got between your legs that is so frightening?" I was trying to play it light, to not show how deeply disturbed I was by the macabre scene before me. Theodosio laughed, and punched me in my shoulder, but the shake in his laugh betrayed his horror as well.

Any attempt at our facade was cut short when the corpse of the slave raised her head. Her once-beautiful darkened features had drained to pale with the loss of her blood. A low-pitched moan rattled through the room. Her open eyes didn't seem to focus on anything. She slowly rose to her feet, her arms outstretched towards us, that serpentine dagger still embedded between her bare breasts.

No words needed to be spoken between Theodosio and I; we both leapt back from the doorway, calling for help. It came in the form of the brothel's security man, a former gladiator now living the good life. His reaction time seemed unchanged from when he had championed the pit three years prior. He blew past Theodosio and I into the room, drawing a gladius from his hip, and rammed the gladius into her upward through the belly and into the chest in the classic stab.

That stab had won us an empire. It was the motion of the soldier, the death-thrust anyone who served in the legions or the pits had been trained to deliver.

It was also, in this situation, completely worthless. The dead slave used the former gladiator's momentum to latch her arms around his neck, then ripped his throat out with her teeth. She followed him to the ground as he choked out his death rattle with her chewing on his throat. He fell, and her head slowly rose to level that blank stare at Theodosio and me.

We fled the brothel at that point. Our faces drained to a chalky white as we ran for the street in front of the brothel, where we looked for the nearest legionnaire. A sergeant and some men sat drinking at a wineshop about a block down. They breath reeked as they laughed at our story.

"You're afraid of a whore, boy?" asked the sergeant. "Best give your plums another couple years to drop then."

I tried again to explain to them, but they burst into drunken ribald laughter. I even pointed at my brother, who dressed his wound as we talked. It wasn't until the rest of the patrons and whores from the brothel spilled streaming into the street that they acted. They stood, collected their weapons, and marched in that half-jog the legions always seemed to use down the street toward the brothel.

I felt relief to see the legions engaged. They'd conquered this slave's entire country; surely they could deal with one slave. I tried to shake loose from the horror I had just seen, and I took comfort that the finest soldiers in all the world were handling with the problem. Theodosius and I walked home in silence.

IN THE DAYS THAT FOLLOWED, we heard little from outside our household. Theodosio's wound took septic in our home, and we maintained a death watch over him, as was proper. Despite our father's sacrifice of his prize goat to our household *lares*, the wound worsened. He weakened quickly, and three days after our trip to the brothel, we sent for the priest of Ceres to oversee his travel to the world of the dead.

The priest never arrived.

Theodosio passed into the next realm without assistance, covered in sweat and gasping in pain. As I was, technically, a priest, though not of the death gods, I began placing the two denarii over his eyes to pay the boatman.

Suddenly, his hand came up and snatched at my wrist. I whipped my arm away and jumped back. His eyes had the same unfocused look I had seen in the slave's, and I took no chances with that expression. I ran back through the doorway, slamming it behind me and holding it shut, whispering a prayer to the *lares* of the household as I did.

"Theo!" I cried out. "What are you doing? Why?"

Theo hit the door hard, slamming into it, pounding it with

his whole body. He had the weight, and I had the speed, so I decided against holding the door. Running seemed better. I gathered myself and sprinted down the hall to our family room, where my father spent his time.

I shouted "Run!" at father, but he looked at me quizzically. Theodosio took him from behind, gripping his head and ripping it backward, then chewing at his neck. It was a grizzly sight, and I stared at it for longer than I should have. My decision to run instead of hold had just cost my father his life. I let the guilt of that wash over me.

I dashed into the streets looking for a legionary, anyone with the proper equipment to put up a fight. I found none; the streets in the patrician section contained naught but the wind.

My brother followed me into the street.

As did my father.

That's when I understood the true nature of the curse laid on us by that foreign whore. Anyone bitten by one of the dead rose again. If the incident at the brothel had continued to go badly, the plebian section of town was likely significantly infested by now. That meant my best chance to find the legions lay there. I sprinted toward the plebian section, my brother and father shambling behind me.

I FOUND what remained of the legion holding a crude barricade toward the plebian section of town.

"Help!" I shouted as I ran toward them. The centurion spun to look at me. I dashed up next to him, panting.

"What's the matter, boy?" the centurion asked. He was an older man, and he kept his voice professional and calm despite the battle raging in front of him.

"My father, my brother... they're dead. And following me."

"Where?"

I gestured behind me, still catching my breath.

"Mars take us all. *Optio!*" On the barricade, a man whose crest indicated that rank turned to look at the centurion.

"Pick three men and get on our flank; there's a couple of 'em coming from behind." The optio banged his fist against his breastplate, and then shouted out three names. Meanwhile, the fight on the barricade continued.

"We stabbed them." said the centurion calmly, with a grim determination in his voice. "Didn't do us any good. We lost a lot of men that way. They gained a lot."

Some of the shambling corpses coming at the barricade wore the *lorica segmentata,* the breastplate of the legion, with the same insignia as the men fighting. Now they were no different from the women, children, and men in their togas, their breechcloths, or in nothing at all. They came as a steady, reeking wave, arms outstretched. That low moan hummed in my ears, never ceasing, sometimes varying in pitch or intensity.

"Now we know. Don't stab, swing for the head." On top of the barricades, a legionnaire did just that, swinging an axe down on the head of a shambling corpse. The corpse dropped to the ground, inert.

"Some of our auxiliaries have axes; those have been good," said the centurion. The gladius sometimes isn't heavy enough to crack the skull."

"But you can fight them now, right?" I said. And they're so slow; you should be able to handle this without a problem."

He shook his head. "Afraid not, boy. If you can get out of town, do it. All I can do here is buy some time; there's too many of them, and my men are getting tired. We can hold them here for another day. Maybe, if we show some serious Julian-style fortitude, we can hold two. But we'll tire out, and that's when they'll take us. In the end, I'm going to be slouching and moaning just like those poor sons of whores out there."

Dear Gods - this man was telling me that our city was doomed.

Time to go. I began walking back up the empty street, back to my now-empty home to pack what belongings I could, a hollow pit forming in my stomach as the city I loved writhed in restless death.

That's when it got me.

A cold arm shot out from the building corner I was about to round, a low moan hit my ears. I tried to jump away, and the bite aimed at my neck hit me on the arm instead. The teeth sunk in and I pulled away, backing off from the evil thing.

Once, she'd looked beautiful. She wore a breechcloth only, her breasts still firm but exposed for the world to see. It would, in another context, have been arousing. She continued to shamble after me, but I was much faster. I ran down the street, back toward my home, so I could wait to die.

I WAS DOOMED, and I knew it. Already I could feel my pulse quicken, my brow heat. That bite had condemned me as surely as Theodosio. Now it only mattered what I did with the days I had left.

Fleeing the city was no longer an option. If this... contagion managed to escape, the whole of the Roman empire could be in danger.

Knowing that, then, made the decision easy. I looked up the mountain; if I was to die, I would do so at the temple of my chosen God. I would breathe my last in his presence, that he might know me for his faithful servant in the end. There was nothing to rebuild, now; there was only to die correctly.

For two days I made my way up the side of the mountain. Usually I could make the temple in the side of the mountain in the space of half a day, but the illness wracked my body. By the end of the second day, I crawled on my knees, shuddering with the chills that the fever brought on, my brow drenched in sweat. I dragged myself into the small cave with the altar to Vulcanis in it.

Then I sat, and waited to die.

As I did, I looked down on my city. Once she had been the gem of the Rome, the pleasure-palace for the whole world. She and I had been reborn together, and now we died together.

Now she, like I, would be reborn one last time. We would be the death of the empire, of the world. This contagion could only spread out, beyond the borders of the city, throughout the empire, growing ever larger. The legions would not contain it. Once the joyous pulse of Rome, my city was now going to be the dark, lifeless heart of an empire of the dead. I shuddered from the thought and from the pain wracking my innards, and then I turned to the altar.

During Vulcanalia, we used the knife on the altar to sacrifice a fish in place of a human to our God, that he might be pleased with our sacrifice. Now I looked at the knife, and saw in it possible salvation.

"Vulcanis!" I cried with what little strength was left in me. "I beseech thee to listen to the last prayer of your faithful servant. I die here, before your altar. My city, a city of your consort Venus, dies below. We have been cursed by the foreign god Khenti-Amentiu..." Here I broke off. I never would figure out who that god was; the intellectual side of me sighed in disappointment. No matter.

"We have been cursed by this foreign god to die, and rise, and bring eternal death to the whole of the Empire. This must not be! I beseech you; if we are to die, then let us die. But *do not let us rise!*"

As I said this, I heard a rumbling beneath me in the mountain. The smell of sulfur, hot from the cracks in the cave side, blew around me in a sudden rush. The presence of

Vulcanis surrounded me, responding to my prayer and my sacrifice. I choked on the breath of the mountain, then took the blade in my hand and brought it toward my throat.

I gazed over my shoulder for the final time at the city that would die with me. From here, I could not see the rot at her heart. From here, she was still the beauty that I had loved my whole life.

"Farewell, Pompeii," I whispered, and then I drew the blade across my throat and collapsed. The stone beneath me rose up to catch me as Vulcan bellowed forth his acceptance of my sacrifice. I smiled as his force and heat took me. Then all the world went dark.

THE HIDDEN SPEAR

Steampunk is, for us, one of the hardest genres to write in. It's a genre based mostly around an aesthetic, which makes it tough to get our brains around. But when Phyllis Irene Radford asks you to submit a steampunk story, well... you write a steampunk story.

You may notice a pattern with us, in that anytime we're given a genre to write in, we do something to twist it. With "Curse of Khenti-Amentiu," we took zombie fiction and put it in ancient Rome. With "Dumpster Diving," we spun the idea of a werewolf around on its head.

With steampunk, the classic steampunk story is Victorian English. It's got that Jules Verne sort of feel. But if you look at the entirety of the world, the Britain of the late 1800s is an imperialist horror, and for some reason that never gets brought out. So instead of writing the traditional steampunk tale, we instead wrote a short story that occurs from the Zulu standpoint.

"The Hidden Spear" is a steampunk rewrite of an actual, historical event. The Battle of Isandlwana is one of the greatest defeats the British Army suffered during this period of time—and while the steampunk devices are obviously fictional, it was a battle where numbers and speed on the part of the Zulu overwhelmed superior weaponry on the part of the British. We tried to capture that essence, here, in a steampunk version—and to give our own tip of the hat to one of the most successful people to spit in the face of British imperialism in history.

3
THE HIDDEN SPEAR

LINDIWE ADJUSTED HER GOGGLES, leaned back on the altitude lever, and brought her *inyoni* closer to the rolling grass hills of midland *Kwa-Zulu*. The mountains nestling her village in loomed to her north, The bottom of her little two person airship skimmed just above the grass undulating seeds. She reveled in the hot wind whipping through her open cockpit, causing her beaded hair to clatter. In the gauges, she could see the reflection of her own ebony face, and glimpse the white beads threaded through her shoulder-length hair.

Her *inyoni* was shaped like a spear; built to be sleek and fast, with a low profile. It had a pointed front and sharp fins stabilizing the cockpit on either side, tapering into a point at the back. Today, she flew without a co-pilot, but there was an empty seat behind her. Usually, it would've been the co-pilot's job to keep an eye on the pressure gauges. Instead, she leveled out the ship and toggled the pressure valve, letting out a cloud of steam into the dry, summer heat.

Off in the distance, flashes of light and something which rumbled like thunder appeared on the horizon, but the sky was clear. Lindiwe altered her course to come closer, trying to discern the source. Even though she worried she knew already. The British had issued their ultimatum just three days ago. They demanded her people submit to British rule, disband all armies, and swear fealty to the crown... or face obliteration. From the thunder, it sounded like the red soldiers hadn't wasted any time acting on their threat.

She crested the hill, still hugging the ground, and looked down on the battlefield below. A cloud tank sat out in front of a group of British foot soldiers. The red soldiers fired with hand-held steam cannons into a band of Zulu. Hoses from the cloud tank snaked through the field, powering the soldiers' weapons. Zulu scouts trapped against a rock outcropping tried to fend off the soldiers as best they could with spears and long shields made of cow hide.

The tank had its own weapons as well. Lindiwe could easily see two rapid-fire guns. Also, a main cannon on a rotary crank which was made from a set of three telescoping metal tubes, and crowned by a large targeting focus welded on the end.

With a sudden whirring of gears, the turret swiveled, bringing its barrels around and firing a blast of steam shrouded scattershot. Two of the Zulu warriors managed to dodge aside, but three more crumpled brokenly to the earth and lay still.

Lindiwe cringed. They were obviously overpowered. She started to turn her ship away, so she wouldn't have to watch, but then one *impi* ran out in front, dodging the British fire and circling around the red soldiers to cut off the hoses. He swung the sharp tip of his *iklwa* around by its wooden shaft, taking one British soldier in the chest, and cutting through another hose. He finished the move by knocking a soldier out with the butt of the weapon.

The *impi* reset his stance, blocked an incoming bayonet blow with his shield, and then used the soldier's own momentum to throw him onto his back and finish him. As he stabbed the fallen soldier, another came up behind him and fired at his back.

The ball grazed his ribcage. He spun, slicing open the soldier's gun hand, and stabbing down into the hose. A haze of steam hissed up around them. The last of his fellow warriors took a cannon round to the chest and fell.

Suddenly, he stood alone on the field, still surrounded by hostile red soldiers. He grabbed onto the nearest red coat, stabbing with his *iklwa* while throwing the soldier to the side and into three more red soldiers lined up to take a shot at him. He broke into a run, weaving through the hail of projectiles and explosions.

Lindiwe bit her lip. She was supposed to be strictly on a reconnaissance mission, but the warrior was seriously outmatched. The red soldiers showed no signs that they were interested in his surrender. They kept shooting, still trying to bring him down.

Her village elders took their responsibilities very seriously; her instructions were not to be seen by the British or any of the other Zulu warriors. If she did anything to help him, she would be breaking one of her village's most serious taboos. In a worst case scenario, they might even exile her for showing her ship to outsiders... but she couldn't watch the British run the last warrior down right in front of her eyes if she could help it.

She made a snap decision, opened the throttle, threw all of the steam generators to max, and screamed down into the battlefield. At the last minute, she pulled the *inyoni* up and leveled it out next to the running warrior.

"Jump in behind me!" she yelled, holding out a hand to pull him up beside her.

He gave her a wild eyed look for half a second, and then one of the projectiles clanged off of the airship, causing her to swerve. Lindiwe swore, brought it back under control, and held her hand back out to the warrior. She ducked down lower over the controls as more projectiles shot over the airship.

"If you want to live," she urged, "Come with me. They are

too strong to fight alone. We will come back a different day, and make them pay for these deaths." He hesitated. "Please come." she said. "Do not make me leave you here for the red soldiers to kill." She shook her offered hand at him. He reached up and grasped it. She pulled him up beside her, and pushed the altitude lever as far forward as it would go. They shot up into the sky. Once they were well out of the red soldier's range, she eased up on the throttle and the altitude lever, slowing them down, and bringing them back to a horizontal flight path.

"We are well away now." she said. "Sorry to shock you like that." There was no response from the warrior. She glanced back at the co-pilot chair. He slumped forward in the seat like a rag doll, completely unconscious, blood seeping from the wound in his side and dripping all over the controls .

She couldn't bandage midair, and if she didn't get him some help quickly, she worried he might still die. She found a sheltered plateau in the foothills the Lubombo mountains, landed her *inyoni* long enough to do a quick field bandage, then turned her ship further northward toward home. Maybe if the elders saw the impacts of the invasion with their own eyes, they might listen to her.

Lindiwe's *inyoni* came to the mountain swiftly. She turned the inyoni, navigating along the rivers and climbing the hidden passes leading to her village. Lindiwe came out circling the highest peak, deftly threading the inyoni through the rift that lead into Izulu village.

The village appeared before her suddenly, like someone had just unfurled a map. Platforms and huts were set into the narrow valleys walls, with bridges and handlines stretching between them. Lindiwe swooped down over sky village, navigating among the many lines and platforms. The village couldn't be found on foot at all, as the entrance was too far up on a sheer mountain face. Trees provided shade, and there was a well and water wheel which pumped water from a nearby spring to various hangars and gardens. Weather vanes and windsocks stuck out of the trees' branches marking the direction of the wind. Lindiwe blinked the lights on the underside of her airship, signaling her approach, and brought the *inyoni* to the landing platform outside the elder's hut. The warrior in the back seat moaned, but was still unconscious.

Her mechanic, Cebisile, came running out of the hut as soon as Lindiwe landed. She started to call her typical greeting, and then noticed the *impi* slumped in the co-pilot seat.

"Lindiwe, the elders will have your head on a platter for bringing an outsider here." she said.

"He is Zulu," Lindiwe said defensively. "He would have died at the hands of the invaders if I hadn't intervened."

"But he is not from Izulu. You know we are not allowed to bring any of the other tribes here. The elders will say you have violated the trust placed in us by King Shaka."

"There have been three kings since King Shaka sat on the Zulu throne, and the elders still hide behind his edict rather than entrusting this village's fate to the new monarchs. The elders enjoy being hidden." Lindiwe scoffed. The warrior groaned and his shoulders twitched.

"We should at least get him inside and get his wound treated." Cebisile decided. "If you are going to be reprimanded for bringing him here anyway, it would be a double tragedy if he died. I will help carry him inside."

Working together, they maneuvered him onto a woven grass stretcher, and then moved him into an adjacent hut where a young *sangoma* performed healing rituals with herb-laden smoke and bound the wounds tightly to stop the bleeding. Lindiwe thought some color may have been coming back into his face, but it was difficult to tell in the shifting gas light of the hut.

Once it was obvious that they were not needed, Cebisile grabbed onto Lindiwe's shirt by the beads and started hauling her out of the hut. "You are coming with me to wash out that cockpit you just filled with blood. Do you know what I will do to you if any of the blood got into the pressure sensors? You are fortunate none of them malfunctioned on the way here. Your engine could have over-pressurized or you could have fallen right out of the sky."

"I should go report to the elders," Lindiwe said doubtfully.

"You should let everyone else who just saw us haul that *impi* into the hut tell the elders, and then wait for them to summon you. If you're lucky, they'll have had some time to cool off." Cebisile contradicted.

Lindiwe ended up helping her scour the blood off the dials, levers, and switches in the rear seat. Once they confirmed all the sensors functioned to Cebisile's satisfaction, Lindiwe strode back toward the *sangoma's* hut, since she had still not received the expected summons.

Lindiwe ducked inside. The warrior was sitting up on a mat in the middle of the room. He must be less hurt than she feared, if he was already sitting up. She gave a small breath of relief. His torso was wrapped in large white bandages, but he was already stretching his arms up above his head experimentally. He stopped as soon as he saw her. Lindiwe speculated the *sangoma* wouldn't approve.

"*Sawubona,*" she said in greeting. "I am called Lindiwe kaSiphiso. How are you feeling?"

"*Sawubona,*" he repeated. "I am Ntshingwayo kaMahole Khoza. I have been better, but I could have been much worse. The *sangoma's* medicines and rituals were effective. Thank you for your assistance. What is this village?"

"We are in Izulu village."

"I have not heard of such a village."

"We have been hidden for many years. Do you remember coming here?"

"I am not sure. I dreamed that we flew."

"You did not dream. When you are well, I will show you. This village was founded by Shaka himself. You have not seen nor heard of it, because it is sheltered in a valley behind a sheer cliff, high in the Lubombo and can only be reached from the sky."

"I would very much like to see this village," Khoza said, struggling to rise.

"You should still rest." Lindiwe cautioned.

"I am not badly hurt. The *sangoma's* medicines have revived me," Khoza insisted. "I would see King Shaka's village." Lindiwe acquiesced, helping him to his feet, and led him out onto the platform. They were high up on the wall of the valley, with the hut and its platform built around it in arching graceful lines. You could look out over the village and see platform after platform of houses, landing pads for inyoni, the ornate cranks for hoists and elevators, the lightening cracking around the electric generator, and the quiet whirr of clockworks.

"This must be the magic of the ancestors." Khoza whispered in awe.

"Not their magic, just their knowledge." Lindiwe answered.

"Then their knowledge is magical." he insisted.

Another *inyoni* returned from patrol, swooping down only a foot away from where they were standing, and landing on a platform that was part of a tall building lower down in the village.

"We have been the silent protection of the Zulu people for many years, but we have not been in contact with the King since Shaka was killed. In order to help the Zulu fight off the new invaders, I need to speak to the King. Can you tell me where he is?" Lindiwe asked.

Khoza immediately became wary. "Why do you need to speak to the King?" he asked.

"The elders will let us use the *inyoni*, the fliers, to openly aid the Zulu, but only if the King orders it. I need to go to the King to tell him of this. Otherwise the elders will not act. Shaka bid us hide ourselves, and we have. They will continue to hide unless the King orders otherwise. If I cannot see the King, this village may remain hidden forever, no matter what invaders come."

"How do I know you are not an evil spirit that is trying to harm the King?"

"I am not an evil spirit. This is a village full of Zulu. We are the hidden weapon of the Zulu people. King Shaka founded Izulu village inside this valley, so it could only be reached from the sky. Izulu helped him form the Zulu empire. Before King Shaka died, he ordered us to hide the village and our *inyoni.*"

"You look Zulu," Khoza said cautiously, "but none of this magic I see looks Zulu. You are unlike any shaman I have seen."

"We are not shaman." Lindiwe said again. "The things you see are tools, just like spears or shields. They do not have spirits. They are the power and knowledge that Shaka hid from the world, so it could not be abused."

"If it looks like you are doing anything to harm the King, or my people, I will stop you."

"That is only natural. Thank you."

Cebisile rounded the corner at full charge, and checked when she saw Khoza and Lindiwe. Her mouth opened and closed a few times like she couldn't really decide what she wanted to say. Finally she settled for, "The elders are waiting for you. I will take the warrior to get some food, that his wounds heal faster."

"Thank you, Cebisile." Lindiwe swung across several platforms, and then ducked inside the elder's hut. She was confronted by the village's three most senior matriarchs. All of them were old, gnarled Zulu with skin that looked like weathered leather, and white frizzy hair. Funani was the oldest, and the most honored. She fixed Lindiwe with an icy glare and began speaking.

"Izulu has remained hidden since the reign of Shaka. By his own edict, we have remained hidden. We have upheld his wish that we watch over Zulu lands, and not give our expertise to any one tribe, or allow them to gain our power. And now you have brought a member of one of the outside tribes here. Why would you break our trust and bring an outsider here?"

"Elders," Lindiwe said carefully, "As you know, red soldiers from across the sea wish to claim Zulu lands as their own. They are hunting and killing the Zulu to make them give up their land. The warrior I brought here was valiantly fighting against great odds. I brought him here so that the invaders would not cost us another Zulu life."

Funani made a harrumphing sound. "The tribes have been through many wars, since Shaka's time, and never have they come close to being wiped out. They do not need our intervention. We will remain neutral and hidden from these troubles."

"These invaders have power similar to our own," Lindiwe countered. "If we stay hidden, they will overpower the tribes with their cloud tanks and cannons."

"It still remains that our last edict from a true Zulu King was for the *inyoni* to remain hidden. We cannot break the promise made by our ancestors just because you say that these invaders will do the impossible." Funani intoned.

"The King who sits on the Zulu throne is of Shaka's blood, but he cannot update any edicts or forgive any vows because we are hidden from him."

"His father's brother assassinated King Shaka." Funani grumbled irritably.

"And as you know very well, his father killed that assassin. If we remain hidden while the British invaders burn Zulu villages, kill Zulu warriors, and crush the Zulu people, then can we still call ourselves Zulu? Zulu means the people of the sky because of this village. Can we still say we are all people of the sky if we would abandon the other tribes to be slaughtered, while we remain safe and hidden?"

Funani sat and stared at Lindiwe with penetrating eyes, not saying anything for a full five minutes. Lindiwe tried not to squirm.

"There is some truth in what you say." Funani finally concluded. "We have cut ourselves off from receiving further direction from the throne. But I will not commit our village to war because of raids by foreign soldiers. I shall send an envoy to learn the King's will in this matter. As you have already made contact with an outside tribe member, Lindiwe, I will have you return with him to the outside. Go to King Cetschwayo and find out his will. Should he wish our help in repelling the invaders, then we shall provide it."

The other two elders did not look happy, but nodded their assent.

"Thank you for your graciousness." Lindiwe said. "I will go see if the warrior is ready to travel again. The British invasion proceeds swiftly. If he is awake, I will leave as soon as he may be convinced to take me to the King. I will report when I return."

Lindiwe left the elders' hut, and went to find Cebisile and the rescued warrior.

Cebisile was sitting outside of the medical hut, with her feet dangling over the edge of the platform and a broken throttle she was fixing in her lap. She hummed under her breath as she worked.

"Cebisile!" Lindiwe called. "I have come to see the warrior. Do you know if he wakes?"

"I see you must have survived your explanations to the elders." Cebisile grinned. "Are you forgiven?"

"I am forgiven and headed back to the King Cetschwayo with the wounded one. We are going to war. We will need all the *inyoni* to be in working order, so I am sure they will be calling you shortly. You will be busy. They have finally recognized this invasion as a threat to the Zulu."

Cebisile's head snapped up. "I'd better get back then. Your *inyoni* will be ready and waiting. I have a premonition that the rest of my day will be spent battle-fitting the rest of the *inyoni*."

She waved and took off running, leaping from the platform and catching onto the long handles of a pullied rope-slide in one fluid motion, and riding it directly down to the mechanics' level.

The King's camp at Ulundi was in chaos. Tents, and hastily built lodges made with cow hide, lined the horizon as far as the eye could see. Favor had smiled on the Zulu in one thing only; when the British issued their ultimatum, every able-bodied warrior had been assembled at Ulundi for the yearly festival to pay homage to the King. Now those warriors prepared to march out to meet the British forces and defy the foreign ultimatum. More warriors than Lindiwe could count milled through the camp, Some sat and sharpened spears around campfires. Others danced and chanted to the ancestors for favor in the battle to come.

Lindiwe spotted a flat spot to land the *inyoni* and Khoza shouted down to the warriors, so they would not think they were under attack. Despite the wide swath of bandages across his torso, Khoza confidently strode across the camp, and Lindiwe hurried to keep up. He seemed to take on a bigger than life presence at this camp, and the change startled her. He must be much less hurt that she originally feared. Although she guessed he was the type of warrior who would put his best face forward, even if he couldn't walk.

"Khoza!" one of the warriors cat-called as they passed. "You risk the wrath of the ancestors by capturing a shaman; did she fly with you all night? You should lend her to me."

Lindiwe immediately rounded on the heckler, stalking over to glare at him, and stopping just a few inches from his chest.

A little steel blade from the spring-loaded holster on her wrist flashed into her hand, and she held it to his chest over his heart, making sure he could see. "I am not captured," she bit out. "Nor would I ever 'fly' with you. If you speak to me thus again, you will be the one risking my wrath."

The warrior looked at Khoza with wide eyes.

"Don't look at me," he said. "This one is a warrior to her very fingertips. And she brings knowledge of the ancestors to our king. You are the one who angered her. I do not wish to anger the ancestors."

Lindiwe lowered her knife. "Just as long someone realizes women can be *impi*," she grumbled. "And I am not a shaman. I do not speak to the ancestors, I just bring their knowledge."

"I do not see a difference." Khoza said affably. He waved to the group of staring warriors looking between Lindiwe and the airship, and steered her back toward the center of camp, wincing slightly as he walked.

"Who do we need to consult to gain audience with the King?" she asked.

"We need consult no one," he answered. "King Cetschwayo is my half-brother." He flashed a grin. "The ancestors led you to save the right person."

She couldn't think of anything to deny that, so she let it be.

Khoza acknowledged the guards at the tent and strode in.

There was a stocky man sitting in a chair with maps spread out in front of him, a circlet on his brow, and furs around his shoulders. He looked up when Khoza entered the room.

"Khoza!" he exclaimed. "I thought you dead."

"I fear the rest of my *ibutho* is," Khoza replied. "We were attacked by a squadron of red soldiers with a cloud tank. I took some wounds, but this person was able to help me evade capture or death. Her name is Lindiwe KaSiphiso." He motioned Lindiwe forward.

"Greetings your Majesty." she said. "It is a great honor to

meet you. I bring news from the lost village of Izulu. It was my honor to aid Khoza on the battlefield."

The monarch stared at her with an arrested look. "You say you are from Izulu? I have not heard that name since my father died, and even then, only in stories. Tell me about your people."

"My people's village is nestled in a deep valley in the Lubombo mountains. Our last orders from King Shaka were to stay hidden along with our flying machines, and so we have done. However, none of the monarchs since that time have contacted us, so we have become concerned we were forgotten. I apologize if I bring offense by not staying hidden as ordered and coming here today. The Izulu elders sent me to discover your will in this matter. We have three hundred *inyoni*, flying machines, in the village. They are at your disposal should you wish it."

The King leaned back in his chair, and crossed his arms over his chest. "I would love to take your word at face value, but it seems very convenient that you show up on my doorstep the eve of battle and say you can offer me a weapon beyond imagining."

"As weapons, your majesty, they do not have much fire power. They are very fast, and can transport warriors anywhere in the battle at least five times faster than normally possible. They do have some small rapid-fire guns on hand cranks. However, you will want to concentrate them on areas of the battle that have cloud tanks, as they can attack from above where the tank's turret cannot reach."

"How can I trust that you truly have them?" the King questioned.

"Khoza has been to Izulu village, your majesty. While he did not count how many there were, he can vouch that the *inyoni* are there as I say. Also, I have transported us here in one of them, so you are welcome to inspect it if you wish."

The King leaned forward, immediately intrigued, and his

eyes became more shrewd. Lindiwe could easily guess he was envisioning himself with three hundred *inyoni*. "I would love to see it." he replied.

They walked out to the *inyoni* as a group.

"This is the flying machine, your majesty." Lindiwe said, gesturing at the dark, sleek machine.

"And you have ridden in it?" King Cetschwayo asked Khoza. Khoza nodded. "Was it safe?"

"It seems to be." Khoza said. "I have ridden in it twice now."

"It is very safe, your highness. Would you like to go up in it briefly?"

The King shook his head and sighed with regret. "Sadly, I believe if I did, all of my advisers would weep blood. I cannot put my person in the hands of an unknown, no matter what type of good news she brings."

"Understood, your majesty." Lindiwe acceded. "Your advisers are very wise, and I would not want to cause them additional worries in these tense times. I can still explain some of its abilities if you like?"

"Please do."

"The airship holds two people. The front seat is for the pilot that handles where the ship goes and how fast. The second seat is for a co-pilot or a passenger. From the backseat you can monitor how much power the *inyoni* is generating, and also fire the rotary cannon, which is right here." She said pointing. "The spear shape is because it cuts through the air faster, like the point of your *iklwa.*"

"It would not shock me if my Great-Uncle Shaka built them with that in mind." King Cetschwayo mused. "He highly regarded the *iklwa* as an all-purpose weapon."

"Just so." Lindiwe agreed. "These gauges show how high you are in the sky, and how your engine is functioning."

King Cetschwayo seemed to be lost in thought, so Lindiwe paused in her explanations. After standing and staring at the craft for some time, King Cetschwayo finally seemed to come to a conclusion.

"Invaders come at the Zulu from all sides. I have the British on one side, the Dutch on another, and some of my own brothers and sisters would like to revolt. I am still not convinced that your village is truly my ally. However, you may tell you elders I rescind the order for them to stay hidden, at least long enough for them to aid us at the coming battle. I will utilize all of these flying machines you can bring me. After the battle, have your elders present themselves to me, and we will discuss the future role of Izulu."

"Yes, Majesty," She replied.

"Be at Islandlwana at dawn. Khoza will give your people orders from there. I will use your machines as the two flanking forces for our charging buffalo attack."

He paused to ask, "Do you know that tactic?"

Lindiwe nodded.

"Good. If you are not there I will know you were false, and if I ever see you again, you will be driven from Zulu lands. Khoza will lead the main body of our Zulu *impi*. If you need to coordinate, I will leave you to speak to him."

They spoke strategy briefly, and then Lindiwe had to leave so she could be back at the village in time to arrange for everyone to be back at dawn.

"Until the battle," Khoza said.

"Until the battle," Lindiwe repeated and pulled the *inyoni* up into the sky.

The day of battle dawned clear and cold. The ranks from Izulu arrived a little early, and were dispatched into their two opposite deployment spots for the flanking maneuver. Lindiwe had been tempted to run a reconnaissance flight over the British camp, but she couldn't be sure that the steam tank squadron she had saved Khoza from hadn't warned the British troops to be watching the sky.

The British discovered their hiding place just after dawn, and Khoza initiated the attack. The main force surged forward, and the first guns fired. Lindiwe gave her squad the signal, pulled on her goggles, and they lifted into the air. The air shook and reverberated with the sound of gunfire, *inyoni* engines, the tank's whistles, and shouted commands.

Lindiwe shut out the noise as best she could and surveyed the field, dodging fire from a squad of foot soldiers. Cebisile was her co-pilot today, winding the large crank on the rapid-fire gun and keeping an eye on the engine pressure, so Lindiwe could concentrate on maneuvering the *inyoni* wherever was most advantageous.

The red soldiers looked to be about eight hundred strong, so with over eighteen hundred *impi*, the Zulu had the advantage in numbers. But the red soldiers had rifles, cloud tanks, hand-cannons, and rocket batteries to make up for their lack of numbers. Fortunately, the *inyoni* were much, much faster than the cloud tanks or artillery pieces. "Rocket battery to the right!" Lindiwe yelled as she swooped down behind the soldiers manning it. Cebisile fired a stream of lead into them. The soldiers cried out, crumpling to the earth. A red pool quickly spread from where they lay, and the rocket battery splintered.

The *inyoni* squadrons pinched the British in between them, cutting off any means of escape, and the Zulu warriors swarmed in cutting off any escape from the front. For every Zulu that the British hand-cannons took down another two ran forward to take their place. The British were completely unprepared. From the looks of it, they had not been expecting any kind of an organized resistance, or the sheer numbers the Zulu had managed to pull together on short notice.

Then the cloud tanks fired. The warriors had wiped out the British foot troops; but the tanks themselves proved impenetrable, and any time one of the shells actually hit its target, fifty Zulu fell. The right side of the main column suffered horrible casualties. Lindiwe watched with horror as the bodies of her people started to pile up. The large tread of the cloud tanks ground the bodies of both sides' fallen down into the dirt whether they still breathed or no.

One *impi* after another rushed at the tanks trying to pry away at their metal armor to get at the steam generator inside. Their *iklwa* scarcely made a dent before they were shot down. In the middle of the carnage, Lindiwe saw Khoza spinning in a tight circle, taking out any red solder who came near. His spear was an ever moving arc of silver death.

A cloud tank moved in, taking aim at him, and prepared to fire.

"Hold on," Lindiwe yelled to Cebisile. "We're going in to take out that tank!"

"With what?" Cebisile yelled back.

"With the *inyoni* if we have to, but I'm sure we'll think of something."

"You will NOT, repeat, WILL NOT crash my baby into that tank" Cebisile warned. "If you do, I am never, ever, repairing anything for you ever again."

"So, new plan. We jettison the anchor, catch it onto the tank, open up the throttle as far as she'll go and try to flip the thing."

"Not better. If we do that, we just crash the *inyoni* into the ground. We don't have enough pull." Cebisile protested.

"Fine, I guess we do it the hard way."

Lindiwe buzzed the tank, and Cebisile used the rotary gun to strafe the top of the tank behind the main cannon. Lindiwe swung back around for a second pass. Most of the bullets had just scarred the surface armor and ricocheted off, but at the very top of the tank, to the back and right of the main cannon, there were some bullet holes that were shooting a jet of steam up into the morning air.

"Do you see that? We can do this!" Cebisile shouted excitedly. "They didn't armor the pressure vessel for the steam enough! If we make another pass, and open that vessel up completely, they won't be able to move or have enough pressure to fire." Lindiwe lined them up for another pass, but one of the other tanks moved to intercept, firing a shot that went wide streaking past the right wing of the *inyoni*. The cloud tank corrected its aim and fired a cannon round straight at the *inyoni*, forcing Lindiwe to evade. Since she was forced to change directions anyway, Lindiwe punched the accelerator, so they shot over the top of the firing tank. Cebisile fired some precisely aimed bullets down into its pressure vessel. A cloud of angry steam rose up to meet them. Lindiwe already aligned the *inyoni* to disable the next tank.

Khoza had seen the British open the hatch and bail out of the first tank. He moved swiftly toward it, killing a wide swath of the red soldiers with his *iklwa*. He cleared the last of the red soldiers defending the tank with a triumphant shout, just as Lindiwe brought the *inyoni* around from disabling yet another tank. The underside of her *inyoni* was scarred from stray bullets, but so far, she was still in the air, and everything seemed to be functioning.

The two remaining steam tanks beat a hasty retreat. Cebisile managed to blow a few holes in one of them. It limped away. Lindiwe, her fellow *inyoni*'s, and the rest of the Zulu *impi* cleansed the field of the remaining red soldiers with disturbing ease.

Lindiwe set the *inyoni* down, to talk to Khoza. He looked relieved to see them unharmed. He'd sent an *ibutho* of warriors in pursuit of the few British and was about to take news of the battle back to King Cetschwayo.

"Why don't you go report with him?" Cebisile suggested. "It will be faster, and I want to take a closer look at these cloud tanks. You can come back and pick me up later, or I'll come back with the *impi*."

Khoza nodded his assent, and he and Cebisile switched

places. Cebisile waved to them as they lifted from the battlefield, then immediately began exploring inside the open tank.

With the *inyoni's* help, the victory had been resounding. The bodies of the invaders littered the battlefield.

"Today, we have redeemed the honor of the Zulu! These instigators of war have bitten off more than they can chew, thanks to your village. I am grateful to the ancestors for bringing you to us to defend our lands." Khoza exclaimed as they watched the scenery flash past, leaving the battlefield behind them.

"We have always been here. We are the defenders of the Zulu," Lindiwe said. "We are all people of the sky. My village only strives to keep its brothers and sisters free."

"Even so, I will tell my brother of your village's great valor and prowess on the field of battle. You do not fight as normal Zulu do, but you have the Zulu heart."

Lindiwe flashed a grin at him. "I am glad to hear that our long absence from our fellow tribes has not changed our hearts."

She landed at the King's temporary command situated between the battlefield and Ulundi, and Khoza made a full report to King Cetschwayo about the battle, including the cloud tank's fatal weakness. The King instructed her to bring the Izulu elders with her when she returned to his camp next. Lindiwe took her leave, and pulled the *inyoni* into the sky, to report to the elders as well.

She did stop by the battlefield and pick up Cebisile, who was reluctant to leave her new project. She finally relented, when Lindiwe pointed out that many of the *inyoni* were in desperate need of repairs from the battle. Given Cebisile's lingering look back at the tanks, Lindiwe predicted that there would be quite a few flights in her mechanic's future. She took a wide route back home which took them over the wide beaches of the

Northeastern coastline. She wanted to avoid any straggling British forces, if she could help it.

As they flew out over the coast, something winked on the horizon, and Lindiwe pulled the altitude lever back, and let the *inyoni* skim closer to the grass. The sun created a glare on the water, but there was something else as well.

She swerved out over the ocean, so she could get a better look, and her stomach sank to her knees. Far out in the horizon, but only a few days' sail away, she could just make out the glint of the sun off the sails of at least one hundred ships. It did not take a genius to know they were either full of supplies for the invaders, or more red soldiers...

"It looks like our battle with the invaders is not over yet," Lindiwe sighed, pointing at the sails.

"We should hurry to the elders, and then back to the King." Cebisile warned. "They need to know they bring more ships to our lands."

Lindiwe nodded. She pulled back on the altitude lever, and the inyoni short forward. The sails became a speck on the horizon once more as they headed to rendezvous with the elders in Izulu.

END OF THE LONG HAUL

I am so excited for this one.

"End of the Long Haul" comes originally from an anthology called How Beer Saved the World, one of the top-selling anthologies we've been in. It's an anthology that came from CampCon, a gathering of authors in the woods near Mt. Hood in Oregon—and mostly came out of Phyllis Irene Radford saying "Hey, that would make a great anthology" when someone said the title in another context.

Be very careful about talking around authors. You never know when it's turning into an anthology.

Anyways, I'd been wanting to try something sort of Hemingway-esque. To tell an entire story via dialogue. I also wanted to spin the title around a bit and have beer as a physical object, and not necessarily the consumption of beer, be the thing that saved the world.

So, of course, I wrote a transcript of what is essentially CB traffic between space truckers.

This is a fun story, but it ran into a problem with its original publication. The transcript is annotated with footnotes from the person compiling this evidence, and those footnotes are often used to translate the space-trucker slang, and other times to land a joke. But if you pick up a copy of the Sky Warrior printing of How Beer Saved the World, the publisher was forced to insert them into the volume as endnotes, meaning that the reader had to flip back and forth pages to get the jokes.

I am so happy to have it here, in a written volume whose footnotes are in the correct place. It will finally give the reader the experience of reading it as it is meant to be read. For most of our stories, this anthology is a trip down nostalgia road. Here, it's a celebration of finally being able to tell the story right.

4

END OF THE LONG HAUL

UNITED SPACE PATROL

REPORT OF INCIDENT #GA-435-U26

SUPPLEMENT B: TRANSCRIPT OF
COMMUNICATIONS LOG, LASER RELAY STATION
EU-28

Note from Patrick Lerenor, Investigating Officer:
What follows is a transcript of live communications sent
and received by the EU-28, a tight-beam communications
satellite around Europa. It presents a real-time perspective of
the events of E.C. 6-08-2967, beginning at 22:31 system
standard time. It was at this time the ship piloted by Murray
Laverne Williams, aka "Fat Squirrel" arrived within range of
this communications satellite, en route to Europa.

The majority of communications on this frequency are to
and from merchant shipping pilots. These "truckers," as they

colloquially refer to themselves, spend most of their time alone in their cabs, and have taken to using relayed tight-beam communications to socialize with one another. I have attempted to provide translations of their jargon where necessary. Truckers are logged by the communications satellite according to their ship's license numbers, which appear at the beginning of every communication.

- TRANSCRIPT BEGINS -

EA-29384XB: Breaker, Breaker, one-niner-six, this is Fat Squirrel, coming in off the long haul from the blue dot.[1] Who's out there in Europa local tonight?

EU-4356: Fat Squirrel, this is Hot Chicken. Been a while since we've seen you kicking around the crush ball.[2] What're you haulin'?

EA-29384XB: Hot damn, Gladys. Good to see you're still riding the vacuum. I'm bringing in about one and a half teralitres from Big Larch brewing company for offload at Delta Station.

CA-936: Fat Squirrel, this is Puddlestomper. Did I hear you tellin' us that you're bringing actual beer in?

EA-29384XB: That's an affirm, Puddlestomper.

CA-936: Hot diggity. They've been dishing out greengrog[3] for way too long. Tastes like yer' gettin' drunk off a salmon's ass.

EU-4356: (laughs) Copy that, Puddlestomper. I'm on the backside right now, but I'm picking up a load of vat sealant, then I'll be bound for Delta soon as I can. Murray, can you

---

1. "Long haul from the Blue Dot" - Jargon for making the trip from Earth to the colonies on the Jovian Moons.
2. Jupiter.
3. Slang for the fermented kelp beverage currently used as the primary intoxicant on the Jovian moons.

confirm they'll be selling that brew up in the EUX Truck Stop on Delta once you tank in?

EA-29384XB: I'm not sure on that. If anyone's got the line to Jenny at the EUX, maybe they could give her a direct call. I've just started my deceleration; ETA is 1:32 at Delta.

CA-936: I've got that number. I'll check in with Jenny. If she's serving once you're tanked, I'm buying a round for everyone at the stop.

IO-3698: Breaker, breaker one-nine-six. This is Old Henry.

EU-4356: Copy Old Henry, this is Hot Chicken. Did you hear the news from Murray?

IO-3698: That's a negative Chicken. Are we talking about Fat Squirrel here?

EA-29384XB: That's affirm, Hank. How you doin' this fine evening?

IO-3698: Murray! Can't complain. So what brings a homeboy[4] like you out to the crush ball?

CA-936: This here's Puddlestomper, and I'm back y'all. I have a big ol' confirm from Jenny. I'm a gonna repeat that so's I know you all heard me. Jenny at the EUX on Delta will be serving Big Larch Lager for as long as it lasts, once Fat Squirrel there can get himself to Delta Station and tank off.

IO-3698: Well, well. Murray's bootlegging.

EA-29384XB: Ain't no bootlegging, Hank. Running the first leg off of permits. You Jovians have a hell of a time growing grain, so Big Larch has the contract to deliver the good stuff. I'll be making the long haul for a long time, thanks to that contract.

IO-3698: That's a mighty fine deal you have for yourself, there.

EU-4356: I don't know, Hank. That's a long haul with nothing but empty air[5] to keep you company.

---

4. Someone who works primarily from Earth.

5. "Empty air" does not refer to actual air. Rather, it refers to the "air waves" of

EA-29384XB: Yeah, but once the burn is made you can just leave Newton in the driver's seat and do's you like. I've been tying my own flies; next cycle I get off, going to head to the woods for some trout fishin.

EU-4356: I guess if that's your thing. Me, I like the short hops between the pinballs.[6] Good money, decent company.

CA-936: And now actual beer!

IO-3698: I am sad to miss that. I'm burning outcycle[7] from the Flaming Pincushion[8] to the New Kid[9] with another load of hydroponic equipment.

CA-936: Hank, them rebs is just filling your wallet, ain't they?

IO-3698: Heh, that's an affirm, Jimmy. Every time the militants torch another station, I get to make another run. Their little crusade against dependence on the inner moons is just crazy talk, but it is lucrative.

EA-29384XB: Hey, Hank, I haven't been keeping up on you pinballs. What's going on over on the New Kid?

IO-3698: Oh, nothing but the usual. Every time there's a new colony, at some point they decide to get all political. It's fool-talk if you ask me, to call yourself independent and then blow up the machinery what keeps you fed.

EU-4356: Ain't nothing but a lot of hogwash. They'll settle down, soon enough. Once more people move to a colony, it starts to get domestic-like. It's just that the sort of folk who like to be first to colonize are also the sort of folk who don't want anyone to be second. It'll sort out in the long run.

---

the late twentieth century, where atmospheric radio communications were the primary method of communication. Empty air simply means no one to talk to.

6. Jovian moons.

7. To a higher orbit around Jupiter.

8. Io, so named because of its many mountains and volcanoes.

9. Ganymede, so named due to its very recent colonization.

IO-3698: In the meantime, I get to haul replacement equipment.

CA-936: Time you get back, like as not Jenny'll be sold out of Fat Squirrel's load.

IO-3698: What the hell was that?

CA-936: Aw, shucks Hank, I'se just pullin' yer chain. I'll make sure we save a drop of...

IO-3698: No, not you. I mean what in tarnation just went past me? I had something long and narrow just buzz my rig.

EU-4356: Joyguzzlers?[10]

IO-3698: Maybe. They look to be on course for the Whisky Cooler,[11] but if so they're way past Rubicon and still accelerating.

CA-936: Drunk Joyguzzlers? You think one of the Skypigs[12] can get them towed off collision?

IO-3698: Not sure. I'm about to head out of range of this sat, though; if someone else wants to try to get ahold of Skypig local about it, maybe.

EU-4356: Copy that, Old Henry. I'm on it. You have a good flight.

(Investigator's Note: It was at this point in time that Gladys McHavernathy, aka Hot Chicken, contacted Space Patrol HQ on Europa via direct com channel. Please refer to this report's Supplement C for a full transcript of that conversation. A pause occurs in the laser relay's recordings at this point, roughly the length of that phone conversation. It appears that the timestamps on our inboard calls and the laser relay station match.)

---

10. A person who drives at maximum acceleration until Rubicon, then maximum deceleration. A practice reviled by the truckers, as it tends to be out-of-control wealthy teenagers who can afford the massive fuel expense.
11. Europa; presumably so named because it is a giant ball of ice.
12. That would be us, the Space Patrol.

EU-4356: Alright, the Skypigs are looking into Old Henry's contact. We'll let them deal with it.

GA-54: Breaker, breaker one-nine-six. This is Firebarrel. I just passed Old Henry goin' the other way; any you have word on them joyguzzlers of his on a foxtrot-six[13] with the Whisky Cooler?

CA-936: Firebarrel, this is Puddlestomper. Always good to see your fine self flying into Europa local. I believe Hot Chicken's been on the line with the Skypigs about them joyguzzlers. You headed for an offload at Delta station?

GA-54: That's an affirm, Puddlestomper. You going to try to invite me for another round of greengrog? I don't recall the last time going so well.

CA-936: I think it went alright, but that's none to the point. We got us Fat Squirrel here in Europa local, and he's about to fill up Delta Station with honest-to-God beer from the blue dot.

GA-54: Jimmy, if you're pulling my leg I'm going to find you on Delta and smack you so hard your last remaining teeth will...

EA-29384XB: Firebarrel, this is Fat Squirrel. I can't vouch none for Jimmy's tolerableness on a date, but he ain't lyin' about the beer. I've got me a teralitre and a half of Big Larch Lager on it's way to Delta, ETA 1:32.

GA-54: Well, if that ain't just a thing to get a girl's attention. Jimmy, I do believe I'll take you up on your offer to buy me one.

EA-29384XB: Puddlestomper, I think you owe me for getting you a second date.

CA-936: That's an affirm, Fat Squirrel. We'll catch up on Delta. Maybe I can set you up with my cousin Doreen. She's not as pretty as Leslie out there, but she's got most'er teeth an' she

---

13. Collision Course. "Foxtrot" hear bears the same meaning it does in the more common term "Charlie Foxtrot." "Six" refers to direction. Thus, putting oneself on a course for a foxtrot-six means, delicately, to invite fornication from the rear.

cooks a fine stew. Maybe I'll get her on a shuttle up to Delta, see's if you two...

SP-1: This is an activation of the Emergency Lightcast System. This is not a test. Please stay tuned to this channel for further instructions. Repeat. This is an activation of the Emergency Lightcast System. This is not a test. Please stay tuned to this channel for further instructions.

(Investigator's Note: This announcement is followed by a standard fifteen-second two-tone alarm. Once the ELS is activated, inbound and outbound signals from the relay station are blocked for the duration of the emergency broadcast. Therefore, we have no recordings of the assorted trucker's transmissions during this time.)

SP-1: This is the Emergency Lightcast System. An object accelerating at a high rate of speed towards the crust of Europa is hereby confirmed to be a rebel missile. Current analysis suggests that this missile is of the planet-cracking variety. We ask all citizens not to panic. We do not have Space Patrol craft on course capable of interception. We ask all citizens not to panic. All spacefaring vehicles in Europa Local, please forward vehicle specification and current vectors to 65.334.2305.67 for immediate processing. Repeat...

(Investigator's note: This message repeats itself three times prior to allowing normal conversation to resume. In the interest of brevity, I have not included all three repetitions in transcribing this recording. However, they should be taken into account given any potential analysis of timing.)

GA-54: Did he just say planet-cracker?

CA-936: That's an affirm, Leslie. New plan, how's about you and I burn our vector up to high orbit around the crush ball?

GA-54: Nice thought, Jimmy, but I'm way past Rubicon on the Ice to Ice run.[14] Gonna reaccelerate incycle and try to burn to low orbit.

CA-936: Damn it all, we just turned into ships passing in the night. T'ain't nearly as romantic-like as it sounds.

EU-4356: Give it up, Jimmy, it was never meant to be anyways. Firebarrel, I'm going to be joining you on that incycle burn; I'm swinging around towards Delta station and am about to burn to break orbit. Fat Squirrel, you got yourself an way out?

EA-29384XB: Well, I'm coming in hot, figure I'll bust past and back outcycle with Jimmy if I...

SP-1: EA-29384XB, This is Space Patrol One. Please copy.

EA-29384XB: Shit, boys, I think I'm in trouble for something. Ok, SP-1, this is EA-29384XB, Fat Squirrel in the driver's seat. I copy.

SP-1: Er, yes. Mr. Squirrel, you are hereby requested to vector towards X thirty-five degrees, Y seventy-two degrees, Z negative forty-eight degrees. Please confirm.

EA-29384XB: Uh, SP-1, this is Fat Squirrel. I copy your request of X thirty-five, Y seventy-two, Z negative forty-eight. Is this an official order? I am currently on a course confirmed in flight plan number...

SP-1: Standby.

(Investigator's Note: Sergeant Greg Wilicutty's report is available as supplement A. Based on timestamps it is reasonable to say that during the interim period when Sgt. Wilicutty is absent from this transcript, he is confirming the requisition order from his superior officers.)

---

14. The run between Ganymede and Europa.

EU-4356: Murray, them Skypigs trying to pull you over[15] in the middle of a planet-cracking attack? That don't seem right at all.

EA-29384XB: Not sure. They just went all quiet on me.

GA-54: Odds are the vacuum porkers[16] didn't even listen to their own emergency notice. Fat Squirrel's gonna get a load ticket, and we're gonna watch the Whisky Cooler blow while he does. Typical.

CA-936: Dammit all, Murray, just get the hell out of there. Let them match your vector if they want to board. Don't let them get you...

SP-1: This is Space Patrol One to EA-29384XB. Fat Squirrel, you are hereby ordered, not requested, to set vector as previously mentioned, with an additional negative one-point-five Z.

EA-29384XB: Uh, SP-1, Fat Squirrel here. I copy your order and am complying. Course adjusting now. Can I ask the reason for this board?

SP-1: Mr. Squirrel, this is not a request to allow boarding. This is a requisition order under Space Patrol Charter, Section...

EA-29384XB: A requisition? What do the Skypigs need with a teralitre and a half of beer?

CA-936: Greedy sons of bitches, them Skypigs.

EU-4356: Hush now, Jimmy. Let the adults talk.

SP-1: Mr. Squirrel, please confirm that you have adopted the new heading and re-send vector data.

EA-29384XB: Uh, copy. Confirmed and complying, SP-1.

SP-1: Roger that. We are going to need you to make a 3.5G acceleration burn for thirty seconds at t-minus twenty-five...

EA-29384XB: 3.5G? That's max burn forward! SP-1, I am

---

15. Another term adopted from ground-based trucking. Colloquialism for executing a standard boarding check.
16. i.e., Space Pig. Us again.

currently attempting deceleration for in-system docking... that kind of burn is going to wreak havoc with Delta station.

SP-1: EA-29384XB, acknowledge 3.5G acceleration burn in t-minus thirteen...

EA-29384XB: On your head be it, then. Order acknowledged.

GA-54: Holy crap, anyone else look at the flight vectors on that burn?

SP-1: t-minus five

EA-29384XB: Firebarrel, this is Fat Squirrel, what do you...

SP-1: Initiate burn.

EA-29384XB: Burn Initiated. Firebarrel, what do you mean the flight vectors?

GA-54: Fat Squirrel, pull all incoming up on navcomp. I think the Skypigs are putting you on foxtrot six with the planet cracker.

(Investigator's Note: A moment of silence follows this. An examination of the consoles of Leslie Malera aka Firebarrel, James Wotenheim aka Puddlestomper, and Gladys McHavernathy aka Hot Chicken show they all ran this simulation at roughly the same time. Judging by the following transmission, Mr. Williams ran a similar program, but due to the EM pulse of the blast we were unable to reconstruct his navcomp's memory.)

EA-29384XB: Well, I'll be. SP-1, you got any idea how I'm gonna...

CA-936: SP-1, this is CA-936, Puddlestomper piloting. Request that I be given vector to foxtrot six with incoming missile instead of Fat Squirrel.

GA-54: Jimmy! That's one hell of an offer. You sure you want to do that?

CA-936: We can just emergency blow away from our loads

once the course is set; shouldn't get us caught in the blast. Only problem is, Murray's about to blow up the first chance we had at *real beer*. I ain't gonna drink no more kelp ifn's I can help it.

SP-1: Puddlestomper, that's a negative on your request. EA-29384XB is the closest vessel. In addition, we show that the cargo of EA-29384XB is almost entirely liquid, which should provide less dangerous shrapnel post-explosion. Fat Squirrel, we show appropriate course and speed. You may detach your cab at any time.

CA-936: . . .

(Investigator's note: At this point in the recording, there is an open transmission from CA-936. No actual words can be heard, but closer inspection reveals a choked sob at one point during the transmission.)

EA-29384XB: Cargo away.

EU-4356: Goodbye, sweet lager. We hardly knew ye.

CA-936: And flights of angels sing thee to thy rest.

GA-54: Jimmy, you know Shakespeare?

CA-936: Who?

GA-54: Nevermind.

EA-29384XB: SP-1, permission to vector away and burn an acceleration to avoid that blast?

SP-1: Standby.

EA-29384XB: Ummmm... SP-1? What, exactly, do you mean "standby"?

SP-1: Projected impact in t-minus three...

EA-29384XB: Oh, shi....

(Investigator's note: At this point, the impact occurred. See our main report as well as the vector analysis of the remaining beer in Supplement D and the meteorological report detailing the pattern of the rain of beer on Europa for details on the explosion.)

EU-4356: Murray?

(Investigator's note: A thirty-second silence follows this.)

EU-4356: Fat Squirrel, this is Hot Chicken, please respond. Repeat, Fat Squirrel this is Hot Chicken, respond.

GA-54: I'm coming in from that side of the Whisky Cooler. Space Patrol One, this is GA-54, Firebarrel piloting. Request vector information to make visual check on projected intercept with Fat Squirrel.

SP-1: Standby.

GA-54: Of course. Another Standby.

(Investigator's note: While there is a significant amount of displeasure at Sgt. Wilicutty displayed in this transcript, a review of this report as a whole should recommend him for significant commendation in his quick calculations. It is this investigator's opinion that, without the heroic actions of Sgt. Wilicutty, Europa may very well have been victim to the Ganymedean rebel attack.)

EU-4356: Sons-of-bitches.

GA-54: Exactly. Ooo, I can see the blast site on my scope now. It's a giant, expanding star, made of freezing beer. Here, I'm streaming it; check your visuals.

CA-936: It's... beautiful.

SP-1: Firebarrel, permission to vector granted. Come to X negative twenty-two, Y twelve, Z eleven.

GA-54: Roger that. Initiating vector shift.

EU-4356: You see him, Leslie?

GA-54: Ummm... not yet. SP-1, do I have an ETA on contact?

SP-1: Stand...

GA-54: ...by? How did I not see that coming. Ooo, there's his cab. Pulling it up on scope now.

EU-4356: Do you see Murray? Is he OK?

GA-54: No, not yet. It's pretty dark in... wait, there he is! He's got a handlight, shining back and forth. It looks like he's alive, but no power systems. SP-1, are you copying this? Fat Squirrel is alive but stranded on your projected course. No idea how much air he has in there.

SP-1: Copy that, Firebarrel. Deploying fast rescue units now.

EU-4356: Oh, thank God.

CA-936: Hey, SP-1, when you haul him outta that dead can of his, can you get us an ETA on the next shipment he'll have coming in?

SP-1: Uh... standby.

(Investigator's note: This transcript largely confirms all other reports contained herein. However, it does specifically contain the requisition language Big Larch Brewing has asked about. It would appear that, given Mr. William's reticence to respond prior to being ordered, we are liable to Big Larch for the cost of one tanker truck and 1.5 Tl of beer. As this investigator is currently quartered on Delta Station, it is requested that recompensation be made with all due haste).

- END TRANSCRIPT -

WAKE-ING UP

This delightful little fairy tale is the result of Esther's strange imagination.

I'd taken point on "End of the Long Haul," the piece we'd placed into the first Beer volume. But How Beer Saved the World sold really, really well, and sure enough we ended up getting together for a Volume 2. And I'd gotten to take point the first time... so this time, it fell to Esther to take point.

The result is a classic fairy tale... sort of.

Beer fairies are, perhaps, one of my favorite fantasy races now. But if there can be cobbler fairies, why not brewing fairies? For a story about the loss of a loved one, and the passing of a legacy... this one's a poignant exploration filled with humor and catharsis. It's one of my favorites of our stories, and I'm glad to be republishing it.

5

WAKE-ING UP

THE BLESSING, and the curse, of a small town is that everybody knows everybody else. On every corner she walked past, someone offered her well-meant sympathies or condolences. Amberlyn just wanted to hide for a few minutes. She could find no relief from the constant pressure and expectations. Alone, maybe, just maybe, she could start to deal the giant wall of grief that threatened her with every step.

Strange how a fraction of a minute could change the course of her whole family. One car accident stole her mother, father and older brother in less time than it took to order take-out. At twenty-two, she had suddenly become the guardian of her two younger siblings, one brewery, and the livelihood of close to twenty employees. Everything rested on her untried shoulders, now.

That terrified her enough, even without the added burden of everyone's eyes. Amberlyn's head seemed yards above the rest of her body, attached balloon-like by a thin thread as her feet continued to bobble down the sidewalk.

She found herself headed back to the one place she knew *no one* would be. The brewery, where her father should have been checking on the vats and preparing for the next bottling, stood dark and opaque against the horizon.

The brewery consisted of a large, old timber-pole building with a corrugated metal grain silo and storage shed attached. If you weren't from town, the faded sign reading *Gilles Brewers family owned and operated since 1906,* was easily missed.

Amberlyn didn't have time to break down like a normal person, not if she was going to keep the brewery alive. Dad had always kept the vats running at full capacity. She couldn't do that, but she could sell what he'd already made and use those proceeds to make it through the next month. One month to care for her siblings. One month to learn the craft of brewing. One month to figure out whether she could pay her employees in the future.

A sliver of light shown out from under the brewery door. Muffled voices buzzed in her ears as she got closer.

Who could be here at this time? Anyone who had a key should have been resting at home after the funeral. Of course, that included herself.

Perhaps someone else sought solace, or one last memory, in these old wooden walls.

Amberlyn turned her key in the lock, then pushed open the heavy door.

A hoard of impossibly tiny people—about ten inches tall, with an equally impossible rainbow of hair colors—crammed into every inch of the brewery, hefting pint glasses nearly as large as themselves, and swilling down Gilles' beer. They sat on vats, swung off pipes and spigots, lined the conveyer belt for the bottler, and sprawled across every possible horizontal surface in the place, obviously as shocked by the interruption as she was.

Amberlyn didn't know how to process what she saw. A list of possible labels scrolled through her mind: elves, pixies, imps, brownies, fay, wee folk. None of which were *real.*

In front of the nearest storage vat--containing beer on which next month's solvency rested-- a tiny yellow-bearded man embraced a mug. A steady flow of yeasty, dark merchandise flowed into the mug from the vat. An impish female in a short, green dress with a mop of fire-red hair straddled vat's test-spigot, holding the valve open. The yellow-bearded wee person standing under the spigot rolled a large copper-green eye at her in question, but otherwise remained stock-still.

Or at least, he remained motionless until his mug started overflowing, spilling the irreplaceable, dark liquid across the floor. He yelled in alarm, before plunging his face into the mug as he tried to slurp up the beer. The female above hastily shut off the spigot and then stared at Amberlyn as if daring her to notice the man's struggles.

Amberlyn had no idea how to actually *remake* any of the beer currently in this storehouse.

The brewery had always operated on a shoestring budget. She needed to *sell* this beer if she wanted to have a chance in hell of keeping the place open long enough for her to actually learn how to *produce* it. Hot anger surged up her spine.

"Hey! That's my father's beer! Get away. Shoo, all you!" As if her shout had broken some spell, mayhem broke out everywhere. Amberlyn charged forward, intending to herd the small creatures away from her father and brother's precious last efforts. The tiny horde scattered, shouting in alarm, hoisting their mugs above their heads and dodging away from her, more of her inventory sloshing and slopping onto the hard concrete floor.

Amberlyn slid to a halt in front of the storage vat and put her hand over her eyes, struggling to deal with the conflicting emotions surging through her. None of this could be real. This had to be some sort of sick nightmare hallucination brought on by her feelings of inadequacy. Grief, anger, despair, and helplessness fought in a never ending knot in the center of her chest.

She felt a small tug on the pinky finger of her left hand. She looked down to find a small, youthful-looking wee person with long, bright-white hair proffering her its mug of ale with a rueful nudge. Could hallucinations involve all five senses? She might be headed for a full-on psychotic break at this rate. Amberlyn accepted the mug with numb fingers, still trying to comprehend the scene in front of her.

"Your Da was a good man," the wee person said in a high, fluting tone. "Your brother too. They were part of our family. Couldn't have found better tall folk anywhere to keep the old traditions alive.   They brewed the best of the best. Irreplaceable, that's what they are." The sprite broke off, choked up.   A new voice shouted from out in the crowd. "To the Gilleses! May they rest in peace where the beer flows without end." The toast was taken up and echoed until it became a roar throughout the room. Mugs clinked as the horde of tiny people celebrated her family with a fervor that had been totally absent during the recent, long, nightmare of a funeral.

She gripped the smooth handle of the mug. Inside the glass, thick, frothy beer sloshed. Beer her father and brother had spent long hours crafting and perfecting.

Shame to waste it.

Tipping the mug back, she let the nutty, slightly sweet, rich flavors of her family roll across her tongue and flow down her throat. The taste brought memories of summers sitting around the barbeque or bonfire, spring storms on the back porch, and homey dinners with her family's laughter ringing around the table. Gilleses followed the craft of brewing, but even more, Gilleses loved sharing the fruits of their labors.

If she was going to hallucinate a brewery full of little people, she might as well join what looked to be a much more fitting celebration of her family's lives.   They deserved a wake.

Nothing spoke more about how the Gilles family lived and loved than their beers.

"More," she told the wee red-head who still sat hugging the spigot. Thick beer swirled into a glass. Amberlyn tipped it back, letting the tears finally run down her face. She brought her empty glass back down in front of the spigot. "Hit me again." The wee person topped off Amberlyn's glass, giving it a good, frothy head.

Tiny people began to creep back out of the corners of the brewery, carefully balancing their mugs. The small white-haired person who'd surrendered her glass to Amberlyn ran off and returned with a clean mug, looking at Amberlyn expectantly.

Amberlyn raised her glass in a toast. "My family makes the best damn ale anywhere. Here's to Jevlyn, Marianne, and Thomas Gilles. May they rest in peace and enjoy many a fine glass in the afterlife."

The sprites mimicked her motion with a boisterous cheer of "To Jev! To Mari! To Tom! Gilles beer forever!" before draining their own mugs with mind-boggling swiftness. She threw back her own glass, and suddenly all was forgiven; the party sprang back in riotous, full-swing.

Everywhere Amberlyn looked the metal, glass, and the old timber beams of the weathered storehouse were covered in capering wee folk, beer mugs, and hops flowers floating lazily around the room. One of the tiny people had found the row of hops barrels behind the boilers, belly-flopped down into its contents, and a cloud of the buds sprayed into the air, staying improbably suspended. The air brimmed with the pungent aromas of hops, yeast, and malted barley.

AMBERLYN WOKE UP, her head pounding, her cheek pressed against the cool concrete of the floor.

Or, upon further experimentation, her face stuck in some kind of sticky pool to the cool concrete of the floor. Her skin broke loose of the mess with a zippering sensation, and she sat up, her eyes squeezed shut. A whole drum corps beat away between her temples.

Water. She needed water. That, and some aspirin. Then she would try to make sense of whatever mental break-down had made her dream up a wake full of carousing small people. Or sprites, as her mind had labelled them as the party progressed last night.

Amberlyn staggered over to the utility sink and rinsed out one of a mountain of beer mugs piled in it. Filling it with water, she limped over to her father's desk and rummaged through his top drawer. Pushing aside the small person slumbering in the pen tray, she located the economy-sized jug of aspirin her father kept for emergencies, then at the sprite's muttered protest, re-shut the drawer against the light. Amberlyn tossed four aspirin back, chugged down the water, and waited for her gray matter to regroup.

Wait.

Amberlyn carefully re-opened the drawer to her father's desk. A small sprite with wild, blueberry-colored hair, green tunic and brown leggings, curled in the left side of the pen tray. It opened one liquid-copper eye at her, squinting against the light, and groaned before turning its face away into shadow.

"Too early," it muttered audibly. "Humans always want to be so diurnal. It isn't decent."

She apologized automatically and shut the drawer again. Panic began to boil in her stomach and push its way up her throat.

Last night had been a dream. None of it could be real. Especially the part where the party drank until the storage vats went completely dry. That part *couldn't be real.* She ran for the row of vats that were supposed to provide product for the already impossible next few weeks.

She checked each one with rising desperation, but all the vats stood hollow, empty. Reality set in with a vengeance; wee folk still infested her brewery.

Evidence of the events of the previous night lay everywhere. The floor was a sticky mess littered with hops, the tuns empty, the mash strewn like graffiti on tanks and walls. Fresh barley heaped on the floor under the silo chute, ground into the under layer of sticky wort and spilled beer. In places, she could make out the outlines where sprites had lain and made "barley angels."

No. No. No.

This wasn't how she was supposed to start her tenure as the master brewer. She hadn't trained as the apprentice. She didn't know how to do this job. And now everything, all the product that should have at least seen her through the first rocky month lay destroyed by one night of spritely revelry.

She had siblings to support, bills to pay, employees expecting checks for work already completed.

During that moment, the lowest point in her twenty-two years of life, the brewery in shambles, Amberlyn heard the main door push open. Of course, she hadn't locked it when she came in. *Of course,* someone would stop by now, at the absolute worst time, when she had no idea how to explain herself or what had happened here.

She turned slowly, pasting a sheepish smile on her face, hoping for her siblings in search of their older sister. Instead she saw the prim-suited form of Mr. Vickrit, from the local bank. As he gazed around the brewery, Amberlyn watched his face transform from sympathetic condolence and lengthen in disappointment.

"Mr. Vickrit," she tried weakly, taking a few steps toward him, "This looks bad, I know."

"Amberlyn Gilles, I knew your grandfather. I've known you, your father, and your brother since you were babies. My heart breaks for you."

"Thank you for your kind words. I really appreciate them, but you've caught me at a bad time. If you could come back, sometime later?"

The man shifted awkwardly and lowered his eyes before admitting, "That's not the only reason I came today, Amberlyn. I know it's not a good time for this, but in the past the bank has offered this brewery a large amount of credit. While your father was alive, I was able to convince my bosses that the brewery was a good investment; however, you have no similar experience with brewing or running a business of this size. The bank has decided not to offer you the same credit lines they extended to your father. I'm so sorry to bring this bad news, especially right now."

"It's ok, Mr. Vickrit. Thanks for telling me personally. It'll be tough without further credit, but I'll think of something." Amberlyn's head throbbed.

"I'm afraid you're not understanding the full scope. It's worse news than the brewery not being able to take out new loans," he said apologetically.

"What do you mean?"

"Since the brewery's credit has been revoked, all your father's loans will come due as part of his probate. I wish there was something I could do, but I've talked to the loan managers, and they wouldn't budge. Amberlyn, I don't see how you can pay any of it with the brewery in this state. As your friend, I advise you to sell and be done with it."

"You can't mean that."

"It's not an easy recommendation to make, I assure you."

"Exactly how much had my father borrowed?" Mr. Vickrit

named a number that made all of Amberlyn's blood fall into the pit of her stomach and then flare back up into her face. Impossible. That number was impossible. Even if she'd had the inventory from yesterday, that number was daunting. Now that she didn't... it was abysmal.

"You need to find a buyer," Mr. Vickrit advised gently, "Someone who already knows how to run this business. You aren't doing yourself, your family, or your employees any favors by letting the brewery get into this state."

"I'm going to clean up now. This place and myself—"

"You don't have to try to explain it to me; you might just want to be sure no one else sees the brewery like this. You have your younger siblings relying on you now, you know. Wish I had better news for you."

Mr. Vickrit gave her a sudden quick hug, and then turned, jerking open the door. As he left, he threw one last parting remark over his shoulder, cutting Amberlyn to the core. "Sell the brewery, Amberlyn."

For the second time in twenty-four hours, Amberlyn stood stunned just inside her family's brewery. *Gilles Brewers, family owned and operated since 1906.* She knew she was no brewer, but she had to make it work. She was a Gilles too.

Now, more than ever, this brewery needed to be making money again.

Regardless of anything else, Mr. Vickrit was right that she couldn't brew in a place as filthy as this. It *all* had to be cleaned and sterilized before anything else could happen. And she was the only one who could do that, now. She hosed herself down with the nozzle for cleaning the vats, shivering in the cold water and sending a few more hungover sprites scrambling for cover.

Mr. Vickrit hadn't mentioned the sprites during his visit. Amberlyn assumed that meant she *was* hallucinating, after all. She should probably go see a doctor, but she couldn't afford the time or money such a dire neurological event would require at the moment.

She changed into one of Thomas' old coveralls, rolling up the legs and sleeves, and wadding her own foul clothes in a bag to take home and wash later.

Amberlyn swept up the hops and grain that could be pried loose from the floor, and deposited all of it in one of the large dust bins. What a waste.

She started hosing the mash off of the vats and tanks, shepherding the mess into the drains on the floor. Some of it had dried on in a surprising short amount time, making her scour and scrub before she could even think about sterilizing. Hours later, Amberlyn's back was screaming, but the brewery actually looked functional.

Unfortunately, with all of the vats and fermenters empty, functional did not mean *functioning*. She needed to have product to sell if she was going to have enough money to pay off the brewery's debts. She needed to brew new inventory. Any more slacking off would be this brewery's death knell.

This was on her. Time to start replacing the inventory wasted during her (hopefully temporary) madness. Time to prove she could run this brewery. Time to provide for her siblings. Time to be there for the farmers, salesmen, and distributors who relied on this brewery for their livelihoods.

She pried the lids off the hops barrels, and found only one had been wasted. A quick inspection of the cold storage showed the brewing yeast remained untouched. Despite the barley spilled last night, there was still plenty of usable barley in the malter, and more waiting to be malted in the silo.

So she had ingredients, but no finished product to sell. There were really only four main ingredients in any decent brew: malted barley, hops, water, and yeast. She knew that much. Guesstimating on the ratios, she added malted barley and water to the mash mixer and watched it cook the grain and water into a dense slurry.

She stared at it. How long was she supposed to let it mix? An hour? Two hours? She was so very screwed. How exactly did transferring the mix to the lauter tun work anyway? A quick search on her smart phone for brewing times yielded a list of gravities and ratios that might as well have been in another language.

In fact, none of the fancy equipment in her father's brewery came with an operating manual, and she couldn't afford to call any employees in. Paying them what they were owed was already an issue.

While she waited for the mash to either be ready or explode into a literal hot mess, she tackled the mountain of dirty mugs in the sink. The mugs jostled and clinked as she washed them, some of the hot, sudsy water sloshing over the side.

After about an hour, she decided to try to hook up the transfer between the mixer and the lauter tun. She dragged over a large hose that looked like it *might* actually be for that purpose, and hooked it up to a coupling on the side of the masher. She draped the opposite end into the hatch on the lauter tun and said a prayer. Mash sprayed out from around the mis-matched coupling, coating her, her newly cleaned floors, and the masher tank. Swearing, she struggled to cut off the flow, while coated in uncomfortably hot, sticky mash.

"Hey," a sprite spluttered, poking its head out from under a nearby tank with part of its moss-green hair plastered down to its skull by a lump of mash. "I'm hung over; keep it down, will you? Some people are trying to sleep here. And I can bathe myself in something way nicer than that, thanks."

"Deal with it," Amberlyn snapped, frustrated, still struggling with the stupid hose.

The sprite gave a disparaging hrrump, but staggered out to inspect the former contents of the mash mixer now coating the floor. "I'm awake now anyhow," it grumbled, "Might as well see what you're up to."

"I am trying to *save* this brewery, no thanks to all of you. To stay open we need beer. Beer we all drank last night. So I'm making more."

"Doesn't look like you're being very successful at it," the sprite observed. "You know you shouldn't be trying to hook up the hose there, right?"

Amberlyn, dripping in mash, stared at the sprite. It met her stare for a moment and then resumed its commentary, unfazed.

"Not that it would have mattered even if you had found the pump and hooked it up right to get that pap into the lauter tun. Saddest excuse for mash, I've ever seen. You'd never even make a wort out of that weak stuff."

"Thank you for the criticisms from the peanut gallery."

"You need a better ratio than that, lassie. It's simple truth, especially if you're looking to turn out a quick pale ale to replenish stores."

Amberlyn stopped struggling with the hose and stepped away, letting the mash continue to spray uselessly onto the floor. She wiped a sticky hand down her face, to clear as much mash as possible out of her eyes, and glowered at the sprite. "And I suppose you know more about beer than how to drink it, then?" She was going to have to clean all of this up *again*. But the sprite had caught her attention. She *needed* beer.

"Why, we Sprites are as much a part of this brewery as the Gilleses. We can work just as hard as we drink, lass."

The last of the mash leaked weakly onto the floor as Amberlyn squeezed her eyes shut, trying to breathe through an imminent panic attack. Could she trust that such tiny people could really have the skills she desperately needed to learn?

"How come I've never seen you guys when I've visited here before?" Amberlyn asked, "No one ever mentioned you, either."

"We've always had an arrangement exclusively with the

brewmaster himself," the sprite intoned officiously. "Our presence here is very hush-hush. Need to know only."

"Last night didn't look like any arrangement I've ever seen, and I think I deserved to be in the need-to-know category." Amberlyn crossed her arms over her chest.

The sprite rubbed his hand down his face, and scratched his head. "Well, that's the thing. *We* didn't know if we had a new brew master until you showed up and could see us, after all. It wouldn't have been fitting *not* to drink to the dead. And with the brewery suffering three deaths at once, you have to drink thrice as much to give everyone their proper due. But there may be a wee bit of a mess to clean up, sure."

"A wee bit? I broke my back cleaning this place today!" Amberlyn swung her arm wide to encompass the whole brewery. "And, I guess I'll be cleaning this up now too," she pointed at her dismal brewing attempt, coating the masher and floor.

"We would've cleaned the place ourselves tonight," the sprite muttered. "Why humans always want to do a thing when any decent body'd be sleeping is beyond me. Besides, you drank just as much as the rest of us all. You can sure put them back, lassie. Formidable stamina, for a tall folk. It truly impressed everyone, it did."

"This can't happen again," Amberlyn warned direly. "I have to start all over from scratch now. *If* I can."

The small sprite stared up at her, an affronted look on his face. "Of course that was a one-time-only deal. You can't worry about practical stuff like reserves and cleanliness at a wake, after all. Like I said, we'll negotiate for our take."

"Your take, huh? Well, as the new brew master, I guess that means you negotiate with me." Amberlyn pointed at her own soggy chest with her thumb. He nodded expectantly, apparently waiting for her to put forward some kind of an offer.

The silence stretched. "So... how does this work?" she acceded finally.

"Jev gave us beer from the first storage tank, there, as the family's homage to the wee folk. In return, we'd help with the malt and other tasks around the brewery." He indicated the storage tank closest to the door that the red-headed sprite had been pouring from at the beginning of last night.

"If I give you the beer from that storage tank as it's ready, can you help me learn how to brew *and fast*, so we can keep this place open? You all must promise to leave the rest of the vats' contents for selling, and I'll set aside the product in that storage vat for sprites only. This is all contingent on you teaching me and letting me sell the rest of the beer. I have to have a lot, and I do mean *a lot* of beer ready and sold before the end of the month." She stuck out a hand. "Do we have a deal?"

The sprite slapped his small hand into hers excitedly, shaking vigorously, "You have a deal! We'll show you how to brew beer right proper. Fast too."

His face lit with joy as he ran across the floor, shouting, "The new brew master will give us *all* the beer from the first storage vat in return for keeping this place running! Get up you lazy buggers! This place has to be spotless! The brew master must brew starting *now*! Beer and Gilleses forever!"

Amberlyn watched in dumbfounded awe as the brewery erupted with activity, sprites emerging from equipment all over. The small people cleaned every possible surface, including the remains of her disastrous mash, all in a matter of minutes.

"Apparently, they really liked that deal," Amberlyn observed under her breath finally, letting the events of last night and this morning tick through her mind. Of course, fey folk always had a reputation for getting the best bargain possible.

If you believed in the old tales.

Which she kinda had to, now. It beat believing she'd gone

completely looney-bin crazy. And this deal actually still worked heavily in her favor.

Now she just had to trust that with the sprites' help, they'd be able turn out product fast enough to pay off the bank situation.

With the cleaning finished in a record time, a group of sprites waved her over to where they dangled and clambered over the mash-mixer.

"So tonight we're going to be steeping the mash and making the wort," the moss-haired bargainer instructed. "We're going to go for several quick pales because they can be cloudy without affecting quality, and can be kegged instead of bottled to speed up the carbonation and conditioning process. You should be able sell the kegs to the pubs and taverns on your Da's list for top dollar with no problem once we're done. But you have to be very exact with your starting wort ratios or you'll end up with undrinkable swill rather than Gilles beer. Observe what we do carefully here, and we'll let you try measuring the next batch." Amberlyn watched teams of two sprites heft scoops of barley as large as they were, measuring out the malted barley to into the mash mixer.

"So when you say 'quick,' when will it be ready to sell? Not to be panicky, but we have no beer right now and no money."

"Ah, don't fret yourself so much, Ammie. We have a bargain, and sprites always honor their promises. Generosity requires a return, it does. We can start the next batch of mash in four hours when this goes to the lauter tun, and you'll have kegs ready to start going out to your customers in six days. You can start taking orders for it now, even. Cross my heart or poke me with iron." The sprite held up a hand, its fingers arranged in what Amberlyn presumed must be some archaic symbol of honor. "And once we get all your bills paid to the bank-man, we can start showin' you how to do even better beers. Make your family proud and keep this place hummin' for sure." The sprite chuckled excitedly, already making plans of all the beers it wanted to craft in the future.

Amberlyn blew out a long breath. It looked like she had a lot to learn, an incredibly short time-line and some very capable, if small, teachers. She had to blink rapidly in order to keep the sprites from becoming blurry.

For the first time since realizing she had just inherited all of her parents' responsibilities, she believed she might have the capability to fufill her family's traditions and obligations. Her skin prickled with gratitude and relief. Her salvation came as an unexpected and unlikely inheritance.

Beer and Gilleses forever.

THE DRAGON WENT DOWN TO DYFI

I'm not actually a fan of Country Music.

That said, when I was in high school there we did a talent show. And a group of us—Kiyomi, Jesse, Ibra, Kelly, Eric, you know who you are—sat down and took "The Devil Went Down to Georgia" apart with a fine-toothed comb in order for those five to reproduce it on stage. Possibly the best thing that's ever been put on as part of a high school talent show, as we put a lot of work into deciphering the music, and they put a lot of work into reproducing it.

It was a real team effort, and it indelibly engraved every note of that song into the inside of my skull.

Fast forward to the great Superstars Writing Seminar. This gathering, hosted by the great Kevin J. Anderson, is a fabulous crash-course in the business of being an author. I recommend it highly, by the way. Anyways, the "tribe," as we participants in that conference call ourselves, puts together an anthology every once in a while as a way to fund scholarships to the conference.

Dragon Writers is one such anthology. It features such

authors as Brandon Sanderson, Todd McCaffery, David Farland, Jodie Lynn Nye... and Frog Jones. This is the one story that Esther and I submitted under our individual names, as we both decided to submit individually to this anthology for some reason that I don't honestly remember.

The theme of the anthology was dragons. And creativity. Had to be both. Now, based on the title, and based on the fact that it's coming from a writing seminar, I figured that there'd be a lot of dragons-and-writing stories (and I wasn't wrong). So, I decided to take my other creative obsession—music—and write about that, instead.

I thought about the old Welsh Eisteddfod, and thought about the great Red Dragon of Wales—it shows up on the flag— showing up to compete. And I said to myself, "You know, sort of like 'The Devil Went Down to Georgia,'" except with a dragon and harps.

And then my eyebrows flew up as I realized how awesome what I'd said was. The rest of this story wrote itself, and got itself published.

6
THE DRAGON WENT DOWN
TO DYFI

JONATHAN STRODE to the center of the amphitheater without hesitation. Soft dirt scratched beneath his doeskin boots. His bright blue tabard hung over a flawlessly clean linen tunic. His wide-brimmed hat shone with bright plumage that whispered quietly in the soft breeze coming off the Dyfi River.

The Eisteddfod, the great competition of bards, had been a mere formality for several years. Jonathan felt no anxiety entering the competition. He knew his victory to be a foregone conclusion. The purple-robed Prifardd, the head of the Bardic Guild, looked on with mild interest. His high-backed wooden chair was carved with the image of Y Ddraig Goch, the Red Dragon, the heraldry of the kingdom of Gwynedd, and the words eisteddfod aberdyfi. It was a chair that, by all rights, should have belonged to Jonathan.

The Prifardd stood slowly, then announced the only performance that mattered. "Our final act is Jonathan Evans," he said in a tepid tone.

Despite his lack of enthusiasm, the crowd erupted in applause, stomping and hooting. The only silent ones wore the blue tabard; the other bards who'd performed in the amphitheater before him.

Everyone knew they'd been competing for *second* place.

Jonathan took his seat on the old, wooden stump, worn smooth by years of bards sitting in this very place. He brought his harp to his lap and began to play.

The tune that flowed forth was, technically, perfect. His hands followed the strings, but his eyes remained fixed on the Prifardd's. Jonathan should have held that honorable title, but the Prifardd refused to join the competition. Thus, Jonathan could enter the Eisteddfod every year, demonstrating to one and all that no bard could match his playing. But he could not sit the chair.

His hands, calloused from practice, flew over the strings with a will of their own, leaving his mind free to dwell on the greatest crowd the Aberdyfi Eisteddfod had ever drawn. They'd come to watch *him*. He may not wear the purple robe or sit the bardic chair, but no other harper commanded the price of Jonathan Evans in the inns of Gwynedd.

Jonathan did not listen to himself. Music, as a finished product, lacked significance; the note he had just produced was nowhere near as important as the string he had yet to pluck. His hands wove complicated melodies on the right, while his left danced along the big bass strings further away. His flawless performance concluded, and the crowd erupted in applause.

The Prifardd stood, shaking his head, and declared Jonathan the greatest competitor of the day.

"I challenge the Prifardd!" Jonathan said in a formal cadence. This, too, was tradition. The Prifardd could choose to defend his title or to decline.

The bard begin to shake his head.

"Coward!" shouted Jonathan. This was distinctly *not* tradition. He leaped to his feet, swinging his harp by its shoulder with his right hand, pointing at the Prifardd with his left. "Every year for four years I stand before these people, and every year for four years you declare me the victor. Aberdyfi knows, Gwynedd knows—*you* know—that I should sit that chair. You dishonor your robes by hiding. I say you are a coward."

The crowd grew silent.

The old bard simply tossed the victory pouch in the dirt of the amphitheater floor, turned his back on Jonathan, and left the auditorium. The crowd, hushed, followed him.

Jonathan Evans, four-time champion of the Aberdyfi Eisteddfod, stood alone in the amphitheater, holding his harp.

NOT EVEN THE fastest harp in Gwynedd could defeat the Bardic Guild. No crowd he could draw was worth being placed on the guild's blacklist, and so no innkeeper would let him through the door. For a full year, Jonathan played for pennies near the fisherman's wharf.

He kept his harp tuned, and his fingers still knew their path across the strings, but his eyes were dim and his head sagged low. His bright, plumed hat and elaborate hose were replaced by simple, rustic clothes. The gray wool of his tattered pants and shirt clashed with the fine polished carving on his harp. He made his home on a pallet under the wharf. The rank smell of dead fish and rotting seaweed filled his nostrils, and the cold air off the sea chilled his joints into a constant, stiff ache.

He still drew a crowd, but they no longer cheered for him. Instead, they gathered to see the "Beggar Bard." A rough clay bowl sat in front of him to catch the occasional penny from the crowd, a pitiful homage to the complex melodies and harmonies his fingers plucked.

Once again, the people gathered for the Eisteddfod, but Jonathan, the once-great champion, could no longer enter the amphitheater.

A small, blond-haired boy, towed by his mother, stopped in front of him. "Mama, look!" said the boy. "It's Evans the Harp! He's playing outside this year."

The mother shot a distasteful glance at Jonathan, then moved her son to the other side. "Never you mind him. We're here to see the *real* bards."

"But, Mama!" said the boy. "He *is* a real bard. He wins *all the time!*"

Jonathan smiled at the boy, then favored the woman with a nod.

"Your mother's got the right of it, boyo. I'm just a harper on the street. Go in and listen; mayhap you'll get to hear the Prifardd himself take the stage. He hasn't done that in five years, you know. Me, all I ask is a coin these days."

The woman frowned, but she placed a penny into his bowl. "Your coin, sir. Now come along, Bran. They're about to begin."

Bran kept his eyes on Jonathan as his mother pulled him into the amphitheater.

After the first round of applause, Jonathan's fingers stilled, and he placed his harp into its well-oiled leather case. He closed his eyes to listen.

To hear the "acceptable" bards, the ones approved by the Guild, grated on him like broken glass. The soft breeze off the Dyfi carried their tunes to him, and he picked their flaws from the air and wallowed in them.

Too slow. Missed the fingering. Bad accent. Jonathan's knuckles turned white as he clutched his harp case and listened to the grand display of mediocrity.

Eventually, his senses bruised to the point of assault, he shook his head, picked up his harp, and walked off. There would be no more pennies today; the Beggar Bard had earned his last.

And so, while all the people of Aberdyfi gathered to hear the bards of the Eisteddfod, it was Jonathan Evans who first saw the dragon.

Y DDRAIG GOCH. The Red Dragon.

There were songs about the dragon. No bard in living memory had seen it, but all the old lays agreed that it slept in a rocky cave high atop Cadair Idris. Some songs lauded Y Ddraig Goch as the defender of Gwynedd. Even High King Cadwalader had placed the Red Dragon on his banner, claiming the great beast's patronage.

But other tales were not so kindly.

The Red Dragon took all the sheep from a village and left the people to starve. The Red Dragon enslaved the people of a town and demand tribute. The Red Dragon unleashed his fiery breath upon a castle, destroying it simply because it could.

Yet all the stories agreed that Y Ddraig Goch was a being of immense power.

And now it flew in the skies above Cadair Idris. It circled the mountain, coiling upward into the air with its long, serpentine body and great red wings.

Then, Y Ddraig Goch spread his wings wide and began to soar, straight at the village of Aberdyfi.

Jonathan could only stare as the great beast approached. He heard the lackluster performances of the Eisteddfod stop and the cries of the villagers begin, but he was mesmerized by the great beauty of the dragon. Its horns swept back and away from its head, fading from a deep red to a pinkish-white. Its snout sharpened almost to a beak, and the scaly plates about the dragon's face added to its avian appearance.

The neck and body, however, were pure reptile. Four scaled legs curled back against its body in flight, and the leathery-red coating of its wings was shot through with deep scarlet veins and thick bones. The sun glinted off the dragon's scales, reflecting as from a shattered, bloodstained mirror.

Jonathan heard screams erupting behind him. Y Ddraig Goch circled the town, then flapped its wings and landed in the amphitheater, its red body disappearing into the sunken stadium.

Jonathan heard screams erupting, and the townspeople of Aberdyfi boiled over the lip of the amphitheater, in panicked flight away from the terrible, awesome creature.

"Stop." The command was issued in a pitch so low it could not be—and most certainly wasn't—human.

Jonathan savored the rich, bass timbre of Y Ddraig Goch's voice as it rumbled through his entire body.

"Be seated."

The people, feeling the same force, stopped in their tracks and turned back toward the amphitheater. Jonathan could not resist, either. The Beggar Bard had little life left to preserve.

Jonathan looked over the lip of the amphitheater. The dragon's right front claw rested on the bardic stump where Jonathan had so often sat. The beast craned its neck to bring himself face-to-face with the Prifardd.

"Tell me, Prifardd. Who here shall champion Aberdyfi in the Eisteddfod?"

The Prifardd's eyebrows rose, and he shrank back into his seat, under the carving of the very beast who addressed him. "Champion?" he asked, his voice high and shaking.

"Champion. I desire to place a challenge to this village. None in Gwynedd can claim superiority to me. In Degannwy, they bragged once of their impregnable castle, which I broke upon their heads. In Aberffaw, they claimed their woolen sheep as the greatest in the land, so I did feast upon them. Here, you claim the prowess of your string-pluckers. I shall not have my people thinking that I may be bested in

anything. For I am Y Ddraig Goch—the true Lord of Gwynedd and all Wales. And I shall not be outdone."

The Prifardd swallowed hard. To his credit, though, he stood tall before the dragon. "If you wish to enter the Eisteddfod, then by all means, I shall permit—"

"Permit? You permit nothing, mortal. I am here to place a challenge before the greatest harper in the land, not to stand in line. Come, Prifardd. Name your champion. I shall even set stakes. In the unlikely event that your champion best me with his song, he shall have my harp."

At this, the dragon raised its front leg from the stump and wove intricate patterns in the air. A great, golden harp, perfectly fitted for the sheer mass of the dragon, appeared. Its strings were separated enough to allow gargantuan claws to pluck with ease, making the grade of the sound box shallower than usual. This lengthened the harp to a proportion that made Jonathan blink with the strangeness of it.

The strings themselves glinted steely gray, and Jonathan wondered what material could take a pluck from those claws and sound true instead of snap. Whatever it was, when combined with the gold framework of the harp itself, and given the immense size of the instrument, Jonathan could only begin to guess at its value. He stared at the dragon's harp longingly, then looked down at his oiled-leather case.

"Of course, in the event of a loss, I shall burn your village and seize your champion. He shall be chained in Cadair Idris, eating only of my scraps and playing songs of my glory whenever I wish it. If you have no champion, then I shall simply burn the village for its arrogance and leave it at that. Come—who among you thinks yourself the greatest of the string-pluckers? Who shall test me in this contest of art?"

Silence fell over the auditorium. All the bards gathered in line for the Eisteddfod looked at each other, then at the dragon. None of them moved to volunteer. The Prifardd stood stock-still, staring at the dragon as though the power of his gaze alone could protect Aberdyfi from this terror.

Jonathan strode down the aisle.

"Y Ddraig Goch! My name is Jonathan Evans!" he shouted, his voice piercing the silence. The crowd turned to stare at the Beggar Bard as he worked his way down to the amphitheater floor. "I am banned from competition in the Eisteddfod, and therefore engaging with you may be tantamount to sacrilege. Nevertheless, I accept your wager. I believe you shall come to rue this day, for I am the greatest harper the world has ever seen."

"Faugh! This beggar is the best you can send, Prifardd? Is he truly your choice of Champion? Or do you mean to doom a madman rather than risk one of your own?"

The Prifardd turned to the dragon and said, "You are mistaken, Sir Ddraig. He who stands before you is Evans the Harp, the Beggar Bard, and the most skilled harper Gwynedd has ever seen. If you seek a challenger, he is our choice. Only, I beg you to allow for a single day before the competition so that he may be once again inducted into the guild. Otherwise, as he says, his participation in the Eisteddfod would be sacrilege. Not even the great Y Ddraig Goch would choose to offend the Gods, I believe?"

The dragon snorted, and a cloud of acrid smoke engulfed the Prifardd.

"A single day. At nightfall tomorrow, we shall test the harp of the Beggar Bard against the harp of Y Ddraig Goch. And the world will see that no human shall ever be the equal of me."

Y Ddraig Goch unfurled its red wings, poised itself, then sprung into the air and away from the amphitheater, leaving Jonathan standing in the aisle, harp already halfway out of its satchel, staring at the Prifardd.

"What need have you of a day? The last time I joined the Bard's Guild, it was but a simple ceremony."

The old man strode toward Jonathan. When close, he bent his head and whispered. "Hush, man. Do you want that drake to hear you and circle back? Take a day; tomorrow is the hardest competition you're ever like to have. Come to the Three Princes Inn. Let me buy you a supper and an ale, that your fingers will not tremble. You should be prepared." The Prifardd glanced pointedly around at the crowd of villagers still in the amphitheater. "We should *all* be prepared."

Jonathan understood. "And let the villagers clear out?"

"Those who can. You are a great harper, Jonathan, though you lack somewhat. But let us bet with the lives of as few as possible."

Jonathan nodded, conceding the point. As much as he wanted to hear what the dragon could do with that titanic harp, he did not want the deaths of the villagers on his head.

"The Three Princes, then."

THE THREE PRINCES drew the best-paying crowds in Aberdyfi. The inn was built out of hewn lumber, the same as most of the town, its furniture simple and rough. However, the innkeeper had insisted on a maniacal fastidiousness from his employees.

Thus, when the Beggar Bard entered the inn, the patrons all turned to stare at him. Wearing his ragged clothing, and smelling very much as though he belonged in one of the town's lesser establishments, Jonathan tried to keep his head high. The innkeeper met Jonathan's eyes, then jerked his head up the steps.

Jonathan nodded his thanks and proceeded upstairs.

The Prifardd had left the door to a room open; he sat inside next to a small, wooden desk. Two candles flickered their meager light in the dark, windowless room. On the bed lay a set of fresh clothes, and next to the bed a steaming tub of water had been drawn.

Jonathan eyed the tub with longing.

"Go ahead," said the Prifardd. "You should look—and smell—your best to play in the Eisteddfod tomorrow."

A year ago, Jonathan would have turned up his nose at such charity. To strip down in front of a man he held in contempt would have humiliated him into rage. But the Beggar Bard's desire to slough off a year's worth of filth and rejoin the ranks of humanity overrode any lingering sense of pride. He quickly pulled off his reeking rags and lowered himself into the steaming water.

"So," said the Prifardd. "Do you truly believe you can best Y Ddraig Goch?"

Jonathan stared at the Prifardd for a long minute before answering. "You feared to play against me in the amphitheater. Do you now doubt that I am the best hope for the village?"

The last time Jonathan had accused the Prifardd of cowardice, it had shattered his life. He braced himself, waiting for rage, rejection or exasperation. When the Prifardd instead cracked a half-smile and shook his head, Jonathan found himself breathing in relief.

"Best hope? Yes, you are that. But just because a rat is grander than a mouse does not mean he has good odds against the cat."

Jonathan leaned his head back into the tub and let his eyes follow the flickering candlelight as it danced on the exposed wooden rafters. "Aye, that's true. But a life in chains in a dragon's lair, living off scraps, can't be much worse than the life of the Beggar Bard."

"And knowing the rest of the village burned?"

"I didn't hear anyone else volunteer. Those who can flee are on their way away from here. At least I bought them some time."

The Prifardd shook his head. "You didn't do this for the village. You've never cared about the village. The only thing Jonathan Evans has ever cared about is his own pride. So why volunteer? Tell me the truth."

"Because I am the best," said Jonathan. "I'm the best harper to walk the streets of Aberdyfi, and if any harp is fit to challenge Y Ddraig Goch, it's mine. I did it for my pride."

"And that is why you will lose," said the Prifardd.

Jonathan shook his head. "A bard's pride is what holds him together. Without pride, your hands twitch and tremble on the strings. Without pride, your voice shakes with the trepidation of the performance. Pride is the lifeblood of a bard, and you call it my weakness?"

"No," said the Prifardd. "Your weakness is not your pride; it is your reluctance to feel anything *other* than pride."

"How else can I play against a beast as mighty as Y Ddraig Goch?"

"Your music has always been the music of arrogance. Fast, perfect, splendid. You play the harp in a grand style, a style that makes you seem larger than life, that makes the audience feel your pride as though it were their own. When your fingers dance the strings, you convey the only emotion you have ever wanted to convey."

"And I do it well. So speak your problem."

"My problem is this: Not even the pride of the great Evans the Harp, four-time champion of the Eisteddfod, can match the pride of Y Ddraig Goch. You are pitting yourself against a beast whose pride has lasted for eons, whose every interaction with man seems to be bent on ensuring that man keep his place beneath the wings of the dragon. You are up against a being whose pride you simply cannot surpass. If you try to impress the audience, what few remain, with your pride tomorrow, then you will be remembered only as the foolish slave who challenged the Red Dragon."

"So what would you have me do, old man? Weep for the crowd? Fear the dragon and the doom it brings? I am who I am, Prifardd. And if you truly believe your way superior, you would have met my challenge in the amphitheater."

"And I would have lost. Oh, I admit it. Had I accepted your challenge, you would wear the purple robes and sit the wooden seat, and I would simply have gone back to being Davies the Song. But our art would have lost all depth in the process, and the guild would have suffered for it. You are brilliant, but you are only brilliant at conveying one thing."

"So let me *do* what I am brilliant at," Jonathan said, sliding his upper torso out of the tub and locking eyes with the Prifardd.

"You are the moon before the sun. Make this a competition of beauty, not brightness." With that, the Prifardd rose from his seat. At the doorway, he turned his head and said over his shoulder, "At least think on the last year, and whether remaining a beggar or a slave is truly your desire."

Jonathan scoffed and lowered himself back down into the warm, soothing water. If this was to be his last, free night, he would certainly make sure to enjoy it.

Y DDRAIG GOCH'S teeth shone bright white against his crimson-scaled face as Jonathan entered the sparsely-populated amphitheater. Jonathan kept his gaze fixed on the dragon's, not flinching from the great beast.

The Prifardd, seated on his wooden chair, broke the silence. "Y Ddraig Goch challenges and shall therefore perform first. Evans, step to the wings. Sir Ddraig, begin at your leisure."

The great dragon stretched its wings over those few for whom witnessing this competition was worth the risk of the dragon's rage. It brought its claws up for its spell-weaving, adding those deep, guttural tones. This time, when the harp appeared, it was joined by a number of others. There were lap-harps, such as Jonathan's, great floor harps, and wire clairseach lining the floor of the amphitheater.

"Very well, Prifardd. I shall present my challenge. Let all here witness that no human bard can compete with me, for I am Y Ddraig Goch, the greatest being in Wales."

The floor harps started playing on their own, their low tones creating a powerful bass line. The sound resonated among the stone seats of the amphitheater, bouncing back and forth and combining with the deep sound boxes. The lap harps and the clairseach began weaving a counterpoint to the bass.

Then Y Ddraig Goch set talon to string, and began to play its great golden instrument.

Power.

The power of the dragon shone in its music, filling the auditorium with a sense of awe and wonder. The dragon played with head high, and the music it made struck hard, fast, and true. It was a song of glory in battle, in competition. A song of dragons, not men.

Jonathan could hear the weakness in his own species, in *humanity,* thrumming through his body as Y Ddraig Goch channeled all its draconic arrogance into a rhythm of climbing, rising, self-glorifying crescendo. The final notes, a stately challenge to all, left Jonathan breathless, with one thought firmly in his mind.

I cannot win.

He stared down at his lone harp. The tool of one man, and a traveling man at that, could weave no such interdependent harmony as Y Ddraig Goch had put forth. His harp could not to compete on the same stage as the Red Dragon. As the dragon backed away, ceding him the amphitheater with a sneer, Jonathan trembled.

How can I follow this act?

"You are the moon before the sun. Make this a competition of beauty, not brightness."

And what was beauty? Jonathan pondered that question on his slow walk to the player's stump, now rough from the claws of the dragon. How did one make something beautiful without brightness? He sat on the stump. What could he possibly put into his music that Y Ddraig Goch could not?

He looked out over the crowd and caught the eyes of the small child Bran. His mother, head bowed low, did not meet his eyes. Why had she stayed? Why had she allowed Bran to stay? Their doom had been sealed by his arrogance, as had the doom of all those who surrounded him, waiting for his feeble response to the wall of sound that still seemed to reverberate in the very stones of the amphitheater.

Jonathan took a breath, then reached forward his left hand and plucked a single, low string. It rang true, the old sound box of polished wood giving warmth to the single note. He had exactly one performance left in his life, and he knew it. He could not waste it.

He plucked again, moving a step and a half higher. His right hand ran a pentatonic scale, more out of habit than desire. He moved slowly, in a bittersweet haze, savoring each note as it rang. Each pitch sounded clear, true, and simple, and a tear made its way down Jonathan's cheek as he began his final performance for any human ear.

And there, in the wetness the tear left atop his harp's shoulder, lay his answer. His left hand hit a minor chord, and he began a slow, mournful melody.

He could not match arrogance with arrogance, but the dragon was a being who had never known sorrow. He grasped at his pain in desperation, the pain of his potential loss, and then, as his confidence began to grow, the pain of his year spent on the streets. He let all of it flow onto his strings, and his hands danced a pattern they'd never traced before, shifting in and out of minor keys in a slow dirge.

And then hope. It had a different flavor from the bombastic flair of his previous performances. His arrogant strut that came from technical perfection had been replaced by a soaring rise, moving out of the minor key. His left hand traced a rapid bass line while his right kept to the pentatonic scale, playing a clean, simple melody over the pounding bass as he channeled the ability to overcome imperfection into the music.

And it was this the dragon lacked. Jonathan's music did not boast of perfection, but rather of tenacity. He played the song of hope, not pride, and as he locked eyes with Y Ddraig Goch, he let his music tell the dragon that humankind's beauty lay not in being without flaw, but rather in overcoming. In triumph. His final coda sang with the joy of it, a bouncing reel that washed away any wall between audience and performer, and he saw that even one of the dragon's mighty talons had begun to tap along with the music.

When he finished, he simply bowed to the dragon. Y Ddraig Goch lowered his head and craned his long, serpentine neck out to Jonathan.

They froze in a tableau. The giant, perfect drake and the smiling, imperfect human, gazes locked. The only sounds were the rustle of the cold breeze off the Dyfi and the rumbling breath of the dragon.

After a long minute, the Red Dragon pulled its head back, then slowly pushed the great, golden harp in front of Jonathan. Wordlessly, Y Ddraig Goch spread its wings to take to the air once more.

"Dragon!" shouted Jonathan.

The great beast stopped, mid-flap, to turn its gaze back to Jonathan.

"Thank you for your challenge. It was an honor to Aberdyfi. If you choose to join us for the Eisteddfod next year, I would be

FROG JONES & ESTHER JONES

happy to join you once again on the floor of the amphitheater to test our songs against one another. Perhaps next time no wager of harp against town will be necessary."

Y Ddraig Goch snorted, a gout of smoke billowing from its nostrils. It made no verbal response, but rather beat its wings, launching into the air. However, instead of flying back directly, the great Red Dragon circled the village, dipping his wings as he did.

Next year's Eisteddfod was sure to draw the biggest crowd yet.

DUMPSTER DIVING

Esther took point on this one, and when she first came up with the concept it absolutely sent me into gales of laughter.

"Dumpster Diving" twists the werewolf tale. A werewolf, of course, is half-canine, half-human. We all know that if you're bitten by a werewolf, you become one. The very simple question Dumpster Diving asked was... what if that's just as true for dogs as it is humans?

What happens when a scrappy little stray gets bitten by a werewolf?

"Dumpster Diving" is the story of Heyboy—because it's told in the first person, and that is how the dog understands his name. He's loyal to the boy who regularly slips him treats, and otherwise is a purely greedy little mutt.

At Westercon in 2019, the master of urban fantasy, Laurell K. Hamilton herself, fell in love with Heyboy and ended up purchasing an entire copy of Tales of the Pack, the original anthology he appeared in. So, you know... that's the selling point. It's urban werewolf fiction good enough that one of the Queens of urban werewolf fiction wanted a copy.

One of these days, we're going to write the further adventures of Heyboy. We've thought about doing it as an illustrated children's book, although if we do that he'll have to remember to wear clothes when he shifts into his human form. He's too good a character to leave sitting there, waiting to appear once more and make me double over laughing again.

7

DUMPSTER DIVING

I STALKED toward the dumpster in the early dawn light. Its alluring smells drifted down the alley, directly into my empty belly. My stomach cramped with hunger. It had already been a whole day and night since I'd begged a few scraps of bacon from the boy. He usually waited for the big yellow thing to come pick him up a few blocks from here. We had an arrangement.

I had a small frame for a street mutt. My father may have been a poodle, but I was a terrier all the way to the tips of my claws. The point is, head-to-head I can't stand up against the bigger strays. It's why I loved begging. Trouble was, not enough humans were susceptible. Kids were much better, but usually gave less food. A few scraps, nothing more.

I won most of my food by being quick and sneaky.

I slunk up on the far side of the big blue container, sniffing. I'd claw my way up and in if I had to. I placed my paws on its shiny surface, stretching my nose up toward the lid. I took a moment to savor the aromas of old meat and juices leaking out.

A rustling on the other side of dumpster caught my attention. I cocked my head, my ears lifting. Fight of flight? Fight. I strained my haunches and hopped on top of the dumpster before anyone else could claim my prize. Obviously, once I was on the top of the dumpster, I was bigger than anything else out here. Any scavengers would *have* to give up against my superior height.

Besides, my stomach demanded I not give this one up. I'd gotten on top. I was bigger now. The garbage was *my* feast.

A dirty, bedraggled human came out around the front of the dumpster. Not bothered by my superiority, he started to lift the lid. It was typical human behavior, but always supremely aggravating.

My sense of injustice rose.

Humans could walk into one of the buildings lined with food and get a whole bag of meat! Multiple bags, sometimes. I'd tried to check it out myself, and been chased out by a lady with a broom. Those buildings were apparently for humans only. There was no reason to poach my dumpster. Besides, he looked pretty scrawny. I was, after all, on top of the dumpster.

I'd make him 'shoo' like the humans were always doing to me, for once.

I raised my light brown fur and growled low in my chest, signaling my ownership. I lowered my bushy brown forelocks over my eyes, trying to look as scary as possible for a terrier with slightly curly hair.

The human looked up and glared at me. He said something to me in a low gutteral voice, something that sounded like, "Retep dog! Get away rommi ya vaderc. Eckl ip remit!" He sounded really upset at that last part.

Now, I'm not stupid, but I've only bothered to learn the words in the human language that seemed useful. For instance, "Heyboy," is me. "Want some?" or "Goodboy" means the human is going to feed me. "Stupid mutt," and any number of other expletives, generally means the human is angry and wants me to go away.

Learning the rest just seemed like a bother.

Anyway, this human was rude. The dumpster was way bigger than he was, and since I was above it, so was I. Clearly, the contents were mine! I *demanded* respect.

I bared my teeth in an act of warning and snapped at the arm holding open the other side of container.

This human didn't react the way I expected. A normal response would have included snatching back his arm from my indisputably vicious bite while backing away from my show of superior strength. Which of course, would concede the dumpster to me.

Instead of jerking his arm away and jumping back though, he snarled at me. His body seemed to move under his cloths, his eyes going feral.

My terrier teeth savaged a full inch and a half of his wrist.

Then I froze.

His shoulders shot upward with a sudden spurt, gaining three feet of height over my perch on the dumpster. His face and teeth elongated. His shoulders, arms, and legs bulked up with muscles, his skin now covered with dark, matted fur.

The wrist in my mouth tasted strangely gamey. I rolled an eye toward his fingers and was rewarded by the sight of his gleaming three inch claws. Way, way bigger than my own modest scratchers.

I gingerly started to unlatch my jaw, but too slow. The slavering not-human latched those huge, ridiculously sharp canines onto my back left leg. He swept me off the dumpster, ripping my mouth away from his wrist like he didn't even feel it. Then, with my leg still trapped and bleeding, he worried me back and forth over the grungy pavement until all the blood rushed to my head.

Trapped in those jaws, I saw all the meals I'd ever eaten flash before my eyes.

Just when I thought he was truly going to eat me, he threw me against the alley wall with one last violent thrash of his head. I bashed into the concrete with an undignified squeal, stars pricking the edges of my vision. I fell to the ground, landing on three paws. Now that I was back down at street level, I was noticeably much smaller than him. *Damn.* For now, he had the upper hand. I would have to leave this dumpster for another day. I tore down the alley away from him as fast as my little body would go.

Risking a last glance over my shoulder, I looked back and saw the not-human digging through the dumpster with his hulking claws and teeth, feasting on *my* breakfast.

I TRIED to go up to a human for help, but he backed away. Then he just stood there, talking into a little black square with unfamiliar words. I was hurting, so I simply crawled back to my cardboard box under the Fourth Street Bridge feeling light-headed and mangled, dragging my left leg behind me.

I'd tucked the box under one of the bridge supports, so it was like a cave. I didn't want to get my cardboard abode all soggy, so I sat outside and tried to lick the wound to get it to stop bleeding.

The ravaged inside of my thigh reminded me rather sickeningly of a raw chicken leg I'd seen once. Looking on the bright side, I wasn't really hungry anymore.

No, wait. I was.

I was just too tired to care anymore, so I closed my eyes instead.

When I opened them again, it was to excruciating pain, and not just in my leg. My head pounded; it felt like my limbs were trying to go through another growth spurt. I should have been done with those years ago.

I put my paw in front of my nose, but it did not look like my paw. This paw was giant and tipped with lengthy claws. They reminded me of the silvery knives humans sometimes carried. The paw was attached to an equally beefy foreleg.

The fur wasn't right either. My fur was a light, fluffy honey-brown, always messing up my street mutt credibility. This fur was the right color, but coarse, stringy, and long. Not mine at all.

I ran my tongue over my teeth. They were so sharp, I nicked it on accident. I wondered if I should even be able to bite my tongue if I wasn't trying to chew. It didn't seem right.

I lumbered up, placing my weight on all four paws, but that didn't feel right either. I looked down at the giant, corded muscles in my legs, and tried standing up right. My cardboard home seemed weirdly small and far away where it sat on the pavement. I stumbled over to a puddle on too-big feet. Propping myself up against the wall, I squinted at the snarling giant in the reflection. Nothing was normal, but I didn't care. I was huge. I immediately started making plans to hunt down a cow or a horse and eat it.

Unfortunately, my plans were cut short when another seizure of pain hit me. I scrabbled at the pavement trying to hold on to the big brawny frame. With that form, I could eat anything, go anywhere, and beat up the feline bully on Main Street. He had it coming.

After the wave of pain passed, I lay panting for a moment. I knew I had shrunk, the massive muscles of a minute before no longer present, but I didn't feel like my normal doggy self. I reached a paw out, seeing if it would take my weight, and did a double take.

My paw was pink. Pink and hairless.

Kind of like it was... human? I tried that idea on for size. I was human.

I wiggled the digits where my claws should have been. Human paws were so weird. I sat up and looked at the pink hind legs spayed out in front of me. They were so long. It must be like walking on poles.

Oh yeah-- what about the bite?

I poked my left thigh. Where there should have been a raw bite mark, there was puckered flesh that didn't quite look like the rest. But it wasn't bleeding. That was good, I guessed, although I'd never had a cut heal so fast before.

A third seizure hit me, and all of a sudden I was back to my usual, tiny, street mutt self.

I looked at my paws on the ground for a moment. My thigh still seemed healed. I trotted in and out of my box cave a couple times, and everything was in working order. Huh.

I thought about the not-human from this morning. He had looked like a human before I bit him. Then he changed forms, bit me, and I started changing forms.

Obviously, the human himself had been nothing special. I'd been winning our confrontation, hands-down. Then he cheated, changing forms to win. Anything that scrawny excuse for a human could do, I bet I could do better.

Being human would be *very* useful...

I squeezed my eyes shut and focused on wanting to be human. Humans could eat meat, and chicken, and no one *ever* told them to 'shoo'. Slowly, I felt my bones begin to lengthen and my limbs straightened. I opened my eyes and looked down at my pink flesh gleefully. That hadn't been too hard. I sprawled on the ground and rolled with joy.

This was going to be awesome.

Now for the hard part. Passing myself off as human meant I could only walk on my hind legs. This seemed silly, but since humans' forelegs were so much shorter, it kind of made sense.

I braced my paws against the pavement and got my both my hind and forelegs underneath me. Then using my strange new paws I grabbed the wall until I was totally upright. The ground was a long way down.

This is just like being on a dumpster. No wonder humans never shoo.

My balance seemed pretty wobbly at first. I walked up and down in front of my box with the wall's help, getting more confident each time. Turns out walking on two feet was a lot like when I would bound from my hind legs to my forelegs in running. Only, as a human you landed on one paw instead of two. Once I got the hang of it, it wasn't too bad.

I glanced at the sky outside the bridge, and froze, shocked. The sun was high, too much time had passed. If I didn't leave now, I was going to miss the boy with the bacon. He *always* had bacon for Heyboy.

I scrambled out from under the bridge, stopping too quickly on my new feet and almost over correcting. It was only four blocks to where he always waited.

Even in this form I could make it.

Driven by the thought of bacon, I almost knocked over a little old lady who looked at me with wide eyes. Trying to avoid knocking into her, I nearly fell over again. At the last possible second I managed throw my weight to the side, swerving around her and keeping my feet. I kept going.

I was almost there. Many humans on the street were yelling what I thought must be encouragement. I supposed they were impressed with how fast I could run, seeing as I went past all of them.

There was the boy, the boy with the bacon. I charged him and the other children at the corner, proud I arrived before the yellow thing took them away. I squatted down in front of him and shoved my nose at pocket of his jacket, where I knew he kept the bacon.

I drooled. He screamed.

I reeled back, confused. All the children were screaming now. I didn't have a tail to wag, to show I meant no harm. I did the next non-aggressive thing I could think of and licked his face. I really wanted bacon.

He started crying and the older girl next to him hit me with her backpack. She forced herself in between me and him and started bashing me with the backpack, again and again. I winced and put up my forepaws to shield my face.

I whimpered and rolled onto my back, showing my unprotected belly, so they'd know I wasn't challenging their pack. I just wanted bacon. A loud bellow pierced the screams, and I looked over to see one of the humans in blue running over. He looked angry. I knew what humans in uniforms did, though. I'd run into them before.

They were dog catchers!

I rolled up onto my hind legs and went for my normal dog catcher routine. I sprinted out between the traffic, causing the cars to honk. Dog catchers usually didn't chase you in between the vehicles. Clearly, they were slower and afraid of things that honked. This one was persistent, though. I spun around a corner in front of him and then dropped and slid underneath a parked van, hiding until he ran past.

They'd known I was a dog.

I wasn't sure how they'd figured it out so quickly. I hadn't even gotten the bacon.

I'D THOUGHT LONG and hard about the humans I'd seen before today, and finally came up with the difference. I didn't have any fake cloth fur like they did. All the humans, even the one at the dumpster this morning, put huge importance on the cloths they wore over their skin. Apparently, when I hadn't worn any, they'd known I was an imposter.

The custom didn't make sense to me, but if it would keep them from seeing through to my dogginess, I'd give it a shot.

I knew exactly where to go. A while ago, I'd found out the hard way not all dumpsters have food in them. I'd seen humans taking bags of things to a big blue dumpster with a red symbol on it. I thought it must be food, because then a second human would come take the things from the dumpster and carry them all inside another building. Other people came out of the building with bags, but before they went in, they never had bags. Food had seemed like the only answer, so I'd waited until nightfall, and then jumped in the dumpster to root around.

The bags had been full of the stupid fake fur cloths and nothing else. *All* of the bags. Not even one had food in it. It was a completely wasted night.

Or so I'd thought. It was going to be really useful for my human disguise now. I snuck up to the cloths dumpster, and found a black chest cloth with some human writing across the front. Then I found a leg cloth with a stretchy top, black with white strips down the side, and leg tubes that looked about the right length for my new hind legs. Putting these cloths on was a lot harder than it looked. After a few false tries, I got my hind legs into the tubes properly. If you didn't do it right, it was impossible to walk.

Having figured out the tunnel system on the hind leg one, the chest one *was* much easier, although my head tried to go through one of the foreleg holes first.

I emerged in my new cloths, a little out of sorts.

I sauntered down the street, trying to stay casual, watching for the humans reactions. My shoulders felt twitchy. I kept expecting someone to point at me and sick the dog catcher on me again. However, after walking around several blocks and sitting down next to a few humans with no one paying any attention to me, I began to feel more confident.

Perfect. The disguise worked. Everyone believed I was a human. Everything was falling into place exactly how I wanted.

There was one place I really, really wanted to go. Humans

went in with nothing all the time and came out with bags and bags of food. Sometimes when the humans had too many bags they even had to have baskets instead. Sometimes, the baskets were so very large and held so much, they had to have wheels.

But the doors didn't open for dogs. I'd tried before and had to sneak in after a human triggered it. In the brief moments I'd been inside, I'd seen row after row of food. Then I got chased out.

The memory was bittersweet.

I STOOD FOR A MOMENT, and watched the humans coming in and out of the food building with their giant wheeled baskets. Today, I would get inside, and *I* would be the one leaving with delicious smells wafting up from *my* bags of food. Today, I would make up for all the times I had been denied admittance to this banquet, just because I happened to be born on four legs. Today, there would be *justice*.

My heart in my mouth, I walked up to the entrance with a confidence I did not feel. You never show uncertainty to the pack unless you want them to rub your nose in it.

Everyone else was taking one, so I took one of the big baskets on wheels in an attempt to blend in. The hallowed doors to the food building hissed open as I passed, and I had a spike of glee as I realized it recognized me as human.

I was in now, behind my wheeled basket. I hadn't had time for a good look before. My eyes bulged out of their sockets. Food of every type lined the walls. Surely this was enough food for a year or even two, with a full belly every night.

They had the store divided up into food-lined alleys. I ignored the alleys with plants in them. I didn't know why you would ever choose to eat plants on purpose. I'd tried to eat weeds when I was starving before, and it hadn't worked out well. I threw up much more than I kept down. Filling my belly with water worked much better for those days. I steered my cart far away from all that green stuff. Some of the alleys had boxes and bags of powder in them. It didn't look like the boxes contained meat or anything. A lot of the boxes showed pictures of kids on them, but I knew humans don't eat their young. The pictures didn't make much sense. They also had shiny metal containers with pictures of more things I didn't recognize. That was ok, because it would hurt a lot to bite through the metal anyway.

All of this food was overwhelming and great, but really I was after one thing, and one thing only. I sniffed the air, looking for the meat. I knew it was here, but I couldn't smell it. Human noses were so dull.

I wandered around the building, pushing the wheeled basket in front of me in hopes I would find it. Obviously, they knew how precious it was because they'd protected it at the back of the store in its very own double-sided alley. I gasped, craning my head from side to side as I went down the alley. My heart leapt and pounded. I had never seen so much meat in one place.

I couldn't believe it. There was an entire --I had to blink and look again to make sure -- *an entire wall* of meat. Meat in either direction, as far as my eyes could see. It glistened under the lights. I ran up to the nearest shelves, leaving my basket abandoned by the alley entrance. The whole area hummed, and little holes blew cold wind down on the meat. The shelves for the meat went all the way up the wall *on both sides,* and they'd lined the meat up in little packages, so you could just reach out and *take* it.

My eyes teared up. *How can a place like this exist? And how often can I come back?*

The alley walls had shelves cut into them so every inch was used. The meats were stacked three or four deep. And they were of all shapes and sizes. Thin meats, thick meats, round meats, rectangular meats, sliced meats, cubed meats, stripped meats. I saw ground meat. Lots of ground meat, with different marbling and in different colors.

They had meats with *bones* in them. Some looked like the leg of the animal they'd been taken off of. Some packages had hooves or tails in them. Then they had meat with skins, and meats without skins. They had bones by themselves and meats where the bones had been removed. Red meats, pink meats, white meats.

And sausages. Oh, so many different types of sausages. Little ones, big ones, skinny ones, long ones, short ones. Round sausages, looped sausages – they even had sausages tied in knots. I didn't know why knots made sausages better, but I was going to find out.

They even had fish. All colors of fish.

That wasn't even counting the meats set aside in a glass case. Those meats *looked* the same as the ones in the little packages, but weren't wrapped in plastic like the others. I didn't know how to get at those ones. Since they looked the same, I reluctantly decided to go for the individually packaged meat rather than try to figure out the case.

Some of the meats were already cooked, although surely they wouldn't be as juicy as the others. I scorned those, because they just weren't as good as everything else.

I heaped all the most delicious looking meats in the wheeled basket. I saw now why the basket was a really good idea. I could put *much* more in it than I could carry. Each person had one; it seemed you could only take as much out of the store as you can fit in the basket. That made sense. Otherwise, what would keep someone from taking the whole wall for themselves?

I knew I wanted to.

There was no way I was going to be able to fit everything I wanted into the wheeled basket, but I tried my hardest. I grabbed the bone in, dark red meat with rim of fat from the shelves, the cold air running over my paws. I wasn't sure what all of these meats were, but they all looked delicious. I also grabbed big haunches of red meat on the bone, and giant brown, oblong pieces of meat showing all pink meat all around the bone, plus sliced pale pink meat marbled with fat, striped strips of meat (it sort of reminded me of a paler version of the bacon the boy brought each morning), and so, so many sausages. I loved sausages. I took all the sausages. I looked at my mountain of meat packages with a very deep and abiding satisfaction. I wasn't going be hungry again for a very, very long time.

Grunting, but feeling very happy, I pushed my cart up back up toward the doors at the front of the store. As I wheeled past other humans in the food building, I realized humans who left the food building all stopped and let another human count the food in their basket first. That's when it got put into the bags. I lined up behind the nearest human. She turned a little when I stepped up behind her, and eyed my cart. She said something in an amused tone. I panicked.

It sounded like, "Hey, Mu tin oo ef init meat, ickner?"

That threw me. I didn't want to break my cover after I was so close to having all this food. I didn't know any words that seemed appropriate. "Damn dog," was right out. In desperation, I mimicked another male human I'd observed while in the building. While trying to keep a casual expression on my face, I jerked my head up and down once. "M-hmm." I muttered.

To my great relief, she seemed to accept that. She quirked an eyebrow, and turned back to her own basket of food. A moving band in the counter paraded each human's food before the food building person, which seemed really nifty. I bet in my terrier form that would be an awesome thing to run on.

I turned slightly, trying not to stare. I ended up looking at the wheeled basket behind me. I recoiled in horror. The human behind me had a giant blue bag with a picture of a terrier head on it in his basket. *Surely, that couldn't be... they wouldn't, would they?*

I turned back to the front, determined not to think about it. I just needed them to count my meat, and I was out of here.

My turn was next, and I helped the food-building person empty my basket. She pushed the food across a glass plate and another human put it in bags.

It seemed like a strange custom. I knew what the bags were for, I'd seen enough humans walking around with them. But the counting of food was strange.

Unless... they used it to know how many more pieces of meat to have on the wall tomorrow. That kind of made sense. The food building person said something to me, and I realized all of my meat was bagged and back in the basket.

I nodded, smiling happily and started pushing the basket out of the store. The humans around me started shouting, and one put a hand on my shoulder. I looked around. The humans all looked upset. None of the things they were saying were words I knew.

One of them began yelling into a black rectangle tethered to the counter. I realized I had messed up *again*. Somehow, I hadn't done the ritual right. They'd all figured out I was a dog. I glanced despairingly at all that meat. I was *so* close to the doors. My stomach burbled in protest.

Screw it. I would take what I could before the dog catcher came.

Before they could stop me, I surged forward with the wheeled basket. I knocked the restraining human away and ran with all my might for the doors. This meat *would be mine*.

I didn't understand why these humans were so unwilling to share their food, but they were really, really angry and determined to get it back. There were three of them giving chase behind me. One jumped at me from the front, grabbing onto the wheeled cart before I could force it out the doors.

There was no time. I grabbed the top two bags, one in each hand and sprinted away into the bright sun. I wove around the parked cars, trying to lose the humans, but every time another human found me. Another of the building's people tried to grab me, throwing his arms out wide, and I stumbled.

If I stayed in this form, they were going to catch me. My heart felt torn open. I'd lost my beautiful mountain of marbled meat and sausages. I didn't even know which meats I was currently running with. *What if I'd left the sausages?*

I dodged away from the next human, and ran all out getting away from him, my lungs burning. They were getting closer; close enough I worried they might catch me and take away *all* the meat.

With a howl of wretchedness, I cornered hard, running behind the building. As I entered the shadow of the building, I skidded between two vehicles, concentrating on becoming myself.

I returned to my own form with an almost audible pop. I tried to pick up both bags in my jaws, but they were just too heavy. I couldn't drag both of them home.

A shout warned me the food building person was about to find my hiding place. I picked up the remaining bag of meat and ran underneath the cars until I was far, far, away from the food building and the angry humans.

That night, as I sat in my cardboard cave, my belly distended with meat, I decided that being a human really wasn't for me. Humans were just too confusing with all their customs. I liked being a dog better.

Besides, the cloths really weren't that comfortable, and I'd have to find new ones, since my old ones got left in the parking lot alongside the other bag of meat. The meat had been delicious even though I had left the sausages, but then there had been that bag of terrier...

Not worth it. I'd just go back to begging, like usual. I

hadn't realized just how precious meat was to the humans. I couldn't be mad about it though. If I had that much meat, I wouldn't share it either. I'd hoard it too. Tomorrow, I would thank the boy for always bringing me some of the bacon from his stockpile. I hoped he'd still come after what happened today.

I huffed out a breath and went to sleep pondering all of the humans' peculiarities. I dreamt of the beautiful haunches of meat I'd left behind all night.

I SCOPED out the situation before I trotted up to the boy the next morning. Everything looked cool. No one was screaming or pointing. I trotted on up and waited for him to notice me.

"Heyboy," he said. "Want some?" *Yes, oh yes.* This was how the exchange was supposed to go. I wagged my tail indicating my approval. Thanks to the bag of meat yesterday, I wasn't near as hungry as usual, but I didn't want to break our little arrangement. I'd worried after yesterday, he might not bring my treat today, after all.

He held out the crisp strips. Just as I reached out to daintily take the bacon, a thing barreled out of the side street, much like I had yesterday, straight toward children.

It took me a fraction of a second to track him, but I recognized the not-human in his giant wolf form. He swiped at a small human, and I watched it crumple to the ground. He glanced at it for a half a moment then kept streaking right toward me and the boy.

I barked a warning. The boy jumped back, surprised. He pulled several of the other children back with him, his eyes wide.

The not-human flew forward in its giant wolf form, rearing up on its sinewy hind legs and trying to catch at the boy with teeth and claws. His fangs snapped shut just short of the boy's face.

I snarled a warning at the not-human. He might have stolen my breakfast yesterday, but one meal was a lot less important to me than the boy. Besides, today was a whole different situation.

I thought of the long pointed ears, the narrow snout filled with sharp pointed teeth, the coarse hair and large bulk of the giant wolf. As I felt my bones rearrange and gain mass, I launched myself into the not-human, body-blocking him back from the boy.

The not-human tried to dodge around me to make another attempt. I wrapped a long arm around his waist, grappling him. He savaged one of my arms with his claws. I bit into his shoulder, since I couldn't reach his neck, trying to keep him in place.

His eyes were fixed on the children and even more crazed than when we met yesterday. I didn't understand why the boy would be a target, but he was mine to protect.

When it came down to it, I was his Heyboy, and he was my kid. That's all I needed to know.

I twisted, trying to bring the formshifter down with me. My feet slipped on the concrete, my claws not finding purchase.

The not-human used my lack of balance against me, raking his claws across my face.

My eyes filled with blood, blinding me. I scrabbled at my eyes with the back of my paws.

The human boy cried. I instinctively tried to turn toward him. The formshifter's teeth snapped shut so close to my neck, I felt his hot, fetid breath.

The not-human's failed lunge over-extended his balance. I used his own momentum to pin him down. Following him down, I savaged his neck with my crushing jaws. The bones gave out under my teeth with a sharp sounding snap. I looked up from my grizzly prize with a quiet shock.

I'd never killed anything before. I was too small for it to even be an issue.

"Heyboy?" the boy's voice came tentatively.

I looked over at him, and concentrated on becoming his goofy- looking terrier with slightly curly hair. Once I was back to normal, I trotted over, and we stood together looking at the giant wolf.

The blue-clothed person came, but didn't try to catch me. He talked to all the children before bundling up and carting off the carcass. I knew they were talking about me, because was a lot of pointing to me from the kids, and a lot of head shaking from the adults.

Eventually, the boy looked down at the bacon still clutched in his hand, and said, "Oh yeah, want some?"

Yes. Of course I did.

THE LLANTHONY LIVESTOCK
LITIGATION

The story of how It's Your Cow came to be is a long and bizarre one. It involves me building a catapult in my garage. It involves nearly killing a friend's steer with a coconut launched from said catapult. It involves the launch party for Sanan Kolva's amazing epic fantasy series The Shrouded Sky. And it involves me shooting my mouth off in front of Frances Pauli, which as it turns out is a good way to end up editing an anthology.

"The Llanthony Livestock Litigation" is the story that we wrote for Cow. In case you couldn't tell by the very, very Welsh name, I took point. But the discussion between us in making this one was pretty extensive.

I have always been fascinated by the Welsh tradition of the Mari Lwyd. If you don't know, it's a horse skull on a stick, and the person holding the skull is draped in sackcloth so that it looks like the ghost of a horse is mucking about. The Mari Lwyd then goes house to house, followed by others.

Once at a house, the Mari Lwyd requests entry… by singing. The owners of the home sing a response, denying entry. After this, a sort of folk-singing rap battle begins in which the Mari

Lwyd and the homeowner sing back and forth to one another in a debate as to whether the homeowner should let the Grey Mare in. If the homeowner relents or can't think of something to sing, the homeowner lets the Mari Lwyd and its followers inside and gives them food and drink.

Sounds like a cool Halloween tradition, right? Wrong. Because the Mari Lwyd is south Wales' version of Christmas caroling.

There's all kinds of theories as to how this got started. It may be an ancient pagan tradition, it may not. But in my mind, song-fighting a horse ghost doesn't really seem like a traditionally Christian tradition either. Yet there it is, nestled amongst Christianity in South Wales.

The Llanthony Livestock Litigation is really about the way that Wales' pagan identity has sort of enmeshed itself with its Christian one. It's about the soul of the region, and about how its people came to embrace this entwining of traditions. The idea has always fascinated me, and this story gave me an opportunity to sort of explore that.

Reading it out loud is a real feat, by the way. Any time I do a reading of this story, I have to remember the pronunciation of all the Latin. I even managed to give one of our Catholic authors flashbacks to his youth with some of the traditional Latin in this story. That's always amused me any time I dust it off.

8

THE LLANTHONY LIVESTOCK LITIGATION

"Are we sure this is a good idea?" asked Camy, her bright wings bringing her to rest atop the massive beast's rump.

"Well," said Canhem. "It's your cow." The young male sprite picked up a stick from the ground just behind the bovine and hefted it over his shoulder, deftly avoiding his fluttering wings.

"They're all my cows," said Camy, her voice rising in both pitch and tempo as she gestured across the green hillside toward the herd of cattle. "Whenever I want them to be."

"Yes, love," said Canhem. "So where's the harm in a bit of fun with one or two?"

Camy settled down to sit on the bovine's haunches to ponder this. She shook a strand of her long, red hair out of her face and folded her shimmering wings behind her. "I'm just not sure we've thought this through," she said after a moment.

"Um, love?" said Canhem. His bare chest rippled with the effort of lifting the small branch, and his wings began to lift both sprite and stick off the ground. "You're Camymddwyn and I'm Canhem. We are sprites, and our job is mischief and mayhem. So, no. We haven't thought this through at all. It honestly makes me concerned that you want to."

Camy shrugged. "That's all well and good where the Cymri are involved. But I'm worried about the cows."

"Ha!" said Canhem, beginning to fly forward, stick outstretched like a tiny lance. "The cows should be fine."

And with that, he buried the rough length of wood firmly into the bovine anus before him.

The cow reacted both immediately and predictably. The big animal lurched forward in a mad dash. Camy fell for a moment, then caught herself on her iridescent wings. Hovering in mid-aid, the two sprites watched as one bovine's madness spread through the herd, turning a once-docile mass of cud-chewing docility into a rolling wave of panic, galloping down the hillside in a mud-churning flurry of hooves and insanity.

"See?" said Canhem. "Now that's a good day's work."

THE NICE THING about being otherworldly creatures of magic—or, at least, one of the nice things—is that the cruising air speed of a sprite is far faster than one might expect given their diminuitive physiology. So as the stampede approached the construction site around Llanthony Priory, the two sprites sat perched atop the half-built stonework of their target.

"You know," said Camy, "it's pretty impressive what these people can put together when they decide on a goal."

"You know we're here to oppose this building, right?" responded Canhem.

"Well, obviously," said Camy. "But still. You have to admit, awful lot of effort to bring all this stone here and stack it up like this."

"Oh, aye," said Canhem. "Their God keeps having them build things. Build the churches to bind their beliefs. Build the fences to cage the beasts, build mills to harness the river. They build their weapons out of iron, iron, to aid them in killing both each other and us. And everything they build drags them further and further away from who they were."

Camy looked down at the stonework. The massive priory had rooms, but no ceiling as yet. And all around it, the builder's huts and a small chapel to the God of the Normans and the Saxons stood. Those huts were little more than sticks, with a thatched roof. Looking up the hill at the bovine tide on the way with her far-seeing eyes, Camy didn't put a lot of odds on anything but this stonework surviving.

"Well," Camy said, "that's all true. But if they're willing to put that much effort into building things, maybe we should learn to reach into their buildings. After all, there's only so much we can do to stop it."

"But, these are the Cymri!" said Canhem. "They are our people! Ever since the alliance of Pryderi and Arawn, the Cymri have been our allies among the mortals. And now, they begin to turn away from us to this Saxon God. This Norman God. And this is Calan Mai. Today, of all days, the straw men should be hanged. The warriors of Winter and Summer should duel. We may not be able to stop their building, but we can at the least remind them who we are."

Below the two sprites, the workers bustled, pointing up at the hillside. The distant thunder of hoofbeats grew louder, joined by maddened lowing and the occasional clank of a bell. Workers fled or ducked into the unroofed stone walls as the wave of angry beef bore through their tents and over their personal belongings.

GOD WAS ANGRY.

Brother Cledwyn did not know why the Lord of Lords had chosen to visit his displeasure on the monks of Llanthony. He found himself especially confused as to why it would happen today of all days. Was this not the Feast of Saint Bertha of Kent, the holy Lady responsible for bringing the Word of the Lord to the British Isles in the first place? Why, on her feast day of all days, would Saint Bertha turn her back on her people?

Brother Cledwyn could not fathom it, and tried only for a moment. The ways of God were mysterious, and if He should choose to test his followers with a stampede of black Welsh cattle, Brother Cledwyn could but persevere. He pressed himself to the unfinished wall of stone sheltering him from the raging herd, pulled the long string of wooden beads from his waist band, made the sign of the cross, and began to pray.

"Credo in Deum Patrem omnipotentem, Creatorem caeli et terrae—"

As he prayed, a high-pitched, female voice sounded out of nowhere. "What're you doing?" it asked.

He ignored it. "Et in Iesum Christum, Filium eius unicum, Dominum nostrum, qui conceptus est de Spiritu Sancto—"

"Those are really funny-sounding words," the voice said.

Was this the holy Saint Bertha, speaking directly to him from heaven? Had he been rewarded for his faith? He continued his prayer. "natus ex Maria Virgine, passus sub Pontio Pilato, crucifixus, mortuus, et sepultus, descendit ad infernos, tertia die resurrexit a mortuis, ascendit ad caelos, sedet ad dexteram Dei Patris omnipotentis—"

"You know, it's really rather rude to talk to someone else when I'm here."

This could not be Saint Bertha. That holy lady would never interrupt someone in prayer like this. And no women had joined the Brotherhood in their labors to build the Priory of Llanthony, so that could only mean one thing. The Devil was afoot and had driven these bovines down to stampede amongst the Brotherhood. Now all made sense, for he and his brethren were clearly being tested like Job, as a plaything between God and Satan. Like Job, Brother Cledwyn resolved to meet this test.

"—inde venturus est iudicare vivos et mortuos. Credo in Spiritum Sanctum, sanctam Ecclesiam catholicam, sanctorum communionem, remissionem peccatorum, carnis resurrectionem, vitam aeternam. Amen."

"Ooo, an 'amen.' I know that one," continued the voice of Satan. "That one means you're done, right?"

Brother Cledwyn ignored the voice, moving onward to the bead above the cross and continuing to chant. "Pater Noster, qui es in caelis, sanctificetur nomen tuum. Adveniat regnum tuum—"

"Oh," said the Devil. "You're doing the bead thing. I've heard of this. It'll take a while, won't it? I mean, the cows are long past by now, but if you're going to keep sitting there and mumbling weird words, I can wait. Go on."

Brother Cledwyn did not believe the Devil would react so passively to these prayers. After all, Brother Cledwyn had taught that prayer horrified the Devil, driving him back before the power of the Almighty God. He expected Satan to continue her interruptions, to pester him away from the Peace that was God's.

Instead, he circled the Rosary without further interruption from the feminine voice. The power of his prayer victorious, he put aside the temptations of the Dark One. He focused only on the holy blessings that were his and his brotherhoods. His mind focused, cleared, and prepared itself for the labor of cleaning the camp after the evil works which had been wrought about it, and his spirit celebrated once again the greater task of constructing the Pryory.

"—Per eundem Christum Dominum nostrum. Amen," he finished, and opened his eyes.

Before him, standing upon an uneven stone in the rock wall,

stood a small figure with iridescent wings and a shining nimbus.

Brother Cledwyn's spirit soared.

HER LOVER HAD FLOWN off in a bit of a huff before the strange man had finished with his hand on the cross, leaving Camy alone to watch the robed Cymri men.

This Saxon God seemed like a pretty demanding fellow. Camy stood upon the wall and watched the Cymri man pray, eyes closed, to his deity. She couldn't fathom why he repeated the same words over and over again, but as she didn't understand the Roman language he spoke she couldn't comment on the contents.

She tried, early on, to get one of them to speak back to her, but the Saxon God apparently demanded absolute obedience and attention. She knew she shouldn't be surprised about this; the Saxon God had always been something of a domineering stick-in-the-mud, and he apparently demanded the same from his followers. But rudeness did not necessitate rudeness in response, and Camy's curiosity got the better of her.

So she leaned herself against the rough-hewn stone of the Priory wall, and waited for the man to circle his beads.

And as she watched, she became fascinated. Because the prayer did seem to be having an effect. The man's muscles relaxed, and his breathing evened. The corners of his lips began to turn upward, and his eyebrow unfurrowed into an expression of peace and relaxation. Camy looked about the ruins of the tent city and saw the same effect on the other men. Slowly, they began to rise to their feet.

And the man before her stood and opened his eyes.

He took a step back from Camy, his eyebrows flying up. Then he fell back to his knees and pressed his forehead into the ground. Camy, confused, flew down to ground level to stand next to his ear.

"Hello?" she asked tentatively.

"Oh holy messenger, forgive my behavior should it affront you."

"Um…" said Camy, not sure how to respond to this. "Well, we did figure the stampede would be a lot more upsetting than this. Canhem's going to be more affronted than I am about that, though. I'll pass your words along?"

"Canhem? An angel of mayhem?" asked the man.

"What? No!" she recoiled. "Canhem's like me. Do you not even recognize a sprite?"

The man raised his torso up from the ground, resting himself in a kneeling position, and looked squarely at Camy.

"You are not an angelic messenger of the Heavenly Father?"

"Ew. No," said Camy, her face contorted in disgust. "What a terrible life. No genitals, complete servitude. No thanks."

"So you are a devil," the man grabbed his cross again, holding it in between Camy and himself.

"Were you not listening?" asked Camy in an irritated tone. She flew up and lighted upon the cross itself. "I'm not an angel, and I'm not a devil. I'm a sprite. Camymddwyn is my common name. You can call me Camy."

"Mischief?" asked the man.

"If you're going to use the Saxon tongue for things, yes. It felt like a good enough moniker. Now, I've given you something to call me. It's only polite you return the favor, you know."

"You know," he said, "if you were a demon, you'd likely lie to me about it."

"Maybe," said Camy. "I don't know much about demons. Hmm, let's see… could a demon do this?"

Camy swung her right leg in an arc as she crouched with her left. She hooked her right ankle behind the cross and spun, sliding down and spinning with a dancer's grace to end resting her buttocks upon the cross-beam of the icon, her arms embracing the top of it. She reached into her memory while embracing the cross, then repeated the sounds she'd heard the man making earlier.

"Credo in Deum Patrem omnipotentem, Creatorem caeli—"

"Agh!" shouted the priest, and he shook her free of his cross.

"Could a demon do that?" Camy asked him, hovering now with slow flaps of her wings.

The robed man sat, staring. She'd flummoxed him with that move; that was good. "I, uh... no," he said. "I don't believe one could. Are you really a Christian?"

"A follower of your Saxon God? Hardly," said Camy. "I told you, I'm a sprite."

"But you just said you believed—"

"Did I?" asked Camy. "I really have no idea what those Roman words mean. I remembered the sound of you saying them, is all. Now, since you know I'm not a demon, can I please know what I should call you."

He stared at her for a moment, and Camy could not tell what thoughts went through his head. Finally, he seemed to relent, and he half-smiled as he said, "I, uh, I'm Brother Cledwyn of Llanthony Priory. Or, at least, I will be once we build Llanthony Priory. So, if you are neither angel nor demon..what are you?"

Camy rolled her eyes with an exaggerated head motion. She sighed deeply, then said, "Have you not been listening to me at all? I'm a sprite."

"Yes, of course I've heard you say that. But, well... what's a sprite?"

"Are you not Cymri?" Camy asked, her voice rising with her exasperation. "You know the meaning of my name, and of Canhem's. Do you no longer tell the tales of Arawn's kingdom?"

"Arawn? You mean, the faeries? Those are just peasant

superstitions, tales for mothers to tell their children. There is only One True God," Brother Cledwyn kept talking. Camy gave him a flat and increasingly angry stare, but he did not appear to notice as he continued to ramble. "Stamping out that kind of superstition is the reason we're building this Priory here in Wales. The Word of God must—oh," he cut off suddenly.

"And the lightning strikes at last," said Camy through clenched teeth. "You know Arawn's Court is fully aware of your intent to "stamp out" any belief in us. Although," she paused to look about the destroyed remnants of the monks' tent city. "I think the stamping has gone the other way for the moment."

"Fairies are real?" Brother Cledwyn asked.

"Flying right in front of you," said Camy. "Right here. That you even have to ask shows me how in violation of the pact between Arawn and Pryderi you are."

"Pact?" said Cledwyn. "I don't remember any pact."

"Look," said Camy, her irritation at this clueless, insulting human in front of her hitting its peak. "There's a pact. You're in violation of it. And for so long as you continue your disrespect of Arawn's Court, Canhem and I are tasked to make your life miserable. Your little string of beads can't save you or your Priory. Only your compliance."

And with that, Camy flitted off to join Canhem.

BROTHER CLEDWYN TOOK a long time to wrap his head around what had just happened.

It couldn't have been a demon. No demon would be able to touch a holy cross while reciting the Apostle's Creed, regardless of whether she understood the words or not. Still, that left the problem of who this sprite was, and what pact she referred to.

Around him, his Brothers were beginning to pick up the remains of their tents. The canvas had been ripped apart by hooves, and no other shelter save the unfinished walls of the Priory remained.

"Brothers," he called. "Let us gather for a moment, and discuss the situation."

"The situation?" said Brother Anarawd. He was a great, black-bearded fellow, with broad shoulders and a deep voice that would normally have been soothing. "God has shown his displeasure with us. The only question remains whether we suffer here, or attempt to journey to shelter ere night falls."

"It's a seven-mile walk to Abergavenny," said Cledwyn. "Mid-day is already past us, and we are without horses or even a donkey. I do not believe all the brethren can make that journey before the fall of night."

"No," said Brother Anarawd. "Likely not. But there's a small farming village not half a mile up the mountain from us. Hasn't a name, but the folk have come down to trade their eggs and milk a time or two. Mayhap they'd be willing to extend a hand."

"Up the mountain?" asked Cledwyn. "That's a pagan village, isn't it?" He could not stop thinking about the little sprite, and her anger with him. "Are we certain we'll be well-received there?"

"Folk seem kindly enough," said Brother Anarawd.

"They're pagans, though," said Cledwyn. "Do you actually think they'll provide succor to us?"

Brother Anarawd shrugged at this. "Don't see why not. They think us curious, but they seem like good folk. Might be God has sent us this test as an opportunity, to let us go and speak with them about the Holy Word."

Should I tell them? thought Brother Cledwyn to himself. The other brothers would likely discount his vision of the sprite, might even go so far as to accuse him of some form of witchcraft, though he rated that unlikely. Still, didn't they have the right to know that it was not God, but Faery, that had shown its displeasure on them? And given that, that a pagan village could present problems?

But Abergavenny lay too far away. The Brothers had nothing with which to survive here. They would walk to the pagans, and would pray to Almighty God for protection.

"Ha!" said Canhem. "Look at that, they're running. Right to our actual people, no less."

"Yes," said Camy. She'd calmed down since talking to Brother Cledwyn. After all, it wasn't his fault he'd never been taught the Pact. Sure, the man had been nothing but pig-headed, but still he'd been willing to listen.

"And on Calan Mai! Let the Straw Men be formed!" asked Canhem.

"Straw men?" she said. "They believe in their God, and they believe in suffering for their God. Do you really want to give them that kind of suffering?"

"Oh, pish," said Canhem. "I doubt that once the straw man is alight that these brothers praise their God. And I certainly don't think he does anything about it. It's Calan Mai, and this is the time for such celebrations!"

Canhem's tone of voice struck Camy as giddy, verging on joyous. Camy, though, wasn't so sure. She remembered the look of peace on Brother Cledwyn's face as he prayed to his bead-thing. He'd just been overrun by a stampede, he and all his brethren's makeshift homes had been destroyed, all their belongings crushed under the hooves of Canhem's vengeance.

But she hadn't seen anger.

Camy prided herself on being a connoisseur of human anguish. She had seen humans yell, and scream, and tear their clothes, and gnash their teeth in response to her and Canhem's ministrations. Brother Cledwyn hadn't expressed any of that. No frustration, no rage; just a calm acceptance. He'd even blamed his God, and then prayed anyway. She couldn't put her finger on why, but she found herself growing more impressed with the pious brother.

So she couldn't bring herself to join in Canhem's glee at the thought of Brother Cledwyn burning in a Straw Man. Instead, she became lost in her thoughts, struggling to reconcile two contrasting worlds. She wished for a solution before Canhem reached the village, but could not think of any.

THE VILLAGERS MET the Brothers just downslope of their small collection of homes. And Brother Cledwyn didn't see food and blankets among them, but rather bows and spears.

"Ho!" shouted Brother Anarawd. "Is Bran among you? Him that brings the eggs and cheeses to trade with us?"

A grizzled-looking pagan in his mid-30's, stepped forward. He wore rough-spun clothes, but carried a rough yew bow with a hunting broadhead nonetheless.

"Ho, Anarawd. I'm here, but you've come to us on Calan Mai. It's not a day for trading eggs."

Calan Mai? thought Cledwyn. The First of May? They still celebrate the old holidays here. To us, it's the Feast of St. Bertha. To them, it's Calan Mai. And that means—oh. Oh, no.

He tried to speak, but could not beat the booming voice of Brother Anarawd. "Calan Mai? A pagan holiday? Well, regardless, it's not trade we're seeking, but succor. A herd of cattle—likely belonging to one of you fine folk—took fear and destroyed our homes."

"Aye," said Bran calmly. "At the behest of the Tylwyth Teg, no less. Mischief and Mayhem have passed a bit of Arawn's judgment on you."

"Well, of course we believe differently; we feel our God is

testing us," said Brother Anarawd. "But this is no time to debate theology. We are without shelter, food, or—"

"Isn't about theology," said Bran.

Cledwyn cringed.

"It's about you pissed off the faeries, and we're not terribly keen to do the same. Mayhem himself brought the word, and we've little choice in the matter. First time in my life we'll have real Straw Men on Calan Mai, but that's the way of it. You calm down and cooperate, we'll get you senseless first."

Anarawd's face grew ashen as he processed Bran's meaning. Cledwyn closed his eyes and bowed his head in prayer. As he chanted the words to his God, his mind raced back, through his past. Back before he'd been given to the Brotherhood, back to his sheep-herding father and all the old tales. The pact with Arawn, the Fair Folk, Calan Mai—there had to be something to stop this tragedy.

Then he had it.

"WAIT!" he shouted, and as he heard his voice joined in the cry by another, higher-pitched and feminine. He opened his eyes and raised his head to see the small, glowing figure hovering between the pagans and the Christians, her eyes locked with his. She gave him a smile, then gestured for him to speak first.

Cledwyn cleared his throat, then raised his voice.

"We seek Judgment before the Stones!"

BROTHER CLEDWYN HAD GOTTEN it right!

Camy heard the invocation of the Stones and could not believe it. She hadn't thought Brother Cledwyn knew enough of the Tylwyth Teg to invoke, thought she'd have to do it for him. But he'd known. Somewhere, under all those layers of Roman chanting and prayer beads, somewhere Brother Cledwyn was, in fact, Cymri.

Hope blossomed within Camy.

"Judgment before the Stones?" asked one of the other brothers, a black-bearded man of significantly larger stature than her Cledwyn. "You would submit yourself to a pagan ritual?"

"Have faith, Brother," said Cledwyn. "Did not Elijah challenge the prophets of Baal in their own ritual? Judgment is for the Lord our God, and will be his whether we stand before a Stone or an Altar, will it not?"

"You are willing to go before the Stones?" she asked aloud, so that both the groups of Cymri could hear her. "It is the judgment of Arawn you seek, then, and not your Norman God."

Grumblings from some of the other brethren at this, but Brother Cledwyn simply smiled at her. "My faith says otherwise," he said. "Lead on."

Camy's frustration warred with her amusement at this man. Even here, even now, the brother exuded a sense of calm acceptance. Canhem wanted him to burn, but Camy simply wanted him to bend. The fate of the priests, as it always had been, would be for the judgment of Arawn.

The trek to the Judgment Stones that lay uphill of the village took but minutes. The three Stones themselves had simply been laid in a small circle; Bran and Brother Cledwyn sat upon two, and a third remained empty.

For a short time.

The air began to shimmer over the third stone, and out of the air itself stepped Arawn. Camy saw that he had chosen, this time, to appear as a man, more slender than any human in proportion. He wore intricate armor of boiled leather, dyed to a glossy black, that interlocked and moved quietly in perfection. A black cape flowed off one shoulder only, and a long witchwood sword slung at his hip. He quietly moved to sit upon the Judgment Stone.

Camy took a deep breath, then flitted to alight on his right shoulder just as Canhem arrived and lighted on his left.

I have been called in Judgment. Arawn's mouth did not open, and no noise issued forth. But Camy heard his words nonetheless, and based on the ashen faces of the Llanthony Brotherhood, they did as well. And I have answered, for my servants do not agree.

Camy looked away from her lord, blushing slightly. At best, this sort of intervention ranked as one of the more embarrassing moments in her life. If Judgment went against her —well, it would be worse.

Speak your case, Mayhem, said the Lord of Annwyn.

"My Lord," said Canhem, "These men, who used to be Cymri, are building a place to worship their Norman God. They have turned from their compact with you and seek to turn other Cymri away from you. It is Calan Mai, and we can stop this now."

"No," said Camy, "We can't."

All eyes, save those of Arawn's, turned to her.

"We can't stop them. They've won. We can burn these unarmed brothers, sure. But what happens to Bran and his people when the steel-suited ones find out and bring cold iron to purge us? We once reigned over all this island, and now we have these mountains in Cymru, but nothing more. We can't stop them."

Do you argue, then, to not punish a violation of the pact where we see it? said Arawn. Even should we agree that the steel-bearers cannot be resisted, why should we leave such an insult unanswered when it is in front of us?

"Exactly!" cried Canhem. "Exactly my point. The Pact is broken, and the oathbreakers must pay."

"My lord," spoke Bran, and Camy took a deep breath at the

sound of a Cymri entering the discussion. "What you say is true, but I would tell you that these Brothers have been nothing but kind to us, even though they worship the Norman God. They have traded in good faith, they have never spoken in ill will toward us. Aye, they've sought to turn us to their God, but only by words, not steel. Surely this counts for somewhat. Let them re-swear the pact with you, take the damage to their homes as their punishment, and continue living."

The Lord of Annwyn sat long in silence. Camy felt her nerves sing while the King of the Faeries determined the fate of Brother Cledwyn.

"My king!" said Canhem, interrupting the silence. "These monks will continue to break the oaths their forefathers made, even after today, should you let them live. They will return to their Pryory, and they will begin their work anew."

Is this true? asked Arawn, for the first time turning his head to stare directly at Brother Cledwyn.

"Yes," said Brother Cledwyn, his voice still calm and accepting. Camy gawked at the strength to look Arawn in the eye and admit something like this.

"Yes," said Brother Cledwyn again. "Yes, we will continue to build the Priory, for that is our holy mission from our God. And we will continue to educate all around us in the Word of our Lord, for so we have been instructed. If that alone is enough to burn us, then by all means burn us. We shall join Saint Stephen and face your flames as he faced the stones. I am sorry, my lord, but I will tell the truth. My faith is with the Lord."

Brother Cledwyn's voice trembled as he said this. Behind him, the other brothers shook as their leader pronounced what certainly must be their death sentence, but none gainsayed him. Camy could not cry, could not breathe, could not act for what seemed an eternity after such a stunning act of faith.

"Lord," she said at last, "must the Pact be exclusive with their actions? Do you see their strength, and how it drives them?"

"Ego sum Dominus Deus tuus qui eduxi te de terra Aegypti de domo servitutis non habebis deos alienos coram me," said the black-bearded Brother.

"I am the Lord thy God," translated Brother Cledwyn, "who brought you out of the Land of Egypt, out of the house bondage. You shall have no other gods before me." He took a breath at this, then continued. "And so we are commanded. We cannot worship Arawn, even though he be real, and seated before us. We are commanded to worship one god alone."

The Pact is not one of worship, nor do I lay any claim to Godhood, said Arawn. I am a King, and I demand fealty, not piety. Worship whatever God you choose to believe in. But you shall respect my people, and work in tandem with them. You shall light the straw man in remembrance of them, and you shall tell their tales. You shall feast on Calan Awst, burn the fires on Calan Gaef, hang the straw man on Calan Mai, and dance the Mari Llwyd during Alban Arthan. You shall bring no steel into the Rings, nor refuse hospitality when asked of the Tylwyth Teg. Does your God forbid these things?

THE PAVED STREET before the Chepstow Museum had been cleared of cars, and crowds of people gathered, waiting. On top of the small, half-circle awning, Camymddwyn and Canhem perched.

"A thousand years," said Canhem.

"Not quite a thousand, yet," said Camy. "Still, you have to admit it's largely worked out. In a choice between extermination and adaptation, I think we chose correctly. I mean, look what happened to the Irish fey when Fionnbharr went all nutty."

Down the street, a parade of horse-skulls began to move. Men carried the grim things on poles, cloth draping down to cover all but the bottom portions of their legs. The skulls bounced up and down, lit by the streetlights above them. Here and there, one of the Grey Mares would dip, approaching the face of some small child, who would recoil and squeal in terror and delight.

"The Mari-Llwyd," said Canhem. "Still dancing, after all this time."

"Aye," said Camy. "They worship their God, and they respect their otherworldly King. The Pact holds."

Canhem shook his head, and smiled. "That it does. But still, we are who we are. Shall we have some fun?"

KAMPGROUND OF ANDROMEDA

So, Beer was a great success. Beer 2 also did quite well. And we still had CampCon going on. There was still a large group of science fiction/fantasy authors gathering around a campfire at night. And we'd had a couple of hits with anthologies produced within the group.

That's really what prompted the Campcon Anthologies.

Tales from an Alien Campfire came from that. The Beer stories had happened largely by accident. Alien Campfire was an anthology designed with intent to be an anthology specifically born of camping. And as a result, its theme was camping. But camping in a science fiction universe.

This all had the misfortune of coming up after my first "camping" trip with my cousins, the Ovens family.

Let me back up. In my youth, I was a hardcore, avid camper. A full-on, legit Eagle Scout. I did the wilderness survival training. I've been chased by a moose. That sort of thing. So camping to me has a special meaning, and even though I'm old and fat now I still love going out to the wilderness. I spent two summers teaching at a Boy Scout Summer Camp (the Cowles Scout Reservation).

The Ovens family had just started with their camping, though, and when they invited my wife and I to meet them at a "campground," I didn't know that they meant a "Kampground of America" facility.

I spend the entire trip griping about how the fact that Kamping was to Camping as Krab meat is to Crab meat.

So naturally, given a story about camping in the future, I couldn't help but take my shot, and the "Kampground of Andromeda" was born. It's a very deliberate skewering of the Kamping my cousins took us on.

Since then, the Ovens family has become much better about their camping practices.

Alien Campfire had a sort of awkward cover to it, and so this hasn't been one of our more popular stories. Which is too bad, because it holds a special place near and dear to the camp counselor within me. I'm happy to see it dusted off and presented here, because Blondie (as my fellow counselors knew me) still loves me.

9

KAMPGROUND OF ANDROMEDA

W<small>HEN</small> J<small>EFF</small> "C<small>HOPIN</small>" Grogan had gone into cryostasis mere seconds ago from his perspective, he had expected that he would dream. After all, everyone said the whole process felt like going to sleep. What they didn't tell you, what no one told you, was that you woke up feeling like you'd played chicken with a glacier. And lost.

He tried to open his eyes, then immediately experience searing pain. It seemed, from the split second he'd blinked them open, as though someone had created their own heatless, miniature sun and suspended it inches from his face. The light seared its way through his eyes into the back of his skull.

Someone talked to him, a low, soothing male voice, but Jeff couldn't make out the words. He shook his head, desperately grasping to find his bearings. Water inside his eardrums broke its surface tension and ran down his face; the voice became intelligible.

"-ffrey? Can you hear me? Nod if you understand."

Chopin opened his mouth to tell the moron that he could talk just fine, only to find his throat completely dry and incapacitated. Chopin wasn't one for panic, but the growing list of body parts that were not working started to concern him. He nodded, shakily.

"Ah. Good. Some of these early preps, the finer tissues come out all damaged. Growing you a new eardrum would add significantly to your bill."

Bill? He'd been insured for this, he thought. Nevermind that; time to worry about finances later. At the moment, there was blindness, muteness, and the looming spectre of his brain tumor to worry about. Bankruptcy seemed a far cry.

He blinked his eyes again, and was rewarded with slightly less pain than before. As he squinted, letting his thawed-out eyeballs adjust to the light, a blurry spectre began to come into focus. He was an older—well, older than Chopin—man. Early thirties, Chopin guessed. He was a rotund man, with dark brown hair and a patchy beard, wearing a white jumpsuit.

"Can you see yet? How many fingers am I holding up?"

Three. Chopin still couldn't talk, so he mimicked the gesture.

"Good, good. Well, you'll be happy to know the brain tumor is taken care of. Simple procedure, nowadays; we did it in transit. Doesn't look like you suffered any permanent damage up there, though we'll never really be sure. Not like I can ask you if there's anything you don't remember, eh?" Chopin shook his head. And not like I'd miss it unless I knew. Make the best of what you have in the situation. Chopin had never been able to plan out his life very well, but the converse of that was his ability to deal with what was in front of him. Whatever—whenever—he was, he'd adapt. Fit yourself into your environment; only way to survive.

"Alright. Let's see... nineteen years old, yep. 5'9", skinny, dirty blonde, scar above the right eye. Unemployed, not that it matters now."

I was employed, thought Chopin. Just not in winter. The life of a summer camp counselor is, by its nature, seasonal. Still, those who do the job tend to think of themselves as camp staff first, layabouts second.

His brain tumor had hit early in the year. The doctors proposed a surgery so risky that betting one's life savings on a game of bingo seemed like a good idea in comparison. The other choice was cryoprep, being frozen for some future treatment. In the early 21st century, cryo was a joke. By the time Chopin went on ice in 2081, it had been a viable form of treatment.

The doctor – or whoever he was – handed Chopin a glass of water. He drank greedily, the cool liquid bathing his parched throat. He swallowed three, then four times, and lowered the glass.

"Where am I?" Chopin asked, vocal chords straining from disuse.

"That's a complicated question. You're aboard the medical frigate Fleming, which is itself in orbit around the third planet of the Loranis system."

In orbit? Loranis system? In Chopin's time, interplanetary travel had been restricted to the very rich; interstellar travel had been experimental at best. This set of facts diverted Chopin's attention away from his where to a more pressing question.

"When am I?"

"2096."

Fifteen years? That didn't seem right. Something had happened in the last fifteen years to drastically catapult humanity's technolo—

"Oop, sorry. You're from back in the Judeo-Christian notation. We judge time from the founding of the Galactic Council, now. You're in 2096 G.C. Let's see if I remember my history. 1 G.C. happens at...well around 6,000 C.E. Give or take. You've been down and out for somewhere in the ballpark of eight thousand years earth standard."

Eight thousand years. Chopin wondered what had

happened to his family, his friends. His Camp. All gone, now, he supposed.

"Your vitals check out. You're going to be a bit wobbly for the rest of the day, but I'm clearing you for duty."

"What du—"

A sparkling light flashed in front of Chopin's eyes, blinding him all over again.

WHEN HE BLINKED AGAIN, he was no longer in the white medical-style room. Instead, he sat in a wood-paneled office, lined with assorted degrees and diplomas. A short, skinny balding man with a dyed-black hair in a bad combover sat behind a desk. Brain tumor, no problem. Male pattern baldness, still an issue. Check.

"Mr. Grogan, yes? Good. I am Ternal Hurnot, Loranis system administrator. Welcome to the frontier."

"Frontier?" asked Chopin.

"Well, that's what they think of us back in the Milky Way. Out here in Andromeda, everything's totally wild. This is where they go to 'get away from it all.'" So, here we are. Our files tell us you've got some experience in organized campgrounds, a field for which we have little experience."

"Andromeda? I'm... in a different galaxy?"

"Different than what? From the one you started in? Yes, quite. Of course, there you were little more than another cryobrick. Here, you have a chance to live again. You're welcome for that, by the way."

"Oh, um... thanks?" So, they'd have left me on ice otherwise. I can tell we're going to get along.

"Your thanks will come in a particular form. Let's see, you've been under for seven thousand, nine hundred and fifty-three years, two months, and twelve days. Of that, the first forty-eight years, six months, and three days were covered by Indigo Cross, your health insurance. They went bankrupt, and their... ah... "assets" were acquired by the Eukaryota Conglomerate, of which we are an extension. None of their liabilities were transferred in the bankruptcy, however."

Chopin's head spun. Hurnot's dry, nasal tones carried this information rapidly, in a manner that suggested Hurnot did not care if his subject understood the information he conveyed.

"Your debt to the Eukaryota Conglomerate, charged at the contractual rate at the time of your freezing, with the standard interest for non-payment... is, and I'm rounding down here, thirteen point oh-nine-two times ten to the thirty-third power in Galactic credits. That compound interest can get really nasty, can't it?"

Ten to the thirty-third? Chopin tried to remember what the name for that number was, but couldn't come up with it. How much was a Galactic credit, anyways?

"And how will you be paying today?"

Chopin stared at Hurnot with a slack jaw. Paying? Chopin had never owned a Galactic credit in his life, let alone ten to the thirty-third of them. Then he heard Hurnot's laugh. It was a raspy, nasal thing, creating more noise on the inhale than the exhale. Even his laugh is irritating, thought Chopin.

"I'm kidding, of course. Obviously you are currently incapable of payment. This is why you have been transferred to our section of the E.C. It is, in fact, why you are here, why you are awake." Hurnot stood from his desk, though rising from the chair seemed to change his height by a mere six or so inches. "Come," he said. "Come and see."

Hurnot led Chopin to a window, then slid it open. Chopin looked out from high in the sky of a planet he did not know, but that looked surprisingly like Earth. Except, of course, for the vast number of small, metal bubbles beneath him, dotting the landscape as though the land itself had grown smallpox, punctuated by the occasional massive building labeled "Holo-Vision theater," "Zero-G Waterpark," and "Snack Stand."

"Welcome to your new home, Mr. Grogan. Welcome to the Kampground of Andromeda."

Chopin swore he could hear the K.

WHEN HE'D WORKED at Grizzly, Chopin was a Scoutcraft counselor. He instructed the scouts at camp in the merit badges concerning life in the outdoors: pioneering, orienteering, wilderness survival. As a senior staff member, Chopin had managed to avoid the more basic courses; camping, knot-tying, fire-building. Those classes tended to be filled with wet-behind-the-ears eleven-year-olds who spent half their time wishing for Mommy. No, Chopin's classes were for the scouts on the path to Eagle. Wilderness Survival courses involved spending the night away from tents, sleeping bags, or really any of the comforts of life. As an example, Chopin himself would live in the woods outside of Scoutcraft, packing nothing his time at Camp that didn't fit into a fanny pack.

Sitting in a polished office in a poofy chair on the third story of the "Kampground Administration Center," it was hard for Chopin to feel like he'd actually landed on a Camp.

From his window, what he saw resembled more of a vast parking lot. On it, spherical ships roughly the size of the split-level home he'd once lived in with his parents landed in designated areas, controlled by the Launch Control team on level 2. A family would step out from the ship, look around at the sea of concrete about them, admire the trees growing from the mountains visible on the horizon, then step back into the ship. Rarely did a family spend more time outside of these galactic RVs than that.

So, how do you counsel a Kamp?

For the last three months, Jeff had done nothing but sit in this office, then retire to his equally luxurious apartment and play games with the built-in holosuite. The Kampground used his image, his story, in all their advertising material, but apart from the occasional fighting couple who mistook the meaning of the term "Kamp Counselor" he'd yet to do anything.

A light next to a button on his desk flashed. That was new. Startled, he stared at it for a moment, then pressed it.

Hurnot's head sprang into existence, hovering about a foot above his desk.

"Ah, Chopin. I just wanted to call in for your quarterly performance review."

"Performance review?"

"Yes, well. As an employee of the E.C., you are to be reviewed once per quarter to determine your ongoing viability as an employee."

"Viability?"

"A technical term. You needn't worry about it; you are clearly an asset to this company. Bookings for the Kampground have increased dramatically; we've been able to raise our price in order to allow demand to meet supply. There's been a twelve percent increase in the Kampground's profitability since you joined our staff. Well done, Chopin. Well done."

"But... I haven't done anything," said Chopin.

"You've boosted revenue twelve percent! That's hardly nothing."

"Well, ok. But I just sat here. I haven't actually taught any classes on camping."

"Classes? Who needs to be taught about camping? You fly there, let the autopilot land the ship, then take off on your departure time. It's not rocket science."

It's a lot more like rocket science than it is camping, thought Chopin. He didn't say it. Instead, he adopted that soft tone of voice used by a teenaged camp counselor who knew more than the first-time adult Scoutmaster in front of him, but could not appear to know more, lest he offend the adult.

"There are parts of this planet that aren't developed yet, am I correct?"

"Aren't you ambitious! We're working on it as fast as we can, but you're quite right. Three-quarters of the land on the planet, as well as the entirety of the ocean floors, remain undeveloped. We're turning them into Kampground slots as quickly as we can, but for now our volume is limited. I like your spirit, though."

He thought I was complaining about that, thought Chopin.

"So, not developed, but terraformed?"

"Of course. The nanotech that terraforms does the whole planet at once; it's easier to create a realistic, viable biosphere that way. We just don't have it fine-tuned enough to provide high-tech facilities, so the development takes longer."

"So, three-quarters of this planet is undeveloped, earth-like wilderness, am I correct?"

"Yes."

"How many of your campers go into that wilderness?"

Hurnot's eyebrows flew up in a startled expression. "Why in the galaxy would they do that? It's dangerous out there, you know. To do a full biosphere, we've got all the earth-creatures packed in. It's like your old proverb – lions, tigers, and bears, oh my."

"That's not a pro- nevermind." How to hook Hurnot on this idea? Ah, yes. Of course. "How would you feel about doing a media event?"

"A media event? With you? You've been good for advertisement so far, so I'm listening."

"It won't cost you much. You'll just need to be able to film me. I'll need one fanny pack, and inside of it..."

CHOPIN BREATHED IN DEEPLY. The tangy scent of the conifers filled his nostrils. He stood, in the middle of the forest, wearing his fanny-pack. For the first time since he awoke, he began to feel at home. No machine-hum from the high-tech office suite, no holo-vids, no automatic meals, no zero-G waterparks. All of those false, artificial comforts had been stripped away, leaving Chopin alone in the wilderness with himself. It had been too long.

There was one exception. Floating next to him was a "Julie-vision" camera, a holo-imager designed to follow his every move. This camera had been meticulously sculpted to resemble a small, black pug. Chopin had been told this was to make the viewer more comfortable speaking to the camera, but the floating, motionless pug had something of a reverse effect. Still, it was a small price to pay to get himself back into the forest where he belonged.

"Alright. Here I am," he said out loud. The woods were entirely empty, but he knew his class was watching through the mechanical eyes of the floating pug. "It's a nice, dense forest, and by the smell of it there's been some rain recently. I know the teleporter sent me somewhere within fifty miles of the Kampground, but I wasn't told exactly where. So, my priority is finding out where I am, then getting back home. I've got my fanny-pack, which has an attached water bottle. That pack contains my basic survival kit, the contents of which are available as additional information on your holo-viewer; for now, the item I want to talk about is this map." Here he unfolded the paper map for the holos to pick up. "It gives me my magnetic declination for this planet, as well as a topographical layout of the countryside. So all I need to do is get to a high point, orient this map with my compass, and compare it to my surroundings. And the nearest high point is... there," he pointed to the top of a mountain.

"Now, most of this mountain is covered in underbrush.

Nasty stuff to walk through. So the first thing I'm going to do it head for the ridge line, there," he pointed. "That'll let me hike the ridge up to the summit, avoid all that brush."

Hiking through the forest, with no trail and no bearings, came as a relief to Chopin. Home. Obviously, not Camp Grizzly. No dining-hall songs or silly games, but still. Home. The forest opened beneath his feet and welcomed him to the place he belonged. He found himself watching his footing as though it were a second nature, picking his path up the ridge with alacrity. Finding his footing, moving as a living, breathing part of the forest came naturally to him; some things even eight thousand years and a brain tumor can't erase.

It took the better part of the day to summit, and then give Julie another lecture on orienting a map. Forty-two miles to the north, through mountainous terrain, was the southern edge of the Kampground. He knew where he was going, now; he turned to the floating pug-cam.

"Now, that's not a full day's work. I've got several hours left before sunset, and in that time I need to worry about making it through the night. So here's what we're going to do."

He then took the holo-viewers through a description of the basic needs for survival. Need number one: water. He began to descend from the peak towards a ravine, describing the pattern water takes over topography and laying his bets on finding a source of water. Within half an hour, though, he was giving a different lecture.

"See, topography is a tricky thing. Since these maps were made, it appears that some of this hillside has broken free in a rockslide, which has created this very beautiful cliff on which I stand." Chopin judged it about a hundred and fifty foot sheer drop off a granite cliff. He'd never actually free-climbed down that far; liability rules precluded it. Still, he didn't need to free-climb.

"This is about a hundred feet of what we called parachute

cord back in the day," he said, removing the cordage from his fanny pack. In the back of his mind, he noted a slight regret that he hadn't asked for something more high-tech, but he'd wanted to keep his fanny-pack as close to original as possible, for authenticity. "Cordage is about one of the most useful things you can have in the woods, and I'll show you why." He began braiding the cords into a rope strong enough (he hoped) to hold him.

"This rope isn't long enough to rapel down, but I can use it to secure me during the descent." In theory, anyways. Practice rarely worked out that way, but he had to pretend. He did a long-tailed trucker's hitch around the base of a tree on the side of the cliff, then began to climb down.

The rocky face of the cliff was, fortunately, freshly broken and still craggy. Weather hadn't had the eons to wear it to smoothness, and so it was not as difficult a climb as it could have been. Once down his ten feet, he pulled the tail on the hitch, freeing his line, then found a rock formation to repeat the process on. After four repetitions of this process, he found himself a third of the way down.

That is when he slipped.

Hiking boots and rock climbing shoes are very different things. A hiking boot is built for support and stability; a climbing shoe is built for flexibility and grip. These things are almost exact opposites, and with the boot on, Chopin's foot thought it had found solid footing.

He plummeted off the cliff side, then felt the jerk on his belt as his improvised safety line caught him. Immediately, he grabbed a handhold, then made the other three points of contact. Julie followed him, hovering anxiously over his shoulder. He pulled the line down and inspected it, then raised his voice to the pug and her attendant audience.

"You can see here, if the camera zooms in, how my line has frayed where it looped around the rock. The edge must have cut into it. For this to continue to be usable, I need to rebraid it. And I can't do that while hanging off the side of the mountain, so we're down to free-climbing. That was my one get-out-of-death-free card."

He took the rest of the climb very, very slowly; twenty feet off the ground, and dusk was beginning to set in.

"Time to speed this up," he announced to his faux-canine companion, looking at the pile of scree below him. It was sharp and jagged, but the fall had pulverized the stone down to small pieces, and the angle of the scree was steep.

Chopin pushed off the cliff side, letting himself drop the remaining twenty feet towards the scree pile. He twisted, lining his hips parallel with the slope instead of perpendicular, and slid as he hit the scree. Too fast; his torso moved faster than his feet could slide, and he dropped his shoulder into a roll. He could feel his back getting cut up by the sharp gravel as he rolled and came back to his feet, finishing his slide.

"So," he said calmly, keeping his terror hidden from the campers he knew were watching him. "That's done. Time to get some water."

Once at the stream, he did what he could to clean his cuts, then crafted a lean-to using fallen tree branches, then gave a demonstration of fire-building using a hand-drill. He had matches in his fanny-pack, if he needed them, but better to put on a show.

He spent that first night hungry, but it was a welcome deprivation. Waking in the morning with that gnawing sensation in his gut, he explained to the holo that food was important, but not as important as water. He re-filled his bottle from the stream, purified it, and headed North down the side of the stream. It would add several miles to his trek, but staying streamside had a number of survival advantages.

That evening, when he came upon the pond surrounded by cattails, he gave Julie a demonstration of those advantages by harvesting their roots and hearts. The firecake from the root combined with the roasted heart was bland, tasteless, and absolutely lovely for it.

He wove a shoulder-slung bag from their reeds, then filled it with food. He spent a full day next to this pond, and finished that day by using a makeshift pole to catch a couple small bluegill, putting protein into his system for dinner before resuming his trek.

After that, it became simply a matter of mileage. He had a full food supply, a consistent water supply, and a location. The rest of the trip took several days, covering mileage over hard terrain, but it was simple drudgery.

Just like coming home again.

HE HADN'T BEEN EXPECTING the crowd waiting for him on the southern edge of the Kampground. As he emerged from the trees onto the concrete slab, a veritable horde of children and their parents began applauding. The kids rushed forward, trying to ask him questions or even to touch him. He waved his hands in a vague defensive gesture, but was too exhausted to run for it.

Fortunately, the teleporter caught him before he was swarmed under. He found himself once again seated in Hurnot's office.

"That... was extraordinary. To be honest, I did not expect you to survive the trip. It would have served a marketing purpose, of course, but this? I'm getting a deluge of people wanting to set up appointments to go do this with you. They are offering top-credit to do it, too. You're something of an intergalactic sensation, you know. You may actually get your debt paid off during your lifetime. Can you do it? Take others along with you?"

"In small enough groups, yes. Larger groups I could give some basic classes to, take out for a night or so, but you can only forage for so many people off one area of land before you just starve."

"Fine, then. Larger groups, shorter trips most of the time, and special trips for high-paying clients on demand. Yes, that will work nicely." Hurnot's greed-fueled grin crossed his face below narrow, squinting eyes.

Adapt to your environment, and it will serve you, though Chopin, smiling to himself. *I'll turn this into a proper Camp yet.*

SOME KIND OF WAY OUT OF HERE

The CampCon stories continue!

We'd done Beer and Beer 2. We'd done Kampground. This time, it was the great Manny Frishberg who stepped up, and his idea was a little more esoteric.

For those of you who haven't read any of Manny's stuff, you really should. He's one of the finest short story authors I've ever had the pleasure of reading. I've often said that the trick to a short story is that you have one punch to throw, and you have to throw it well. Manny has the capability to knock you tail-over-teakettle when he throws his punches, so it was really exciting to be in an anthology he edited.

Horseshoes, Hand-Grenades, and Magic is his first anthology stepping into the role of editor. And his idea for a theme certainly was a bit more esoteric. Basically, it's an anthology of genre fiction in which the theme of the story is "close is good enough."

Some Kind of Way Out of Here follows that description. This was a really fun story to write, though it took us more revisions than most to hit the beats just right. The result has drawn attention to it, though, and a graphic-novel type retelling of this story is going to appear in the upcoming Tales from the Cockerel's Fist put out by Silver Phoenix Publishing.

10

SOME KIND OF WAY OUT
OF HERE

RODERICK DID NOT, as a general rule, trust assassins.

In the past, he'd paired up with pickpockets, smooth talkers, bandits, and the occasional honest-faced merchant. Everyone with any connection to the underworld knew Roderick was the best sneak-thief anywhere in the Five Kingdoms, and he'd worked with them all to get a significant cut of the loot.

His tall, lanky build helped him up many a wall, and his long, delicate fingers picked locks perfectly. He kept his dark hair close-cropped, to provide less motion in shadows of the night.

Across the table from him, Braedun the Blade sat. In person, Braedun stood much shorter than Roderick would have imagined him, and his rough woolen clothing hung loosely over his body, concealing what Roderick imagined to be any number of nasty implements of the assassin's trade. The server at the smoke-filled inn had placed two mugs of weak ale before them, but neither man had touched it.

Inns on Gurante's waterfront were not known for their quality or their honesty; their reputation as convenient meeting places for people like Roderick and Braedun, however... Cheap, sure, and the plank walls and floor couldn't hold back a light breeze, but the staff studiously never paid attention to detail.

"I'm no assassin," Roderick said. He felt it best to get that on the table as quickly as possible. Every criminal had a level to which they would not sink; the con-men looked down on the sneak-thieves, the sneak-thieves looked down on the 'pockets, and the 'pockets looked down on the thugs. Everyone looked askance at the assassins; looking down on people who made a living out of peddling death rarely made good business sense.

"Of course not," said Braedun. "That's my job. But you're a sneak-thief, and I've got information that you may find... valuable."

"I'm listening. I'm not committing, mind you. But I'm listening."

"Of course," said Braedun. His tone was soft and silky as he waved his hand in a non-chalant gesture. "But I can get you into the Royal Vault of Gurante. And I know how to get back out again."

Roderick sucked in his breath.

Mistake.

Never a good idea to let the other person know he'd grabbed your interest; it rang of simply bad bargaining strategy. Rockerick sat back from the table, and toyed with his beer in feigned disinterest. Braedun's slight grin let him know he was fooling no one.

"The Royal Vault's six hells' of a target, no doubt. But what's it to you if I get in? I'll not give a large cut to an information-broker, and I'll not pay up front for information."

"Pay? Cut? You misunderstand me! I only ask that you raid the vault in exactly one fortnight."

"Too soon," Roderick said immediately.

"Surande the Sly burgled the Vault of Rymona in a day, did he not?"

"Ha! I knew a man who apprenticed under one of Surande's students, and the bards have embellished that tale up a bit. Oh, it makes great telling in an inn, gets the ale flowing. Few bards want to tell the story of the thief who meticulously mapped out the timing of each guard's path, planning and plotting for months to pull off the heist."

"I have guard uniforms, a written schedule of patrols and shift changes I prepared myself, and this," Braedun pulled a large key on a lanyard from around his neck. "The key to the vault, made from a wax impression. I have, as you say, *been* planning for months."

"And I'm simply supposed to trust your planning?"

"Not at all! You have a fortnight; put on the uniform, test the schedule. You will find it accurate to the detail."

Roderick thought on this. "I've still got a couple of problems. First off, you've neglected a major part of my business. *Getting in* is never the hard part. I'm sure with the uniform, and the schedule, and the key I could make it in. I could spend the next couple of weeks testing them out, and be ready to *get in*."

Braedun nodded along, appearing pleased he had his mark on the hook.

"But *in* isn't the hard part. You assassins; you never try to carry anything out *with* you. You cause confusion, then escape. That's easy. The trick to what I do isn't the *in*, it's the *out*. I need to leave the castle with a satchel of treasure; even with a guard uniform on, they're not about to simply let me walk out with a bag of loot."

A smile crossed Braedun's face; here came the twist. "But you will do exactly that, anyways. In the treasury is the Staff of Nazerlith."

Roderick raised an eyebrow and stared at Braedun.

"I once used the Staff myself; it opens a portal into the Chapel of the Six in Nazerlith. Remember the change of

Archbishop there a year and a half ago?" Braedun's smile unnerved Roderick. "The Staff was payment in part for that job. I managed to get it 'confiscated' when I entered Gurante. The troops wouldn't put an artifact like that anywhere *but* the Royal Vault, which means it's sitting there, waiting for you to make good your escape."

"What's it look like?" asked Roderick.

"It's a long staff with arcane runes all over it. What more do you want? Fill your bag with loot, tap the butt of the staff on the floor, step through the portal, and you'll be a full kingdom away from Gurante with your bag full of treasure. Open the vault, lock yourself in, and while the guard is beating away on the door, steal as you please, then just step through the portal."

Get-rich-quick. Roderick had seen the con work before, had even teamed up with a man who promised instant riches to investors.

"And what do *you* get? If you don't want a cut, and you don't want payment, then what are you looking for?"

"Honestly? A distraction. You step into the vault, slam the door behind you. The guard responds at the vault, piles up outside and waits to catch you. The Royal Guard of Gurante runs to the basement. This leaves other areas in Castle Gurante more... available than they would otherwise be."

Right. Assassin. "I take the loot, stir up the guards, you make a kill?"

"I get paid by my employer. You get paid in whatever you can take—I'm sure a thief of your standing can figure out how to best make use of this opportunity. We both make out like bandits, pardon the phrase."

Roderick stared at his mug of cheap ale. Houses, mansions, warehouses, stables... these he had burgled. A royal vault, though; you *never* hit one of those. It had been generations since Surande the Sly, and thieves were *still* talking about him. It sounded too good to be true. But he couldn't pass up the chance Rockerick'd check out the information to the best he could. He'd do his reconnaissance. But he'd do it. And Braedun knew it. As the assassin's grimy teeth flashed in a wide grin, they both knew. Against his better judgment, Roderick had a date with a royal vault.

RODERICK STARED AT THE WALL, trying to comprehend the number of staves he saw. Forty-three. Forty-three staves.

I knew that bastard was selling me out. If Braedun wanted a distraction, how much better if Roderick stuck around? Got caught? *Took the blame for the murder* he's *about to commit?* Damn it, he should've known better. Never trust an assassin; they just weren't as honorable as thieves.

The guards beat against the vault door, rattling it on it hinges. Up to this point, everything had gone precisely to plan. Now, Roderick stared at the back wall of the royal vault, and its forty-three staves. A gilt pot also sat along the back wall, containing smaller sticks, also coated in runes, shelves of rings, belts, necklaces, and one live chicken. The chicken made no noise, but simply stared at him, head cocked to the side.

Nazerlith. Think. The people of Nazerlith rarely used the old rune systems or spoke in Kellemaric. Taking those staves out of the equation cut the total down to about twenty-two staves. Three of those were heavily gilt; he could eliminate them as well. Nobody on their way to Nazerlith carried *that* much wealth on them openly.

Nineteen staves left. Nothing for it. Roderick grabbed a staff off the wall and tapped it three times into the floor.

He felt a brief surge of hope as a portal sprang into existence before him, but the flames licking their way out from the edges of the portal didn't seem correct. That was confirmed a moment later when a small, flat-nosed, dog-like creature stepped through. It had the shape of a lady's lapdog, its front nose pushed in to the point of flatness, and its skin wrinked and furrowed. It had no fur, however, and glowed a dull red from within that rose to brilliant orange in the crevices where it folded in on itself. The portal snapped shut behind the beast Roderick dubbed a hellpup.

The demonic creature looked at him for a moment, before its flaming tongue lolled out of its mouth. Then it looked towards the front of the vault, gave three barks so low-pitched and loud that Roderick felt them in his gut more than heard them, and began pawing at the closed vault door.

Not the Staff of Nazerlith. Staff of Hellpup? Whatever. Next...

Before Roderick could try the next staff, however, the pup stepped back, looked at the door, and then belched forth a fireball that heated the entire vault. The door itself melted to slag, and he heard cries of surprise on the other side of the smoke cloud as the guards leapt back away from the door to avoid the puddle of hot liquid metal. This left Roderick with an open doorway where once there was a vault door, and at the stone wall of the opposite side of the hallway. The hallway itself ran perpendicular to the vault door, so Roderick saw no portions of the hallway not filled with molten metal. The Gurante Royal Guards, he knew, would be waiting on either side of that slag puddle, down both sides of the basement passage.

Roderick himself took caution with the puddle of slag. The chicken, caged as it was, began flapping its wings and squawking; Roderick caught a glimpse of gold eggs as it flapped its wings as though to hold back the slagged metal. *Gold.*

The acrid stench of the melted door went surprisingly well with the copper taste of panic in his mouth. Soon, that slag puddle would cool, and then the guards would be on him. He was backed into a box, with nowhere to go and no way out.

Damn you, Braedun.

No time for regrets. Think. This back wall of the vault contained little that *wasn't* magic of some form or another. That vase of sticks resembled wands, and the rings, belts, and amulets on shelves had been meticulously separated from the piles of treasure in the rest of the vault. No way he'd get through testing the eighteen remaining staves before that metal cooled; it was time to improvise.

Taking staves was out. Too bulky. But the rest of it looked portable enough. He began slipping on various belts, rings, and amulets, then grabbed a handful of wands and stuffed them in his pocket. He spared only a wistful glance at the gold-laying chicken. Surely it was the most profitable thing in the vault, but transporting a live chicken in a last-ditch escape attempt seemed too likely to slow him down.

The trick here would be to cross the slag pond *before* the guards could bottleneck him. They'd be waiting, taking their time; their prey was trapped, and they knew it. There would be a moment where the metal was *probably* safe, but the guards would want to make sure. In that safety margin lay the one window of opportunity Roderick would have. So he stood at the edge of the puddle.

Now!

He stepped over the slag puddle and into the hall, pulling out two wands at random and stretched his arms out to either side, waving them where he knew his captors-to-be waited.

The guard on his left turned into a black rabbit roughly a foot and a half in length. On his right, several gallons of wine sprayed out, coating the hallway but doing little to impede the progress of the guard charging him.

Right. Well, I've got one that's useful. Rabbit wand. Huh.

He dodged towards the rabbit. It hopped about in a confused

pattern. He stowed the flowing-wine-wand (which he decided would be useful *after* his escape), then turned and flicked the rabbit-wand at the one remaining guard.

This time, the guard changed from a Royal Guard of Gurante into a nine-foot snarling cave bear, which continued to hurtle down the hallway at Roderick.

Animal wand. Not a rabbit wand.

Oops.

Roderick had only a split second for his eyes to widen in surprise before the bear crashed into him in a headlong charge. He tumbled backward into the corner of the hallway, then came to a rest by cracking the back of his head into the rough stone wall. This left him dazed, in a sitting position, and facing his now-ursine aggressor.

He fumbled at his belt-pouch for another wand. *Because the last one worked so well.* The guard-bear reared back on two legs, the top of its head nearly striking the stone ceiling. It swiped at him with a massive paw. Roderick raised his arms in a futile-but-instinctive gesture to cover his face, but the bear's attack stopped short of landing.

Instead, a violet force field sprung up around Roderick, and the bear shot backwards, landing a good way down the hallway. Roderick clambered to his feet during the unexpected reprieve, and as he did a purple gem fell off one of his new belts and shattered against the floor. He looked down at the belt – only three more gems adorned it. *Well, that was at least useful.*

The bear shook his massive head, layers of fat down his body rippling with the motion. Then he charged again, barreling down on Roderick.

Roderick, not wanting to chance a second impact, turned to his right and ran. The bear negotiated the corner Roderick had vacated with less than total grace, impacting the wall with a force that shook and rattled even the heavy stone. Roderick's fingers found purchase on a wand at last, and he waved it at the bear in the blind hope that something useful would happen.

A jet of sparks left the tip of the wand, creating a dazzling, multi-colored display. Brilliant reds, greens, blues, and golds showered the stone hall, including the shaggy beast at its end. Bits of Guard Bear's fur ignited, and he roared with rage and pain. The hallway filled with the acrid stench of burning bear, but the shower of sparks did little to deter the beast from its attack. Regaining its feet, it moved at Roderick once again, who turned and ran some more.

Better stick to your feet, here. Roderick hurtled through the labyrinth of basement passages that surrounded the Royal Vault, taking turns wherever he could to outpace the bear. He heard shouting coming from his right, from the center of the castle. *Wasn't planning on heading to the center, anyways.*

He sprinted down a long hallway at full speed, and as he did a ring he'd slipped on his left hand began to warm up. Suddenly, Roderick found himself accelerating as fast as a galloping horse down the hallway. Then faster. A smile broke out on his face as the ring propelled him at a speed beyond that any pursuer could hope to achieve down the corridor.

That smile vanished as the hallway ended in a T-shaped intersection, and Roderick found himself hurtling directly at another stone wall. He tried to stop his feet, but his momentum ended up sending him tail-over-teakettle. He tumbled to a crashing halt at the end of the hallway. Jumping instinctively to his feet, he took a moment of amazement that he remained uninjured.

As he did, two more gems fell from the belt that had created the forcefield which had repelled the bear attack. He slipped the now-warm speed ring off his finger and into a pouch, then looked down to his protection belt. One gem left.

Suddenly, the purple forcefield glowed, then faded. The final gem dropped, as did the belt. A glance over his shoulder revealed a crossbow bolt laying harmlessly on the floor, and a liveried guard standing in the hall, working the windlass to reload his weapon. No more gems remained.

Time to gamble again. He grabbed at a wand from his pouch, then wove it in the direction of the guard. A slight chill settled over him. The exposed hairs on his arm stood on end, and goosebumps coated his skin as he shivered, but he could see no other effect. He shook it again; no effect. Great. He tossed the worthless dud of a wand to the side.

The guard's crossbow now loaded, Roderick darted down the hallway to his left before the guard could look up and take aim, or notice the bear charging down the hall behind him.

Damn you, Braedun, for getting me into this. Now I'm launching a full-scale escape from this bleeding castle, and naught to show but some magical doohickies. Even if I make it out of here, Gods willing, I'm still the most wanted man in Gurante.

The hallway turned into stairs, leading upward. Roderick felt his spirits lift a little bit; these steps should be taking him up to the surface level, instead of continuing to run about the basement at vault-level. As the stairway spiraled upward, he could taste the crisp evening air on his tongue. Good; the stairs should open up to the outside, most likely into the castle's courtyard. One step closer to freedom.

He screeched to a halt at the top of the steps. Ten guards stood in a line, facing him. Five held swords in one hand, torches in the other, lighting the exit from the stairs far better than the shining moon could. The other five held crossbows, pointed directly at him.

Well. Bollocks. That was that. He hung his head and raised his hands, slowly. Maybe he could convince his Royal Majesty he hadn't killed any guards, or curry some favor by handing in Braedun. *Hell, I'd settle for seeing that assassin swing from the gallows before me at this point.* Despite his wild hopes of escape, he knew he was caught.

"Right, lads!" said the man on the end in a commanding tone. Roderick dubbed this man the Sergeant of the bunch, though he couldn't read the military rank based on the uniform. "We know he's headed this way, an' we know he's armed t'the teeth. His Nibs don't much care about the blackheart makin' it ta the dungeons alive, and you give 'im a blink, Gods alone know what could happen. So be lively on them triggers, and end him 'fore he gets the chance to give us any o' his malice."

Roderick raised an eyebrow at this speech. By this logic, he should already be filled with bolts, but the guards continued to stare at him with intensity. The Sergeant issued him no orders, and the *twang* he expected never sounded in the crisp night air.

Experimentally, Roderick slowly sidestepped one large step to the left. The guards' crossbows didn't track after him, and their eyelines stayed fixed on the stairwell. Another step, then another.

They don't see me!

Slowly, he made his way around the squad of men, who paid him no notice as they maintained their useless watch.

Roderick kept his steps slow and quiet as he crossed the courtyard. No magic, that; for once since this debacle started, his skills as a thief came into play. He chose his steps carefully, not knowing whether the guards could hear him. Clearly, they couldn't see him. The guards earlier had, though... what changed?

The goosebumps on his arm, raised by the wave of the last wand, began to fade. The chill that had settled over him faded, being replaced by the simple snap of the night air against his skin.

"There he is!" came a shout from the top of the outer wall. "Right middle of the courtyard!"

The sound of at least a dozen men in chain mail turning to point their crossbows at Roderick echoed through the courtyard. Rockerick held his hands up to the air, going down to his knees. Easier to escape a dungeon later than to fight the inevitable.

"I surrender! Don't shoot!"

The guard captain rolled his eyes, apparently disappointed at being denied the opportunity to do *just that*. Instead, he approached Roderick, pulling a pair of shackles from his waistband as he did so. "Alright, you blaggard. Let's see 'im wrists and get you chained proper."

Roderick held out his wrists, then chanced a question. "That's fine. Say, is there a visiting dignitary in the castle? Some important person not normally here?"

The captain raised his eyebrow at Roderick as he clamped the first shackle tightly about Roderick's wrist. "Are you talkin' o' Prince Haren? And why d'you care a whit f'r that? You went f'r t'treasury, not the Royal Guest 'partments." His eyes trailed upward to a tower in the castle.

Because that's Braedun's target.

Before the second shackle could be fastened about Roderick's wrist, a loud, snuffling, snort resounded from the castle entrance. Guard Bear trundled into the courtyard behind the guards, then paced to stand in line with his fellows.

The Royal Guard of Gurante was not prepared for this. They turned to stare at the peculiar sight, half in fear, half in wonder. Roderick saw his chance.

No time for individual tests. Roderick simply grabbed all his remaining wands and waved them downward in the general direction of the guards.

GLYNHADAAL THE THIRD, by the Grace of God, King of Gurante, stared down at Roderick from his throne. "The Crown of Gurante thanks you for your service in saving the life of Prince Haren of Rymona. Your actions in leading the Royal Guard to catch the villainous assassin Braedun the Blade have saved the Kingdom considerable embarrassment. The bounty on Braedun is ten thousand golds, for which you will be rewarded. In addition, Prince Haren has added a bounty of five thousand, in appreciation." The king's voice betrayed little in the way of enthusiasm with his otherwise-congratulatory speech.

The King was a steely-eyed man in his late forties. The bags below his highness' eyes marked the only sign that he had been unexpectedly roused from bed in the middle of the night. He'd dressed in a simple, severe grey tunic and pants, well-fit but plainly adorned. The king's stubbly face was partially hidden behind steepled hands, fingers intertwined in front of his mouth, as he paused and surveyed his guards.

The Captain who had finally managed to arrest Roderick stood, back stiff, staring straight ahead, at perfect, dignified attention. This was particularly impressive given the number of small rips and tears on his tabard, scratches across his face, and his general coating of loose feathers. Standing next to him, a taller liveried man's beard slowly melted away from massive icicles. He held a rope in his hand, which was in turn fastened about the ankle of another guard, floating ever-upwards above the heads of the rest. Next in line to him, a guard's face was mottled in brilliant pink and green, with his hair continuing to smolder.

On the end, also standing to attention, were Guards Bear and Bunny. The Rabbit Guard had managed to escape most of the chaos, but Guard Bear's stomach fur had been etched with some sort of elaborate map, including a marked "X." Roderick's eyes kept straying to the map, trying to burn it into his memory before the court mage repaired the damage.

None of the guards looked particularly ready to cheer on Roderick's heroic rescue of Crown Prince Haren of Rymona. The Prince himself, though, stood positively beaming at Roderick. *And therein lies my salvation. He hails me as a hero, and they need him to conclude whatever business they're about. So I'm a hero, not the villain.*

"Now, we get to the problems. While your rescue and apprehension was both gallant and valued, your methods were... less than ideal. I will assume your assault on the vault was merely a method of gaining the attention of my guard, and not the product of ill-motive. I will also assume your knowledge of the impending assassination came to you through perfectly legitimate channels." The King's eyes bore down on Roderick, and his voice carried a hard edge of finality; it was clear that he assumed no such things. Roderick nodded vigorously, and both men accepted the conveniently diplomatic lie for what it was.

"However, your... unconventional methods of gaining the guard's attention have cost us a great deal. The vault door you slagged was worth three thousand, five hundred, sixty-two gold pieces. Another two hundred for damages to the guards' uniforms and mail. The court mage estimates that he will have to expend five thousand, eight hundred and thirty-nine gold pieces' worth of magical components to restore some of the damage to the guards themselves, including polymorphs, uncontrolled levitation, and other assorted issues. While the herd of cattle may have had value after being butchered, sadly they dis-incorporated, leaving only a hallway full of trampled tapestries and damaged rugs. That brings your total bill to..." The King paused, as if to add his figures together.

Roderick knew the old politician wouldn't let him off easily.

"Exactly fifteen thousand, two hundred and six gold pieces. Your bounties are hereby forfeit to cover the bulk of the expenses; I will allow you to speak to my Master of Coinage to arrange for payment of the balance."

The King's gaze bored into Roderick, daring him to protest. Roderick knew better. He simply nodded, accepting this as a light sentence compared to the gallows that awaited Braedun.

"Very well," said the King. "You are dismissed."

As Roderick walked back along the line of guardsmen/animals, he felt in his waistband for the one ring he'd managed to conceal.

I successfully burgled the Royal Vault of Gurante. Granted, long odds the ring held more than two hundred and six gold pieces' value, but he'd still pulled of a heist that bards could sing tales about. Or, at least something close enough.

VAPORS AND VALOR

OK, this is the final CampCon specific story. There *are* other Campcon anthologies, but after this one we started running out of time to work on them.

Steam and Dragons is a very self-explanatory title that Blaze Ward came up with. It's an anthology where every story revolves around Dragons and the element of steam.

I knew, when I sat down to take point on this one, that most of the stories were going to be steampunk or steamy romance. So I tossed out both of those, and just set the story in a room that would naturally be filled with steam.

The rest of this thing wrote itself. It's a different sort of story; it's a dialogue between two characters with very different perspectives on how to go through life.

The thing you need to know about this story is that, to date, it is still absolutely my favorite thing to read out loud. Any time I'm doing a reading, I have to decide whether or not to read from the thing I'm trying to sell in that moment, or to read this. And it's always a toss up.

Our dragon has a very deep, rich, slow voice. Our knight has an almost nasal, self-important voice. And switching between the two quickly as they speak to one another is just too much fun for me to handle. So often I will read this story even though I'm trying to sell something completely different.

Steam and Dragons is out of print, and so I haven't even had a thin excuse to read it recently. We haven't had copies of it to sell. So one of the (many) reasons I'm super happy to have *Unmitigated Chaos* finally complete is that it'll give me an excuse to continue doing readings of "Vapors and Valor."

11

VAPORS AND VALOR

A HOT, dank mist filled the cave as Sir Hubert descended in search of his quarry.

His torch flickered and danced about, throwing its light onto the fog and no further. A gentle lapping sound told of a pool of water ahead, though Sir Hubert did not know how far. His shield, adorned with the rampant stag of his house, stayed slung across his back in favor of his torch, and his sword, the sword of his family, rested within its scabbard. His right arm stayed on the cave wall, and he moved his feet slowly, ever downward, blindly. The steel plates of his armor clashed and clanked as he stumbled over an unseen stone, and the metallic echo filled the cavern.

"Ah, a guest! Please, do come in and make yourself comfortable," said a low rumbling voice from within the mists.

Sir Hubert froze. He'd been caught already. Slowly, he crouched toward the ground, setting his torch down, then readied his sword and shield. He'd hoped against hope that the beast was away, wanted to set a trap for the creature. But now destiny had decreed that he face his foe head-on, and let his mettle see him to victory.

"Oh, come now. I can hear all that, and there's hardly a need for it. Come down, come in; I so rarely get visitors."

Sir Hubert waited, prepared for the craven monster to strike. His nerves hummed and sang. All his years of training had led him here, to this moment. The time had come, once and for all, for him to be tested. Fear and excitement twined within him, quickening his heart and increasing his breathing as he waited for the opening blow.

"Really?" said the voice, its tone still calm and even. A splashing sound followed this, followed by a resumption of the gentle lapping that filled the cave. "Well, it's your choice to stand there, I suppose. I assure you things are far more comfortable down here, though. I can wait."

Time stretched itself as Sir Hubert stood motionless. He lost track of how long he held his stance, perfectly, as though he still drilled with Master Therilon. But his muscles, though hardened with years of toil and practice, began to sing out in discomfort with the prolonged wait.

"Still there?" that rich, bass voice asked. "I don't like to harp on the point, but there's really no sense in that. I'm quite comfortable here, thank you very much. I'm not sure what you've been told, but so long as any blade is sheathed, you've naught to fear from me."

Sir Hubert hadn't been trained for this eventuality. He'd trained in all the military arts. The Order held classes on philosophy and ethics, on communication, but these had never been his interest. Nobody won their circle in a debate with the enemy; no honor to be had from talking. So now, confronted with talking instead of fighting, he found himself not entirely sure what to do.

He could leave, of course. But leaving would admit defeat. He'd accepted his Task, agreed to slay a dragon in order to be awarded the Fifth Circle, the highest level of honor of his Order. To turn back now would be cowardice, and would at best leave him without a chance at the Fifth. At worst, he could be ejected from the Order, as cowards never fared well amongst knights.

Retreat was no option at all. Remaining here, on guard, seemed like a bad choice as well. Even Sir Hubert, the greatest physical specimen of his generation, could not hold against the aches building in his muscles. And like as not, the beast was waiting for the opportunity to strike.

Dragons were not to be trusted. So he raised his voice and called back into the mist:

"How can I be sure of your hospitality?"

"Well, that's simply rude. You have my word on it, sworn on the shell of the egg that hatched me. For so long as no blade of yours comes free of its sheathe in my presence, no harm shall come to you. No oath is more binding amongst my people. Have you made no study of us at all?"

Study? Yes. But the nature of oaths amongst dragons had never come up. Still, it seemed the only real opportunity Sir Hubert had. He slid his sword back into his sheathe.

"Ah, good. Please, do come down. I imagine you're a bit stiff, standing there. Here, let me clear a path and turn on some light. Stay to the inside of that corner for a moment."

A scorching wind suddenly whipped its way up the cave, followed by a gout of searing flame curling its way along the outer wall of the curve. The wind blew clear most of the mist, and certain rocks, becoming heated, began to throw a soft, pale light, illuminating the cave.

"Now, come. I hunger for news of the world above, and for a decent conversation."

THE DRAGON LOOKED a great deal smaller than Sir Hubert expected. His dreams of valiantly leaping atop the back of a

Great Wyrm simply would not work with the creature before him. Oh, it was still larger than Sir Hubert, perhaps ten feet from nostrils to tail by his guess.

It *was* a guess, though, for Sir Hubert could not see the end of that tail. The dragon's turquoise scales gleamed and glittered on its upper chest and neck, but everything below its lower abdomen lay beneath the surface of a steaming pool of water that would put the Roman baths to shame. The beast had folded his wings behind him and sat upright, reclining in the water. His left claw stretched out along the rim of the pool. His right held a very plain, ceramic goblet roughly the size of a small soup tureen. The dragon drank deeply of its contents as Sir Hubert looked on, mouth agape.

After the beast had finished his draught, he lifted his glass in a casual salute to Sir Hubert. "Come, in, come in," the dragon said. "Allow me to introduce myself properly. My name is Graxentheroniarantashanifar. A mouthful, yes? Terrible thing to have attached to one's identity. You can simply call me Grax."

Silence. Sir Hubert continued to stare at the reclined dragon. The serpent's eyes never broke their gaze with him, but Grax tipped his wine back for another draught.

Right. Manners.

"I am Sir Hubert Berrynton, Protector of the Feywood, Champion of the Fourth Ring of Saint Vigianus, and sixteenth Lord of Derbinshire." Sir Hubert made a bow, his steel armor clanking as he did.

"Ah, well. I should be less ashamed of Graxentheroniarantashanifar, then, shouldn't I?" The dragon let out a low chuckle, and his laughter reverberated through the high, stone ceilings of the bathing cavern. "Shall I just call you Hubert, then?"

Sir Hubert's back straightened a bit at this. To accept such familiarity with a mere beast seemed beyond the pale!

"Well, Hubert," Grax continued in that calm, pleasant bass.

"The wine barrel is over there, and there's some cups near it that may be to your liking. I keep them around in case of company, though it's rare I get some. You may need to give it a rinse-off, but the wine itself is simply delicious. Been aging it for ten years now, right in the barrel. Seemed like a good time to breach the cask, yes?"

Hubert's mind struggled to keep up. The heroic Quest for his Fifth Circle seemed completely out of balance at this point. Should he draw his sword and challenge the creature right now?

"Hubert, you're here. You've got my guarantee of safe passage. I don't know what's making you so jumpy, but I can assure you the wine will help. You have my hospitality; I suggest you take advantage of it."

Hubert inhaled once, deeply. Grax did not seem like such a threat. Was there honor in challenging something—some*one* as they reclined in a bath drinking wine? It didn't seem worthy of the Fifth Circle.

So, instead, he found the wine cask. The human-sized goblets needed a fair bit more than simply "rinsing out," as Grax had said. Layers of dust adorned the plain ceramic, with cobwebs stretched across the mouth of the goblets. Still, a quick moment by the heated pool and Hubert had a perfectly clean vessel.

Which he proceeded to fill, then sip.

"Good, isn't it?" asked Grax.

It was. Oh, it was. Hubert didn't know where exactly Grax had found this particular cask. No doubt it had been looted from some poor vintner in a torrent of destruction, but Hubert could do little about that. And the wine itself was delicious.

"Yes," Hubert said, his voice hesitant as he addressed his host. "Yes, that's quite nice. Thank you."

"Oh, oh," said Grax. "I have to admit, I'm ever so happy you think so. I've been growing the grapes for this wine for a while now, and made some changes to the varieties in this blend. I really think it turned out to be quite something, but you never can rely on just yourself, can you? I mean, of course *I* think it's good, but I'm glad for the second opinion."

Hubert took another sip, then walked to stand by the lip of the pool. The rich, caramel taste filled his mouth and rolled back into his palate, a barrage of spices and flavors coming on with its finish. "You made this?"

"Yes; it's been quite the ordeal getting my grapes up. They're in a different cavern—one with more light, obviously —and it's really taken some doing. But I do think they've done very well."

"You," Hubert hesitated here, "You, uh, you didn't simply steal it?"

"Heavens, no! Why would I do such a thing? If a dragon wanders about up on the surface stealing things from humans, and they get quite upset. Do I look like a Great Wyrm to you? I'm not about to draw a bunch of you knights down to seek your righteous vengeance on me. No, no; I simply live my little life."

"But, all dragons—"

"All dragons! Pfah!" A hiss of steam billowed up from Grax's nostrils. "Tell me, do all humans do anything the same? Are all of them bound by codes of honor like you? Do all humans go about holy quests, or do some of them stay home and bake bread instead?"

"Well—"

"Of course they're different. So are we. Oh, there are big strong ones who fly about and feel very good about themselves while your peasants scatter below. Bunch of arrogant saps never stop to consider what that does to the rest of us. Bullies, you know? Picking on the weak to make themselves feel more important."

"Umm—" Hubert looked down at his sheathed sword, and then looked at the relaxing small dragon, surely one of the weakest of his species. Hubert had the sense to avert his eyes as he considered Grax's words.

"Noticed something about our current situation, did you?" asked Grax. "Oh, I know what you came here to do. And no doubt you could, too; it's not like I'm much in a fight, eh? But tell me, is there really honor in killing me?"

Was there? Hubert couldn't tell. Kill a dragon, that'd been his mission. And he'd been sent here, specifically, because there'd been reports of a dragon. Still... if he murdered Grax, would that truly be a worthy deed?

The fact that he himself deemed it "murder" answered the question for him. He shook his head.

"A head! The man has a head on his shoulders. Such a relief," Grax stretched his left arm alongside the rim of the pool as well. "Come, come in. You must be sore from wearing all that steel. Since we're agreed that you won't kill me, and your blades are still sheathed, why don't you join me for a soak? It's wonderful in here, just the thing for loosening those tense muscles of yours."

Hubert looked down at the pool, then at his armor.

"Oh, come. Get all that steel off you. It's doing you naught at all down here, and keeping it on isn't worth skipping this fine bath. There's a reason I claimed these caves as my own, you know."

Absurdity.

But on the other hand, Grax was right. Attacking this dragon would be a pointless gesture, one without honor. And the soft steam rising up off the hot spring's surface called out to his aching muscles. After a moment Hubert shrugged, then began unbuckling his armor.

"Oh, good man. You won't regret it, I promise."

He didn't, either. Hubert slipped his naked form into the pool; his muscles immediately responded to the heat. He tipped his head back against the rim of the pool and closed his eyes, breathing in the steam and feeling his knots working themselves out.

AFTER SEVERAL MINUTES of quiet contemplation, Grax's bass voice rumbled through the cavern once again. "So, what now for you? Will your Order deem a bit of relaxation with a new friend an act of cowardice?"

"Honestly?" said Hubert, his mind grasping its way up from a pleasant fugue of warmth and wine, "I have no idea. I've sworn an oath to kill a dragon to gain my Fifth Circle."

"Any, uh, any dragon in *specific?*" asked Grax.

"Well, no. My master told me about rumors of a dragon here, so here I am."

"Here you are, indeed. And here you are welcome to stay, or go, as you please. You don't have to return to your Order, you know. I have food, I have wine, and I have a lovely pool made from a hot spring. It's a good life, down here."

"My life—isn't so simple." Hubert said.

"*Make* it simple," said Grax. "There is no joy in complication. Tell me, when you received your First Circle—yes, yes, I know about the Circles—when you received the First Circle, were you happy?"

The question took Hubert aback. He considered it for a moment, remembered how he felt when Master Therilon handed him his first ring. "Yes. For a time."

"For a time," said Grax. "Until you realized it wasn't the Second."

"Yes," said Hubert. "But that drove me to attain the Second."

Here Grax rumbled that low, chortling laugh of his. "So it did, so it did," he said. "And after the Second, you needed the Third. After the Third, the Fourth. And now you seek the Fifth. So tell me, are you happy?"

Hubert leaned back into the warm water and stared at the ceiling.

"When I complete—"

Grax cut him off. "When you complete your Circles there will, without a doubt, *be something else*. I am not your father, but I have lived on this earth for thousands of years. And achievements will never give you happiness, because there will always be *one more thing* to achieve."

Grax's words hit Hubert harder than any swipe of the talons could have. He sunk his head down below the waterline, letting the warmth envelop his face and wash away any tears that he might have shed.

"So, again; live here, with me. Be happy. Eat, drink, soak. We will speak on many things, you and I, and we will smile and laugh. And when, in your dotage, you pass from the earth you will have enjoyed your time here."

Hubert shook his head. "I am sorry. You seem like a very nice, uh, dragon, and I'm sure the life you describe would be pleasant. Indeed, it *is* pleasant, for tonight I live it. Master Therilon had me swear an oath to attain the Fifth Circle, and I could not be happy as an oathbreaker."

"You could not find a village, wait for a dragon to attack, and simply defend it?"

"It's rare to have such attacks these days. No, if I am to fulfill my oath, I must find my target."

"And so you will hunt a dragon to gain your Fifth Circle?"

"Yes."

Grax took a deep breath and sighed. "So be it, then," he said. "I wish it were otherwise, but so be it. Let us at least enjoy tonight."

There they sat, unlikely friends, and for hours Grax asked Hubert about the world above. Hubert told him about the King, about his training. Grax told Hubert stories of lore, of the first meeting between their people. He spoke in sorrow of his diminishing race, of eggs constantly under siege and a reproductive rate that simply could not keep up with humanity's.

Grax's scales glittered and shone as he spun around to face the pool edge. He stretched his wings out over the water for a moment, then walked on all fours up out of the water. Hubert made to follow him, but Grax's soft, soothing voice stopped him. "No, no. You stay there. I'll be back with momentarily, and we can dine together."

Hubert sank back into the water. He hadn't expected Grax, hadn't expected the kindness or the civility. Hadn't expected the complete peace he felt in this moment. A part of him wondered whether or not humans and dragons could live like this, could learn to speak and be spoken to.

Then he remembered his oath, and firmed himself against the thought. He'd sworn to kill a dragon, not to dine with one. Grax was a pleasant fellow, true, but surely unique among his kind.

The warm smells of roasted mutton invaded Hubert's nostrils, and his stomach growled a reminder of hunger. He'd breakfasted but little that morning, to stay light on his feet for the approaching battle. As Grax set the platter beside him on the pool's rim, saliva began to fill his mouth. It was a generous slab, and it smelled as though it had been slowly, perfectly cooked.

Grax placed a similar, if larger, platter next to his spot in the pool, then slid back in. He used his sharp talons to slice through the meat, lifting each succulent portion to his lips and smacking them in obvious enjoyment.

Hubert looked at his fingers, then looked at the meat. Everything else he'd received from Grax today had been perfection, and he had no doubt by the aroma that this was, too. Grax may be small and underpowered, but the drake had a true knack as a bon vivant. Impolite to simply pick up the massive slab of mutton and chew on it, but Grax had provided no utensils.

Easily remedied. He hopped out of the pool and took two steps to grab his belt knife. His eyes fixed on the meat as he pulled the blade out of—

Sir Hubert Berrynton, Protector of the Feywood, Champion of the Fourth Ring of Saint Vigianus, and sixteenth Lord of Derbinshire, died in a blazing inferno, stark naked. His flesh seared from his bones in an instant; he had no time to even consider the reason for his death.

His unsheathed belt knife clattered to the stone floor of the cavern, its naked blade blackened with soot.

GRAX SIGHED, climbed back out of the pool, then took hold of the knight's crested shield. He paced back, through his cave, past his small vineyard and his cooking ovens, past the small pens where he raised his sheep and the cavern of fungus which he used as their feed. He came to a small room, one he could not even fit in himself, and craned his neck to look in at its occupant.

Master Therilon, Champion of the Fifth Ring of Saint Vigianus, met his eyes. His face still held hope, excitement. Grax stared back, then looked at the floor and shook his head. He passed Hubert's shield into the small space, and Master Therilon's face fell as he took its meaning.

"I'm sorry, Therilon," Grax said. "But he failed."

THE END.

INTERVENTION WITH A VAMPIRE

Inspiration is a fickle beast. Sometimes it refuses to show up when you want it to. Other times, it horns its way into your thoughts without so much as a by-your-leave and makes you write something you have absolutely no use for.

Every other piece in this collection, I've identified for you the anthology it was originally associated with. In some cases (The Mentor) it didn't make it into that anthology. In other cases (Sixty-eight), it ended up in a different anthology than it was intended for. And in one case (Awakening), it's for an anthology that has yet to exist.

This piece isn't like this.

This piece had no goal. I drafted it because, at a Radcon, I misheard another author—I'm pretty sure it was Manny Frishberg—when he was speaking to someone else. He was talking, of course, about *Interview with a Vampire*. For some reason, my brain heard *Intervention with a Vampire*, and I was off and running. The idea of vampirism has always, in my mind, been closely linked to the idea of substance abuse, so the idea of hosting an intervention for one just tickled me.

And so I wrote this. And then I put it in a drawer and forgot about it, until now. Now I dust it off and include it here, because it insisted it had to be written, and I've been waiting for the opportunity to share it with others.

12

INTERVENTION WITH A VAMPIRE

DARREN KNEW what was going on as soon as he stepped into the room.

His own living room, usually coated in dirty underwear and scattered video-game cases, had been meticulously cleaned. His second-hand furniture, still beaten and worn, had been cleared of their layers of bachelor detritus. They now contained something much, much worse.

His family.

Marta, Darren's ex-girlfriend, sat on the broken burnt-orange recliner. Her thin arms were crossed over her tank-topped chest, and the ice-green eyes set in her pinched-up face glared at him as though their last fight had never ended. Next to her, on the far end of the rough lime-green couch, Darren's father had positioned himself. Father's face was stern and stark under his bald head, and his slightly tubby frame maintained the rigid, militaristic posture years of service had ingrained into it. His right arm looped about the neck of Darren's mother, who had obviously been crying. Her once-precisely-applied makeup no longer hid the damage age and worry had wreaked across her features, and the result was the look of a woman too old for the perfectly colored and styled blonde hair that perched on her head.

Janice, Darren's baby sister, had claimed the near end of the couch. While the other three all struggled with their emotions (hatred, anger, sorrow), Janice's perfect teenage face was obscured somewhat by her eternally-present smartphone. Her thumbs moved deftly across the screen, carrying on a conversation that clearly interested her far more than the agenda in this room.

A folding chair had been taken from the kitchen/dining table and dragged to the near end of the couch. Seated on its padded-metal frame was a man whose girth threatened to devastate the flimsy structure supporting him with the barest movement. This behemoth was the only stranger in the room, but his round spectacles and full beard over a shirt and tie marked him as something of an academic type.

Darren didn't know the *identity* of this fat interloper, but as Father rose to make an introduction, it became immediately clear what his *function* was.

"Darren, this is Mr. Durlitzer. We've asked him to join us here to—"

Darren spun on his heel. An intervention was *not* on his to-do list for the day. How dare his family ambush him like this! Ambushes like this required fight or flight, and he loved his family just enough to take a pass on the former option.

Dad moved fast, but Darren was out the door before he closed the gap. Two flights of outdoor stairs led down to the parking lot below, and Darren cleared them two at a time. The reverberation of cheap cast-iron shaking told him Father was following.

His rusted-out Chevy Aveo sat faithfully in the parking lot, door unlocked. A quick reach into the door panel revealed a pack of cheap cigarettes. Darren fumbled with the pack, hands shaking, then pulled a lighter from his pocket and began flicking it, coaxing forth flame with all the desperation of a freezing man.

"Darren, come back upstairs." Father's voice was calm, steady, and implacable, if punctuated by heavy breathing. It carried an authority he assumed into existence from nothing.

The fire finally responded to Darren's fumbling hand, and he brought it to the end of his cigarette. He drew his breath in, drawing the chemical relief into his lungs and holding on to it like a life preserver. The nicotine didn't come close to satisfying all his cravings, but it stopped his hands from shaking and kept his voice level when he turned to face Father.

"Fuck you."

"Fuck me? Darren, your whole family is here to talk to you. You don't want to listen?"

"You didn't tell me there was going to be an intervention. This is bullshit."

"You wouldn't have come if we'd told you." Father's voice was rising slightly in volume, his disciplined control beginning to slip into one of his rages. Darren knew if he could just provoke a little bit more, he could end this confrontation and make it Father's fault. He was so close to that freedom he could taste it; he just needed a little push.

"You're goddamned right I wouldn't. You have no idea what it's like to be me."

"Darren, just—" Father's voice was right on the brink, but then his bald head turned away from Darren. He took a deep breath, held it, then turned back. "Look, just come inside. Hear what we have to say. If you don't like it, you can leave when we're done. But you owe us that much."

Darren took a long, slow pull on his cigarette. He'd never seen Father head off one of his rages like that. It was new, outside the pattern. Hard to deal with. If he left now, there was no way to place blame later. Nothing for it, then. He'd need to buy some time before getting a clean way out.

The tableau inside the apartment remained, remarkably, unchanged since his dramatic exit. Noone but Father had moved. The sole difference was that Janice's cell phone had disappeared, presumably into the recesses of her all-too-stylish handbag. The sour looks Janice was not-very-furtively shooting toward their wet-eyed matriarch left little doubt as to the reason for this disappearance.

Mr. Durlitzer heaved himself upward and shook Darren's hand, then gestured toward the couch. At this prearranged signal, Mom cuddled in close with Father, and Janice scooched toward the edge, leaving a narrow gap in between them as the only location in the room for Darren to sit. Briefly, he considered grabbing Durlitzer's chair just to be an ass about it, but he decided not to risk sending the fat man into that narrow gap.

Mom hugged him as soon as he sank back against the faux-crushed-velvet. It was physically unavoidable – his left side was firmly up against Mom, and (more dangerously), Janice's lithe body pressed into his right.

Darren began to salivate.

"Darren, your family asked me here because they just love you like heck." Durlitzer's voice was low and soft, like a man trying to gentle a wild dog. "They've been meeting with me for the last couple of days, and they really feel like they've lost you. They want to get you back, and they're here to ask you to join in that fight."

Darren snorted in derision at this obviously-scripted platitude.

"So they've all written you a letter, and we're going to let them say what they're going to say, then we'll have you say what you're going to say, then we'll be done. Ok?"

Being done was the goal for Darren. He nodded mutely.

"Let's start with your mother, then."

Mom pulled a folded piece of paper from her purse. As she

did so, the rest of this improvised press-gang of a family pulled out similar folded letters. Mom's voice was raspy, and she paused occasionally for a choke or a sob.

"Darren, your addiction has affected my life negatively in the following ways:" Pause, sob, eye dab, and a quick gasp for air. "One: You killed your Uncle Bob."

"Oh, this is crap!" shouted Darren. "He's the one who hid his heart condition from us! If I'd have known, I never would have taken that much."

"Darren, you took two pints." The sadness in Mom's voice was starting to harden into icy anger.

"So? I take that much from you, like, once a week. You're still alive. If Uncle Bob had *told* me about his heart condition, maybe he'd be alive. Not my fault."

Mom paused here, meeting Darren's gaze evenly for the first time. An uneasy silence held the room, daring someone to break it. Deliberately, then, Mom raised her letter back and continued to read.

"Two: I am constantly anemic. I can't go out with my friends anymore, I can't have my own life. As soon as I start to regain my energy, then you come along and drain me again."

Darren was still unmoved. "You're the one who told me not to get my blood on the streets. Never know what's in street-red; could get AIDS, or Hep, or something. You got all worried, made sure I drank at home. You breaking that agreement now?"

"Darren, we need you to stop drinking human blood entirely. That's why we're here."

"No blood? Mom, I'm a *vampire*. You just want me to fucking die? Is that it? Break a leg off the coffee table and stake me, then, if you want me dead."

"Darren!" shouted Dad. "Respect! Just shut up and—"

"Now, now," said Durlitzer. "We're not here to shame. Darren, I'm a vampire. You know perfectly well that we can live off animal blood. Most butcher shops are happy to sell cow's blood or pig's blood at a discount. I've been clean of human blood for fifteen years, now."

Darren couldn't believe his ears. Animal blood. These bastards wanted to take away everything that fueled him. He stood from his chair, and he felt his anger began to take over.

"You don't understand!" he screamed. "None of you understand. Cow's blood? You haven't fed on a human for fifteen years? Have you forgotten the difference? You say you love me, and you want to *neuter* me?" He stormed towards the door, not willing to hear anything else from these people.

It was Mother that followed him out to the parking lot. "Honey," she said in her calm, pseudo-caring voice. "Just... come back inside and listen to what we have to—"

Darren wheeled on her, fangs out. No human blood, indeed. He'd show her. He'd been toning it down, doing his family a *favor,* and did they appreciate him? Did they see how hard this was on him? No. Ungrateful, that's what she was—and he meant to show her the error by draining her right here, right now.

And that's when she held up the cross.

Darren recoiled at the instinctual fear the symbol provoked in him. "A cross, mom?" he asked. "What the *fuck?*"

"Darren, come back inside. Right now. We have to talk to you, and you need to listen to us."

He seethed inside. She'd brought a cross along. What else did she have in that purse of hers? Garlic? Holy water? Was she actually packing a stake? How far did they intend this to go?

"*Fine,*" he said. "I'll come. I'll listen to your little letters. But I'm not stopping human blood. I've got it under control. Uncle Bob was just a fluke. It's not like I've killed anyone else."

"Just come back," she said. "Just come back and listen."

He huffed, but followed. He did love his mother after all, and she *was* a very useful source for his blood. He could listen to her whining for a bit if it meant keeping her around.

As they re-entered the room, Durlitzer smiled that fake

smile of his at Darren. "Welcome back," the fat man said. "Go ahead and have a seat right where you were. Mom, I think we were on your letter still."

Mom nodded. Janice rolled her eyes and looked up from her cell phone. Father kept his face passive.

"OK," Mom said. "Darren, I'm asking you to accept this gift today—"

"Gift?" asked Darren. "What gift."

"You want to hear about it?" asked Durlitzer.

Darren gave the fat man a non-commital shrug.

"Well, your family has arranged for you to come with me. There's a lovely treatment center in San Diego that—"

"San Diego? You're sending me to one of the sunniest spots in the U.S.? How long do you want me to be there?"

"It's a ninety day program," said Durlitzer, unflustered by Darren's ranting. "And it's a very good facility. UV shading on all the windows, no garlic, ample supplies of pig and cow blood, and a really good staff to help you really work through things."

"I don't need to get locked up for ninety days! If you all don't want me to get my blood from you, then I'll have to get it elsewhere. That's fine."

"Well," said Durlitzer. "Mom, why don't you go ahead and read the consequence portion of your letter?"

Mom sighed. She paused. Darren felt her lack of resolve for a moment, and hoped he'd found a weakness. But then she spoke, and after she'd gathered herself her voice came out clear and firm. "If you choose not to accept this gift, I can no longer support your addiction," she said. "This means that I will not allow myself to be bitten any more. I will not help you with your rent. You will not contact me or your father."

"Oh, I see how it is. You're blackmailing me?"

"It's not blackmail, Darren!" shouted Marta, broken free from her silence at last. "Jesus, you're not safe! You keep threatening to turn our kids into vampires, too! How can I let you around the children if you keep acting this way?"

"Now you're taking away my *kids?*" asked Darren. "I'm trying to make them *immortal*. How is that a bad thing?"

Durlitzer sighed. "Darren, all of these people love you like crazy. I spent most of yesterday with them, and I heard how much they love you. Marta wants you to have your kids... she just doesn't want them in danger. And you're out of control. You and I both know what human blood does to us. You think I don't remember? But you're hurting everyone around you, and they're just saying they're done with your addiction. Now, you can choose to be done with your addiction too, or you can choose to be done with them. Nobody's forcing you to do anything—"

"Nobody's *forcing?* They're making it so I don't have a choice!" screamed Darren. The blood-rage boiled behind his eyes. He looked at the humans all stacked up nice and neat in his home, ready to be eaten at a moment's notice.

"No. They're making their own choices," said Durlitzer. "They have that right. Now it's time for you to make yours. What's it going to be, Darren?"

"I can't do ninety days!" said Darren—and then he lunged for Marta. As he did, she quickly brought a small spray bottle out of her purse and doused him with it like he was a cat getting too frisky with the houseplants.

He felt the rash set in immediately. *"Holy water?"* he asked. "You're using *holy water* on me now?" He began scratching and clawing at his face.

Durlitzer handed him a rag. "You were going to drain her," he said, still calmly. "You should know that everyone here has been equipped and trained to make sure that you can't do that. You made the choice to attack—what you're feeling now is a natural consequence of that choice. Accept this gift, Darren.

Learn to live without human blood. Life is so much more than just stalking your next victim."

"I can't do ninety days. Maybe, I don't know. Maybe I can go to meetings or something."

"You need more than that," said Durlitzer. "You've heard the terms of the offer. This isn't a negotiation. They all have their bottom lines, and they're going to stick to them. If you stick to yours, then we're done. But if you take what they're offering, what they all want you to have, then you get a whole new life. So what's it going to be?"

"I don't think I have a choice…" said Darren.

"You've got a choice," said Durlitzer. "Might not be one you want to make, but you've got it."

"Fine," said Darren with a huff. "I'll go."

"You will?" asked Mom. Her voice broke Darren's heart; the fearful hope she had that maybe this would work. It snapped his resolve like a twig, and he couldn't do anything but nod.

Of course he'd go.

SIXTY-EIGHT

This story appeared long before I was even aware of the amazing light novel series/anime/manga IP *86 Eighty-Six*. It has nothing to do with that IP. That happens to be one of my favorite IPs at the moment, so I thought I should just throw that disclaimer right here in case you know me or have read any of my online posting.

Esther took point on this one, and she wrote it originally for the *Alternative Truths* anthology for B-cubed press. It's easily our most political work to date. Politically, Esther and I are both moderates. We don't really take strident positions, but rather try to work things through rationally. And so when asked to do a political story about the dark future heralded by the Trump presidency, we were a little put off.

Instead of tackling something from the perspective of the right or the left, we looked at the basic flaws in the system. And to us, the biggest flaw—on both sides—is the way a for-profit news company can steer the electorate that best profits that news company. Whether it's Fox News or MSNBC, we're now living in an age where it's the news company and not the news that controls the decisions of most of the country.

So we did a cyberpunk story exploring *that*.

It wasn't quite what B-cubed was looking for in *Alternative Truths*, though, and it does not appear in that anthology. But Bob Brown still liked the story, and he put it into *After the Orange*, an Anthology of post-Trump cyberpunky stories edited by Manny Frishberg.

I like that we wrote this story almost as much as I dislike reading it. Not because it's bad—just because the concept of it still seems a little too possible, and that scares the heck out of me. Remember as you read this that it's a story meant as a warning, and not as a prophecy. At least, I hope it is.

13
SIXTY-EIGHT

SPECIAL AGENT DANA LIU ran toward the weather-beaten warehouse, weapon drawn. Her thick-soled boots barely made a sound despite the gravel and dead grass impeding her way.

Carefully halting outside the loading door, Dana quickly scanned the area. No surveillance cameras, no drones, no robotic guards, no signs of occupation adorned the outside the building. But her instincts told her: *Here. Her quarry would be here.*

She didn't dare wait for back up, either. Every second that passed had the potential to create irreparable damage to the whole nation, possibly for generations.

The back of her neck pulsed with tension, and she relied on her training to force her stressed muscles and breathing to calm.

Once her breath and heartbeat steadied, Dana carefully pried the cover loose from the loading door's security panel. Its interface had a neural line jack but no wireless capability, and no uplink to the neural net. A local network only then. She estimated the technology at least fifty years out-of-date, but in pristine condition. If the warehouse had truly been abandoned, it's internal servers should have given out long ago.

Dana snorted. No doubt the out-dated tech had been installed recently to keep the insurgents' location hidden. Her lips quirked. A cocky blunder on their part.

The building's absence from the neural net made it difficult to locate, but now that she had, it would be that much easier to hack and control.

Holstering her weapon, Dana tapped the temporal bone behind her ear, just above her mastoid process, releasing the neural line stored there. She let the cord unspool, then plugged it into the jack, merging directly with the building's main operating system.

The surface programs were all dormant; as one would expect from a warehouse not currently in use. Under the surface, though, lay a second set of protocols, blocked by a fire wall. She made quick work of unlocking loading doors next to her and then turned her attention to the hidden code beneath.

A fine sweat broke out across Dana's forehead and her brow wrinkled as she struggled to penetrate the much more sophisticated code locking the second set of protocols away from her, her brain churning through possible code combinations as fast as thought.

By the time the firewall finally parted, Dana's temples throbbed with the effort. But she had access to the warehouse's true security protocols and schematics. Her eyes closed, she played them back in front of her mind's eye, and a room hidden in the building's north wall caught her attention. The warehouse electrically systems routed extra power there, but no cameras filmed outside its entrance, no mention of it at all on the warehouse's manifest... She unhooked her neural line form the control panel, letting it spool back up inside her head. Her target would most likely be there.

Dana redrew her weapon and cautiously entered the

warehouse using the tall, wall-to-ceiling shelving as cover. No lights illuminated the massive cavernous space, old, discarded farm machinery from before wireless neural automation glinted dully on some of the shelves.

A bullet ricocheted off a shelf, two feet above her head, throwing a spark in the gloom. Dana pivoted and crouched, keeping the shelving between herself and the shooter, sighting down her own weapon, into the darkness.

A muzzle flashed, and she jerked her aim up to hit presumed center mass below the flash. Dana squeezed, her weapon barking and bucking in her grip.

Her ears rang; she had no way of knowing if she'd truly hit. Dana waited the space of ten heartbeats, but no other deafening flashes appeared.

SHE MOVED QUICKLY and carefully to the shelves shielding the hidden doorway, tensed for shots that did not come. Dana knelt, then triggered the hidden latch on the bottom shelf.

The door swung open silently.

Light spilled out from a laboratory-looking room where a man sat, his hands calmly folded over his lap. He wore a well-tailored, light-colored suit, and his dark hair had been cleanly cut. Next to him, a virtual reality tank labeled "68" told Dana she'd finally found the right place. She steadied her aim on the man.

Silently, Dana activated her connection to the neural net, immediately informing her superiors, *"Destiny located. Transmitting exact GPS coordinates. On first visual, Lyceum and passenger appear undamaged. One possible hostile on site. Will attempt to engage until reinforcements arrive."*

Out loud, Dana said only, "Secret Service. Keep your hands where I can see them."

"Ah, Agent Liu, I see you made it. I was hoping we'd have a

chance to chat." The man remained still, his hands neatly folded his lap.

Shock and surprise at her own name passing the terrorist's lips swept through Dana, and she struggled to keep her expression neutral.

"I'm not *joining* you for anything," Dana said. "The only person I care about here occupies that VR tank behind you. I will be leaving as soon as you stand down, and I assure myself of Sixty-Eight's safety."

"Anika's quite safe; I assure you. No need to be rude. Anyway, Dana—can I call you Dana? My name—well, for all intents and purposes, anyhow—is Ven."

Dana frowned. Something here felt off, but she couldn't put her finger on it.

Ven slowly reached his left hand into a drawer next to him. Dana gestured with her weapon, and he raised his right hand in sign of surrender, but did not withdraw his left.

"It rarely pays to be so hasty, you know." Ven said, his tone mildly chiding. He pulled a bottle of what appeared to be a very old single-malt Scotch from a distillery called "Ardbeg" out of the desk along with two glasses, all held by the long, agile fingers of his left hand. He placed the whisky on the table, opened it, and began to pour, all still with his left hand.

Dana held herself ready, but waited for Ven to prove himself an overt threat.

"I'm merely suggesting we engage in some conversation before you rush on your way. You're already here, after all." Ven slid a glass across the desk toward Dana, then took a sip from his own.

Dana clenched her jaw, ignoring the (possibly poisoned) glass before her. "There are much easier ways to get my attention if all you want to do is talk," she said in a sharp tone. "As it is, the only thing I'll be discussing with you is whether you've harmed the minor behind you."

"Harmed? Of course I haven't!" Ven took a long, slow sip from his glass. "I don't want to harm anyone, Dana. I simply believe in freedom."

"Sixty-Eight wasn't being held captive, *Ven*. You *stole* her from her rightful home and custodian," Dana corrected the kidnapper crisply, debating her options. She needed information on this abductor's splinter group. And Sixty-Eight did not appear in immediate danger...

"Sixty-eight?" asked Ven. "You know, she *does* have a name. Anika, I'm told. And I 'stole' her from the 34th floor of the Coast-to-Coast media network. Not exactly a pair of loving parents there, eh?" He shook his head.

Dana pressed her lips together tightly, trying to contain her irritation. "She was with her legal guardian. State News One has invested every bit as much time, care, and education into Sixty-Eight as any traditional parent, Ven." Dana measured the distance between the VR tank and herself with her eyes, debating whether she could close the distance if he made any sudden moves.

Ven shook his head, his voice taking on a overly solicitous tone, "Has Anika ever rode a bike? Scraped a knee? Even left that VR tank?"

Dana blew out an exasperated breath, and took a small step closer to Sixty-Eight, angling to keep herself out of Ven's reach. His air of quiet confidence confused her, made her wary of underestimating the situation.

She responded to his question to buy herself time to think. "The American public spends the majority of their time in VR tanks, just like that one, plugged into the neural net."

"Yes," said Ven. "I'm quite aware of that particular tragedy. But you claim that State News One is an appropriate custodian to raise young Anika, here. And I merely point out that she isn't exactly getting a normal childhood in her artificial environment."

"That VR tank is far less dangerous and more effective in conveying experiences to its user than a traditional upbringing. It allows a candidate to learn and absorb knowledge at an accelerated rate. True, it's not a *normal* education; rather, it's an extraordinary one for a very gifted individual, Ven. A future leader. A person whose mind is capable of shaping the very future of this country."

"So State News One shapes the girl, and the girl shapes the country. Funny how the shape of the country appears awfully like the shape of State News One." Ven watched her expectantly, a friendly smile curling his lips.

"Our elections are decided by everyone casting their vote." Dana said, not willing to get caught up by his affable facade.

"And yet, Anika's tank is labelled '68' as though she'd already taken office, is it not?" Ven smiled, beatifically. "You've even repeatedly called her by that title in your conversation with me. And yet. She's twenty years away from Constitutional eligibility, and you've got her number already. In twenty-four years' time, she *will* be President of the United States. Hence, an upstanding Secret Service agent like yourself has already been assigned to her. Hardly seems like a free, open election to me."

"You can't blame the population for electing the most qualified candidate presented to them." Dana took another step closer to Sixty-Eight's VR tank.

"But who really decides the most qualified candidate? We're currently electing the 65th POTUS, and yet there are Secret Service agents assigned for VR tanks, just like this one, all the way up to 70? Does that really seem to indicate a free and unskewed election? A true expression of democracy?"

"I don't know who's been leaking you your intel, but State News One doesn't force anyone to vote against their conscience, nor does it cook ballots or in any way falsify the election results. Everyone's vote is cast and counted as intended." As she said the words, Dana heard an echo in her mind, as if someone else had said that to her once, but she couldn't remember who.

"Ah, I see." Ven smiled again, his eyes crinkling as if he didn't have a care in the world. Dana's eyes narrowed with suspicion, and she sharpened her focus, dragging her foot back another step closer to the tank.

Ven continued talking, seeming to ignore Dana's inching toward the tank. "I suppose in some ways you may be right. But, let's explore idea that shall we?" he said.

Ven slowly brought his fingers up and steepled them, watching Dana with bright eyes. "Our first voter, Elda, is a widow living on a fixed income. Her church and her grandbabies are her social circle, and the riskiest pastime she enjoys is the penny slots at the local casino on the ten-dollar senior buffet day."

"You better be going somewhere with this fast. My patience is not limitless." Dana interrupted, her shoulders twinging from maintaining combat readiness.

Ven sighed. "*She* votes for your candidate as the leader who will uphold traditional family values, fight for the 'sanctity' of marriage, and protect all human life from the moment of conception." Ven paused. Dana glowered at him, taking another step toward Sixty-Eight, and the readouts on her VR tank.

Ven shook his head, then continued calmly, "Meanwhile, we have Sven. He's a twenty-something college grad. Sven believes in universally-available social and health services; a woman's right to choose any and all things that happen to her body; and equitable access to opportunity regardless of race, religion, gender, or sexual preference. He also votes for your candidate, believing her to person whose priorities best mirror his own."

"What's your point?" Dana said. "People vote for candidates for their own reasons all the time."

"Tsk, Tsk," said Ven. "These two people's views are diametrically opposed, but they both chose the same person as their ideal leader. One of them must be wrong about the candidate's actual stance on their issues. Tell me, how is it possible for one person uphold contradictory beliefs, Dana?"

"Access to a whole world of information is available to everyone at the speed of thought. It's not the news network's fault that people only digest the fraction of it they want to hear."

"Is that true, though? Or does the neural net flood the average American flooded with so much information that they naturally gravitate to the people and views that make them feel most secure? Not unlike a drowning person clings to an overturned canoe." Venn's voice held a plaintive note that disturbed Dana, even as she reminded herself that he was a probable domestic terrorist and proven kidnapper.

"No one can control at what threshold or in what way people will react to data overload," Dana said. "There's even a waiver in the terms of use."

Ven merely raised an eyebrow. "And how sad that is. Democracy has been waived away. Would you say then, Dana, that the news each person receives is unbiased? Isn't a custom campaign beamed directly into the skull of each and every citizen? If not, how do all Americans predictably and reliably arrive at the same elected candidate?"

"I don't believe it's nearly that simple," Dana said, then realized she'd forgotten to move and took another step toward Sixty-Eight.

Ven shook his head sadly, for what Dana swore was the fortieth time since she entered the room. "Yet even you speak of your belief, not your knowledge. Tell me Dana, what do you truly know for sure?"

"Looking at historical law enforcement data, I know law-breaking has decreased, rapes have diminished, and hate crimes are at an all-time low. Our healthcare system works. Our economy is strong. We are respected internationally. And our people are *happy*."

"And all of those are laudable goals, I'm sure. But can you really say they've been truly accomplished when the neural net is riddled with pockets of hateful bile once you know where look?"

"The bigots are inflicting their views on others like themselves without causing harm to anyone else." She said, her voice sounding defensive even to her own ears.

"Ah, but who truly bears the price? Young Anika who's locked away in a VR tank, learning to be President from birth? What parent would want that? Can you give Anika the chance to live unconstrained, to make her own destiny?" Ven interjected.

Shock hit Dana as Sixty-Eight's code name, 'Destiny,' passed Venn's lips. "Can anyone truly guarantee that?" she countered, watching his expression, but he didn't appear to be aware of weight behind the word. "Before the neural net, America had some disastrous administrations. Presidents that pushed our country to the brink of chaos and despair. Forty-five practically started a civil war while throwing nukes at North Korea, and that was only the start. Since the Net, all of that has calmed. We're stable. We're happy."

"Do you know that to be true, or has State News One only led you to believe it's true?" Ven asked.

"What?" Dana asked, shaking her head to clear it, her ears suddenly buzzing and popping.

"How much of what goes on before our eyes depends on who is reporting it?" Ven asked, his voice deceptively mild. "Where is your outside source?"

Dana paused.

"I can tell you," Ven said, his voice suddenly gentle, "It doesn't exist. Not anymore. There is no unbiased source; there is only the News. And from that monolithic entity, the power of the people to rule is conned out of them, not freely given."

"These candidates win the Presidency because anyone else

217

would do an inferior job running the country if elected." Dana reiterated. Sixty-Eight was her only concern here, she reminded herself. Nothing this man said mattered.

"The perfect President that State News One nurtured, trained, and put into power. If you take a step back, doesn't that concept seem laughable?"

Dana stared at him, little pin-pricks of light flashing on the edge of her vision light fireworks. She blinked. Had he drugged her somehow and she hadn't realized? She hadn't drunk the whiskey, but her head felt strangely heavy.

Ven's voice took on a persuasive cadence. "We are a dog chasing its tail in ever shortening circles. I *liberated* that child from a greedy corporation. One that's using her to keep a death-grip on the power base they've built. One that most Americans can't even see."

If Ven had truly done something to her, she needed to end this before she became incapacitated. Everything felt slightly out of focus. She blinked.

"But you can. You see it, but you look away from it. You'll probably continue to ignore it." Ven slowly rose from his chair, holding his hands out in front of him and palms upward, as if to display how little threat he was.

She mustn't believe it. He'd stolen from the future President from the bosom of the whole secret service. This man had to be very, very dangerous. He must be.

Ven's voice continued melodically. "All of this technology hiding the fiddler, and yet we all dance to the same tune. Does that seem like a true expression of democracy, free will, and self-determination to you?"

"No, it doesn't." Dana said, frowning at her own words.

"I'm glad to hear we can agree on something." But she didn't agree with this traitor.

She tried again. "In my experience on this side, people need structure, they need rules, they need some 'herd mentality' to keep themselves civilized. Humans were often horrific to each other before the neural net, and certainly still have that capacity. Our current level of technology just means it's not expressed to anyone's detriment."

"So, let me interpret what you're saying. People's views haven't changed. Technology just allows you to divert to who and how they express it. Filth is still just as dirty no matter how expensive a rug is laid over the top you know." Ven's voice took on that chiding tone she hated so much.

"But it keeps the people from treading in it." Dana said.

"It leaves all of society precariously suspended above it, you mean, ready to fall in at anytime. Meanwhile, the media and the big corporate sponsors rake in all the profit from the politicians that no longer 'appear' corrupt, but are even more ineffectual at assisting the people they represent."

"The working public are not unhappy."

"Aren't they? Or do they just not know it?" Ven took another step toward her, and Dana instinctively widened the distance. "Let me ask you. Are you happy, Dana?"

She stared at him, her brain full of white static and cotton.

"Think back to when you first took picked up your secret service badge. Did you ever expect the secrets you hold as you serve to be this massive? Our Presidents are being grown in tanks like artificial protein. And the media convinces everyone to imbibe." Ven gestured at the large tank and Dana realized he stood much too close. He'd approached her, and she hadn't noticed. It hadn't registered as important.

Something was seriously wrong. Her reactions were sluggish, heavy. He must've drugged her, put something in the air vents or on something she touched. It didn't matter what really, keeping Sixty-Eight safe was her responsibility.

"What have you done?" Dana asked Ven, feeling ridiculous the moment the words left her mouth.

"Given America a chance to be free once more, I hope." Ven said.

She brought her gun up, slowly, her arms trembling, and glared at him. "Surrender now, or die by my hand."

Ven shook his head. "Still so violent, I see."

"I am not the one who forcibly abducted a minor." Eliminating the threat before she was incapacitated must be her only priority now. If he wouldn't surrender...

Ven sighed, still much too close for Dana's comfort. "We may as well take this to its inevitable end, then. Embrace each of our destinies as it were." Ven said and lunged suddenly, grabbing at her gun, but caught a fistful of her uniform coat instead, tearing it and throwing her aim downward. But not far enough.

Dana's muscle memory flexed, his chest blossoming into red blood that splattered over her then across the floor. Ven crumpled, his eyes glassing over as he took his last labored breaths.

"Goodbye, Dana," he breathed, and blood foamed his smiling lips.

Dana glowered at him, irritated by the smile that seemed to say he knew something she didn't. She sat down and put her head between her legs, waiting for whatever he'd done to her to pass. Of course he had to have the last word.

Finally, Dana sat up, holstered her weapon, and moved to check the readouts on Sixty-Eight's Lyceum.

The reinforcements finally arrived just as she finished running diagnostics and verifying there was no strange coding added to the VR tank's neural buffer. The new squad fanned out, securing the perimeter and double checking Ven for life signs.

"About time," Dana told the squad leader grumpily. "Take us home will ya? We have some house cleaning to do, I think. That man knew entirely too much about our Presidents."

CAROL FIRLOTTI, chairman of the Luddite Resistance, leaned back in her chair and took a deep breath, swirling the single malt in her glass as she pondered the death of a true patriot. Ven had done his job, had given the agent just enough niggling seeds of doubt that that it would seem natural when the neural virus completely over took over their systems. When President Anika Paulsen and Agent Liu decided to take on the bastards at News One, it would seem entirely natural. Their own well-reasoned decision. This little incident would fall by the wayside in the annals of history, a mere footnote in the great revolution to come.

And only Carol would know exactly how calculated the sacrifice had been. Her brother had remained calm and erudite to the last. She raised her glass to the memory of Ven's sacrifice, and to the Luddite victory, still twenty-four years in the future.

THE MENTOR

This is a story that didn't make it into its intended anthology.

I feel no shame in that. The anthology in question was a tribute anthology to David Farland, aka David Wolverton, one of the great fantasy writers of our time. The number of very talented authors who submitted to that antho—well. Let's just say that David Farland is a man who touched a number of lives very, very deeply.

He wrote amazing stories, true. But more than that. David Farland's true mission in life was shepherding the rest of us. He was a teacher. He was our mentor. And his sudden passing came as a shock to the whole community.

So, yes. This one has been sitting in my drawer since. But I'm not sad we wrote it, because writing it was a kind of therapy. Our way of mourning the passing of a great man whose life touched just about everyone writing fantasy today.

There's really nowhere else I want this submitted to. This is a story about David Farland, even if he's never mentioned. Having it published in a place that didn't acknowledge that would just degrade the emotion I felt while writing it. So I'm really happy we get to include it here, because that allows us to share with the world our feelings regarding a man who so many fantasy authors consider to be The Mentor.

14

THE MENTOR

The Mentor

"Remember, a great tale isn't just about you. Ultimately, the reader should close your book and feel that a connection has been made, to realize with wonder and delight that 'This story is about me.'" – David Farland

"Why, do you think, does each village need a Wizard?" The Mentor stopped walking down the wide forest path and looked down at Roneld with that half-smile on his age-lined face. He had a well-trimmed beard, his slight baldness shone in the sun, and he stood taller than Roneld by a full hand. The long, flowing dark cloak that marked the Mentor in the eyes of all Wizards flew behind him, though to the uninitiated it would simply appear a nice cloak for a traveler.

Roneld had to think on this. Despite the Mentor's kindly tone of voice, Roneld recognized a teaching question when he heard it. He frowned as he thought about it. A slight, cool breeze whispered through the trees around him and fluffed his ill-trimmed, dirty-blond hair into his eyes, breaking his chain of thought. *When in doubt,* he decided, *take a stab at it.*

"Because we heal the sick, bring the rains for the crops, and find the water from the ground?" Roneld ventured.

The Mentor shook his head, and continued to smile that kind, soft smile. "Think on that," he said. "What have I taught you about the sick?"

"That... they mostly get better on their own. Magical healing just sort of speeds up what the body would do anyways."

"Good," said the Mentor. "So why does the village *need* us for that?"

"I..." said Roneld. "I mean, it's better if someone is healed faster, isn't it?"

"It is," said the Mentor. "But is it *needed,* or just *convenient?*"

Roneld sighed. He decided to shift the conversation away from this prodding. "Mentor," he said, "Why are you asking me these things? And why drag me away from the College down this half-forgotten trail? Where are the other candidates? I'm the top of this class. I should, by right, have my pick of assignments."

"Mayhap," said the Mentor. He kept that smile on his face despite Roneld's irritation. "But the *why* is important, as well. If you know *why* you are needed, you will know what decisions need to be made. So, again—with healing, are we *needed,* or just *convenient?*"

"Convenient, I suppose," said Roneld. "Most of what we do could be done by someone who just knew how to clean a wound or set a bone. We can make it go faster, but we're not going to save anyone they couldn't."

"Exactly," said the Mentor. "So, it cannot be that we are needed for healing. What of the crops? What have you learned of the weather?"

"That... the plants have grown to be accustomed to the normal weather patterns, and that making it rain on one day simply means it won't rain the next."

"Exactly. And yet, we all perform the rain ceremony to bring rains after the spring planting, don't we?"

The question seemed absurd. "Of *course,* Mentor. Any village that doesn't have the rain ceremony..."

Roneld trailed off. He'd never put two and two together about this. The rain ceremony had been completely ingrained into him throughout his childhood. He simply *knew* that any village without a rain ceremony was going to have a horrible harvest. And even when presented the new information... he'd never applied it, until this moment.

The Mentor smiled and laughed a little. "Yes. A village without a rain ceremony will survive. They will grow their crops, and they will eat. So... why the Wizard?" The old Wizard let Roneld ponder that, allowing a silence to fall between them. Roneld used the silence to re-arrange the thoughts in his mind, staring off into the distance as this new worldview settled in on his shoulders.

Roneld shook his head, letting his thoughts come back to the present, thankful that the Mentor had given him that silence to process.

The Mentor picked back up. "As to finding water from the ground, what have you learned about that?"

"That it's most efficient to cast a spell to confirm what your measurements tell you," said Roneld promptly. "That water can be found as a result of weather patterns and geography. Casting spells about to find water at random absorbs a great deal more energy and time than using the geography to come up with a best guess, then using the spell to confirm."

"Mmm, good," said the Mentor in his quiet tone. "So... again, what does that mean for the village? Do they *need* magic for this?"

"...No," said Roneld. "It's... convenient, I suppose."

"Just so," said the Mentor. He took a deep breath and inhaled the clean air of the forest. "Which brings me back to my question. Why does a village *need* a Wizard?"

Roneld had to think on this. Before he could answer, though, the Mentor began walking down the path again, and Roneld moved to join him. The Mentor did not press Roneld for an answer, which was good—because Roneld didn't think he had one.

THE PATH LED them in silence to a small little hamlet. Still in the forest, the Mentor slipped his Wizard's chain beneath his shirt, then nodded to Roneld to do the same. Roneld, confused, followed the Mentor's lead, though he couldn't fathom why. These chains announced to the world that the two were trained Wizards. Wielders of power. Keepers of lore and knowledge. Why the Mentor chose to *avoid* that announcement completely escaped Roneld.

The village itself was tiny. No more than a small collection of hovels, with thin streams of smoke rising from the turf-covered roofs. It sat in a small valley, and after leaving the woods the two Wizards still had roughly three furlongs of fields to cross before reaching it.

As they approached the little collection of huts, Roneld asked, "What village is this? I've studied our maps extensively, trying to choose my post, and I don't recall any village being here."

"That's because," said the Mentor, "those maps are incorrect. We do not have enough with the Gift to send a Wizard to each village. We prioritize. We select. But there are hundreds of these small villages that exist without a Wizard... and we don't place them on our maps because we will not be posting a Wizard here. Not every village has a Wizard."

Roneld blinked, processing this. "But..." he said, then trailed off. "But every village *needs* a Wizard."

"Why?" asked the Mentor.

"Because... because they *do*," said Roneld.

"That's not an answer," said the Mentor. "You know that. So, think. Underneath all the rituals. The rain ceremony. The water-dowsing. The healing. The fire festival in the summer, the snow-dance on Midwinter... underneath all of that, what is it that a Wizard provides? What does the village get?"

"I..." Roneld had no answer. But that made no sense. A village's Wizard was the centerpiece. Villages bragged about the strength of their Wizards. The Wizard rarely paid for his drinks in the common-house. Everyone knew a Wizard was the critical, most important piece of the village.

The Mentor smiled down to Roneld. "Well," he said. "Let us then examine a village without a Wizard, and we can see."

The two of them entered the village. Roneld couldn't see a building large enough for a common-room, a gathering place for the people. A small well stood to the side of the village. All the doors to the huts seemed to open onto a muddy area that could, if one were feeling generous, be called the town square. While smoke rose from the huts, there was no bustle about the village. It felt... empty.

And then one of the doors opened, and an older-looking lady stepped out carrying a water-bucket. She took a moment to look at the two men—one aged, one younger—in the middle of her village.

"You two get lost somewhere?" she asked in a tone that approached an accusation without being one.

"Uhh—" said Roneld.

"Not at all," said the Mentor, that kindly smile on his face. "We are simply wandering, seeing what this fine world has to offer us."

"Well, you'd best keep on wanderin', then," said the old

woman. "Not much to offer here other than you help with the chores."

Roneld sighed. This was all getting pointless, and fast.

"Of course we'll help," said the Mentor. He stepped forward and took the water bucket from the aged woman. Roneld could feel his mouth going open. This was the Mentor... the head Wizard of the College of Wizards. Arguably the single most powerful man in the world. Stories were told of the Mentor, of his deeds before he'd held that title, of his immense ability to wield the power of creation. And now... and now the Mentor was using a bucket to fetch water for an old lady who appeared more confused than grateful.

As the woman led them towards the well, the Mentor continued to address her. "So, tell me—what do you all do for fun around here?"

The woman scoffed. "You blind?" she said. "Have you a look around. We scrape our livin' from the dirt. We do our chores. Fun's a thing for children, and even then they ought not to waste their time on it. Best learn to be useful."

Roneld couldn't help but gape at the woman. Her existence... the very fact of her mundane, joyless life... scared the hell out of him. As he looked around, other villagers began to emerge from their homes. Not a single one smiled—they simply went about the tasks of the day. Roneld began to feel as though an ominous weight hung over this poor village.

The Mentor reached the well, hooked the bucket to the line, and dropped it in, then began hauling it back up. "How long until the fire festival?" he asked the old woman, still appearing a man just trying to make pleasant conversation.

"The what now?" asked the old woman. "Mind you don't spill that on the walk back."

The Mentor chuckled a little, gaining a glare from the villager. "Of course, madam," he said.

After the Mentor had completed his water-hauling task, he

looked between Roneld and the woman. "Well," he said. "I do suppose you're right. I think we've seen all we need to see of this village." He turned to look straight at Roneld, then added "Haven't we, candidate?"

Roneld nodded slowly. He had.

On the trail back to the College, the Mentor once again stopped, all of a sudden, and turned to ask Roneld. "So, again. Why do you think each village has a Wizard?"

"Because we provide entertainment?" said Roneld. It tasted bitter when he said it, as though he'd cheapened the profession and the gift he'd put so much work into.

"Hmmm, close," said the Mentor. "We provide *wonder*. Inspiration. People see us work and *know* that the world is a special, magical place. The key to training a good Wizard is not to teach them to *entertain*. It is to teach them to *connect*. To allow each and every villager to touch that special, magical place, even if only on the rare occasion. It isn't about us. It isn't about the magic. It's about the *people*. Because once the people know that there is such a thing as magic, they can feel that magic in their own lives. It's not the healing. It's not the rain. It's not the dowsing. It's the people who come to know wonderment and feel joy in their lives as a result. And *that* is why a village needs a Wizard."

Roneld took a deep breath, then released it. Once again, the Mentor strode down the path, and Roneld could but trail behind, allowing his thoughts to churn as they walked.

THEY HADN'T WALKED but an hour before the Mentor took a sudden left off the path. Roneld followed, and found himself on what appeared to be a game trail.

As they hiked the small path in silence, Roneld began to hear the distant howling of wolves. He readied his defensive spells—

but even with the Mentor, he didn't believe they could fend off an entire pack. He looked nervously at the Mentor's back, but the great Wizard didn't appear worried by the howling at all.

Then they reached a small clearing. The Mentor reached up and unclasped his cloak, then began folding it. "I still haven't answered your question, have I?" he asked.

"Um..." said Roneld. What was the question? He searched his memory, trying to find the last question he'd posed the Mentor.

"I brought you out here alone so that you could see these things and understand them. Most of the time, a Wizard learns this gradually, over the course of time. You, though, are different. You needed to see the issue *now*."

"Why?" The question flew out of Roneld's mouth before he knew he was asking it.

"It's best to show you," said the kindly old man. Without his cloak, it was hard for Roneld to think of him as the Mentor. "Come, do a diagnostic spell on me; particularly on my head."

Roneld nodded. He began to weave his fingers before him in the magic he'd been taught, then placed his hands on either side of the older man's head. He ran his magic through the neurons, then the blood vessels.

And then he stopped, taking a step back. "You're..." he said.

"Yes," said the Mentor, still with that smile on his face. "There's a rather large weak spot in my blood vessel, isn't there? At some point—very soon—I will die. Fortunately, because of my magic, I know this—and that is why I've brought you up here. Because there is one, final spell that you must know."

And here the old Wizard took a series of deep breaths, a calming technique all Wizards were taught in their first year. Roneld had never seen the Mentor need to do that, but this... this wasn't the Mentor.

"I learned this spell in this very clearing," the old man said, his smile saddened and his eyes wet. "I learned it when the man who was my Mentor brought me here, and taught it to me.

Watch well, for I can only perform it once, and you must learn it from that one example."

Roneld blinked. Then the howling of the wolves called out once more, much closer—surrounding them. Roneld's head whipped up to see the great, grey beasts stalking to the edge of the clearing, their yellow eyes intent on the two Wizards within.

"Before I do this," said the man who'd been the Mentor, "I have a gift and a burden for you. The gift is this cloak," he said, then handed over the Mentor's cloak to Roneld.

Roneld, for his part, gasped. His hands shook as he took the folded garment from the old man. "I..." he said, then trailed off, trying to find the words.

"You are one of the best Wizards I've ever had the privilege to train," said the old man. "And I have trained many. So many men and women, using their Power to bring a sense of wonder to their villages. So many smiles. So much laughter. So many lives improved, just a little, by the presence of magic. That is my legacy—but it's one you must continue, now. Because people must never let the magic go out of their lives."

Roneld nodded solemnly.

"Put it on," said the old man.

So Roneld put the cloak about his shoulders. He'd expected it to be too long—his predecessor's height—but he sensed the magic as it changed to fit itself perfectly to his body. He felt it envelop him, become a part of him, and he looked to the old man who'd once worn it and nodded slowly.

"Good," said the old man. "Now. The life of the Mentor is one of service. Your life is bound to the College now. You will do great good—but you will have little freedom. Your life belongs to others in the world. That is the sacrifice that every Mentor makes—to live for the good of all, and not themselves. It is a sacrifice I found worth making, and I believe you will, too."

"I will," he said softly.

The old Wizard sighed, then continued. "And some day, when you are old and you sense your death coming to you, you will select your finest student. You will bring them to a Wizardless village, and show them why the world needs magic. And then you will bring them here."

One of the wolves padded up from the ring about them. Roneld started a bit, but the calm way the wolf approached did not appear like an attack. And Roneld's teacher simply smiled at the wolf as it approached him.

Then the wolf butted its head in a little nuzzle into the old man's stomach. He looked down, tears freely flowing from his face, and scratched the wolf between the ears as Roneld simply gawked.

"Just as my Mentor did with me," the aged Wizard said, keeping his eyes on the massive grey wolf before him. "And you will perform the spell I am about to show you. For this spell is your reward for a life well lived. It will only work if you've done your duty—in a way, the rest of your life will serve as its prerequisites. But you will come here, and you will cast it, and if you have spread enough magic in the world... that magic will allow you freedom at last."

Then he smiled his kind smile one, last time, and began the spell. Roneld watched the streams of magic flow through the old man, whipping about him and surrounding him in a glowing ball of light. He watched bits and pieces of essence streaming in from what must be throughout the known world. Little pieces of magic, of energy, seeded for this very day. Roneld had to actively remind himself to breathe as he sensed the staggering power the old man channeled.

And all around him, the wolves put up their howl. They made no aggressive move, but simply sang their song. Their voices joined and melded with the glowing ball of magic the old man had become, pulsing along with it and weaving their song in and out of the flow of power.

And then the howl subsided, and the magic with it. Where the Mentor had once been, now stood a great, grey wolf, much like the others. It had no more words to give Roneld. Instead, it padded up to him, then leapt up with its two forepaws on Roneld's chest and calmly laid its head on Roneld's shoulder—a last, final goodbye from a great man, now freed.

THE MENTOR WALKED down the path and looked to the College. He wiped the last of the tears from his eyes. He looked once more over his shoulder towards the forest where the pack—and his predecessor—roamed. Then he squared his shoulders and walked back to take up his responsibilities. Because no matter who the Mentor was—the world still needed magic.

BALANCING THE SCALES

Vae Victis.

Those two words are, to my mind, the biggest example of toxic masculinity ever spoken. The story behind them goes back to the sacking of Rome—before Rome was ever an empire. The Gauls raided it, sacked it, and agreed to leave in exchange for 1,000 pounds of gold. The Gauls provided the scales. After a bit, the Romans noticed that the scales seemed to be rigged. They complained to Brennus, the leader of the Gauls, who responded by taking his sword, chucking it onto the counterweight side of the scales, and saying *"Vae Victis."*

Woe to the Vanquished.

In other words, screw you. You lost. We won. That means we get to do what we want. Our use of physical force means you're at our mercy, so shut up and pay us or suffer the consequences. Ancient history is filled with glaring examples of belligerence, but nothing stands out to me so much as that moment.

Lee French of Clockwork Dragon put together an anthology called *Swords, Sorcery, and Self-Rescuing Damsels.* We wanted to tell a story which took the most masculine event we could think of and threw a feminist counterpoint into it. And the story that came immediately to mind was *Vae Victis.*

Esther took point on this, and drafted an incredible fantasy tale that lets the women of Rome get a little back at Brennus, and balance the scales of the *Vae Victis* story.

15

BALANCING THE SCALES

TERTIA'S THROAT felt dry and scratchy as the cart evacuating her father, mother, two sisters, and all of the Scipiones family's wealth, rattled out of the courtyard. Tertia must stay and face the barbarians. The Gallic barbarians had already overtaken and slaughtered the militia, and they would soon fall upon the city, plundering Rome. Tertia thought it unlikely they'd spare one apparently worthless eleven-year-old.

Her eyes burned like coals, full of pain and resentment. Father's clear repudiation of her as he evacuated everything— everyone— else to the Capitoline stung at her like wasps. But her pride wouldn't let her cry. She crouched down where she stood and hid her eyes against her thighs as the wagon creaked away, unwilling watch her family abandon her.

When she could no longer hear the cart, Tertia opened her eyes. She and the remaining servants stared at each other blankly. Father left no instructions for any them. One of the servants started looting food and easily carried household items, and the rest followed in a mad rush to flee. There was no way Tertia could halt the thievery; she snatched bread, cheese, and a small jug of water for herself. She fastened her small bundle of spoils around her neck with twine. Then the servants escaped from the house too, leaving nothing but a quiet shell that had, minutes ago, been home.

Despite her father's words of impending catastrophe, in the short time that passed, not one alien invader had yet shown up to tear down walls. Tertia looked around the deserted courtyard she'd known her whole life and felt tears well up. Whether she willed it or no, her breath came in fits and sobs, and Tertia could not stop shaking. Father said she would die today. She took a deep breath, trying to find space in her head to think.

Far in the distance she heard crashing. Then strange chanting mixed with screams fell faintly on her ears. She began to poke about the courtyard, looking for something to do the job properly with; better to die fighting than to meekly accept whatever the barbarians had in store for her.

Tertia found her mother's weaving rod, sturdy and sharply pointed, next to a pile of discarded work, and hefted it experimentally. It only extended her reach a little, but it would have to do. As the crashing and yelling became louder and more distinct, Tertia crept behind one of the tall pantry bins, squeezing herself into the crevice between it and the wall. Acrid smoke began to tinge the air, and fill Tertia with dread. She waited, her knuckles white from gripping the weaving rod, as the ruckus grew slowly louder.

A shadow fell across the threshold of the house, snatching her attention away from the gated courtyard entrance. A tall, willowy woman, her short-cropped hair wreathed with laurel leaves, sauntered out from inside the hearth's doorway.

The woman raised her arms above her head, stretching. "Whew, it feels *so* good to be free of all those kill-joys! I thought they would never release their grip on me." Her voice was low-pitched and totally relaxed, at great odds with the dissonant chaos threatening to envelope the courtyard.

Tertia hiccupped in shock, gawking. The embroidered tunic

the stranger wore ended at her knees, its edges embellished with grapes and fig leaves. The woman's feet were bare and scarred. And she had come out of Tertia's home as if she owned it, but Tertia had never seen her before. The clamor in the distance moved inexorably louder; now Tertia could hear stomping from many feet, and the clanking of metal, along with the chanting and terrified human or animal screams.

The woman leaned down, eyeing Tertia's hiding spot and weaving rod with a conspiratorial grin. "You may as well come out of there; that hiding place is as weak as a new-born calf," the woman said, still grinning. "It won't fool anyone, least of all those who come after me."

"If you attempt to harm me, I will defend myself," Tertia said, her voice low, thrusting the weaving rod up at the stranger like a sword.

The stranger laughed, a great, booming guffaw. "I do applaud your determination."

The woman's lack of concern would bring the invaders down upon them in minutes if not seconds if she wasn't more careful. "Shhh!" Tertia said, springing forward from her hiding place, attempting to shush the woman's laugh.

Tertia found herself scooped up into a warm embrace instead, the weaving rod deftly twisted out her grip. The woman hefted Tertia up onto one of her shoulders as if Tertia was a much smaller child.

From that vantage, Tertia found herself staring down at laurel leaves nestled in curling dark-brown hair. The woman glanced up at her with a mischievous smile. How could this person be so calm? Tertia wondered.

The air reverberated with the crack of something sundering, much too close, and the smoke in the air thickened. Tertia squeezed her eyes shut against the sting of the smoke, and a tear tracked down her cheek.

"Wipe those eyes, Tullia Tertia Scipiones," the woman

chided, setting Tertia back on her feet, and straightening Tertia's tunic with an easy twitch of fingers. "Aren't you *so* glad all those obnoxious, unimaginative prudes are gone? 'Be pious!' they said. 'You are a Lar. Stop shaming the family,' they said. Who do they think *established* this family!" The woman snorted a laugh.

Tertia gaped, unable to look away. No one had used her *full* name before. She was always just Tertia. The third, the last. The least.

The woman chucked Tertia under the chin and smiled, appearing to ignore the ever-escalating sounds of destruction, now coming from just outside the courtyard.

"Who are you?" Tertia asked. "Are you one of my ancestors? A Lar?"

"Who am I? Why I'm Scipiones, of course. The first. The original. In fact, this family only exists because of me!" Scipiones chuckled, swinging an arm out to encompass the large Roman villa around them. "Which includes you, of course. Tell me, young Tertia: The world is in front of you. What would you like to do?"

"I want to live." Tertia blurted out immediately. "I want to be reunited with my sisters at the Capitoline and not have any of us be killed."

"Oh, delightful!" Scipones exclaimed, leaning in with a conspiratorial grin. "You'll need to be *sneaky*. It so happens that particular trait, ah, runs in your blood," Scipiones winked at Tertia, who could only blink in surprise.

"Shall we start with getting to the Capitoline then?" Scipiones continued blithely, appearing unfazed. "Lesson one: People rarely look *up*." She pointed at the villa's ridge line.

Something that sounded similar to distressed metal squealing reached their ears, followed by the thunderous clap of wood breaking.

Scipiones quickly led Tertia to the sheltered wall of the

courtyard just behind the cistern, then jumped and grabbed onto the yellow brick, swinging her feet up so her toes were leveraged into the small gaps, scrabbling up the vertical wall with apparent ease. The goddess then jumped down, showing Tertia how to cling to the small cracks and crevices in the brick. The goddess then guided Tertia up the wall's seemingly sheer surface for the first few feet, until Tertia started to get the hang of it.

Scipiones clung to the brick easily as Tertia labored, then flawlessly transitioned to the upper story of the villa from the top of the courtyard, leading Tertia by example on this trickier ascent. The villa's decorative arches, ledges, and embellishments formed fewer and even more precarious holds, but even so, Tertia persevered.

"Keep your body low, so it's stable, and stay close to the tiles of the roof itself." Scipones instructed as they approached the top of the villa. "It will make you much harder to see from below, as well." With that advice, Scipiones vanished then reappeared, reclining on the roofing tiles-- where Tertia would hopefully, eventually, land. Outside the courtyard, the sounds of Rome being breached and looted were becoming deafening, but Tertia could not allow herself to look.

Tertia took a deep breath and slowly, carefully crabbed her way up the rest of the villa's second story, then finally to the roof, refusing acknowledge whatever happened below.

Once Tertia lay on the roof next to her, Scipiones pointed across the roofs of the patrician district, toward the hill where the Capitoline sat above the rest. "You can use the canopies or archways between structures to transition from one building to the next."

"I don't know if I can do this," Tertia quavered, her muscles burning and exhausted, as she looked across the narrow alley between the next house over. The distance down to the ground made her stomach jump.

"Then you will die," Scipiones pointed out, her tone matter-of-fact.

Tertia's familial villa stood only two stories high, as did the one next to it, but many of the patrician homes were taller than that. Some soared three or even four stories high with pillars under-pinning lower floor, leaving even fewer hand-holds for scaling.

Tertia gritted her teeth, rolling over onto her stomach as she judged the distance to the next house. If she died today, it would not be because she failed to try.

Scipiones nodded in approval. "Now, the trick, young Tertia, is to only allow yourself to be seen when you want to be," she said, "and if you are seen, only let them perceive what you want them to see. A glint of metal, a bird's shadow, the rustle of the wind against the sun. Now, show me you're worthy of my name." With that, Scipiones vanished like smoke buffeted by sudden wind.

Tertia took a moment to center herself and feel the rough brick and tile under her, then launched herself onto the next rooftop, refusing to look at the distant ground. She felt the mud tile slip under her feet, then pitched her body forward to lower her weight once more.

Then she paused and looked back over her shoulder. Mistake.

Her gaze unwillingly riveted on the alien army flooding up the streets of her neighborhood. She knew she absolutely must keep moving, but fear rooted her body. The Gauls looked nothing like any person Tertia had ever seen. Even the shortest of them stood half again her father's height, like a giant of legend. Those behemoths came, breaking down the barred doors on the smaller dwellings, then throwing their contents in the street, simply trampling what they did not want, taking what they did.

One Gaul, who stood taller than the rest, shouted directions, loosely appearing to direct the chaos. His pale shoulders were striped with blood and blue paint, his torso covered in a leather breastplate. Checked and striped fabric peeked out from underneath. His long hair, pulled up into a mane behind his head, was blinding, brilliantly white, like linen that had been bleached by the sun-- at least where blood had not dyed it scarlet. Around his neck a golden torque glinted in the early evening light and a massive two-handed, iron sword emanated menace in his hands.

Tertia glanced toward the Capitoline. Gathering her strength, she continued scrabbling and launching herself from rooftop to rooftop, trying to stay ahead of the chaos when she could, waiting until the looters were busy when she could not.

Tertia could not help looking down into the courtyards of the last several very affluent villas that lined the road closest to the Capitoline. Elderly patriarchs from Rome's great houses waited for the barbarians outside their respective domiciles. Just below her and to the left she could see her father's friend Marius Papirius, and but there were more silent statesmen in the court years both ahead and behind her. They sat in the carved ivory chairs that overlooked their courtyards and signified their station, but the courtyard gates remained unbarred. Actually on both sides of the road to the Capitoline, she could see open gates. The statesmen she saw had dressed in their ritual best, their long-silvered beards oiled and curled, their cosmetics flawless, ivory staffs held firmly in their weathered and ancient hands.

In a whisper Tertia wondered, "Have they been judged too old, too infirm to defend the Capitoline?"

Scipiones suddenly materialized in the courtyard nearest to Tertia, sitting in the lap of elderly Marius Papirius. His gaze stayed fixed straight ahead, not paying the goddess any mind.

Scipiones looked up at Tertia and answered her question, "They look to find favor for their families with the gods, by offering their lives as sacrifice. They are old, and wise, and perhaps, some of them may become Lares themselves if their will is strong. Their sacrifice is certainly great enough."

Scipiones kissed the weathered cheek of Papirius above his long, oiled beard and turned back into mist. He did not react; had he not seen the Lar?

Tertia had reached the last mansion before the ascent to the Capitoline. Crouching on that rooftop Tertia considered her options. The thick iron gate into the citadel was only thirty feet away, but the rest of the way was totally out in the open, and it had already been locked and barred. An archway two and a half stories tall spanned the road connecting to the mansions on either side, but nothing connected the archway to the gate.

Behind her, the bulk of the strange warriors had reached the houses of the statesmen. Their footsteps slowed as they stared with awed faces at the soaring marble mansions. For several minutes, the invading army just milled up and down the street, glancing through the open gates of the mansions, before returning to their fellows as if suspecting trap, instead of continuing their wave of destruction. They stared in seeming confusion at the carved ivory thrones in the elaborate courtyards, at the dignified elderly men who sat unmoving atop them, but they did not attack.

Tertia wondered if the barbarians thought the old men of the city-state looked just as strange, or stranger, than Gauls did to her, with their blue paint and brilliant-white hair.

One of the Gauls approached Marius Papirius cautiously, walking around his chair of office, and inspecting it from all sides. The whole swarming army had come to a hushed stand-still, appearing unsure of what to do with the open courtyards and their silent inhabitants. The barbarians stopped all looting and a strange, tense hush fell. From Tertia's limited vantage point, none of the Roman statesmen appeared to move, sitting in solemn, formal splendor.

Tertia wondered if the alien army had mistaken the elderly men for Lares in their own right.

Just as she was beginning to hope that the whole invading force might turn around and leave the city of their own volition, the invader nearest Papirius reached out, grabbed a handful of the patriarch's long beard and yanked. Hard.

Papirius lashed out with his staff, dealing the Gaul's head an equally hard blow.

The giant roared in anger, unsheathing his sword and drawing it across Papirius' throat in one fluid motion. Blood splattered on the ground of the courtyard like gruesome rain. Tertia squeezed her eyes shut, queasy. The soft sound of blood spattering across brick seemed to wake the whole army from whatever calming influence they had been under. Descending into a fury of carnage, the barbarians butchered the rest of the statesmen in a matter of minutes, bathing the gutters in blood.

Tertia clamped her eyes and mouth shut, fighting against the nausea in her stomach. If she was ill, the smell would eventually lead them to her, even if the sound did not.

The barbarians dispersed amongst the vast mansions, looting them with abandon. Wonton acts of destruction scattered marble and yellow brick in the street alike. Piles of furniture and household goods were put to the match, sending new gouts of flame and plumes of smoke skyward, blocking out much of the late sun's rays. It helped obscure Tertia's hiding place, and she crept out to the large stone arch than spanned the roadway, hopeful she'd find a way to make it the rest of the way to the Capitoline. But her eyes stung with the smoke, and made it hard for her to squint down into the ruined streets.

Eventually the commander sauntered under the archway where Tertia hid, surrounded by his cohort of fighters. She breathed slowly through her nose, unwilling to let air pass her lips, lest it somehow alert them to her presence.

Behind the barbarians, the looted wagons carrying all their spoils trundled slowly.

A rain of arrows whistled out of the arrow slits of the citadel, sleeting down over the road and sticking of out of the ground and the Gaul's shields like a particularly lethal hail. A few arrows whistled terrifyingly close to Tertia, but thankfully none struck her. Someone laughed, seeming to find the defense of the citadel comical. Tertia's heart hammered in her throat; the efforts of those in the citadel appeared futile to her.

The wagon creaked to a halt in front of the arch, and Tertia crept slowly forward to get a better vantage point. She found the fighters had gathered at the barred gate to the citadel. The commander in front, his army arrayed around him. Glancing about, she did not see that the arrows had had any lasting effect on the invaders.

"Open the gate and your deaths shall be quick," the commander called in a heavily-accented voice to those locked inside. Tertia wondered when and where he'd learned their language. "If you do not, we will dismantle your fortress around you, water its stones with your blood, and piss in the dead eyes of your loved ones."

"We will not allow the City of Rome to be conquered by some nameless invader," came the return call.

"I am Brennus, and we shall see who outlasts the other, then. I am willing to bet, be it today, tomorrow, or a month from now, I will still have the advantage. After all, I have the whole city at my disposal, and you do not." The Gaul army spread out, ringing the Capitoline and settling in for a siege.

Scipiones suddenly appeared on the arch next to Tertia, watching the Gauls' preparations with bright eyes.

"You could walk away now, you know," Scipiones said to Tertia. "Your family has abandoned you once. You have no obligation to save them or any of the other Roman patricians."

Tertia looked at Scipiones solemnly. "I know. I could leave;

no one would miss me. Perhaps they don't *deserve* to be saved." Her father's cold words, her mother's silence, still stabbed at her heart. She closed her eyes and took another deep breath. "Perhaps. But my sisters are there too, and they never did anything to me. The Roman patriarchs did nothing, and yet they died horribly. I cannot leave everyone to die here alone. Not even Father."

"Spoken like a true Scipiones," the Lar said, smiling. "We're going to have to train you as we go. To be successful, you will have to be as imperceptible as the wind. He will not know you've changed his fate. None of them will."

"I can live with that," Tertia said.

"So be it. I do *so* love a challenge," Scipiones said. "We can start tonight."

Tertia turned to reply, but the goddess had already vanished.

TERTIA WOKE ABRUPTLY, certain she was about to tumble off her precarious perch. Instead she found herself clinging to a very amused-looking Scipiones.

"Are you ready for lesson two?" the goddess asked her, before standing on the archway and stretching. It was as if Scipiones had no concerns. For all Tertia knew, she might the only one able to see the Lar.

Tertia nodded, her stomach twisting with nerves.

"If you control the pieces, you control the game," Scipiones said, looking at Tertia expectantly. Scipiones produced a coin out of thin air and handed it to Tertia.

"Close your fist around the coin," the goddess said. Tertia did so, gripping it tightly.

"That coin is yours now, is it not?" Scipiones asked holding Tertia's hand lightly in hers. "You have it trapped in the palm of your hand, yes?"

"Yes, it's in my hand." Tertia squeezed the coin, feeling it press into her palm.

"Are you certain?" Scipiones asked, nodding significantly toward Tertia's fist.

Tertia opened her hand to find she gripped a smooth stone. Scipiones snapped and the golden coin appeared between the goddess' fingers.

For the next few hours, Scipiones demonstrated it again slower, patiently showing Tertia how to pick up and move the coin while not alerting the person who held it.

"Now," Scipiones said, "We're going to send you down there to play similar tricks. Tiny things at first, larger ones as you improve. The rules are the same as before: go where you will not be seen; move silently like the wind, and always cause as much mischief as possible in your wake."

DURING THE NEXT WEEK, under Scipiones tutelage, Tertia became a haunt of the Roman night, creeping silently through sleeping the Gaul army. One of her first acts dyed the city well an ominous, stinking red using pulverized madder root. None of the Gauls had tried to use it in the days since. They had to trek out to the river for water instead.

Then she'd torched the fields outside the city and started stealing the Gaul's rations. Some she'd kept for her own use. Others she'd trampled into the ground as if a wild animal had roamed the army while they slept. The game the Gauls managed to scrounge was meager, and Tertia took every opportunity to spoil any attempts to preserve it.

As she grew bolder, she started stealing the warriors' personal items. She stole this person's sword, that person's axe, a handy belt-knife, wool blankets, drinking horns, and the list went on. Nothing ever went missing while anyone was looking, but she targeted anything that would be keenly missed soon after the theft. Her stash of stolen items grew and had to be spread out on the forum's roof to avoid detection.

Under Scipones' watchful eye, she grew proficient at climbing and spiriting away large, sometimes sharp, objects that the Gauls needed for the siege. She released horses, emptied purses, and then fouled the Gaul's water, over and over again, with dirt and animal dung, but never when someone might see. Tensions in the camp grew and fights started breaking out at the slightest provocation. Her midnight missions complete, she fell asleep in her eyrie just as the dawn's golden light brought the first squabbling disagreements from the camp below. She felt a brushed kiss on her cheek, and Scipiones whispered, "Well done, young Tertia."

TERTIA WOKE to the Gaul commander yelling through gate to the citadel. She crawled to the edge of her favorite arch nearest the Capitoline, looking down at the display below.

"I don't know how you keep sneaking men past my guards or if you employ spirits to do your bidding, but your petty tricks will not work. My men grow hungry, but yours starve outright. We walk for our water, but you have none. Only your deaths or a proper ransom will satisfy," Brennus said.

Father's voice, "Ransom? What kind of ransom?"

"One thousand pounds of gold, and we will leave this place and its cursed, pranking, foreign spirits. Take it or die. Either way, we leave today. You decide whether we leave over your corpses or not."

"You will have your ransom," father said, quickly. The iron door to the citadel slowly groaned open.

"It is done." Brennus confirmed.

Brennus' men produced a giant scale, complete with weights

from the depths of his wagon train. They set up the scales in the plaza in front of the forum, between two of the large pillars. The bottom of the scale stood about a foot off the ground until the weights were placed.

A long line of Romans began depositing all their valuables on the scales. But when they had finished, the balance still leaned heavily in the Gaul's favor.

In front of the scales, her father and Brennus argued about the weight of the ransom.

"We have fulfilled the ransom already," father was protesting. "We have provided far more gold than the required amount. The scales are false."

Brennus stared at her father, his face impassive, his eyes lethal. Then the giant Gaul reached for the sword strapped across his back. Father flinched as Brennus drew the sword, clearly convinced the Gaul meant to use it on him.

Instead, Brennus threw his massive sword onto the Gallic side of the scale with a flourish and a hard, mocking smile. The giant, two-handed sword clanged onto his side of the scale, adding a good seventy pounds to the Gaul's counter-weight, growing Rome's debt in a matter of seconds as their side of the scale inched upward. Brennus continued staring at father in a silent contempt, his gaze unfazed.

"Woe to the vanquished," Brennus said.

Father stared at the Gaul's sword for a moment longer, and then turned, walking off abruptly.

Scipiones appeared next to Tertia, her gaze fixed on the scene below.

"Father is short on gold for the ransom, isn't he?" Tertia asked the goddess. "He's arguing the weights are off because he's already gathered all the gold that Rome has to offer, or so close to it, as makes no difference. Now he must make up the weight somehow or all my efforts will be for naught."

"You have managed much. It's not your fault your father

cannot negotiate a workable bargain. You've reduced the Gaul army to a hungry, contentious, rabble that is nearly as big of a danger to itself as it is to Rome," Scipiones said.

"Brennus hungers for gold to make this siege worthwhile, but he's loathe to waste the energy his army has left or test his control of his men in battle," Tertia said slowly. "But he cannot lose face by accepting a lesser amount or appearing weak in front of a vanquished foe."

"I would agree," Scipiones said.

"Then the scales must balance." Tertia said.

Starting from her stash on the roof of the forum, Tertia tied a sack of bronze statues and other odds and ends to her back. She estimated the sack weighed fifty or sixty pounds. It was not enough, but it was a start. She slid a small knife into her belt and wrapped extra rope around her waist.

From her vantage point, Tertia could see the invaders had set a young Gallic guard in the plaza to keep watch on the gold. Using the pillar farthest from him, she crept carefully down, making sure she stayed out of any eye-line.

Once on the ground, as long as she came in from the back, the bulk of the scale should hide her from his sight and from any of the Gauls gathered in front.

Cautiously circling to the front of the pillar, Tertia dove for the senator's podium directly behind the scale, breathing a prayer to Scipiones. She opened her eyes, confirming no one had spotted her.

The plaza guard was sticking to his post like glue. If she tried to tamper with the weights while he just stood there, he'd notice. Tertia glanced around and saw her sisters, standing at the edge of the plaza into the forum, waiting out of the way of a cart bringing a few more pieces of gold to the scales.

It was risky, but if she could enlist their help... Tertia picked up a pebble, then balanced it in her palm, waiting to throw it until she was *mostly* sure she'd only attract Prima's attention.

The pebble hit Prima's shoulder and fell to the ground with a small clack. Tertia winced.

Her sister turned toward her hiding place. Tertia put one of her fingers to her lips and pointed toward the guard in front of the scales. Prima's eyes grew wide and she gripped Secunda's arm, nodding toward Tertia's hiding place. Secunda's mouth opened in a silent "O" before she clapped a hand over it, looking down. Tertia gave a soft sigh of relief and pointed toward the guard once more. *Please understand*, she begged them internally. She used two of her fingers to mimic walking and pointed toward the guard again.

Prima walked toward the young fighter, wringing her hands, "Sir," she said, "My sister's not feeling well. Can you help please?" She batted her eyes at the young guard.

The young man shook his head doubtfully and shrugged. Prima pointed to where Secunda stood with her hand clapped over her mouth. He stepped toward Secunda, peering at her admittedly pale face.

Tertia crept up next to the pile of the gold on the scales, finding her mother's golden trunk, opening it just far enough to retrieve four of her mother's gold body chains and shove her bag of bronze inside. She then wrapped the chains around several of the yellow bricks scattered about, burying the bricks under the gold at the back of the scale, then hurriedly slitting a burlap bag of coins and laying it on top.

She'd just tied another of the smaller bags of gold coins to her belt when Prima signaled her, panicked. Tertia dodged, hiding inside the nearest senator's podium with her contraband seconds before Brennus and her father rounded the corner. A cart loaded with the last of Rome's gold followed in their wake.

She looked back, realizing she'd left the body chains draped on the ground out of her reach. Brennus meant to weigh the ransom, not count it out gold-piece by gold-piece, but she'd still need to remove the bricks from the scale when Brennus unloaded them.

As father turned away from dumping the last of the gold on the scale, Tertia crept out of the senator's podium. She hugged the floor, heart hammering, then silently grabbed the gold chains where they lay.

The scales slowly settled into an unwilling balance. The Gauls looked around at each other, muttering in surprise, and then turned to Brennus for direction.

Brennus signaled for the unloading of the scales to begin, picking back up his sword. He stepped away, shouting orders, readying their departure. As the Gallic warriors began rapidly unloading the scales--more than ready to be quit of Rome-- Tertia yanked hard on the gold body chains, putting her whole weight into it. The hidden bricks slid off the scale, hitting the ground at the same time the slit burlap sack burst in a raucous shower of coins. Gold cascaded all over the forum floor. Tertia quickly unclasped her gold chains, rolling them up and placing them in her tunic. She waited until the warriors finished picking up the last of the coins, and then slid away to the edge of the plaza, scampering back up a pillar to the safety of the forum's roof.

Scipiones welcomed her there with a beaming smile. "Well done, Tertia. I'm very proud."

Tertia allowed herself a small smile. *Woe to the vanquished,* indeed.

END

PINKERTON'S PREY

I grew up in a small farming town. I grew up surrounded by farmers. Every grocery store had a spinner rack filled with Louis L'Amour books. Every speaker blared country music. Every kid wanted to play "Cowboys and Indians" in the most racist way possible.

Which is all a shorthand way of saying that I normally stay as far away from Westerns as I possibly can. They remind me of the culture I spent my youth trying to escape. Cowboy stories? Hard pass.

Except.

Except when an editor like David Boop asks you to write a story for an anthology he's already contracted with Baen Books, you say yes. And *then* you ask what sort of story he wants. And if he tells you he wants a Weird Western story for an anthology called *Straight Outta Deadwood*, well, you swallow your pride. You reach back into all that cowboy stuff that bombarded you as a child, and you bring forth a Western.

I'll admit that it was sheer, canny greed that gave us the idea for this. *Straight Outta Deadwood* was going to be the widest-distributed anthology we'd been in to date, and so we tied the *Grace* books into it. The characters in this story—well, some of them—are ancestors of the characters in *The Gift of Grace*. It's set in the same world with the same magical rules... it's just the old West.

I grudgingly admit that I like the story that resulted. Thaddeus Neilson first makes his appearance in *Coup de Grace*, and he's a secondary antagonist. He's sort of a jackass. Giving his ancestor a chance to bring a little shine to the Neilson name was a lot of fun, and giving him the reins in this story to do what he wanted to let the character just sort of drag me along to the ending.

I said earlier that "Vapors and Valor" is my favorite thing to read out loud. That's very true, but "Pinkerton's Prey" is a close second. Neilson's cowboy drawl contrasts well with George's overly-formal business speech, and any time I think of George I think of a salsa commercial denigrating *NEW YORK CITY!*

I'm still not a fan of Westerns. But for *Straight Outta Deadwood*, I guess I'll make an exception, because I ended up loving "Pinkerton's Prey."

16

PINKERTON'S PREY

GEORGE E. HOINSCHAUFFER cradled his glass, staring mournfully at the rotgut liquour the refreshment-car bartender had poured him in response to George's request for whiskey. Instead of a rich, amber color, the liquid in his glass shone clear, with only a light brown tint. Where George hoped for an intense bouquet of floral and smoky scents, it assaulted his nostrils with the odor of rotting barley.

"Problem, George?"

From the barstool next to George (and slightly above, given their difference in height), Leonard Neilson looked at him with a wry smile. George shook his head, but said nothing. Neilson shrugged, then tipped his own glass into his mouth with an easy grace that George at once both envied and reviled.

The two men could not have been more dissimilar to look at. Whereas George was short, somewhat pudgy, and certainly balding, Neilson looked tall, lean, and with a thick crop of salt-and-pepper hair peeking out from under his hat. Both wore vests, but where George's had the crisp-clean look of new silk, Neilson's had been made of coarse woven cotton, and showed fray about it. Both wore white shirts underneath; George's had been cleanly pressed, Neilson's had possibly been laundered sometime in the last month. Neilson wore a faded, dusty derby; George's balding pate shone bare.

"The trick," Neilson said, "is to let it hit the back of your throat while spending as little time as possible on the tongue. This ain't the sipping whiskey you New York folk are used to; this here is to be drunk *solely* for effect."

George nodded, then tried bravely to mimic Neilson's smooth shot. He felt the liquid burn his tongue, then the back of his throat. The rancid-barley finish bloomed in his gullet and coated his mouth; he came up coughing.

"There it is," said Neilson. "I like you, George. You're a game sort of fellow. Most of you hoity-toities tend to get upset when presented with a beverage such as this."

"Hoity-toity?" said George. "I've seen what we're paying you for this job. You've no call to—"

"Whoa, there. I am an *employee*, Mr. Hoinschauffer. A servant of the Pinkerton Detective Agency, which in turn has been hired by South Mountain Mining, Limited. You've seen what the Agency is getting paid for my services; I get a percentage, is all."

"How much of a percentage?" asked George, curious.

"Enough to keep me in bad whiskey. Not enough to keep me in good," said Neilson.

George had little response to this, so the two men sat for a while in silence. Neilson seemed perfectly comfortable with that and motioned to the bartender for another round. George felt increasingly awkward sitting next to Neilson and not conversing.

"So... do you think Lorents is actually coming?" George asked as the bartender re-filled Neilson's glass.

"Ha!" said Neilson. "George, for the last three months Randall Lorents has hit every one of South Mountain Mining's payrolls. This here is number four. What in the world makes you think he's going to stop?"

"Well, maybe he knows we hired you to—"

"I sure's fire hope not!" said Neilson. "The anti-summoner branch of the Agency does *not* like to advertise its activities. George, he don't know I'm here. And he sure as hell don't care. Not only is he going to hit this train, I would place five dollars that he does so in the next—"

At this, Leonard Neilson pulled a rather nice, if worn, pocketwatch from his vest.

"—three minutes."

George's back stiffened, and his eyebrows rose at this sudden pronouncement. "Three minutes!" he said.

"Yup," said Neilson calmly. "That's when we'll be in the Lido Gap. Most likely place for an ambush." Neilson turned back to the business at hand as George stared at him in disbelief. The tall Pinkerton simply slammed the second glass of whiskey down, offering no further explanation.

"But—shouldn't you—I mean—three minutes! Shouldn't you be *doing* something?" said George. He'd always known the train would get robbed, but the sudden immediacy caused goosebumps along both his arms.

"Like what?" asked Neilson, calmly.

George could not believe the insufferable laziness before him. "Mr. Neilson, your Agency is contracted with South Mountain Mining to protect its payroll from Randall Lorents and—"

"No," said Neilson. His voice was quiet, but it held a cold edge that arrested George's power of speech, "it ain't."

"It isn't? Then why are you here?" George found himself stunned by the man's demeanor. The Pinkerton Agency had a reputation for getting the job done, not for this. "You have to—"

"Read your contract again, George. It says absolutely rat-squat about protecting this here payroll."

"But—"

"No," said Neilson, gesturing again to the bartender. The

squeeling sound of brakes suddenly intruded upon the conversation, and George snatched at the bar as the sudden deceleration nearly threw him from his stool. Neilson, however, appeared to handle the shift with a peculiar grace.

"That's them!" said George. "Go!"

Instead, Neilson calmly repeated his gesture to the bartender. The man held the bottle, looking at George, but poured.

George's irritation grew, and he felt his face going red. "You cannot simply sit here and drink while—"

"George," Neilson said in that low, cold voice. "That's exactly as I intend to do. And do you know why?"

"I cannot imagine," said George, his volume raised, "what madness would cause you to—"

"The why," said Neilson, his voice staying calm, "is because the Anti-Summoning Division of the Pinkerton Detective Agency never contracts to *stop* a robbery."

"But—" spluttered George. His frustration began to turn to panic as the sounds of shouting, and sporadic gunfire, echoed down to the two men from the front area of the train. Someone had to *do* something.

Neilson threw back his third shot of whiskey, then waved the bartender off a fourth. "George, I am a single man. I am equipped with both a .45 caliber revolver and a lever-action rifle. I flatter myself that I am proficient in the use of these tools. But this train is, as we speak, being robbed by Randall Lorents. A summoner, equipped with the ability to draw on the boundary between our worlds to power his magic. He can move forces and things about as he wills or summon entities from outside our world to his side as allies. And he has planned this robbery out. He is ready."

"Yes!" cried George, seizing the moment. "That's why *we hired you.*"

"You hired the Agency because the Anti-Summoner Division

has a demonstrated record of returning bounties on summoners. Bounties, Mr. Hoinschauffer. Not protection. The only way to deal with a summoner is from as great a distance away as one is comfortable making the shot. I have no intention that Lorents know anything until my bullet pierces his skull, which is why we are here enjoying one another's company instead of getting killed like a pair of fools."

Cheering erupted from ahead of them, and soon after a half-dozen men rode fast past the car, heading back down the tracks out of the Lido gap, in the direction from whence the train had come. George's anger gave way to fear as the summoner and his men passed within feet of George's own person, separated only by thin dining-car windows.

Neilson stood from his stool and walked behind George to the door of the refreshment car. George could only watch as the Pinkerton grabbed his rifle from where it leaned up against the wall. Neilson nodded at the bartender, and then stepped outside. From behind him, George heard the bartender politely cough. The noise catapulted George into motion at last. Anger surged back, covering up his fear as he slapped a bill on the counter and moved to follow the Pinkerton.

Neilson had stepped off the train and moved three cars down, to a stable car. As George stormed towards him, the tall man unlatched and pulled back the door, before leading his own horse onto the bare dirt.

"Well," said Neilson in his matter-of-fact tone, "They took the bait. *Now* I can get to work."

George knew he wasn't in control of himself. He let the anger direct his words, losing any semblance of being a proper gentleman and pointing furiously at the hired gun. *"That's* your plan? Go after them?"

"Well," said Neilson, pausing for a moment, "Yes, I reckon that when you boil it to its core, that's my plan. Go after them, find myself a nice little perch overlooking whatever valley they choose to rathole up in, and kill me a summoner. There's some parts at the end involving getting paid and spending a fair amount of time with the ladies at Miss Sandy's up in Buffalo Creek, but you've struck at the heart of it."

"I'm coming with you," George said, firmly trying to regain control of this situation.

"Well, now," said Neilson. The Pinkerton removed a cheap-looking cheroot from inside his vest and placed it in his mouth. "That does strike me as a singularly terrible idea. I would advise against it." He struck a match.

George let his semblance of self-composure give way, and he yelled at the target of his ire. "Mr. Neilson! You, sir, are contracted with South Mountain Mining, Ltd., of which I am a representative. I have already observed you idling your way through a robbery, and now you announce that your plan is simply to ride off into God-knows-where to do God-knows-what before you claim that you have completed your end of the contract. I will not have this, sir. If my company acknowledges your performance, it will be because I have witnessed it, as I no longer trust that you intend to act in good faith!" He stared at Neilson, trying to display his resolve. Instead, his hands shook, and his breaths came only by panting.

Neilson rose an eyebrow towards George for several seconds. Then he took a deep draw from his cheroot and held it for a moment. The Pinkerton tilted his head backwards and released a billow of smoke upward to the sky, then looked back down at George.

"George," Neilson said, still in that calm, low voice. "You are a damned fool. But I reckon that's just your nature, and there's little to do about it. And I also reckon further that there ain't a way I stop you mounting up and riding after me when I go. That is, no way short of shooting you here and now, an act to which I ain't inclined. So, get your horse and let's get on with it."

George straightened his jacket, regaining his aplomb. By his tally, he'd actually won this round with the imposing Pinkerton. He stepped toward the stable car, and as he began to enter he heard Neilson's voice behind him.

"But, I will remind you again that the Pinkerton Agency has no contract to protect anything here. That's the payroll, sure, but that also means I ain't obligated to save your fool self when you do something stupid. My job is to kill Lorents. All the rest is gravy, far as I'm concerned."

In the privacy of the stable car, George allowed himself a flash of panic. He was about to go after a wanted outlaw—a summoner of great power—with no training, a single derringer pistol, and this lazy, indifferent man at his side. But he could not let Neilson get the better of him, and *he* had been tasked with seeing to the payroll.

"Your warnings are noted, Mr. Neilson," George said, hoping his fear did not show in his voice. He led his horse out of the stable car, then huffed and clambered into the saddle. "Now, shall we be off?"

#

Neilson's method of tracking completely mystified George. He'd read several stories, in the digests of New York, of men who could tell the path of an enemy by no more than a bent twig, or a subtle imprint. He'd secretly delighted in the tales of men who could put their ear to the ground to find a herd of buffalo, or an enemy troop of cavalry.

But Neilson did none of these things. He did not dismount. He simply…rode. The two men kept a steady canter, around this rock and through that valley, based on some guidance that George E. Hoinschauffer simply could not understand.

It was not until the sun began to approach the horizon that Neilson dismounted. He tied his horse to a tree and gestured for George to do the same. He handed George a bucket, then pointed at the small stream running through the valley.

"Fill it, and let it warm a bit before you give it to the horses," Neilson said.

"Shouldn't we push on?" asked George. "They got a head start on us, and likely they're still going." He peered ahead, trying to get a sense of their next destination.

"Not likely," said Neilson. "They're just on the other side of that ridge, there." The tall Pinkerton pointed to a small ridge to their...North? South? In these hills, George had lost all sense of direction.

"How do you—"

"Because the tracks sent them down there, and I pulled us over here tonight. Unless I miss my guess, you should keep your eyes on that ridgeline."

Neilson rubbed down the horses while George fetched the water. Upon returning, George saw a thin stream of smoke from the other side of the ridge.

"Now, that's about right," said Neilson.

"We caught up to them?" George said, still bewildered.

"They left that train at a full gallop," said Neilson. "Gave them a head start, sure, but it was still a damned fool piece of riding. Winded their horses. Never ride a beast that *fast* unless you don't need him to go very *far*, you see?"

"Oh," said George. The pulp-digest heroes galloped everywhere, but what Neilson said made perfect sense.

"So, tonight we'll go without a fire," said Neilson. "No sense letting them know where we are. They'll be getting drunk. Successful robbers *always* get drunk. Tomorrow morning, when Lorents is hung over and stumbles out his tent to make water, I'll be up on that ridge with a rifle. He clears his tent, I shoot him in the head, contract fulfilled. Nice and simple."

This plan sounded like it offered minimal risk to one George E. Hoinschauffer while providing a reasonable chance at recovering the payroll, and therefore he found it acceptable.

The two lay out their bedrolls as the sun descended and gave way to night.

"Where *did* you learn how to track like that?" asked George. "The Agency is known for hiring skilled men, not training them."

"Rode with Buford back in the war," said Neilson, calmly.

"General Buford? You wore the blue?"

"Don't sound so surprised," said Neilson. "Not every rough-and-tumble horseman put on a grey uniform. And Buford was one of the best."

George nodded. "Well, that explains why you'd spend your time hunting summoners," he said after a moment.

"How do you figure?" asked Neilson, a note of genuine curiosity in his voice.

"Wasn't Buford there on the First Day at Gettysburg? When that Reb General—what was his name—Heath? Heth? The man summoned a devil to kill General Reynolds."

"Oh, that mess?" asked Neilson. "I guess so. But it ain't like we had no summoners either; that demon killing General Reynolds was just a fluke. Don't believe what you read in the Times; summoning's just a tool, like being good with this here rifle. Some folk use it to rob, some to help. The Agency pays an extra twenty percent if you go after summoners, and a man who can shoot from a long range makes a good living that way."

That had to have been about the most positive thing George had ever heard anyone say about the practitioners of the dark arts. As to the rest, George found himself disappointed. He wasn't sure why; every other business that men engaged in, his own included, they did so in pursuit of money. Why should being a Pinkerton be any different? And yet, it felt like a life this dramatic should have an equal amount of drama motivating it. Instead, it turned out Neilson functioned like every other man. You offer to pay him, he does a job.

"Now," Neilson said. "If you don't mind, we have something of an early morning tomorrow, so best we turn in."

And with that, the Pinkerton rolled over on to his side and promptly began to snore, leaving George to stare up at the stars as they began to peek out through the twilit sky.

As he did, his thoughts began to turn. This man had waited through the robbery back at the train. Oh, he'd given his reasons, such as they were, but he'd ignored his real purpose. He'd allowed George to come along with him only after George held his contract hostage. And he'd been careful to warn George that George might not live through this little trip.

Now, maybe Neilson was playing straight. But all George had as first-hand evidence was a fire on the other side of the ridge, and that said little about who had started that fire or how. And if Neilson put a bullet into George, and then regretfully report him as a casualty, he could claim the contract complete. After all, George was a man who'd been well and duly warned of the dangers and ignored them to his detriment. South Mountain Mining would pay the Pinkertons, the Pinkertons would pay Neilson, and Lorents would remain at large.

The more he lay there, wrapped in his own thoughts, the more George knew he was right. Neilson had no intention of claiming a bounty or filling a contract. Not when all he had to do was kill George.

George drew the small derringer he kept in his vest pocket, cocked it, and pointed it at the back of Neilson's head.

No.

He had to be sure. If he were going to murder the man, in the middle of the night, while effectively lost, then he'd need to *know*. He slipped the hammer back down and stood from his pallet, leaving his questionable companion at rest.

Then he began to walk up to the ridgeline, using the moonlight as his guide.

Once atop, he looked over a small cliff and saw three large

tents made of thick canvas down below, arranged in a wheel-spoke pattern. A stovepipe poked its way through the top of each tent's roof, happily puffing its smoky release to the night.

How in the hell had they—thought George, then interrupted his own train of logic. *Right. Summoner. That bastard can bring the comfort to them; no need to weigh a horse down with a sleeping roll when you can simply summon a full tent and bed in.* The thought that Randall Lorents and his bandits lived a life of comfort, regardless of where they were, irked George to no extent. The bandits in the digests always lived lives of hard misery, not this kind of portable luxury.

An owl hooted, flying above George. Another, which sounded as though it were perched up the ridge from George, hooted in response. Then a third from below the ridgeline. George couldn't remember if he'd ever heard owls communicating like this, and wondered whether the species was particular to—

And then he found himself in a tent.

No showy flash of light accompanied his teleportation. No slow bending of time, and no sense of anything out of the ordinary happening. One moment, he pondered the sounds of the owls around him. The next, he was sitting on the ground, within the confines of a canvas tent, looking directly at the little Franklin stove in its rear.

"So," said a voice behind him. "You'd best introduce yourself and tell me why you should live through the night."

George tried to spin around, but it was a difficult maneuver while still seated on the ground. Instead, he executed something of a graceless half-fall, half-spin maneuver, coming to rest on his elbows facing the front of the tent and the man who stood in it.

Whoever had drawn Randall Lorents' wanted posted had done a spot-on job. The bandit stood tall and broad-shouldered. His face was coated in stubble, and his dark hair had been slicked back along his head. The faint smell of booze lingered about the tent, but Lorents did not appear mightily affected.

"I, uh—I…" George said.

"You don't look much like a bounty hunter," said Lorents.

"I'm not," said George. "I am a duly appointed representative for the South Mountain Mining Company."

"And you are here to…what, exactly?" asked Lorents. "Negotiate with me? Is there something you have that I'm not already taking?"

"Uh…"George, still trying to get his grasp on the situation, improvised. "Yes, exactly. The Company has authorized me to offer you a, well, let's call it a tribute of sorts. One hundred dollars a month. No risk, no work, just a nice, easy cash stream, and you let our payroll through."

Lorents stared, then stood up and clapped slowly.

"That," said Lorents, "was a very smart play. You saw the opening, and you went for it. I do believe I am impressed at your level of gumption, Mr. Representative. But I know when a man right in front of me is lying. Given your situation, I take no particular offense to it, mind you. Now, you *are* a representative of the Company, that much is true. So, the question becomes… what will they pay to get you back? And, come to think of it, who the hell else is out here with you? Because they sure as damnation didn't send you after a summoner packing only this little toy."

George's derringer appeared in Lorents' hand. George patted at his vest pocket in futility as Lorents stuck the small pistol under his belt, cross-wise in the front.

"So, let's see. Boys!" Lorents shouted.

A couple of gruff-looking men stepped into the tent. Lorents gave them a quick gesture towards George, who shortly found himself hauled to his feet and dragged outside.

"You men keep a watch on our Company Man, here. I need to look for something else."

And, with that, Lorents sat on the ground and closed his eyes. From atop the ridge, George once more heard the hooting of owls.

"A *Pinkerton*," said Lorents. "Now *that* makes sense. Let me guess: long bullet in the morning, kill me before I have a chance to get my Sense up? George, you are traveling with an awful clever man, and it is to my great benefit you had to see me for yourself. Now, let's take care of this."

Lorents took out a stick and scribbled some symbols on the ground. George looked at them, but could not make sense of the strange, angular writing. Lorents then took out a large hunting knife and stepped to George. A lance of pain shot through George as Lorents quickly opened a sizable gash through both shirt and flesh on the back of George's left forearm. George inhaled through clenched teeth, desperate not to show weakness before this predator.

"I am sorry about that," said Lorents. "But I need me some blood, and better it come from you than me. Now, step over here. That's a good lad." The two goons dragged George over to the markings, and Lorents held George's arm above them, shaking it so that he bled onto the script. George saw an additional three men stepping out of their tents to watch as his blood dripped to the earth.

"That'll work," said Lorents after a moment. Then he took a deep breath and, after only a moment the prone, snoring form of Leonard Neilson, Lorents' assassin-to-be, appeared on the ground, laying atop the symbols. George felt his last shred of hope vanish, as he knew now that nothing was going to save him from captivity and likely death at the hand of these bandits.

Neilson, bereft of his warm bedroll, gave a snort, then groggily opened his eyes.

"Well," said Lorents to the waking Pinkerton, "likely you weren't imagining that the two of us would ever converse."

Neilson sat up straight, blinked a couple of times, looked around, and saw George held captive. He gave a half-shrug.

"Nope," said Neilson to the bandit, still blasé. He fetched one of his cheroots out of his vest pocket, then struck a match and lit it, taking a deep draw. "I can't say as this here falls under the category of Plan A."

Lorents gave a chuckle at this. "You're a man knows how to keep his demeanor, Mr. Pinkerton. I respect that."

Neilson shrugged, taking another puff off his cheroot, then looked past Lorents at George. "Mr. Hoinschauffer," he said, "I ain't too sure what happened, but I reckon you and a mighty large dog have recently engaged in unnatural relations with one another. Do you have a mind as to how exactly you plan on living through this here predicament?"

Lorents turned back to George with a wry smile on his face. He gestured towards Neilson with both hands, as though encouraging George to answer.

George could think of nothing. He'd ceased to hope, and merely hung his head, then shook it.

"Right," said Neilson. "Well, I am sorry about that, George. I do believe that this is your fault, but still I ain't pleased at the consequence."

"I would imagine not," said Lorents.

Then Neilson whispered something. George couldn't hear what it was, and apparently neither could Lorents, as the big bandit crouched down to look at Neilson up close.

"What was that, Mr. Pinkerton?"

Neilson didn't say anything. He didn't move, except to look Randall Lorents, master of dark magics and scourge of the South Mountain Mining Company, directly in the eyes and smile.

Then George's derringer, ensconced in the waistband of Lorents' pants, simply discharged itself into Lorents' leg.

"Son of a—" Lorents shouted, as he staggered back up with his good leg.

"Mr. Lorents, what I said was," said Neilson, rising to his own feet. "You half-trained bandit summoners never seem to think about what others can do to you. No defense. You thought you had a captive in front of you, and you left yourself wide open."

The owls hooted once more from behind George, closer now than they had been before. In front of him, Neilson slapped Lorents on the leg, directly on the wound. Then he pushed up his left shirt sleeve with his bloodied hand, coating a tattoo that appeared to be more of those strange symbols. As the feathers of the owls rustled above George's head, a massive bear appeared between Lorents and Neilson, pushing Lorents to the ground. Now in George's line of sight, the owls dove for the ursine combatant. The bear easily swatted down one owl, then another, but the third dove for its face, clawing at the bear's eyes. The big animal reared back on both legs, roaring, as the sharp talons blinded it.

"Jesus!" said the big man holding George's left arm. The goon to George's right remained silent; neither appeared motivated to move into a fray between the two summoners.

Lorents had his eyes closed. George couldn't tell what exactly he was focused on, but he felt a surge of hope as Neilson side-stepped around his ursine companion with his revolver drawn. Behind Lorents, a gateway opened in the air, and something massive and shadowy formed on the other side. But Neilson's gun belched fire and thunder, and Lorent's body simply crumpled to the ground as the portal behind him closed without anything emerging.

The other bandits, including the ones holding George, finally reacted. Judging by the panicked noises the ones next to him were making, George figured they knew any move would be pure desperation.

Each one reached for his pistol. None of them cleared their holster.

Neilson didn't even move the barrel of his gun; he simply pulled the trigger five more times, and the bandits all fell with Neilson's lead in their skulls.

George staggered backward from the carnage, stumbling to the ground.

"You, you're—" he said, looking at Neilson and gibbering.

"A summoner?" asked Neilson, calmly thumbing bullets back into his revolver. "Yes, I am. The Pinkertons don't hire non-summoners to chase summoners; that would be suicide. But we don't let it be known, as folk don't really like summoners now the war's over. And we certainly don't want them we're chasing to know what we can do. So, it's Agency policy to keep this secret, you understand."

"Well, yes," said George, thinking about it. "That makes sense. And you've collected your bounty, here. Well done, I suppose."

"No," said Neilson. "You don't understand. The Agency *does not allow it to be known.* Generally, we ain't accompanied on these little expeditions. I did try to discourage you, George. Told you not to come. Then, after that didn't work, I tried to do things the way the Agency *tells* people we do them. Tried to get the long shot on Lorents without showing my powers off. But you mucked that too, didn't you?"

"Well," said George, "I'm sorry about that. But you should know that I'm very pleased with your eventual result."

Neilson sighed. He shook his head as he slapped the revolver's cylinder back into place. Then he pointed the big hand-cannon point-blank at George's face, and George felt his stomach drop in a sudden rush of understanding.

"No," said the Pinkerton, one final time. "You're not."

APOLOGIES

First Contact Café is one of the coolest anthologies we've ever been included in. It's the brain child of Phyllis Irene Radford.

The First Contact Café is not a café. It's a massive space station run by a completely selfish entity who maintains it as a rental space for alien species to talk to each other. It's Babylon 5 if Babylon 5 were run by a private corporate entity.

The authors of *First Contact Café* were given the description of the station. We were given the first story, and introduced to the people who run the station. We were also given a copy of the Rulebook—the propriety guide for interactions between species in order to avoid catastrophic events. Things like "Do not treat a gift as edible unless specifically instructed to." That sort of thing.

We were then told to invent an entirely new alien race, bring them to the station, and involve them in an incident that added something new to the rulebook.

The result is a *hilarious* anthology.

For our part, we had a friend in college named Gabe. Gabe is, for all intents and purposes, my younger brother. I still love the guy. But back in the day, he had this really unique personality trait. He apologized for *everything*. Literally everything. We couldn't figure out why, but we used to joke with him that the reason was because everything made him angry...and therefore he assumed everything he was doing made other people angry.

When coming up with an alien species for *First Contact Café*, we turned Gabe into an entire species of aliens. The result? Hilarity.

17

APOLOGIES

"Sorry. All is prepared," said Ensign Colis, sitting in the helmsman's chair of the *Bystander*.

I'm not, thought Epizu. He didn't say that, of course. It would certainly have been rude. Everyone on board knew they weren't ready for this. Saying it would simply add to the tension. It would require further apology, or open warfare.

The Tellurants didn't have time for another war before their extinction. They'd just gotten over one, and it had reduced their population by twenty percent. It had raged for a century or so, and their star had continued to degrade in the meantime.

So Epizu, or "Captain" Epizu as he had been styled for this mission, leaned his torso back into his chair.

He brought his four hands together, each hand grasping the wrist of the next with all three fingers and both thumbs. His skin, a deep, healthy shade of green went white with the pressure of his grip.

Organized religion had been dead on Telluran for a while, but superstition had a much longer lifespan. Ensign Colis and Lieutenant Miral, the technology officer, both focused on his ward against danger with their rear-facing eyes. The other two crew members immediately copied the gesture.

It probably didn't do anything, but in situations like this, better to play it safe.

"Sorry," said the helmsman again. *Good secondary apology,* thought Epizu. The helmsman had clearly made all three of them nervous with his announcement. Nervousness triggered the Tellurant fight-or-flight instinct, an instinct sharpened by eons of internal warfare. By taking the blame, Ensign Colis triggered the Tellurant's biological safety valve, allowing the neural pathways of the others to route around their fight-or-flight centers, dispersing the nervous energy that built up in their mind.

Tellurants whose minds had not adapted to accept apologies in this way had gotten themselves killed in the Great Wars long, long ago.

"Sorry," said Epizu, apologizing *in advance* for his next move. "But

go." *Bystander,* the first crewed Tellurant spacecraft in history, turned away from its home planet and made its way into the stars.

<<>>

As the *Bystander* opened up the wormhole to its destination, Epizu could almost hear Urdeth, his bond-partner. He'd come home after being appointed, apologized to her, and then announced his new title.

"Captain of the First Offworld Diplomatic Preservationist Mission? I thought you were *retiring* from the Preservationist movement. I am sorry, Epizu, but this does not sound like an emeritus position."

"Sorry, but this was the whole point of the Preservationist movement. I fought a war for this, we lost a fifth of the population of the planet. I am so sorry, but if the

Preservationists see fit to appoint me Captain of the mission that we fought for, I do not believe I can turn it down."

Urdeth did not seem impressed with this line of patriotism. "I'm sorry, but the Preservationists fought a war because over half the planet voted like idiots. Fatalism was a political movement that told us to *just accept the fact that our star is going to explode.* Those morons decided that, simply because every civilization our Observers have watched rise and fall since the galaxy began venturing into space has eventually fallen, that space travel was suicide. They voted with their fear." A moment passed before, as an afterthought to this rant, she added "Sorry."

"I'm sorry. I do not disagree with your take on Fatalism, though I would point out that we *all* voted on fear. Preservationists feared the explosion of Furnat. Fatalists feared what would happen if Tellurants entered the galaxy. And, sorry, but not just for our people. For the rest of the galaxy. The main Fatalist argument was simply that the wars we've seen here on Tellurant are bad enough. Sorry, but there's some truth there. The rest of the galaxy isn't nearly as good at apologizing for things as we are. And, sorry, we fought the war not because of the vote, but because the Preservationists refused to apologize after losing."

"Sorry, but we had nothing to apologize for."

"But I was there for the meetings. I agreed that no apology be given. As sorry as I am to say it, that was the only way to save our species. But, sorry to say, it was the Preservationists who picked the fight. Without that

apology, the Fatalists would have no choice but violence. How can I not then go on the mission that so many died to make happen? I am sorry, but I am the best-trained diplomat our people have to send. Sorry to ask, but if not me, then who?"

Urdeth sighed at this, but said nothing. Epizu continued.

"Furnat is fat and red in our sky, and likely to supernova soon. Sorry, but we need to send this mission sooner rather than later. And I am trained like no other Tellurant. My training started before the vote, before the war. I trained with a class of thirty other Tellurants, and twenty-nine of them are dead. I am the last one alive, and that means I need to do this. I am sorry."

"I apologize for pointing this out, but you were also last in your class." "Yes, well. Sorry about that, but that also made me last on the
assassination list. I'm the best shot we have. I am sorry, but I need to do this."

In the end, Urdeth had relented. But she still wasn't happy. And now, the entire enterprise rested completely on Epizu. He headed toward the meeting-place in the sky, a place established by the current crop of galactic civilizations to meet and discuss agreements of this nature. He was equipped with blueprints for some basic Tellurant innovations (like the portable wormhole the helmsman was opening up to shove their tiny craft through), two crew members, and a meager set of defensive weaponry (by Tellurant standards). With only this, Epizu had to save his people.

<<>>

The *Bystander* appeared in space next to the strangely-spinning Labyrinthestation. Quickly, Lieutenant Miral set about coordinating the computer of the station with the computer of the *Bystander*.

"It's asking us for our appointment designation," said Miral from the console.

"Appointment designation?" echoed Epizu, trying to think. Tellurants were able to view things from the outside, to monitor communications to some degree. But nobody had thought to set an appointment. After all, the nickname of this place was the First Contact Café—the Tellurants had
taken that to mean that First Contact would actually happen here.

If one called ahead for an appointment, wouldn't that call be

First Contact instead of the meeting? Some on Telluran had suggested an initial communication, but had quickly been talked down. They had apologized for being in the minority, and been apologized to in turn, but it seemed now that perhaps a new round of apologies was due.

Epizu made a mental note of this, then got back to the business at hand. "Sorry, can you access the computer systems to get an appointment?"

Miral snorted. "This computer? It may be running this massive station, but it's got about as much processing power as our atmo scrubbers. We should be able to take control of it pretty easily. Sorry for not doing it sooner." He closed his eyes, fingers resting on his interface.

"*Ugh,*" Miral said after a moment. "Sorry, captain. I've programmed our docking clearance in. Heads-up, though. They still use *jacks* on that station." He shuddered, and his rear-eyes closed for a moment. Miral's interface transmitted through his fingers, as an osmotic interchange of chemical information between the computer and himself. No sense installing things surgically when you could customize the computer to adapt and respond to the internal wiring already available to the user. Jacks were about a couple hundred thousand years outdated, a relic of the dark ages.

Ugh indeed, thought Epizu. Dealing with these new species is going to be a literal headache. Jacked computers. Gravity simulation by centrifuge. Living aboard this station was only a couple steps above a mud-and-wattle hut. *About the only thing I can hope for is a decent atmosphere seal,* he thought.

"Sorry, can you slave their computer to our portable interfaces?" "Yes. Shouldn't be a problem. Sorry about that, all fixed up. Hey, wait

a sec...sorry, we're getting a communication from the station."

"Sorry to ask, but holographic or two-D?" *Just how bad is this tech?*

"Neither. Audio only at this point. Sorry."

Wow, thought Epizu. *Ok. Audio-only. Do we sacrifice livestock to it in order to make it work?* He felt frustration at the tech level beginning to build, turning into resentment and anger. *No. Calm.* These younger species weren't responsible for their ignorance of basic scientific

principles. His Tellurant biology, filled with the fear-driven anger that billions of years of evolution had honed into him, began taking over. *Remember your training. Breathe.* No one was apologizing, nobody providing him with a release from the anger. *Breathe. You trained for this.* The anger-suppression exercises drilled into him during his diplomatic courses began to take effect, taking the edge off, leaving him at least capable of thinking rationally.

Where was I? Oh, right. Audio communication. "Well, sorry all, but I think we need to hear this," he said.

Miral did a reverse-nod of his head, thrusting his chin up so that his rear-eyes dipped down in obedience, then a voice became audible in the cabin.

"There's going to be an additional fee for your unexpected arrival," said the disembodied voice. "And another for breaking into the computer without permission."

Fee? What in Telluran did that mean? The word clearly existed in the Tellurant language, as *Bystander's* translation program had managed it. Rather than admit his ignorance to his ship-mates, he accessed the computer himself, looking for the definition.

Fee: currency-based payment in consideration for services or in penalty for misdeed. Currency based. Lovely. Exchanges in currency had pretty much gone out the window on Telluran several hundred thousand years ago, when the energy-matter matrix had been put into place. Now, all one needed to create just about any resource one might need was enough energy, which could in turn be obtained from other matter.

Money had, after that, seemed somewhat laughable.

Still, the station manager seemed to be interested in it. No reason to fight her on that. "Sorry. Of course. Tell me, what is your preferred currency?"

A pause.

"What species am I dealing with?" came the eventual response from the station.

"Sorry. We are Tellurants, from the Furnat system. I'll send you coordinates." Another pause, as Miral sent the coordinates to Furnat and its orbiting planets.

"New species, then. Good. I am assuming you have no access to galactic credit lines yet, so we will have to take your payment in trade. That will all be negotiated upon your landing. What is your preferred atmosphere?"

Epizu jutted his head at Miral, who sent over the specifications and tolerances for Tellurant life.

"Very good. We will dock you out at HNO 562, not at HNO 131 as you programmed. It's further out from the center of the station, so the gravity may be a bit more than you're used to, but it should be within acceptable limits."

This woman was not apologizing for anything. Epizu felt his Tellurant rage building, fought to keep a grasp on it. Remember your training. Different species. Different customs. Don't destroy the station. You have a world of people to save. Still, the lack of admission that she was doing anything wrong at all, with her ancient levels of technology and her inability to provide suitable accommodations, triggered the basic reflexes honed over millennia of warfare.

Not that the Tellurants couldn't simply alter the gravity to suit their needs, but she didn't know that. And she didn't care to apologize for it.

Ensign Colis' rear eyes were shut tight, and his four hands

gripped the console in front of him knuckle-white hard. *The rage is building in him, too,* thought Epizu. *Better do something about that.*

"This is a hard mission. First contact with a new species is something none of us, in the long history of the Tellurant people, have ever tried. They are crude at best, and not at all polite. I apologize to both of you for subjecting you to such rudeness." There. That would give them an apology, of sorts. A person who had accepted blame, and who had made right on it. That was the key.

<<>>

Looking down the connecting tunnel between airlock and station, Epizu shuddered inwardly as he looked at the being approaching him. Oh, the Tellurants Observers had monitored and archived Labyrinthecommunications, and had constructed a holographic simulation of this being for the briefing file. Ab'nere, that was the name.

He knew who he was looking at, and that she ran the station. Looking at a briefing holo and meeting the real thing was, however, a completely different experience. Ab'nere's sucker-tipped paws protruded from her squat, featureless body. Her ears were folded down, covering the majority of her face. The eyes that peeked out over them were obscured by round circles of glass.

Only two eyes, thought Epizu with a shudder. How can she possibly live without looking backwards?

"May I inquire as to the reason for your presence?" No apologies from the Labrynthian. No greetings. A demand for knowledge.

Breathe.

"I am Epizu of Tellurant, Captain of the First Offworld Diplomatic Preservationsist Mission. Sorry." His apology was tacked on, flawed. In Tellurant society, it could have been taken as rudeness, but Ab'nere seemed simply confused by it.

"I believe that I require further explanation. Your transmission indicated your people to be from the Furnat system, which is home to some barren planets and a red giant that's coming up on supernova. There *are* no life forms in that system. I do not appreciate falsehoods in any negotiations aboard this station."

Falsehoods. It thinks I'm lying, thought Ebizu. *And it did not apologize for the assumption.* He had specifically removed any and all armament from his person for just such an occasion as this. His bottom-left hand caressed the front of his jacket where his disruptor usually sat. He took a step back, a deep breath.

"Sorry," he said. A solid opening gambit. "But could you scan the contents of my ship?"

Ab'nere paused for a moment, but made no external sign of emotion. "This was, in fact, the next matter I had planned on addressing. Your ship appears to be a solid block of matter, with no life forms aboard. I am unsure of the contents, and therefore wary."

Another implied accusation. "Sorry. One moment."

Epizu ducked back inside the cabin, closing his front eyes and taking deep breaths in an attempt to calm his anger. This creature that ran this station was one of the rudest imaginable. His eyes went to his weaponry,

holstered by the door. *No. Training. Breathe. You need to negotiate, to find a place. Killing her does not help your people.*

"Sorry, captain, that you have to do this alone," said Colis. Yes, there it was. This was his crew's fault. They were leaving him alone to deal with this creature. Epizu felt his neural pathways shift in response to the apology, calming his breathing and unclenching his fists. It freed him to deal with Ab'nere in the appropriate, non-violent manner.

"Thank you. And apologies to both of you, but I need you to drop our passive scan shielding."

This was met with a pause that could be construed as

insubordinate. Miral then apologized for the delay, and set about dropping the scan shields. Epizu stepped back onto the gangway to see Ab'nere waiting for him.

"I am sorry about that. Now, can you see our ship?"

Ab'nere paused, obviously getting data from somewhere else. "Yes," she said, her voice trailing off in a soft, wistful manner. She stared into space for a moment, making Epizu wait as she reviewed the scan results. It is the fault of Lieutenant Miral that I am here alone with this creature, Epizu reminded himself. It is his fault and he has apologized for

it. The rage remained cool and distant, the apology reflexes held.

"Now, to business," said Ab'nere abruptly. "I still require an answer to my first question: why did you attempt to deceive me as to your origin, and why did you do it badly?"

"Sorry, but you misconstrued. The scan shield that told you our ship was a solid, inert mass answered both your questions."

The arches above Ab'nere's eyes raised at this, and she took a step in. "Do you mean to tell me there's an entire sentient civilization in orbit around Furnat, with technology of such a level that the entire planet is hidden?"

"Sorry, but yes."

"Furnat is close to supernova."

"You see our problem, then. Sorry, but that does make things quicker." "Yes, well. Hmm. I believe that I could assist you in this, assuming

you are capable of providing an adequate fee."

There was that word again. *Fee.* "Sorry, but I'm not sure what currency

you prefer here. If given the template, I can certainly generate any form of currency you desire."

"Generate? You are not allowed to pay your way here with *forgeries.*

I am insulted you should imply that I would take them."

Damn, thought Epizu. *No one else around to apologize for that gaffe. Who in Furnat's heart uses currency anymore?* "I am sorry. We have brought some basic gifts as a token of our goodwill; perhaps in light of these, you would be willing to waive any exchange of currency?"

"Ah, barter. Yes, barter is perfectly acceptable, especially for non- galactic-faring species. What do you have to offer?"

This, Epizu was ready for. He produced a pocket holo from his uniform with his lower right hand. It displayed a diagram above his hand of an early energy/matter converter. This one was an older model, ancient and obsolete compared to what existed on Telluran. It was only capable of converting energy into hydrogen, the most basic element in the universe. Still, it gave the template for the basics, and would probably be viewed as valuable by the barbarians on this station.

"I am unsure as to what I am looking at," said Ab'nere.

Epizu sighed. "Sorry, but I am not trained as to the inner workings of the energy/mass converstion units."

Ab'nere's breathing quickened slightly. "Energy/mass conversion? You would offer this in exchange for your docking fees, then?" she asked. "Exchange for?" *Right. Fees. Payment.* Epizu had to think on his feet, here. It was ancient tech by Tellurant standards, but to the lesser races it was still a significant leap forward. "Sorry, but I believe this to be worth slightly more than docking fees. Room and board for my crew and I, and an introduction to a species that will allow us access to a nearby world, located a correct distance away from a reasonably young star, with the

appropriate gravity."

Ab'nere let out a long, wistful sigh, then looked at the *Bystander.* "Very well, then," she said in a subdued voice. Another being, this one much taller, and glowing in red and orange, stepped forward. "Number 19 Son will assist you with your rooms," said Ab'nere.

"Son?" questioned Epizu. "Sorry, but who's his father?"

Ab'nere gave him a cold look. "I will also have a copy of the Rules of

Etiquette sent to your ship's computer. You just broke Rule 32. Learn them and follow them."

"Oh," said Epizu. "Sorry."

<<>>

The three Tellurants sat opposite the table from a pair of massive, shaggy beasts. The table itself was divided down the middle by a thin sheet of plastic material. The beasts themselves were jacked into the station's computer; the Tellurants relied on their own translation feed from their ship. Ab'nere had led the delegation here, to this split- atmosphere meeting room. On the other side were beings she called "Prosnoths."

They were massive, half again the size of the Tellurants, and they were covered in fur. They were also breathing a specialized atmosphere which included large amounts of carbon monoxide. Their oversized mouths featured a bottom lip pushed far forward of their top one. Ab'nere had assured the Tellurants that their relative technology level was low, barely interstellar.

Each side had a briefing file in their computer banks prepared by Ab'nere and her children. Epizu's file told him that Prosnoths were a generally friendly race whose atmospheric limitations made it hard for them to "get out much," a phrase not traditionally used in Tellurant society. It moreover detailed the specifications of the Irinile system, of which Prosnan was the second planet in orbit.

The third planet sat at the far edge of the circumstellar habitable zone. It was cold, and it had a problem with meteors. It was far from ideal, but the star was young and the planet itself could be atmospherically adjusted to increase its warmth. The Tellurants hadn't been looking to sign into an inhabited solar system, and Epizu felt his nerves rising as he began to speak with the Prosnoths.

"I am Epizu, Captain of the First Offworld—"

"Right, we know all that," burst in the Prosnoth. "Hey, we got something for ya." The Prosnoth stood and shuffled to the far end of the table, where he placed a two-span box in the atmospheric lock, then sealed his end.

"Sorry," said Epizu, fuming at the rudeness of the Prosnoth. "Ensign Colis, could you get that?"

"Yes, sorry," said Colis. He rose and went to the lock, then removed the box. It was unmarked.

Epizu closed his eyes and touched his fingers to the computer interface inside of his pocket. He was almost sure that...yes, there it was. Rule 38: When providing a gift, provide a detailed chemical formula of the gift as well. Not at the top of Ab'nere's list of Etiquette rules, but still there.

Presumably the Prosnoths had been provided a copy as well. "Sorry," began Epizu cautiously "but—"

"Hey, what's with all the apologizing?" The Prosnoth cut Epizu off again. "Show a little backbone, have a little fun. I'm not sure our species wants to be neighbors with a bunch of saps, you know?"

Oh good, thought Epizu. *A species that frowns upon offering an apology. Somehow I don't see this working out.* The fear and the rage were already boiling in him, pounding against his consciousness. Looking at Miral and Colis, he could see their rear-eyes clenched tight, and all four hands held against each other. *Calm. Breathe. Fight through the anger.*

Before he could apologize to them, Ensign Colis opened the box. The contents of the box aerosolized into a noxious-smelling gas. A quick check with the computer showed it to be non-fatal, but the smell was chokingly strong and brought tears to all of Epizu's eyes.

On the other side of the clear partition, the Prosnoths were laughing, their giant bottom lips bouncing up and down in their mirth.

"Oooo, you should see yourselves. The old rotten-firgola egg trick.

New species fall for it every time. Never stops being funny."

It took every ounce of diplomatic training, of psychological conditioning, for Epizu to not simply order the *Bystander* to break free of its mooring clamps, execute a mass-energy exchange transport for the Tellurants, and obliterate the remaining contents of this room. *Irinile 3 is in a barely habitable zone, but Irinile 2 aka Prosnan is completely viable real estate if the local infestation of these...vermin is removed.* Every long hour of self-control training, of struggle against those most primal and basic of Tellurant instincts, kept Epizu from ordering the absolute destruction of the beasts in this room with him.

Unfortunately, Engineer Miral and Ensign Colis had been given the short-form version of the diplomatic training course.

<<>>

"Sorry, but the station is asking to contact us again." Miral said.

Ab'nere was probably not happy with the use of the matter disruption lance on/through her station. That was fair. Epizu wasn't sure he wanted any more contact with the station.

Diplomacy had failed. Word was spreading over the galactic net that Tellurants were unstable, violent psychopaths. *We followed every Rule to the tee once we knew them,* thought Epizu, but that was apparently unsuitable for the rest of existence.

They'd have to destroy the Prosnoths, of course. Insults on that scale without an apology were not to be tolerated. That meant Tellurant society would unite behind converting the mass in their doomed solar system into a fleet large enough to declare war on that scale, a social side effect that Epizu now thought of as "Plan B." The Fatalists had no argument, now; an offense such as this without an apology demanded an extreme reaction. No one could decry the impact on other species after this deliberate insult.

"Sorry, but she's being very insistent," Miral reminded him.

Epizu paused. *What could she possibly want?* "Fine. Sorry, but put her through."

Ab'nere's voice filled the small cabin. "There is still the matter of damages to the station. Your initial fee did not cover the rather extensive hole you put in several of our bulkheads. In addition, we have lost the ongoing negotiation contract with the Prosnoths due to our inability to ensure their safety."

Still no apology. It was tempting to destroy the station; no purpose could be served by it anymore. Before he could give the order, though, Ab'nere continued.

"Still, I acknowledge that the original violation of the Rules was the Prosnoth's, not your own. Therefore, I do not wish to terminate relations between this station and the Tellurant people. I apologize for any inconvenience, but I am going to request further compensation for the damage your somewhat dramatic reaction caused."

There it is. An apology. The neural pathways routed, the anger dissipated. Epizu's thoughts returned to normal, his breathing slowed.

"We apologize for the damage. Lieutenant Miral, transmit a copy of file...342B to the station." Ancient scan-blocking technology. It would work against the scanners observed on the station and the ships around it. It would also be useless against the Tellurants.

"Will that serve?" he asked Ab'nere.

There was a pause. "I find this adequate. Please, feel free to return at any point, but in the future simply report a violation of the rules to me and I will ensure they are handled."

"Of course," said Epizu. "Sorry."

AWAKENING

We have arrived at the final story. And there's a reason this one is last.

Much like "Intervention with a Vampire" and "The Mentor," "Awakening" is a story that hasn't seen publication until now. There's a different reason for that, though.

"Awakening" represents the beginning of a project. It's a project that I love deeply...and that I have not yet been able to get off the ground.

Digital Glamour is a world I've envisioned. The year is 2197. It's 1,111 years since the Battle of Hastings.

As the Normans took over England, Queen Mab decided that the fey were no longer safe. She case a spell locking them away from time for those 1,111 years. That spell has ended, and the fey are back. Every creature out of the legends of every culture, from the gods of the Incas to the *Kami* in Japan to Baba Yaga in Russia to the Sidhe of the Gaelic stories have re-entered the world. There's a major culture clash about to happen between the world of magic and the world of technology.

I want this to be a *Wild Cards*-like project. Multiple authors, each with a specific focus area. Someone takes *Japan*, and digs into the old stories and faerie tales there to bring back a world of kami and ones and akuma. Someone else takes Africa, and gets into the shamanic tales. Someone else takes the stories of a Native American tribe or two, and brings them to life. Etc, etc. And all of that interacts with a dystopian cyberpunk world run by megacorps. The natural world is overbuilt and gone, but it's about to hit back.

I haven't organized it fully yet. I've made a couple of attempts, but I have yet to pull it off. I really, really want to. For now, though, it's on my to-do list. Nevertheless, you get a taste of it here, because *Awakening* is my proof-of-concept story. It's Chapter 1 of Book 1 of a book that has not been written. It's the end of this book because I deeply want it to be the start of another. So I hope you read this, enjoy, and join me in waiting for the day when I can make *Digital Glamour* a reality.

18

AWAKENING

BUILT into the side of Cadair Idris itself, the Hall of the Mountain King was the last resort of the fairy folk. It required a constant guard, because without it the fey would lack their final remaining refuge. Fengrahf had been assured that Mab did him a major honor assigning him as the Guardian of the Hall. All glory to the *former* General of the Hosts of Our Lady Mab. Fengrahf did not, however, feel honored. He felt left behind. The Host of the Fey had traveled out to aid the Saxons, and left Fengrahf here, standing before this open doorway, attempting to appear fearsome.

As trolls went, Fengrahf did not think himself all *that* scary. After all, he only stood a modest seven-and-a-half-feet tall. His mossy fur laid over his hulking frame, short, dark, and forest green. His beard resembled curling frizz on his cheeks but lengthened down his face. He wore boiled leather armor and carried both a shield and a great cudgel of crafted witchwood. Sure, most humans fled from him on the field. Fengrahf considered that more of a problem with humans than himself.

The tiny air sprite suddenly flying in figure-eights before his eyes did not appear to feel intimidated at all. He slowly focused his eyes on the dizzily bobbing creature. The sprite wore the uniform of the Heralds, an organization of sprites under Queen Mab committed to relaying her messages with haste. Heralds excelled at speed, but sometimes it could be hard to pin down their reliability. This sprite, for instance, did not greet Fengrahf, instead just dancing in the air in front of him. Fengrahf watched ponderously for a bit, hoping she would hail him eventually. Once his patience wore thin, he finally broke the silence.

"What news from Hastings?" Fengrahf rumbled, his frustration at not joining His Lady underpinning his words.

"Ah. Well." The sprite thankfully came to a standstill in front of Fengrahf's face. "Herald Zill, with message for Fengrahf the Troll, Guardian of the Hall of the Mountain King, and former General of the Lady Mab, from Mab, her most gracious—"

"Skip the formal bits, Zill." Impatience began to build through Fengrahf.

The sprite tossed her head, making a little *harumph* noise, but did as Fengrahf bade. "Harold is...overthrown. William reigns in England now."

Fengrahf felt the dark weight of that news sink on him and shook his head. Even with Mab's support, Harold had not managed to hold his shield wall, after all. That was the end, then. The Normans had been sweeping the continent, and now the Isles were going to fall.

He mulled it over, slowly, as trolls do. The Hall would be vulnerable. He now stood in the last remaining bastion of magic left to the fairies on this side of the world. Fey leaders and strongholds elsewhere had already been overpowered by their enemies. The Shuten Doji, Shogun of the Eastern fairies, fell earlier in the century. On the Central Steppes, Baba Yaga's wiley efforts to hold out against Vladimir the Great had crumbled, though she still played cruel pranks on the soldiers there. On the other side of the ocean, the fey folk were not bothered by their stone-wielding humans, but the magic of the Other Continent could not sustain all the fey in the world.

Fengrahf knew what must come, though he wished he did not. He looked at the sprite in front of him.

"Has Mab given any instructions?"

The sprite startled at the sound of the troll's voice. "Well, no. Not to me. But she's coming here now. I'm sure she'll have something for us to do then. She appeared quite upset."

Fengrahf lunged forward, seizing the sprite by its tiny legs and holding the length of them firmly in one of his hands. "This was the sort of information I needed back when the conversation started. Return to Our Lady and tell her that all will be ready for her."

"Ah, yes...that is, of course. Guardian. Sir. Right away. Err. Once you release me."

There was the intimidation. Good to know he hadn't lost it entirely. Fengrahf carefully uncurled his fingers. The sprite zipped off, disappearing into the horizon in less than a blink. Fengrahf turned to enter the Hall.

The troll passed through the traps, trick doorways, and other deadly obstacles laid out in the hall with the ease of long practice. Finally, he arrived at the portal to an open chamber. He ducked to make it through the not-troll-sized opening. The chamber beyond was not much larger. The old stone walls of the circular room, roughly fifteen feet in diameter rose up in a domed ceiling. The top of the dome stood maybe fourteen feet high, but on the outer edges of the room the ceiling started at a mere eight feet. It presented the strange illusion of being both secret and grandiose.

In the center of the room, on a marble pedestal, lay a perfect sphere. Colors swirled, ever-shifting, through the translucent globe. The light of those colors decorated the walls of the Stone Chamber with an ever-changing light show.

Fengrahf ignored this beauty. The Orb belonged to Mab, not

him. He guarded the Hall and left the big magics to the faeries that could handle them. Instead, he walked past the pedestal and lifted a small stone in the back to reveal a hidden nook. Inside this nook rested a small but very decorative pot, filled with oil.

Fengrahf didn't normally use Bachanal Oil; it was very rare, these days. He'd felt it a waste to lubricate all of his devices with the stuff. Besides, a troll doesn't mind using sheep fat once a week instead. It kept the traps just as functional; there was just a little more maintenance involved.

Now, though, was not the time to be stingy. Mab approached, and only one reason would force the Queen to do that. She planned on invoking the Sleep, the thousand-year retreat from the world that only Mab could call. Fengrahf could not remember a time that the Orb of the Mountain had actually been used. They had all suspected that time was coming, though. Back when humans learned to mold iron to their purposes, the doom of the fey had been writ. The only thing to do now was leave the world and hope humanity grew more accepting in a millenium.

That meant, of course, the traps so lovingly maintained by Fengrahf were going to be left alone for a thousand years. Sheep fat simply was not going to be sufficient. Time to bring out the good stuff.

Fengrahf began his normal routine of greasing the traps. The Bachanal Oil had legendary lubricating properties and never needed replacing, unless washed away by wine. Fengrahf took great care to not spill a drop of the rare substance as he ensured his traps would continue to function throughout the next millennium, and beyond if needed. Crafted from stone and witchwood, the traps themselves would outlast time.

Fengrahf finished readying the mechanisms in the space of a couple of hours, then resumed his station at the front entrance, waiting for Mab to arrive. It was likely he had a couple of days before she appeared, but the one thing he could do to prepare, he had done.

He had probably been a little short with that Herald.

TWO DAYS LATER, Mab finally arrived. Her chariot, pulled by twin night-mares, sped towards the Hall at a full gallop. As Fengrahf watched her approach, he noticed men on horseback following Mab's chariot. Had the Saxons provided Mab a rearguard? Fengrahf considered this, then remembered that Saxons did not generally fight from horseback. Normans, then. Normans were, of course, the enemies of the fey. Which meant, concluded Fengrahf, that the horsemen *chased* Mab.

Oh.

Fengrahf's mind strained against the vows holding him to the Hall. If he left his post, he would betray His Lady. If he stayed at his post, then he permitted those ruffians to assault His Lady, which might also be betrayal. If one thought about it, the situation provided very few options to preserve one's honor. This was going to require some pretty careful deliberation before Fengrahf made any kind of move.

The advantage to using a Fengrahf as Guardian lay in the fact that trolls never slept. The disadvantage, however, flowed from that same problem. Trolls were, at the heart of it, creatures of inertia. Fengrahf knew he should be speeding up his thoughts, but he'd been ruminating alone for so long that each thought took him a while. It was hard for him to get moving once he'd been still.

In the end, the length of Fengrahf's ponder made the choice for him. Mab's chariot clattered up to the entrance of the Hall, the horses snorting and steaming in the cold air. She vaulted to the ground in a fluid motion before the vehicle fully stopped.

Fengrahf bowed as Mab strode toward him. Her normally-perfect face showed signs of fatigue. Fengrahf had never seen that look on any of the High Sidhe, let alone on the face of Mab herself.

"The army has scattered," Mab yelled on her way past. "Hold these men off me while I go trigger the Orb."

"And good luck," another voice said. Zill, Herald of Mab, followed the Queen down the corridor, glancing back over her shoulder at the troll.

He stepped more firmly in front of the entrance. Arrows with iron tips clattered about him as he prepared to deal with this small force of Normans should they try to invade the Hall.

He saw Mab had not left the Normans unharmed. It was clear that chasing the Fairie Queen had caused the remaining six men to grow very wary. They fanned out into a semi-circle around him, waiting for someone else to make the first move. That was good. Fengrahf had none of Mab's great magics, but he knew his way around a fight.

The first Norman stepped up holding an iron sword. Actually, iron covered the human. The center of his shield had an iron ball; he wore an iron helm and an iron mail coat. Not exactly a choice opponent for a troll. Of course, iron hurt the *fairies themselves,* but if he caught it against his witchwood it would do very little damage.

Fengrahf raised his shield lazily, deflecting a blow from the Norman. Another stepped in from Fengrahf's left and bent low, swinging the sword at the troll's left ankle. *Bad move,* Fengrahf thought as he raised his leg above the swipe and used it to kick his attacker in the face. The man arced backward with the force of the kick, blood streaming from a broken nose.

The fight was on now. Fengrahf could feel it begin to take him. Normally, Fengrahf did all things very slowly, preserving his strength. He faced six men with iron here, and it was time to access some of his stored energy. Fengrahf began to accelerate, his thoughts and his body responding to the danger.

As his first attacker backed away, Fengrahf pressed his advantage and brought his club around to the side of the man's helmet, caving it in.

Fengrahf *moved* now. His thoughts and his body both sped as his standing inertia gave way to inertia of a different sort entirely. He charged forward, his cudgel clanging down on the upraised shield of the next man. Fengrahf roared mightily as he hooked his own shield underneath his opponent's and pulled up. A step to the side, and the troll brought his cudgel hard into the Norman's now-exposed stomach. The man doubled over, falling.

A searing pain, then the burn of iron, sliced through Fengrahf's shoulder from the rear. He turned, trying to swing his cudgel in an arc at his flanker. Instead, he threw himself off-balance. He realized his arm was no longer attached to his body. Inconvenient, but his thoughts sped past the problems this presented and moved onward.

The new attacker took advantage of Fengrahf's stumble to thrust his sword directly into his eye. The iron tip struck home, and the burning pain of it blinded the big troll.

Now, with most fairies, that kind of pain would immobilize them. Trolls, though, were different. Trolls had *inertia*. It took a long time for a troll to start doing anything, but it also took a long time for them to *stop*. Damage done by iron wouldn't regenerate, but in this moment it didn't matter to Fengrahf. Now that he was *moving*, nothing short of complete dismemberment could stop him against his will. He probably wouldn't live in the end, but his mind ignored that thought like an ox ignored a flea. He needed to kill the enemies of His Lady.

Down to his left eye and arm, Fengrahf slammed the rim of his shield up to knock the blade out of the way, then back down on to the shoulder of the man who had stabbed him. He felt, *heard,* the man's collarbone crunching beneath the blow.

Fengrahf wheeled to the two remaining attackers, loosing another furious roar.

The remaining two thrust their blades at the raging troll. Fengrahf raised his shield, blocking, then brought his massive leg up in a kick aimed to incapacitate any man. He swung his leg into--

--A LARGE, cold, torch?

Whatever it was, it emitted light, like a torch. It was on a stand, bent over his body. But upon making contact with the torch, it failed to burn him. Instead, it simply went flinging out of Fengrahf's line of sight. The press of cloth against his back told him he reclined on some kind of pallet.

Fengrahf tried to mumble something, but then found he had a mask on over his mouth. The mask was made of a clear substance, and a hose led from it back to a small, round metal container. He reached up his right hand, meaning to take off his mask.

As he did so, he noticed two things. The first was a series of images that flashed in front of him. They superimposed themselves over the room and contained a series of words and numbers that zoomed by so fast Fengrahf could not even read them, let alone understand. Then the room was bathed in a gentle blue light and the words, "System Loading," appeared almost directly in front of his face. He tried to recoil back into his bed away from them, but the words moved along with his head, maintaining their position in the air relative to his gaze regardless of where he looked.

The second thing he noticed was the fact that he was using his right arm. He wasn't supposed to have one of those anymore, he thought. Actually, come to think of it, he shouldn't have an eye, either. This was going to require some pondering.

He lay his arm back on the bed, and began thinking about it, instead of even touching his mask.

A voice down the hall interrupted his meditation. "What in the world was all that racket?"

There was something about the language. The Fey, of course, are masters of languages. Even the Goblins can understand almost anything being said by a human. It's hard to contract with people if you don't know their language better than them. Fengrahf was no exception to the rule. This language was different, but human.

"Jesus, this thing knocked over the lamp. It's conscious. Hey, Doc, it's conscious!"

The source of this voice was a young female human, standing at the door wearing blue trousers and matching shirt. No crest was displayed at all, but she wore the old Greek letter "alpha" above her left breast. She simply stood in the doorway of the strange room and stared at him.

He stared back, as this appeared the appropriate etiquette in this place. Suddenly, a thin-lined box drew itself around her face, and her face got bigger. This was interesting. Some words appeared in the air next to the enlarged face: "Jenny Rappenham, R.N.A." R.N.A.? Fengrahf didn't know what that meant, and he stared at it. A second box opened, this one at the bottom of his field of vision, reading "R.N.A.: Registered Nurse's Assistant. A person who is certified to..." The words continued on, sliding themselves upward through the box.

So, she was a Healer, of sorts. That was good. Fengrahf gave her his best toothy grin.

She shrank back from the doorway a bit. Fengrahf sighed. Some humans simply did not get trolls. He held out his right arm, palm open, as a gesture of peace.

Then he noticed his arm. It wasn't his arm at all – it was some form of armor, grafted to his body. It looked metallic, and for a second Fengrahf winced in anticipation of the pain iron always brought.

No pain came. Fengrahf sat up to examine it more thoroughly.

He brought his left arm in front of him to compare. Thankfully, that arm was still covered with his own mossy, green fur. He touched his left hand with his right. He felt the pressure on his right palm, and the warmth, but his left hand touched the hard surface as though it were witchwood.

Which it wasn't. Witchwood reeked of enchantment; this substance had none.

"Oh, he *is* awake! Oh, lovely. Yes. Let us see here..."

Fengrahf re-focused his vision on the older lady who had just entered the room. She stood slightly shorter than Jenny Rappenham, R.N.A., but moved with more authority. Her head, too, became outlined and then enlarged in his vision. The floating text appeared once again, identifying her as Laura Benhoft, M.D. Rappenham seemed to defer to Benhoft, and Fengrahf surmised that he was dealing with a Master Healer now.

Benhoft lifted the mask from Fengrahf's face. "Hello. My name is Doctor Benhoft. Do you understand me?" Benhoft spoke very slowly, as if she spoke to a child.

Fengrahf sat as straight as he could—he could not allow this insult. "Madam, you speak to Troll Fengrahf, Guardian of the Hall, once General of the Hosts of Our Lady Mab. You will not address me as if I were a simpleton. Now, what news of My Lady?" He kept voice level, non-threatening.

"Your lady? I'm sorry, we did not find any other...what did you call yourself? A troll? Oh, the journals will have a field day with this one. Did you know your cells regenerate rapidly? Amazing, that. I took a sample from you, by the way. Azimuth Corp may even promote me if I can incorporate *that* genetic trait. If I can, it would stand to increase Azimuth's market share pretty considerably. But I'm rambling." She was. Fengrahf could not keep up with her words as they sped through the air like a flock of geese.

"So no, no other trolls. We've collected some other pretty weird samples, though. Had this one, only one foot tall. Can you believe it? One foot. Had some proportionately large wings on her, though. Couldn't tell how that was done. Do you think that the model will scale up? Of course not; I'm not even sure how she..."

Dr. Benhoft continued to speak, at length. Fengrahf rested his head on the pillow beneath it. These humans knew nothing of the Fey. That could only mean one thing: the Thousand Years had passed. Mab had stored the Fey away, and they were just re-emerging to the world. That was why the everything seemed so unfamiliar.

It *was*. Or at least, *Fairie* was unfamiliar to *it.*

Fengrahf sat and thought about this. He needed to seek out the Hall, and check to make sure his defenses had held. The Healer had mentioned a fey one foot in height, blue skinned, with wings. An air pixie; if it was in the same place as him, most likely Mab's Herald, Zill.

By Mab's enchantment, Heralds always knew where they were and where they were going; if he could find this one, she could take him to the Hall.

"Where am I?" rumbled Fengrahf.

Dr. Benholt was talking about something called "vivisection," and seemed caught off guard by Fengrahf's question.

"Room 2492. Research. By the way, I see your cybernetics are functioning as intended. That's good; I wasn't sure whether your neural paths would link up or not. Have you tried using the database yet? No, I see not. Really, we could simply initiate a neural transfer. Conversation is just so slow and awkward compared to neural transfer, don't you think? You look confused. Well, I guess you would be, seeing as I had to install the chip myself. You've never done a neural transfer. Silly Benholt; what was I thinking. 'Give the big one some cyber-replacements' they said. 'Let's see if he can be a soldier.' Weaponizing a monster seemed wrong, but it was Azimuth's command. Anyways--"

Fengrahf heard the words of the small, fast-talking woman, and stored them for later reference. His mind was just getting to "vivisection." That was a word for which no equivalent existed. As the meaning of the word exploded into his head, he began to realize that maybe it was time to start cycling up again.

"What are you vivisecting?" His voice didn't so much cut into hers as club it into silence.

"Oh, that little animal, with the wings and the blue skin. She's a precious little thing; someone even taught her to mimic speech. She keeps trying to take a message to someone. We think she's a cross between a parrot and a messenger pigeon. Some brilliant genetics there; I wonder which corp made the lot of you? No, no I don't. Shouldn't wonder. Not my place to get into corporate business. I'm not wondering. Just, you know, silly talk. Ha." This last was said weakly, and Benholt's eyes flicked about the room nervously.

Fengrahf, however, came to the conclusion that Benholt was definitely talking about the air pixie. This human intended to cut apart the Herald while it was still alive. Heralds were, of course, inviolate. They were not to be touched on any field. What Benholt proposed was preposterous.

"Where is the Herald?" Fengrahf's eyes locked onto Dr. Benholt. He realized, for a moment, that there was another box drawn around the doctor, and "TARGET LOCKED" flashed above the box.

Dr. Benholt, noticing some change about him, stepped back and whispered something to Jenny Rappenham, R.N.A., who now cowered outside of the door.

This weird new magic was going to take some pondering. Later. Now, though, he had to get the Herald and find the Hall. That was his priority. He rose from the bed, keeping his eyes on Benholt.

"Take me to the Herald." This was not a question. The time for questions was, for the moment, over. He had enough answers to start spooling up his inertia. He needed to rescue the little air pixie.

"The—the Herald?" said Dr. Benholt. "I don't know what that means! Please don't hurt me!"

Hurt her? Only if she attacked or tried to stop him. He really hadn't threatened her. Well, maybe she saw that "TARGET LOCKED" sign above her. That might be threatening. Not his doing, though.

"The air pixie. One foot tall, wings. You were going to take her apart alive."

"Oh, uh, she's in Research too. Azimuth Corp has asked me to report immediately on her genetic mods, and their effectiveness at scale. I'm afraid that will mean I destroy the sample in the--"

"Take me to her. Now." Fengrahf said, focused intently on the talkative healer.

"But, that's quite impossible. We can't let samples cross-contaminate, you understand. If we did that, we may end up with anomalous results. No, I need you to..."

Benholt *was* resisting. Time to make things clear.

"I am the Guardian of the Hall, appointed there by the hand of Our Lady Mab herself. You are a human. Do as I command and take me to the Herald. Now." Fengrahf came to a seating position, preparing himself.

"But, I can't! Azimuth Corp will terminate me! What about my family?"

"Madam, I do not know who this Mr. Corp is, but he is not here," Fengrahf gestured around and the lack of anyone else in the room. "I am, and I offer you the protection of the Lady of Air and Water herself. You and yours will be fine." Assuming, of course, that Mab could be found. Fengrahf thought it best to skip that part. "But *you* will not be fine if you resist me again. Now, for the last time: Take. Me. To. The. Herald."

"You don't understa--"

As soon as he committed himself to fighting his way past, a set of tubes bound together like a fagot of wood popped out of his shoulder and began spinning, the open end of the tubes pointing toward Dr. Benholt. It made a rapid clicking noise as it spun. Fengrahf was so startled even he turned to look at it.

Benholt ducked, holding her head between her legs and chanting something to herself.

"Doctor!" cried Jenny Rappenham, R.N.A. "It's okay; it's not like we loaded the thing, remember?"

In his field of vision, Fengrahf saw a small, numerical zero with a tiny flashing sign reading "No Ammunition." Ammunition? That was what slingers used, wasn't it?

No matter. The doctor had stopped, and he needed to find the Herald. He quickly exited into a smooth, off-white hallway. A railing lined one side, and certain portions of the ceiling glowed brightly, coating the hall in a soft light. Doors lined the walls of the hallway. Fengrahf's mind stored this all for later meditation. He needed to act.

The big troll began opening doors.

A shrill scream erupted from the first door, and a small elder lady pointed at him with one hand while pushing a button with the other. *Wrong door,* thought Fengrahf. He politely nodded to the lady. He stepped back into the hallway, closing the doorway behind him, and tried the next room.

The next minute of Fengrahf's life could be described as variations on a theme. It was almost as though these people had never seen a troll. Actually, his accelerating brain told him, they probably hadn't. His whole people had been away from the world for a thousand years, after all.

This was going to take a little more delicacy.

"Excuse me," Fengrahf rumbled as he opened the next door. In this room, an older man, maybe forty years of age, merely shrank back into his bed, his eyes wide and his mouth gaping. It was an improvement.

Some white-clad men began running down the hallway at him. The enlarging-face box identified them by name and included the term "orderly." Healer's assistants, then. One of them carried a large needle, but that was the only weapon. Fengrahf ducked into the room with the man.

The troll looked around for a weapon. The nice thing about using a cudgel as your weapon of choice is that it is very easy to find a cudgel in any situation. A chair, built from the same not-iron that now composed his right arm, sat in the corner of the room. A quick stomp on the chair near the joints and Fengrahf had a pair of sticks, a little heavier on one end than the other. He swung them experimentally. Not the best balance, but they would do.

A whimper sounded from the bed.

The orderlies burst into the room, their hands held palm out. Upon seeing that Fengrahf was now armed, the whites of their eyes grew considerably.

"Hold on, now. We don't want any trouble," said the man with the needle. The outlines around him and the floating words identified him as "Roy Herbert, Orderly."

"Good," replied Fengrahf. "Take me to the Herald. Small, winged, blue skin."

"All in good time. All in good time. First, we have to make sure you're healthy. We need to make sure your—erm—blood pressure is stable."

This could not be true. It would be very difficult for this orderly to check the blood pressure of Fengrahf, as Fengrahf's veins flowed with sap. This man *lied* to Fengrahf, and he was not the sort of troll to let that be.

"No. Now. I am Fengrahf, Guardian of the Hall, and you will assist me or stand aside."

"Look, I don't know what kind of weird gengineering was done on you, but you're not stable. We just want you to calm down, take it easy." Herbert's voice was soft and pleasant, but he continued to advance with the needle.

Fengrahf was not about to give up his advantage in range to Roy Herbert. As soon as Herbert stepped into his effective arc, Fengrahf swung his cudgel out and neatly rapped Herbert on the side of his head.

Herbert crumpled to the floor, the needle falling from his hand. The other orderlies burst back into the hall, yelling. It appeared they were running *away* from Fengrahf. Good. The farther away they got, the better.

Fengrahf heard a wailing sound, first faint, then louder. It sounded like a banshee, but it contained none of the compulsion that a banshee's wail did. Up and down the scale it went, without any musicality. It grated on his ears, but he didn't know what to do about it.

The next door down the hall had a small sign on it that read "Dr. Benholt." The Master Healer's private chamber, then; this might do some good. Fengrahf opened the door immediately.

Within the room, the Herald lay in a small, glass case, barely large enough to contain her. Her tiny chest rose and fell with her breathing, but her eyes were closed. The rest of her body was motionless. She was sealed in by a mesh attached to the top of the glass. Iron? No, Fengrahf decided after a close look. Probably more of the same stuff his arm was made of.

"Herald! Are you awake?"

The Herald's eyes opened and looked at him.

"Guardian!" she squeaked excitedly. Her wings tried to flutter in her excitement but slapped fruitlessly against the glass.

Fengrahf ripped the mesh off and lifted the glass lid. The Herald rose out of her confinement. She began flying in mad circles around the troll.

"Oh, thank you, thank you," she chittered. "What happened to you? Your arm, your eye. They look weird."

"Calm down and let us leave this *horrible* place *right now.*"

"Wait. I have a message. Our Lady Mab bids me to tell you that there are only seconds left before she will be able to trigger the Orb, and to continue to hold against the Normans at all costs."

A moment of silence passed as Fengrahf stared at Zill. The pixie was smiling.

Then Fengrahf heard a sound all too familiar. The sound of marching boot steps, many of them, all in a rhythm, echoed up the hallway. He heard the voice of one of the orderlies shouting "In there, it's in Benholt's office."

Fengrahf sighed. He did not want to fight an army; his momentum flowed towards his survival and the survival of the Herald. He looked at the exterior window of Dr. Benholt's office.

This was going to hurt.

The office door flew inward as the soldiers kicked it. The soldiers wore some form of bulky armor, the lead one carrying a tube crafted of the not-metal. Fengrahf was pretty sure it was some kind of weapon but did not know how it was used or how to fight against it. The front of the nearest armor read "Azimuth Corp. Police Services Division."

It wasn't the first time he'd run afoul of the local magistrates.

Fengrahf sprinted toward the window, and used his not-metal arm to crash through it. He launched himself into the air beyond.

Zill followed him.

"Do you think this is such a great idea?" she asked as he fell.

"Unless I land on an iron plate or a fire, I'll regenerate. It'll hurt, but it's better than dealing with soldiers."

"Yes, well...did you notice we're still talking?"

"I did."

"And how fast we're going? I'm having to work pretty hard to slow you down, and it's not really working. My air magic isn't all *that* strong, and you are very heavy."

"I did notice we were going pretty fast."

"Well, that's because of how high up we were. Look up and—oop, nevermind," the Herald said as Fengrahf slammed into the ground below with a resounding *crunch.*

It took a moment for Fengrahf to compose himself. That had hurt, a lot, but he'd been right. There hadn't been any iron or fire. His body reconstructed itself, and he rose. He was still in pain, but he was at least functional.

He turned to look at the building he had leapt from. "Castle" was not the right word. Fengrahf had been in a few castles and thought them large. This, though; this was something else. A massive building, larger than most mountains he had ever seen. It angled itself in towards the top like those pyramids Ra had been so into, and had far too many nooks, crannies, and outcroppings for him to take in at once. One such long outcropping stood far above Fengrahf's impact crater.

"You see?" said Zill. "Really, really big."

Fengrahf shook his head, then resumed his momentum.

"Zill, I need to get back to the Hall that is my charge. I do not know where I am; take me there."

Zill cocked an eyebrow at him.

"You're here. That building is built around Cadair Idris itself. The whole mountain's in there, and so is where the Hall used to be."

"Used to be?"

"Uh...yeah. I woke up inside a chamber these humans call

'janitorial supplies' now. No Hall, just a bunch of bottles, a hose, and some mops."

No Hall. Fengrahf began to lose momentum. His traps had failed, and miserably to judge from the look of this place. Of course, gazing to the left and right of it, this tower was but one in a sea of towers. Small chariots zipped above him, in between the massive buildings. Occasionally one would land on the ground, and a person would emerge. When he thought about what it could mean, he began to get more signs in his field of vision, things like "2059 Toyota Camry." Not really all that useful, he decided.

"What do you suppose Toyota means? I'm not understanding that term," he commented to Zill.

"Where do you see that?" The blue pixie looked around, perplexed.

"The sign, hovering right next to that silver box, over there." Fengraph tried to gesture toward it, and grunted, his healing muscles still very painful.

"I don't see a sign," the Hereald said again, frowning.

"You don't see things being outlined? Getting bigger? Labels and such?" The writing continued to flash in Fengrahf's vision.

"Ummm, no"

"What about 'target locked?' Ever seen that?"

"No. But then, you have that unnatural-looking thing over your eye. You're probably seeing a lot of things."

Eye? Fengrahf reached his left hand, his organic hand, up to his right eye. He tapped his finger against what should have been his eyesocket, but instead found a hard surface. He could watch his finger tapping without even having to blink and it was really very dizzying.

"Oh. Nevermind." He'd ponder it later, when he didn't need to conserve his momentum. "So, I'm not the Guardian of the Hall anymore. Let's go report to Mab and get our instructions."

"About that." The pixie's voice softened, and she cast her eyes downward, staring hard at the ground. "I can't feel Our Lady anymore."

"You can't...is Mab dead?"

"No idea. I just can't find her."

"Oh. Well."

Fengrahf took some time to consider this. Above, two or three chariots with brilliantly-colored, flashing fire adorning them began to streak across the sky towards them. Fengrahf noticed the "Azimuth Corporation Police Services Division" logo on the front of the chariot.

"Let's go find her the old-fashioned way, then. We both need a new assignment." After all, what else could a troll do? He served at Mab's pleasure. Time to find His Lady.

The pixie and the troll raced away from where the Hall should have been, and into the unfamiliar world.

ABOUT THE AUTHORS

Frog and Esther Jones live on Washington State's Olympic Peninsula with their dog, Betty, and a rare, eastern Washington proofreading panda. They have never quite decided what it means to grow up and can be found any particular weekend working on various art or musical projects and pursuing all kinds of nerdery with their whole hearts. They also run their own small press, Impulsive Walrus Books, which is dedicated to publishing lovingly crafted books and supporting the creative spark in all of us.

They can be found at:
www.jonestales.com
www.impulsivewalrusbooks.com